Sexy Beast VIII

Also by Kate Douglas:

Wolf Tales
"Chanku Rising" in *Sexy Beast*
Wolf Tales II
"Camille's Dawn" in *Wild Nights*
Wolf Tales III
"Chanku Fallen" in *Sexy Beast II*
Wolf Tales IV
"Chanku Journey" in *Sexy Beast III*
Wolf Tales V
"Chanku Destiny" in *Sexy Beast IV*
Wolf Tales VI
"Chanku Wild" in *Sexy Beast V*
Wolf Tales VII
"Chanku Honor" in *Sexy Beast VI*
Wolf Tales VIII
"Chanku Challenge" in *Sexy Beast VII*
Wolf Tales 9
"Chanku Spirit" in *Sexy Beast VIII*
Wolf Tales 10

Also by Kathleen Dante:

"Night Pleasures" in *Wild Nights*
"Call of the Wild" in *Sexy Beast II*

Also by Devyn Quinn:

Flesh and the Devil
Sins of the Flesh
Sins of the Night
Embracing Midnight

Sexy Beast VIII

KATE DOUGLAS

KATHLEEN DANTE

DEVYN QUINN

APHRODISIA

KENSINGTON BOOKS

http://www.kensingtonbooks.com

APHRODISIA BOOKS are published by

Kensington Publishing Corp.
119 West 40th Street
New York, NY 10018

All Kensington Titles, Imprints, and Distributed Lines are available at special quantity discounts for bulk purchases for sales promotions, premiums, fund-raising, and educational or institutional use.

Special book excerpts or customized printings can also be created to fit specific needs. For details, write or phone the office of the Kensington special sales manager: Kensington Publishing Corp., 119 West 40th Street, New York, NY 10018, attn: Special Sales Department, Phone: 1-800-221-2647.

Aphrodisia and the A logo Reg. U.S. Pat. & TM Off.

ISBN-13: 978-0-7582-2871-0
ISBN-10: 0-7582-2871-6

First Kensington Trade Paperback Printing: April 2010

10 9 8 7 6 5 4 3 2 1

Printed in the United States of America

CONTENTS

Chanku Spirit

Kate Douglas

Foreword

They live among us, often unaware of their true birthright as they try to exist in a world that, in many ways, forces them to abide by laws and customs contrary to their nature. Ruled by a powerful libido as well as an innate sense of honor and a loyalty to their own kind so deeply ingrained it cannot be denied, they often live lives of quiet desperation until their feral nature is finally, often explosively, unleashed.

Descendants of an ancient race born upon the Tibetan steppe, they are more than human—so much more than they appear to the world around them.

They are shapeshifters.

They are Chanku.

1

A single, low-wattage lamp cast more shadows than light across their sweat-slick bodies. Ulrich Mason's mate lay beneath him, her supple body molded to the contours of his. Tangled and disheveled, Millie's shoulder-length blond hair spread like a rumpled halo across the pillow, though a few strands stuck to the perspiration on her forehead. Her eyes were closed, the look on her face one of blissful completion and utter satiation.

Ulrich held his weight off her as best he could, but he was still buried in her wet heat, and her warm body felt absolutely wonderful pressed close to his. His cock throbbed in perfect harmony with the rhythmic contractions of Millie's powerful vaginal muscles, and while he'd climaxed in a violent paroxysm of absolutely mind-numbing lust, he was still hard.

Though not quite as hard—or as large—as the cock stuffed entirely up his ass. He almost laughed out loud, but that wouldn't be appropriate now, would it? Still, Matt had more than surprised him tonight, especially when the young man so confidently took the dominant role and topped Ric.

When Millie had suggested they invite her young lover to join them after they'd all shifted and run as wolves, Ulrich had assumed he'd be the one in charge. Matt was, after all, a truly nice young man, but not at all the aggressive type. In his midtwenties, he was still a pup—at least in Ulrich's eyes. Though deeply in love with his packmates, Daciana Lupei and Deacon March, Matt hadn't yet bonded with the other two-thirds of his comfortable *ménage à trois*.

His love for the two hadn't kept him away from Millie, either. Ric's mate and Matt had a special bond with one another, a definite friendship with benefits, but it had nothing to do with the deep, loving relationship Matt had with Daci and Deacon.

Ric knew Matt loved them and they loved him. It was a fact of nature—Matt's nature—that their love was such a powerful force holding them together. The fact they'd not taken the next step and completed their mating bond was curious, but knowing how strong-willed Daciana Lupei was, Ric figured there were probably undercurrents he hadn't yet figured out. No matter.

Matt Rodgers was a complicated, fascinating young man. Ric accepted that Matt was almost as much in love with Millie as he was with Daci and Deacon, but there was no risk there, no need for jealousy.

Matt and Millie had a special relationship, one Ulrich encouraged. Hell, he'd been the one to throw them together in the first place. Matt had needed to build his self-confidence just as Millie needed to accept the sexual freedom that was as much a part of her Chanku birthright as the amazing ability to shift from human to wolf.

She'd found it with Matt, and after a night of exploration and discovery, it was more than obvious they'd both come away stronger, more confident in themselves. When Millie had suggested Matt share their bed tonight, Ulrich had been beyond thrilled. His plan was working—she was finally accepting her true nature.

This was a first for Millie—a night of sex with more than one man. Of course, Ric had pictured himself on top, not sandwiched between his mate and her young lover. Not that he was complaining, but for a guy not used to taking the more submissive position, it had required a bit of an adjustment.

Matt might be young, but he was hung like a damned bull moose, with a young man's energy, a young man's strength. Ulrich wondered if he'd be able to sit down come morning.

Matt nuzzled his shoulder and rolled his hips in a slow, lazy thrust that drove his huge cock deeper inside Ulrich. Ric bit back a low groan of pain coupled with a moan of pleasure.

Damn. He'd forgotten how much he loved this. He didn't want Matt to stop, but he didn't want to disturb his mate, either. Millie had gone so quiet, he figured she'd fallen asleep.

"I'm awake," she said. Her eyes stayed closed, but she smiled at him. "Awake and really, really enjoying myself." She tightened her vaginal muscles around his cock. A surge of strength raced from Ric's balls down the length of his shaft.

If he'd been hard a moment ago, he was harder now.

Matt rolled his hips forward once again. *Are you okay? Is this too much?*

Never, Ric said, meaning it now. When he'd gotten his first glimpse of Matt's erection, he'd had second thoughts, especially when he realized the kid fully intended to take the dominant role. Now, though, after hours of some of the best sex he'd had in ages, there was no way Ric wanted to quit. Not yet.

Matt thrust harder, filled him more, forced him deeper inside Millie with the strength of powerful hips and thighs.

Millie sighed.

So did Ric. He'd never been screwed with such respect. He'd known love, he'd known sex for the pleasure of getting off and nothing more, he'd experienced sex as a tool of aggression and dominance, but he realized now why Millie was so fond of Matt.

In spite of his unhappy childhood and youth, the young man loved with all his heart and soul. His was an open, giving spirit. He loved without hesitation—his heart was as unguarded as his beautiful smile. There was no subterfuge, no ulterior motive, no challenge. Ulrich sensed Matt's deep love for Daci, his equally powerful love for Deacon . . . and he'd managed to top Ulrich with so much respect and subtle finesse he'd succeeded before Ric realized what he was doing.

He felt Matt's almost-shy worship of Millie and his powerful respect and love for Ulrich. It was a humbling experience, to feel such strong, selfless love from a man younger than his daughter.

Younger, but somehow older, too. Matt had an old soul, seasoned with a lifetime of pain and need, softened by a heart filled with love. No need to analyze, Ric decided. Better to enjoy, to live for the moment. He caught Matt's rhythm once again and thrust deep inside Millie. She raised her knees on either side of his body and took him all the way, tilting her hips to his powerful penetration.

Ulrich floated on a sensual haze of sensation. Millie's vaginal muscles clasping his thick shaft, her fingers fluttering along his ribs. Her eyes were open now. Mouth parted, she licked her upper lip. Then she closed her eyes once more and moaned with heartfelt pleasure at a particularly deep thrust.

Her thoughts floated freely into Ric's. She loved looking up and seeing his face so close to hers. Loved even more the sight of Matt's eyes watching her over Ric's shoulder. She wanted to crawl inside Matt's head and see what it felt like to take her mate this way—but first she wanted Ulrich's permission.

Why ask? Go for it!

I was afraid you might think it was an intrusion.

Ric leaned close and kissed her. He licked her lower lip, the upper, tasting her sweetness. *Never, Millie, m'love. We have no secrets. None. Let Matt know you want to share his thoughts. I might just go along for the ride.*

How could she possibly appear so young? When Millie grinned in reply, she looked barely sixteen. Then her eyes took on a hazy, unfocused shimmer as she narrowed her thoughts and joined Matt's.

Images and feelings spilled into Ric's mind. Suffused his body with an unfamiliar heat and multilayered levels of sensation—Millie had linked with Matt, and Ric went along for the ride.

He felt the tightness of his sphincter, the way it clung to Matt's thick shaft, gripping him firmly in spite of the condom and plenty of lube. While disease and infections were not a concern to Chanku, they generally used condoms for anal sex. Ric knew Millie appreciated the aesthetics, especially when their lovemaking often went on for many hours and involved penetration of every possible body orifice.

Tonight, though . . . sex with Matt and Ric together, two men loving each other as they loved her, was something entirely new. She shared her own responses, her quivering, shivering need for more, her almost unbearable arousal and absolute joy in every move either man made. She'd never been so turned on in her life. She wanted to do this again, and again.

Making love with Millie while Matt fucked him senseless was something Ric figured he'd better get used to. He'd do anything for Millie, and she was certainly enjoying herself. She bombarded Ric's mind with the multiple images of anal sex from Matt's point of view and vaginal sex as she experienced it. Her arousal spiked, higher, and then higher again.

Ric sensed her fascination with each new impression, her utter absorption with sex through Matt's eyes and nerves, through the sensations enveloping his cock and the pressure in his balls. She was utterly enthralled by the strong clasp of Ric's muscles, the way his ass clamped down on Matt and held his thick shaft so tightly. The heat surprised her, too, as did the emotions spilling out of Matt. The love, the respect, the need for a connection that went beyond mere sex.

He saw Millie and Ric as his family. Just as he loved Daci and Deacon and saw them as his future mates, he accepted Millie and Ric as lovers on an entirely different level. They were the anchors that held him, the roots that grounded him. In such a short time, they had become the family he'd never really had. Accepting, loving, and understanding.

Ric lost himself in the thoughts swirling around in his head, in the amazing tactile experience of making love, of taking love. The clench and ripple deep inside Millie, the dark pleasure verging on pain as Matt's thick cock forged a path inside Ric. Thrust and fill, fill and be filled. Stretching tissues, clenching muscles, the ripple and quiver of hot, wet flesh.

The sounds blended one into the other. The slap of Matt's balls against Ric's ass, the wet, slurping pull as Ulrich's cock slipped almost free of Millie's heat, then filled her once more.

His sensitive nostrils flared with the pungency of sex, the ripe scent of clean sweat and sexual release, of Millie's sweet breath and the vanilla fragrance of her shampoo. Millie's arousal bathed him, Matt's love warmed him, and he was drifting.

Drifting in a world of sensation, his body on fire, his heart full. He floated in a perfect place of physical and emotional passion, of arousal tempered by love, lust fed by desire . . . floating on a wave of sensation until . . .

A tiny tendril of discord touched him. Blinking, body tensing, mind tilting into alertness, Ulrich focused on the thread of thought, worried it until it formed something he could actually follow.

A tiny glimmering strand of anxiety, it took him directly to Matt's subconscious. Moving cautiously, using what stealth and subtlety he possessed, Ric searched for the source of Matt's distress. He sensed one small concern—the pressure Matt felt from Daci and Deacon to complete the mating bond with them.

The even stronger sense that he could not bond yet—not while something held him back.

But what? Curious now, searching even as his body kept up the perfect rhythm of sex with Millie and Matt, Ric continued his quest for answers.

There, lost amid Matt's scattered impressions and thoughts, was something foreign. An alien pressure, separate from Matt's consciousness. Definitely not *of* Matt. Not his thoughts, not his feelings—instead, those of someone else. Someone unfamiliar and unknown. Powerful yet surprisingly filled with love, separate and yet not, voicing a single word. A directive as much as a suggestion, one that Ric absorbed and retained.

Florida.

Why Florida?

Was Matt aware of the presence? Of another consciousness lodged deeply within his own? Did he hear the whisper, or was it a subliminal command gnawing away at his conscious ability to make decisions? Ric hadn't sensed evil intent—just the opposite—but he had definitely felt strength and power behind the voice.

Anton would know. Anton Cheval knew everything—all Ric had to do was ask him. Later. When this amazing night had ended, when his body no longer clung to the man who filled him, no longer embraced the woman he filled.

Yin and yang . . . dark and light, male and female, two sides to the whole.

With Ulrich in the middle. Millie beneath him . . . and Matt, beautiful, loving Matt, for whatever reason, worried about Florida.

Millie heard the phone ring as she turned off the shower, but Ulrich was already out and heading across the room. He wrapped a towel around his trim waist and picked up the phone.

Sunlight filtered through the narrow window blinds and turned his hair silver. Millie felt the familiar little twist of arousal in her womb and had to bite her lips to keep from saying something that would have both of them naked and sweating in no time. She had work to do, a wolf sanctuary to run.

Ulrich held the phone to his ear. "How the hell do you do that?" Laughing, he turned toward Millie. "It's Anton. He must have known I was planning to call."

She watched him as she dried her hair and slipped into a comfortable pair of old sweats. Matt was gone. She'd heard him slip out of bed just before dawn and knew he'd headed back to the cabin he shared with Daci and Deacon.

His troubled thoughts seemed to have remained. She'd sensed them, too. He'd not mentioned why he was thinking of going to Florida, but both she and Ric had picked up his anxiety, his fear that he couldn't complete the mating bond with the two he loved until he'd made the trip.

A journey even Matt didn't understand.

What the hell was going on? Since they'd both been eavesdropping, neither Ric nor Millie felt comfortable bringing it up to Matt. When in doubt, call Anton Cheval—but as usual, he'd beaten them to it.

Ric spoke softly to Anton, nodded his head, gestured with his free hand. He paced across the bedroom, smiled at Millie as he continued his serious conversation with their pack leader.

Goddess how she loved him! Never more than now, when she knew Ric was troubled about Matt. Worried about her lover.

Why did that thought make her want to giggle?

Middle-aged, unmarried Millie West. Now a Chanku shapeshifter, mated to a very sexy man close to her own age, with a lover younger than her son—and both men more than willing to make love to her whenever she wanted either or both, together or separately.

It didn't get any better than this. It couldn't. Absolutely not. Millie was still grinning when she realized the room had gone silent. She raised her head and caught Ric staring at her with a bemused smile on his face, both hands planted firmly on his hips.

Millie cocked one eyebrow. "Well? What's up?"

"Anton's been dreaming about Matt. He's never even seen the boy and yet he described him perfectly to me, right down to the golden color in his wolf form with the darker band around his neck and shoulders. He even mentioned Matt's smile and his quiet human personality . . . and Florida. Anton's dreaming about Florida for some odd reason." Ric laughed. "He's got some property he wants to check on near the Tampa Bay area and figured he'd see if Matt wanted to go with him."

Millie just shook her head. "How does he do that? Weird. It's just way too weird."

Laughing, Ulrich leaned close and kissed her. "No, it's just Anton. Nothing weird at all."

"I don't get it." Daci stared at him with those luminous eyes of hers, and Matt felt like he wanted to throw up.

"I don't, either, Daci." He grabbed both her hands and held on. Too tight. He was crushing her fingers! He loosened his grip and looked up at Deacon, but the Deac was no help. All he did was shrug and stare back. "It's not you guys. I love you both. So much, but there's something pushing me. A feeling I can't explain, but it's like I have to go to Florida."

He shook his head. None of this made sense. Less than a week ago he'd been the one pushing Deacon and Daci to bond. Now they were ready and he was wimping out, and none of it made any sense. Now it was like he had this frickin' voice in his head, coming to him in his dreams, interrupting his thoughts during the day. Hell, he'd even felt it last night in the middle of some of the best sex he'd ever had. Just thinking about doing it with Ric and Millie—what they'd done—made him hard.

Except . . . he couldn't get it out of his head.

Florida. Shit, he'd never been to Florida in his life. Never thought about it, and now all of a sudden he felt like he had to go there? Maybe he was just losing his mind. That was it. Nothing more than a simple, uncomplicated mental breakdown.

Daci raised her head. "Someone's coming. I hear voices."

Deacon peered out the window. "Millie and Ric." He grinned at Matt. "I forgot to ask you how last night went. Sort of like a command performance, to get an invite from the boss."

Matt shook his head. "It's not like that. Not with those two. They're special. Good, loving people. Millie's . . ." He realized his skin was hot and flushed. Hell, just thinking about Millie and the things they'd done . . .

"You're blushing!" Daci leaned over and kissed his cheek as Deacon went to open the front door. "That's really sweet."

Millie stepped through the open door, followed by Ric. The small cabin suddenly felt even smaller. Matt stepped aside to make more room, but with the big bed dominating all the open space in the cabin, there wasn't much room to make.

Millie looked around and grinned. "You know, we do have a larger cabin available if you three would like a little more room to play."

Daci shook her head. "Are you kidding? At least in this place neither one of these guys can get away from me. I think that gives me an enviable advantage."

"There is that." Millie plopped down on the edge of the bed. "We had a message for Matt."

Deacon glanced at Daci and then at Matt. "Do you want us to leave?"

Matt shook his head. "Of course not. What's up?" He

leaned against the cabin wall, aware of a strange tension in the room.

"Anton Cheval called," Ric said. "He's got to make a trip to Florida and wondered if you'd be willing to go with him. Keisha had planned to go, but she doesn't want to leave Lily for a week, and the trip is more business than pleasure."

Ulrich's explanation sort of drifted into space. *Florida.* Why the fuck would Anton, the über-alpha of all the Chanku, a man he'd never even met, suddenly want to take him to Florida? The voice in Matt's head had been decidedly feminine, so it hadn't been Anton's thoughts he'd heard.

What the fuck was going on? Matt shrugged, and wondered if he'd pulled off the nonchalant look. "Sure," he said. "I don't actually know him, but if he wants me to, I'll go."

"Good. I didn't realize you'd never actually met Anton. Not until he called this morning. It's a good chance to get to know the man, and Stefan, too. They're good people. Anton's due to arrive about the same time as you. He said he'd wait for you in a coffee shop at the airport. Stefan's going to meet both of you a day later at your hotel. He's in Seattle at a board meeting for one of their companies right now, but he has a flight booked into Tampa the day after you arrive. Since you've been having dreams about Florida, same as Anton, he figured it only made sense that you should go with him."

"What? How'd you know I was dreaming about . . . ?" Matt shifted his eyes from Ric to Millie. Back to Ric.

Ric merely reached for Millie's hand and tugged her to her feet. "No secrets during sex, m'boy. None at all. At least not with an old dog like me. And no secrets from Anton Cheval, ever." He shook his head. "Before you ask, no. I don't have a clue how he does it. You better pack. Carry-on only, if you can. That way you won't have to wait on luggage. Anton's already e-mailed your tickets and your plane leaves Denver at noon to-morrow."

Ric stretched his arms overhead, arched his back, and changed the subject. "I hope you appreciate the fact that you and Millie just about killed me last night. I need a run to loosen up, so if you kids want to go with us, we're heading out just after dusk." He paused with one hand on the door.

"We'd love to have you join us," Millie said. She turned, glanced over her shoulder, and winked at Matt. Then the two of them left the cabin.

Matt stared at the door long after it closed. The fact they'd picked up on dreams he didn't even understand himself was unsettling. The fact Anton Cheval knew about them, all the way in Montana, totally freaked him out.

As for Millie's saucy wink? She'd left him standing there, hard as a post.

Millie and Ulrich weren't there yet, but Deacon and Daci trotted alongside Matt to the small meadow where they usually started their runs. Beth and Nick waited in the shadows. Nick stepped out to meet them. The guys went through the usual ritual of sniffing butts and noses, peeing on trees and rocks, and generally doing their best to out-alpha one another, at least until Ulrich showed up.

The girls sat quietly and waited. Matt figured they were probably laughing their heads off at the guys, but the instinctive male behavior was half the fun of shifting as far as he was concerned. Nick nipped at his shoulder and Matt jumped him. They tumbled into the brush, leapt to their feet, and squared off with hackles raised. Damn, he was going to miss Nick and Beth, now that they'd accepted an offer from Luc to work directly with the Pack Dynamics crew in San Francisco.

They might even be gone by the time he got home from Florida. The thought sobered him, but he'd known for a long time there was really nothing to hold Beth here at the sanctuary in Colorado.

Her ability to read lies versus truth had become even more powerful since the death of her stepfather. It was almost as if that nightmare had been holding her back, keeping her from becoming the woman she was meant to be.

She and Nick were definitely a lot happier. Nick was stronger, more self-assured. His confidence put him on level footing with his mate, something Matt had originally thought might never happen.

They were good together. Obviously in love, and a well-mated pair. He glanced at Daci and Deacon and caught them watching him. It was so damned obvious they were ready to mate, but they didn't want to do it without Matt. He still couldn't believe they really wanted him to join them, permanently. Loved him enough to wait until he was ready.

There was no doubt in his mind that he loved each of them, equally. So why the hell was he holding back?

Florida.

What the fuck did Florida have to do with anything? Maybe Anton Cheval would know. Damn, he hoped so. Right now he was just flat-out confused and none of this made sense.

Until Millie and Ric trotted into the meadow. Matt looked up and caught sight of the two, and his worries fled. For some reason, Millie had had that effect on him from the beginning. With a nod to Daci and Deacon, he took off along the well-traveled trail, ears forward, tail in the air.

There was something so frickin' amazing about running as a wolf, way beyond the mere fact that it was absolutely surreal and totally impossible. The wolf didn't worry about tomorrow. It didn't care about politics or relationships or what the future might hold. When he ran as a wolf, Matt existed in the here and now. His senses were alive to the forest, from the search for game to potential risks, to any threats that might harm him or his packmates.

Human worries faded away as his feral nature took control.

The September night was cool with the hint of fall. Leaves crackled beneath his big paws, and the scent of dry grasses and blackberries drying on the vines filled his nostrils. Creatures scurried out of his way, small things tunneling through grass and leaves and humus. Tiny bodies squeaked and scrabbled among the roots and rocks and detritus of the forest.

Matt heard them all. Sensed the myriad life forms in the air overhead, on the thick branches of the trees, creeping along the ground. Recognized life, catalogued each creature as to its nature and the place it held in the seething world around him.

When Millie paused with her nose in the air, he stopped as well. Each of them caught the scent of game and connected on a level so far beyond their human capabilities that humanity disappeared entirely.

Focused on the scent, Matt and the pack dissolved as shadows in the forest, each wolf slipping as silent as a wraith through thick undergrowth and tall trees.

When Millie charged the buck, the animal barely had time to react. Her jaws clamped down hard on his throat, and her weight brought the big mule deer to his knees. Daci and Beth attacked from opposite sides. The three females quickly finished the animal.

They stood over their prey, sides heaving, saliva dripping from bloodied jaws. Nick lunged forward, but it was Millie who warned him back. With the other males, Matt paced just outside the invisible yet obvious perimeter established by the females as Millie, Daci, and Beth tore into the animal's soft belly, ripping at thick hide and tearing away mouthfuls of warm flesh and muscle. Muzzles slick with blood, they gorged themselves for long minutes while the males snarled and paced.

When Ulrich, as the alpha male, finally moved in, the others followed. Matt ripped into the dead animal, gulping down huge, bloody chunks. It was good. The food, the kill, the strength of the pack. All of it so good.

The civilized mind of the man who walked on two legs was lost in the frenzied, feral instincts of the beast. Now he moved in absolute confidence on four legs. What mattered was filling his belly, remaining alert to danger. What resonated most were the power of the pack and the bestial instincts that drove him.

Life. Death. Hunger. Sex. Always sex, the drive to mate, to create, to ease the ache of constant arousal, undying need. Now, though, he gorged himself, consumed by his savage, feral nature, by the primitive lust for blood, the smells and the taste and the fading heat of a life just ended. Powerful, untamed needs that overpowered even his ferocious drive for sex.

He was consumed, as well, by something else. Something deeper than his nature, more powerful than his instincts.

The voice.

He *heard* the voice tonight, and it was more than a thread of need, a lingering sense of anxiety. It was more than a subconscious, subliminal directive.

Tonight, it slowly insinuated itself into his conscious mind until it wound about his feral self, holding him tighter, stealing his will.

Leaving him no other option. Matt backed away from the torn and tattered body of the dead deer. Shook his head in bestial denial and whimpered as the voice whispered in his head.

Whispered a powerful directive, an order that grew louder, stronger, until the voice was no longer a whisper, until he sensed it as a clarion call, one he had no choice but to obey.

Florida.

The single word raced along his spine. Raised his hackles. Mesmerized him.

Summoned him.

Aroused him. He felt his cock swell within its sheath. Knew he pulsed hard and hot, reacting to nothing more than the sound of a mysterious yet distinctly feminine voice.

Florida.

Shivers raced along his spine. His ears pressed flat against his broad head. *Impossible. It can't be.*

The voice reassured him.

Not impossible. Florida. Give heed.

Matt realized that everyone had paused. Bloodied muzzles were turned his way, ears pointed in his direction. Eyes stared directly at him. What could he say? How could he explain something he didn't understand himself?

It came to him, then. Such a simple thing and yet as confusing as the ages, as complex as a single moment in time. He raised his head, stared into the nighttime sky. Paused to absorb the intensity of the moment, the power of what he had to do.

Then the golden-hued wolf with the thick dark ruff around his back and neck lifted his nose to the heavens in a long, drawn-out howl, a cry that echoed to the heavens.

The rest of the pack joined in. It was right.

They made a powerful statement, filled with energy, with the joy of their existence.

It was good, and it was right.

How else did one answer the Goddess?

2
_____

They parted ways at the edge of the forest. Millie and Ulrich trotted toward their cabin, Beth and Nick headed to theirs. Deacon and Daci silently followed Matt back to their small cabin.

He still felt shaken. The mysterious voice was silent, as if his howl and those of his packmates, once they'd joined his song of worship, had somehow appeased it for now, but his body thrummed with intense arousal. It was always this way after a run. The burning, desperate need to calm the fires, the raging lust that coursed through his veins, hardened his cock, and fed from his feral nature.

Tonight, though, everything seemed, somehow, *more*—arousal more intense, sexual need more powerful, bestial nature more notable. His thoughts were muddied, so caught up in lust, in the need to . . .

"Matt?"

He glanced up to see Daci standing tall and naked on the back porch. She'd shifted. So had Deacon, yet Matt stood below them on all fours, his mind a seething maelstrom of questions and desire. The voice might be quiet, but carnal need was a panting, slavering creature fighting for release.

Still the wolf, he bounded up the steps and stuck his long snout between Daci's thighs, breathing deeply of her musky, feminine scent. She shrieked with laughter and grabbed his head in both hands. She didn't push him away.

No, she steadied him, held him close while he licked and stroked deep inside her sex, lapping up her sweet cream, shoving his wet nose against her clit while she trembled with one small climax after another. His tongue stretched inside and he stroked the smooth, slick walls of her vaginal passage, curling the tip against her womb, his muzzle buried so deep he finally had to pull back to breathe. He was vaguely aware of Deacon's laughter, Daci's shuddering whimper . . . and then she was gone, tugged away, out of his reach.

"C'mon, Matt. Inside. There's too much risk of someone seeing us out here." Still laughing, Deacon held the door open and pulled Daci across the threshold.

Still on four legs, Matt followed. He leapt up on the bed and stood in the middle, legs braced. Daci and Deacon's voices seemed to come from far away. Deacon's deep laughter, Daci's giggles, the moans and whimpers as they stood beside the bed and stroked one another. Kissed one another, oblivious to Matt's presence.

He growled, low and threatening.

Daci spun around. Her lips were shiny and swollen from Deacon's kisses, her breasts high and proud, her nipples ruched into tightly puckered points. The tuft of dark hair between her legs was matted and wet, as much from his wolven tongue as her own liquid release.

Deacon held her close as if he protected her within the curve of his arm. Protecting Daci from the wolf? Deacon's tall, lean body was pressed close against Daci's feminine curves. His cock stood rampant, resting against her hip.

Matt growled again. He took a step closer to Daci, his eyes focused on the dark triangle of hair and the secrets it guarded. Eyes, hell! His entire existence was focused on that perfect target. Another growl rumbled up out of his chest. He felt the saliva dripping from his parted jaws, imagined Daci's sweet flavor.

Another cautious step, almost to the edge of the mattress. His nostrils flared and his ears flattened even tighter to his skull as the mingled scents of both Daci and Deacon's arousal slammed into him.

Arousal—and fear?

Why should they fear him? He shook his head, vaguely aware of a buzzing in his mind, a voice in his head.

Not the Goddess . . . a familiar voice this time. Daci?

Matt? Are you okay? Why haven't you shifted? You don't want to bond now, do you? Not like this, Matt. It has to be special. Not like this.

Again, he shook his head, confused. Deacon was beside him then, his lanky human body pressed close to Matt's furry one. Deacon threw his arms around Matt's thick neck, buried his face in the thick ruff of fur at his shoulder.

C'mon, buddy. What's wrong? You're acting all weird tonight. Can't you tell us? There's something bothering you, but if you don't tell us what it is, we can't help. You've got walls up neither of us can break through.

Matt shivered. His ears flattened against his skull. He whined, blinking rapidly. As Daci and Deacon's concern filtered into his feral mind, it was as if someone had just pulled a blindfold off his eyes. Slowly raising his head, he looked at Daci's beautiful face with her dark, soulful eyes and the thick tumble of dark brown curls around her shoulders. Deliberately, he studied her, focusing on the slim yet womanly shape of her body, the soft curve of her breasts. His heart thudded slowly in his chest, and he knew love as he'd never known it before.

Not just Daci's. Deacon's, too. Love pouring into him from his dearest friends. Worry, concern, and unlimited love. Ashamed, unsure of what had just happened, Matt shifted. Hanging his head, he stared at his big human feet dangling over the side of the bed and wished he were a million miles away.

"What the fuck happened, man?" Deacon cupped the side of his face in his warm palm and turned Matt's chin so that he couldn't avoid the concern in those dark amber eyes. "You growled like you were really pissed, almost like you were jealous of Daci and me. You're not jealous, are you? We both love you. Daci, you. Me. We're a team, Matt. We're together. The three of us. Always the three of us." He laughed softly. "We're all such odd ducks, we're perfect together."

Deacon was right. They were a most improbable team of misfits. Deacon had been a male prostitute on the streets in San Francisco since he was barely a teenager. Abandoned as a baby, Matt was adopted by a family that had never figured him out, and finally kicked him out of the house. Like Deacon, he'd worked the streets to survive. And Daci, dear, sweet, and beautiful Daciana Lupei, was the illegitimate daughter of the greatest enemy the Chanku had known. Her father was dead now, killed by Ulrich Mason . . . the man who now led their small pack.

Matt might have laughed if he didn't feel like crying. They were a team, all right. Three misfits who somehow clicked, who were stronger together than they'd ever been alone. Deacon and Daci were great, but he . . . shit. He was losing it.

"I don't know what's going on." He hoped they heard his whisper. It wasn't easy, talking past the huge lump in his throat. Daci moved closer until she stood between his knees. She rested her hands on his shoulders. Matt raised his head, looked into her troubled eyes, and sighed. "I don't know if I'm losing my mind or . . ."

"Why?" Daci leaned close and kissed him. The raging lust

had quieted, but he still felt his cock rise with the soft touch of her lips. "Why do you think you're losing it?"

"Voices." He shook his head. "I'm hearing this voice in my head. A woman's voice, and it just keeps whispering 'Florida' as if I should know what that means."

"You're not crazy, Matt." Daci kissed him again. "You're going to Florida tomorrow and you'll find answers. Especially since you're going with Anton Cheval. He understands everything, and if he doesn't, he studies the situation until he knows what's going on. Don't worry. It's all going to work out." She smiled and ran her finger along his jaw. "We'll be here when you come back. Then we're going to bond. I'm not going to risk you leaving us."

He raised his head and frowned. "I love you. Both of you. Why would I leave you? You and Deacon are the best things that ever happened to me."

Daci laughed and twisted her body until she slipped into his lap, trapping his cock between her smooth flank and his belly. It felt so good to be this close, he groaned.

"Oh, maybe if Millie decides she can't live without you. I see how you watch her. And I know you guys are having way too much fun when you're with her . . . and Ulrich."

Matt shook his head, embarrassed. "I don't love Millie that way. Not the way I love you." He wrapped his left arm around Daci's waist and threw his right arm over Deacon's shoulders. "Or you, either, Deac. With Millie and Ric it's . . . well, it's good, but it's not what we have. Not anything close."

"Then why are you holding back?" Daci wrapped her arms around his back and leaned her cheek against his chest. "What's wrong?"

Matt shook his head, lost in the sadness in Daci's eyes. "I don't know. The voice tonight . . . it was different. Before, it's been more a sensation in my mind. Tonight, I heard a woman speak. I didn't recognize her voice, but I heard her as clearly as when you and I are talking." He took a deep, shuddering breath. "You're going to think I'm nuts, but I swear to you, I'm hearing the Goddess."

Daci cocked her head to one side and frowned. "Our Goddess? The one Anton talks about. Did she say her name? Does she even have a name?"

Before Matt could answer, Deacon laughed, but he wasn't teasing or making fun. He was just being Deacon. "Hello, Matt," he said. His voice was low and sexy. "This is your goddess calling."

Matt felt his tension fade away. He jabbed Deacon in the ribs with an elbow and grinned. "Not quite, Deac, but pretty damned close. Somehow, I know that's who was speaking." He shrugged, ready to change the subject. "Daci's right. When I come back from Florida, I should have answers then."

"I'm holding you to that." Daci spun around until she straddled his hips. "But in the meantime, I've got a question."

Matt dropped both arms loosely over her shoulders and rested his forehead against hers. "Oh? What's that?"

Daci rolled her hips, just enough to bring the damp lips of her sex in contact with the underside of his erect shaft. "You gonna share your toys?"

Deacon reached between their bodies and wrapped his long fingers around Matt's cock. "I was wondering the same thing. He doesn't play well with others, does he?" Slowly he slipped his hand down the full length of Matt's shaft, then just as slowly pulled up. He slipped Matt's foreskin over the swollen glans, squeezed gently, then slipped it down again.

Matt groaned. He wrapped his arms around Daci and fell backward on the big mattress. Daci's full breasts pressed against his chest, all soft, womanly, and warm except for the hard tips of her nipples. She undulated against him, dragging those hot little points across his chest.

Matt pivoted his legs toward the foot of the bed with Daci

still sprawled across him, until he lay full length on the bed. She sat up, astride him now, flattened her palms on his chest, and lifted her hips. Deacon still had a tight grasp on Matt's cock. He aimed the broad tip directly into Daci's slick channel. Slowly she eased herself down over Matt's full length.

Even now, after all the months they'd been together, after so many days and nights of lovemaking, so many positions and so many men, Daci was still a tight fit for Matt's huge erection. They'd learned to move slowly, cautiously, when they first connected. Now that he was totally engulfed in her wet heat, the sensation of taut, wet muscles rippling along his length made it well worth the time it took to work himself deep inside her.

Deacon slipped around behind Daci. He straddled Matt's legs, but from Daci's needy whimpers and rough moans of pleasure, it was obvious he wasn't just watching the action.

Matt felt the hard, muscular mouth of her womb against his glans just as Daci sort of wriggled her hips, took a long, deep breath, and relaxed the muscles in her thighs. The weight of her body forced him even deeper. He knew he was huge, but he was all the way inside. Already, Daci was adjusting to his size.

It felt so damned good, it took all his self-control to keep from bucking upward, thrusting deep, but no way was he going to risk hurting his woman. Daci was more than willing to try anything, but he was a big guy and so was Deacon. They loved her too much to risk giving her any discomfort. His body quivered with the strain of keeping himself under control. He took slow, steady breaths and held perfectly still.

Daci tilted forward just a bit, then more, until her tightly puckered nipples brushed his chest. Matt bit back a moan of pure pleasure and concentrated on her face, just inches from his. Daci's eyes were closed, her lips parted.

She was more beautiful than any woman he'd ever seen.

Matt glanced over her shoulder in time to watch Deacon

slowly roll a condom down over his full length. Then he spread thick, clear gel on his fingers.

Matt opened his thoughts to both Deacon and Daci. Daci's mind was filled with sensual images—the thickness of Matt's erection deep inside her vagina, the sense of fullness and the pressure against her womb. Then she added the slick slide of Deacon's fingertips along the deep crease between her buttocks.

Flicking into Deacon's thoughts, Matt saw Daci through Deacon's eyes. The smooth curve of her spine, the rounded swell of her bottom, and the sleek line of her flank. He felt the warmth between her cheeks, the tight little pucker of muscle guarding her anus.

The visual spiked Matt's arousal, the tactile sensations made him harder still. Through Daci's mind, he felt the soft brush of slick fingertips as if they brushed over his own ass, separated his buttocks, slowly forced entrance. Winced at the sharp burn of entry, the easing of taut muscle, the dark, sensual slide into a passage not designed, though sensually perfect, for penetration by a fully erect penis.

Daci tilted forward, still fully impaled on Matt's shaft. She leaned close and licked his chest, running her slick tongue over his collarbone, teasing his mouth with tiny kisses. He trembled with the need to hold perfectly still, to give Daci complete control and time to adjust. Both men were so big, yet she loved to take them both inside her body.

It was only right that she do it on her terms.

She grunted and moved forward. Matt felt the broad head of Deacon's cock through the thin tissues separating Daci's twin channels. Deacon entered her as slowly and carefully as Matt had done, inching his way deeper inside.

Matt felt the flared head of Deacon's cock sliding along the underside of his. Tensed his muscles, holding perfectly still when everything inside begged him to thrust. Quivering with suppressed desire, he closed his eyes and centered himself on the frustratingly slow progress as Deacon entered Daci on a journey that took Matt to the brink of madness.

Finally, Deacon let out a slow breath of air, leaned forward, and rested his forehead against Daci's spine. All of them panted, as if they'd just run a race, yet there were no losers. Only winners, now that Deacon and Matt filled Daci, now that her body slowly rippled and clenched about them both.

Deacon raised his head and grinned at Matt, but his jaw was still clenched, his eyes bright pools of amber fire. Daci slowly rose up along the length of Matt's cock, then came down, just a little faster, impaling herself on Deacon, filling herself with Matt. Again, and then again, with Deacon behind her, inside her.

With Matt before her, buried deep inside her heat, it was as if he and Deacon made love to each other through Daci. The sensation of tightness and heat within Daci's body, multiplied exponentially as they shared individual sensations through a common mental, physical, and emotional link. The amazing sense and slide of two thick cocks, rubbing one against the other through a wall of living flesh barely thicker than the condom Deacon wore.

Heat and stricture, rippling muscles flexing in waves of pressure, contracting, releasing, contracting yet again. Daci sat upright now, taking both men deep inside with each lift and fall of her body. Her thighs trembled with her effort to rise, her breasts jiggled each time she came down hard on Matt's groin. Their pubic hair was wet and matted with her lubricating juices.

She threw her head back, eyes closed, lips parted in a knowing smile with her entire focus on the men who filled her. Daci's thick, dark curls danced across her shoulders and she moved faster, came down harder. Her fingernails dug crescent-shaped furrows into Matt's sides and a light sheen of perspiration covered her skin.

She carried both men with her, taking them to the edge, to a point where unbridled lust threatened to throw all of them over the edge.

And there she held them, slowing her body until both Deacon and Matt hovered, right at the edge of release. Her smile grew with the knowledge she controlled the pace of their lovemaking, the level of arousal. Her thoughts swirled among them, the sense that she loved this too much to let it end, that she loved both men more than she'd ever thought it possible to love anyone or anything.

The knowledge that she, a woman who had lived almost her entire life without love, was now loved by two men she saw as perfect. Two men who met every need she had, every want she might experience. She would never choose between them because she couldn't—they were her men and she loved without reservation.

All this and more swept through Matt's mind. His heart thundered in his chest, his body ached with the need to climax. He clutched at Daci's hips and drove into her, taking control, wresting it away in a single penetrating thrust. Her eyes flashed open and her mouth opened in a perfect O of surprise.

Then Matt slipped his fingers between them, gently caressed the shining curve of her clitoris. Daci's body jerked in response. Her movements were frantic as she tilted her hips forward to press against his fingers even as she struggled to hold on to her fragile control.

Matt felt the sharp coil of heat in the small of his back, the aching pressure in his balls. He fired the sensation of his impending climax to Daci and Deacon, pinching her clitoris between his thumb and forefinger at the same time.

Daci screamed and arched her back, driving Matt deep and

Deacon deeper still. Matt thrust into her clutching, clenching body, felt the jerk and twitch of Deacon's cock against his, and his world went black. Daci's scream, Deacon's cry of pleasure, Matt's long, low groan of completion.

And there, in the minds of all three through their shared link, a new voice. The same voice in Matt's dreams, in his mind, and now in the minds of his lovers.

Joining them. Sharing the sensations of orgasm, whispering once again, the same command to Matt.

Florida.

And then a long, drawn-out cry of completion. A sense of shock, of glorious surprise.

Then nothing.

Deacon sprawled across Daci's slim back, and both of them held Matt to the bed. His cock still pulsed inside Daci. He'd come so hard his semen had spilled out of her spasming sex and now filled the space between their bodies. Sticky and sweaty and reeking of sex, he had absolutely no desire to move.

Deacon managed to raise his head. He peered over Daci's shoulder and stared, wide-eyed, at Matt. "Who the fuck was that?"

It was Daci who answered. Her lips were pressed against Matt's chest, so her voice sounded muffled. "I think we just screwed a goddess."

Deacon nodded. "I was afraid of that." He lowered his head and rested once again on Daci's back.

Matt just lay there and grinned. Deacon and Daci had heard her, too. They knew now. He wasn't cracking up. He was fine. Absolutely fine, once he got past the idea he'd somehow inherited his very own goddess.

Matt wasn't sure how he was going to find which coffee shop Anton wanted to meet in, but within seconds after the plane landed, he realized he didn't have a thing to worry about. Though they'd never met, Anton Cheval's mental greeting was loud and clear. Following the power behind his mindtalking was easier than reading a map.

With his backpack slung over one shoulder, Matt spotted the small restaurant after only a few minutes' walk. Though the shop was filled with customers, there was no mistaking the alpha he'd been told to find.

Anton Cheval sat alone at a small table. Dressed in dark slacks and a white shirt with the long sleeves rolled back along slim wrists, he had an unmistakable presence that was impossible to ignore.

Women filled every one of the nearby tables, and a few blatantly stared at the man. Matt paused a moment and studied the scene. Anton, with his long dark hair and finely chiseled face, looked as if he might be a movie star. Matt knew he'd been a famous magician years ago, but the women trying to get his attention now were Matt's age or younger.

Didn't they realize Anton was in his fifties? Of course, he didn't look that old, but . . .

Anton raised his head and waved to Matt. Laughter filtered into his mind. *Kiss me as if you're my lover when you reach the table. Then the women will leave us alone. If not, once they see you we'll never get away from them.*

This guy was okay. Matt's nerves fled. He walked boldly into the coffee shop, past tables of staring women and straight to Anton Cheval. Anton looked up and smiled.

Matt leaned over and kissed him full on the mouth. He felt Anton's fingers at the nape of his neck, the soft press of his perfect lips on Matt's, and they both heard the collective sigh of disappointed women.

Laughing at their private joke, Matt slipped into the empty chair. Anton reached across the small table and took his hand.

"It's a pleasure to meet you, Matt." Anton frowned. His eyes narrowed and he stared directly into Matt's eyes.

"Interesting. I sense the goddess in you."

Matt shook his head. "She was there last night. There's nothing quite like a simultaneous orgasm with two partners and suddenly realizing you've been joined by a third."

Anton covered his face with his hand. Matt was sure he was trying not to laugh.

"I am, and I'm not succeeding." Chuckling, he raised his head. "She was there? During sex as well?"

Matt glanced up as a waitress approached and flipped over the clean coffee cup in front of him. She filled his and Anton's as well. When she'd moved on to the next table, Matt turned to Anton. "She must have been, though I wasn't aware of her at first. Not until the actual climax. It's a little disconcerting to have a strange woman's sigh of pleasure joining in."

"Better than a complaint, I would imagine." Anton sipped his coffee.

"There is that. Why, though? Why Florida? And how did you know I was having the dreams?"

"Finish your coffee." Anton glanced about the small shop. Customers were coming and going, and an entirely new group of women were taking the vacated chairs nearby. "I think you're a bigger draw than I am. The female population must be suffering a dearth of eligible males. Let's go where we can talk privately."

Matt finished his coffee. Anton paid the bill and they headed out to the parking garage where a rental car waited. It wasn't until they were on the freeway, heading out of town, that Matt even thought to ask where they were going.

He'd been totally mesmerized by the man beside him. A man he'd known now for less than an hour, one whose single kiss, given in jest, still had him aroused and ready for whatever might come.

* * *

"It's been years since I last drove these roads."

Matt turned away from the window he'd been staring out of for the past half hour. "Did you used to live here?"

Anton nodded. "I was young, then, about your age. Had no idea of my Chanku birthright. I was a magician in a second-rate circus. Did my magic tricks and pursued women with a single-minded dedication. I kept thinking that somehow, someday, I'd finally break out, make my fame on stage."

He turned and grinned at Matt. His smile lit up his entire face. "I was gonna be a big star," he said, laughing. Then he shook his head and turned his attention back to the road.

"And were you?"

"What?"

"A big star?" Matt watched Anton's face and tried to read the slow grin that spread across his face.

"Of course. Would you expect anything less of me?" Anton laughed. "No, I guess you wouldn't expect anything. You don't know me well enough to have experienced what my mate refers to as my insufferable ego. Matt, I never do anything halfway, so yes, to answer your question, I was a very big star. I worked the stage in Las Vegas, had a television special that did well. I was at the peak of my career, and then I walked away from it."

"Wow. Do you miss it?" Matt realized he could easily picture Anton onstage, holding the audience enthralled. His voice alone had a mesmerizing quality that drew Matt into his words and had him picturing the big crowds, the bright lights, the cameras.

"Never." Anton shook his head. "I can honestly say I have never missed it a single day. My life is full, and I have more than I ever expected. My mate, my daughter, the pack . . ."

Anton's voice broke. Matt jerked around and stared at the guy's sharp profile. His jaw was clenched, and he took a long, deep breath as if reaching for control.

"They are everything to me," he said. Matt strained to catch the roughly spoken words. "Everything. Money, fame, the adoration of fans . . . none of it can compare. Nothing."

Matt watched him for a few moments longer. Then he turned back in his seat and watched the road ahead. He realized that he felt the same way as Anton. Daci, Deacon . . . the pack. They were everything to him. Nothing could compare. Nothing.

"Matt . . . ?"

"What?" Matt blinked rapidly. He must have been dozing. The road had narrowed and he had no idea where they were, but then he had no idea where they were going, either.

Anton took a deep breath. "Something weird happened today, and it has to do with you. I was reminded of something I shouldn't have forgotten, and that makes me nervous. That I forgot something so important to me."

"I don't get it." Matt turned in his seat, better to see the man beside him. Anton was frowning now, as if trying to organize convoluted thoughts.

He flashed Matt a quick grin. "I'm sorry. I'm thinking out loud. It was when we kissed," he said, keeping his eyes on the traffic ahead, "and yes, that was purely to confuse the growing crowd of women, but I got more than I expected. I told you I sensed a presence in you." He glanced toward Matt once again, then back at the road. "A presence I think I recognize. One I had forgotten about. Perhaps the forgetting was her doing, perhaps my own sense of self-preservation. I'm not certain. What I am certain of is that the same entity calling you to Florida is the same one who came to me, here, many years ago. She came to me for nothing more than sex, and when she was finally satiated, she left."

Matt frowned. "What did you do? How did you feel when she left?"

Anton shook his head. "As hard as it is to believe, I don't re-member. I had forgotten her entirely until today. Even now I can only recall small bits and pieces of the time we spent to-gether, but those memories must have been buried pretty deep for me to forget them." He sighed. "I don't forget easily. Nor do I like the idea that my memories might have been manipu-lated, my free will taken from me."

"Just like I don't like hearing voices telling me to do things, making me feel as if I have no choice." Matt crossed his arms over his chest and sat back in the comfortable seat.

Anton nodded, and Matt knew he understood. Then Anton's thoughts flowed into his mind, and he finally realized why everyone looked to this man with such reverence. There was power here. Unbelievable power, and yet he opened him-self to Matt as if they were equals.

And Anton wasn't any happier with what was going on now than he'd been so many years ago.

He was remembering the woman, and wondering how he could have ever forgotten the time they'd spent together. But he had. He'd forgotten it entirely until a couple of hours ago, when he'd shared that kiss in jest with Matt. She was there. The sense of her, of the Goddess, in Matt.

It had to be her. Only, when he'd first known her, she hadn't been the Goddess.

She'd been *the woman.*

There'd been so many women during those years. They came and went like the ebb and flow of the sea. Dancers and ac-robats, tumblers, even the occasional clown. Trapeze artists, makeup artists, animal trainers, and whores, coming and going so that after a while they'd all run together, a montage of bellies and breasts and cunts—shaved or not—until he'd no longer been able to recall a face or a name or even the sex.

And, until now, he'd not been able to define a single point in time, a single instance when he'd felt anything other than relief for easing an immediate need.

There'd been one, though. Had he dreamed her? The face no longer existed, no matter how hard he tried to recall. No name, not even the sense of her body, not her age or race or size, but now, since kissing Matt, he recalled the sense of her.

Had she come to him in his dreams? Did she really exist? Anton turned and studied the young man sitting beside him. Matt quietly watched him in return, listening for whatever Anton intended to share. Matt's mind was open, his every thought clear to Anton's search. He was wondering about the man beside him, wondered about the voice in his head.

Wondering, most of all, who the woman was who commanded him. Why he'd been chosen and what he needed to do to satisfy her enough to leave him alone.

"I think you need to fuck her."

"What?" Matt blinked. He stared at Anton. "What did you say?"

"You were wondering why the Goddess had called you here to Florida. What she wanted of you. How to get her out of your head." He shrugged and turned his attention fully to the road for a moment as the traffic slowed, bunched up, and then moved on ahead. "I think you need to fuck her. Open to her presence, invite her in, and make love to her." Anton checked the rearview mirror and then turned off at the entrance to a luxury resort beside a perfectly manicured golf course.

Matt stared at him. He couldn't have meant that literally? Could he? Fuck the Goddess? *Shit.*

Matt was still trying to wrap his head around that when Anton continued. "I'm remembering now. Not everything, but some of what happened between us is coming back."

He pulled under a covered archway near the office of a resort that absolutely reeked of luxury. With his mind spinning in a million directions at once, Matt stared wide-eyed out the open window of the rental car. It was easier than making sense of what Anton had just suggested.

Much easier.

Anton touched his shoulder. "It's simple, really," he said, smiling confidentially at Matt. "She's our Goddess, but she is very, very lonely. If I'm correct, I think she draws her strength from sex. Matt, I believe she's chosen you as her lover."

3

Matt tossed his shirt on the closed toilet seat and ran his fingers through the drying sweat on his chest. The air conditioning didn't make a sound, but he knew it had to be on. It was cooler here by at least twenty degrees, the air comfortably dry after the cloying humidity outside. He turned on the cold water tap and washed his face in a bathroom more luxurious than anything he'd ever seen in his life. When he raised his head from the marble sink and stared into the mirror that had to be at least twelve feet wide, he didn't know whether he wanted to laugh or cry or just run away and hide.

They hadn't gotten a room in the hotel. Shit, no. The owner of the place didn't stay in something as mundane as a room or even a suite. Anton had his own private digs away from the main buildings. Matt glanced around, at the bathroom that was almost as big as the whole fucking cabin he shared with Daci and Deacon, and couldn't believe Anton had the balls to call the mansion they were staying in a "cottage."

Two bedrooms the size of most apartments, each with a private bathroom big enough to house a family. There was a fully stocked kitchen and a main room that was all glass on one side with a view of a perfectly manicured swamp.

That was the only way he could describe it. The damned jungle looked like something a landscape artist might have designed, it was so beautiful, so utterly impossible.

And it was still easier to concentrate on the cottage and the jungle and the fact Anton Cheval owned this whole fucking place than it was to think about the other thing he really didn't want to consider.

The fact that he felt like a fucking sacrificial lamb. The fact that the voice in his head was the voice of a goddess. Not a woman, but a damned Goddess with a capital G . . . and she wanted him.

Matt stared at himself in the mirror and wondered why in the hell she'd chosen him. He wasn't anything special. Yeah, he was tall and built okay, and he didn't look like a freak, but he was just a guy.

A guy who was desperately in love with a beautiful woman and a man who was the best friend and most amazing lover he'd ever known in his life.

Two people he missed so badly he thought his heart might break. Missed their smiles and their laughter, the love that was part of everything they did, every word they said.

"Don't you understand?" His whisper sounded pathetic, even to him. What must the Goddess think? Did she even hear him? "I love Daci and Deacon. I've never loved anyone in my life the way I love them. No one's ever loved me, but those two do. I love them, they love me. Get it?"

He planted his palms on the edge of the sink and stared at the water running down the drain.

Sort of how he felt right now. Like his entire life, everything he'd finally allowed himself to dream about, was swirling down the drain like wasted water, headed for the sewer. And damn but he missed his lovers. Missed them more than he'd imagined he could miss anyone.

A sharp rap shocked him out of his misery. Matt's head jerked up and he stared at the closed door. "Yeah? It's unlocked."

Anton stepped into the room. He'd changed into a clean pair of dark slacks and a fresh white cotton shirt. No tie. It was too hot and humid for that, and when you were as rich as Anton Cheval, Matt figured you could wear whatever you wanted.

Anton grinned. "You're right. And I do."

Would he ever get used to the way this guy could read his thoughts? It was downright freaky.

"You will. I promise." Anton laughed. "I do apologize, but I don't always realize I'm reading, not hearing. Drives my mate nuts, but Keisha's gotten pretty good at blocking me. Stefan just ignores me. He's really good at that. It's probably why we're such good friends." Anton leaned against the counter, his back to the mirror and his arms folded across his chest.

The direct look he gave Matt was more than a little unsettling, knowing how easy it was for Anton to see everything he thought. There didn't seem to be any point trying to block him. It wasn't like Matt had anything to hide.

"For what it's worth," Anton said, "I was the Goddess's lover many years ago. An affair I thought lasted for weeks actually appears to have passed in little more than a heartbeat. To be precise, during the break between my first evening show and the second. No one even realized I'd been gone." He shook his head. There was a bemused expression on his face, unusual in a man so self-confident.

"All these years . . . I didn't even realize I'd been gone." His voice had dropped to a whisper. "I didn't know I'd made love to a goddess. Our Goddess. Not until today, after I kissed you and the memories began filtering back."

Anton rested his hand on Matt's shoulder. Warmth and a sense of connection between himself and a man he'd met only a few hours ago slammed into him. Matt's body thrummed with arousal, with such a powerful rush of need he was almost afraid to admit the sensation to himself, much less to the one who caused it—as if Anton didn't already know. To make matters even worse, Matt's eyes filled with tears. He didn't want to cry.

He swallowed back the huge lump in his throat.

"For what it's worth, Matt, she's always been all about goodness and love. I've never felt threatened by her. Whether she's our creator or our caretaker . . ." Anton shrugged. Shook his head. "Hell, Matt. I don't know. You're here because she called you. I'm here because I feel as if I'm the one who was supposed to bring you. I have questions I hope to find answers to. Maybe you're going to be part of the answer. I don't know."

Matt felt as if he'd stepped into some sort of alternate world, a dimension apart from the only reality he'd ever truly embraced—his life as a Chanku shapeshifter, as Daci and Deacon's lover. The years before were filled with memories best forgotten—an adoptive family that couldn't figure out the odd child they'd raised, a life on the streets where he'd often felt less than a word, a breath, a heartbeat from disaster.

Now he stood in what he could only describe as a truly sybaritic bathroom discussing his future as the lover of a goddess with a man he'd known for only a couple of hours.

A man whose simple, caring gesture left his body aching and aroused, his heart thundering in his chest. Pounding out a cadence of need, of want and desire so powerful it took his breath. He needed to touch Anton, and he did. He raised his hand and pressed his palm over the man's heart.

Matt felt the cadence of Anton's heart beating against his hand, a steady *thump, thump, thump*—exactly the same rhythm as his. Matt stared at his fingers, so tan and dark against the pristine shirt. He felt the connection, the warmth of Anton's right hand resting on his left shoulder, the heat beneath his right palm pressed against the taut muscle over Anton's heart.

A circle, complete and entirely whole. He stared at his fingers, the way they splayed over the smooth, white cotton shirt. Anton's heart seemed to beat faster, harder.

Matt's sped up as well. Without thinking, he slid his fingers up the smooth cotton, over Anton's collarbone and around the back of his neck beneath the neatly tied queue of dark hair. They were both large men, physically almost equals, yet Matt hesitated for a moment as he spread his fingers slowly across Anton's skull and pulled his face close.

There'd been no planning in this kiss. No audience to act for, no underlying need beyond the pure power of desire, the need Matt felt in himself, the need he couldn't ignore in Anton. It was really such a simple thing, to touch his lips to Anton's, to feel the smooth texture, sense his lips parting, inhale the sweet taste of mint, of man.

Two men—one comfortable in his power, the other still learning his body's capabilities, one in his fifties, the other in his twenties yet each a perfect physical specimen, each connected through their common heritage.

Their common desire.

Anton's left hand moved slowly over Matt's shoulder, down his biceps. Moved to his back, the fingers splayed wide as he exerted just enough pressure to pull their bodies close, until Matt's naked chest touched the smooth cotton covering Anton's.

Matt groaned and shifted his legs, widening his stance and wrapping his left arm around Anton's slim waist. They met now, fused from mouth to chest to groin, their shared desire pulsing between them, the need spiraling up, higher.

Matt opened his mouth to Anton's tongue, to the intimate thrust and retreat that was a mere prelude to the sex each of them wanted. His cock pressed painfully against the zipper of his jeans. Anton's erection was just as hard, a hot length of powerful muscle trapped behind neatly fitted slacks, pressing alongside Matt's denim-bound shaft.

He thought of moving to the big bed just outside the door, but that would require breaking the connection, separating their bodies for the moment in time it would take to cross the few feet of open space between bathroom and bed.

The simple act of kissing pulled Matt into a maelstrom of lust. His body trembled, muscles clenched as he slowly, methodically made love to Anton's mouth, as he absorbed the matching need spilling out of another man, the sense that this was as it should be, this act at this moment. Their bodies bound together by pure, carnal need.

Power seemed to pulse between them. Power and a sense of something alien, yet familiar. Matt closed his eyes and opened himself to the moment, to Anton's hands stroking his sides, to Anton's lips moving over his, to the damp sweep of his tongue over the edge of his teeth, across the sensitive ridged surface at the roof of Matt's mouth.

Drowning in sensation, Matt knew he was suffocating with the need to breathe deeply of Anton's scent, to taste and touch and understand the planes and valleys of his perfect body. He gasped, momentarily blinded by an odd disconnect from the physical sensations and powerful lust coursing through him.

Confused, blinking to clear his vision of the impossible, Matt looked down on the two of them. Two men holding one another, their legs tangled, their arms wrapped around each other's bodies, hips undulating, one against the other in a sensual dance that left him clinging to the edge of reason.

Impossible. It can't be! Matt glanced to his left and sensed Anton beside him.

It can. It is. This has happened before. With Adam Wolf. And for Adam, with others in the pack. But somehow, this is . . .

Light flashed. A burst of sunshine, an explosion of flame,

and Matt knelt on a green carpet of freshly mowed lawn. Knelt beside Anton. Both of them naked, both heavily aroused.

Both of them on their knees, with heads lowered before a woman of such beauty, of such power and strength and light, they could only bow their heads in awe.

Matt had no idea how long he knelt there, terrified yet thankful Anton was beside him. His heart hammered against his ribs, his lungs ached with the need to draw more air. The light around them shimmered, dimmed, and then shifted to the natural light of a softly sunlit day.

Matt raised his head. The woman who looked down at him was definitely gorgeous, though not as awesome, not as frightening, as she'd been only moments ago. She wore a simple white shift that fell beyond her ankles. He had no control over his eyes as he visually worshipped her body from top to bottom. Her feet were bare. Perfectly shaped toes peeked out beneath the hem. She smiled at him, and then she turned to Anton and held out her hand.

"I've missed you, my love."

Blinking owlishly, Anton took her hand and rose to his feet. He gave her a courtly bow and a smile that made his face as beautiful as the woman's. "If I'd been allowed to remember, I know I would have missed you as well."

Her laughter sounded like bells ringing in the forest. "It was for the best." Her smile dimmed and she said, very softly, "It is always for the best that you forget. Besides, you have your beloved Keisha."

Anton nodded. "I do, and even now, with the memory of your love returned, she fills my heart, Goddess."

"As she should."

Still holding Anton's hand, she turned her attention to Matt. He trembled as understanding raced through him. This was the Goddess. The one they prayed to, the one they cursed.

The one who haunted his dreams.

She held out her hand. Matt placed his fingers in hers, surprised to feel warm flesh, the strength of muscles and bones beneath the skin.

"For now, yes," she said.

Matt stood before her. Towered over her, but their hands remained tightly clasped. "For now?" he asked.

She smiled.

He blinked, awed once more by her beauty.

"Warm flesh. Strong, tensile muscles. I have taken corporeal form, for now. As I did with Anton, so many of your years ago. Come."

She released her grasp on their hands and turned away. Matt glanced at Anton just as Anton turned his way. He winked and Matt shrugged. Then they turned and followed the Goddess along a narrow path through trees older than time.

Matt reached for Anton's thoughts, but the connection was gone. There was no sense of blocking, merely the feeling that their mindtalking didn't work here . . . wherever *here* was.

They stepped out of the forest and entered a small meadow filled with wildflowers. Bees buzzed. Birdsong filled the air. The Goddess paused in the center near a bubbling creek that bisected the meadow. With the flick of her fingers, she released some sort of catch on the shoulder of her gown. The fabric fell away to reveal a body as womanly and perfect as any Matt had ever seen.

She was of average height with shimmering blond hair that framed her full breasts, brushed her perfectly smooth thighs and flowed over full, rounded hips. Her waist was narrow, her belly softly rounded. A perfect triangle of blond curls marked the gateway to her feminine secrets. Her eyes seemed to change color, from green, to gray, to brilliant amber. She held perfectly still while Matt and Anton gazed at her. Then she smiled at them again. "Run with me," she said.

And then she shifted.

The wolf was silver. Not merely a pale shade of gray, but the color of fine sterling. Her thick coat gleamed, and the impossible color rippled and flowed like molten metal.

Anton shifted. So did Matt, though he'd hardly been aware of making the choice to change from human to wolf. The moment his front paws touched the ground, she was off.

Anton yipped and followed. Matt raced behind them, his mind spinning, trying to make sense of what was happening. It had to be an hallucination, a dream of some sort.

Wasn't he still in that luxurious bathroom, holding Anton? Kissing him?

They ran for what felt like hours. Following trails through a forest that couldn't possibly exist, beneath trees so tall their tops were lost in the perfect blue sky glimpsed through the thick canopy of green.

The air was cool, without the cloying humidity he'd felt in Florida. The grass, so spongy and damp, compressed beneath his big paws, and rather than feel tired after running so far and so fast, Matt's body seemed energized, as if he could run forever beside Anton and his Goddess.

But after a while, Matt began to wonder if they might run forever. His energy began to fade. He had no idea where they were, no idea how long they'd run. His sides heaved with each breath of air he sucked into his lungs and his muscles were quivering from strain when the silver wolf finally stopped. She stood motionless, posing like a silver statue in a sunlit meadow surrounding a shimmering, bubbling pool of crystal clear water.

She shifted once again and paused beside the pool, standing as if in prayer, hands out, head bowed. She didn't look their way. Didn't speak. After a moment, she lowered her hands and stepped into the water. Matt watched as she waded out from shore, deeper and deeper until she floated like a pale lily on the surface with her hair fanned all about in a golden arc.

Matt followed Anton, wading into the cool water until the gravelly bottom suddenly dropped from beneath his feet. Shocked, he stroked wildly before he caught a rhythm with hands and feet that held his head out of the water.

Sputtering and laughing, Matt shook the water out of his eyes. He moved his arms and legs slowly, just enough to stay afloat. Bubbles burst around him with a natural effervescence, and the cool pulse and flow soothed his tired muscles. Treading water beside Anton and the Goddess, his questions surfaced once again.

When they'd run, he'd thought as a wolf. Behaved as a wolf. It made him uncomfortable to realize he'd run for miles, following the silver bitch without a single thought of either Daci or Deacon or the little cabin in Colorado.

He hadn't thought of Ric or Millie, of the wolf sanctuary, of Nick or Beth. Nor had he picked up a single thought from Anton. Frowning, Matt turned to his right and caught Anton looking his way. "Are you blocking my thoughts?"

Anton shook his head. "For some reason, we can't communicate with our minds here." He turned to the Goddess, who watched them both warily, almost as if she feared them.

"Why is that, My Lady? The way we communicate in our world doesn't work in yours. Is it your will?"

She smiled. The wariness disappeared and she waved her hand. Anton's perceptions and impressions suddenly popped into Matt's head. So many questions, so much excitement, that Matt almost laughed at Anton's frustration and convoluted thoughts.

Thoughts that disappeared the instant the Goddess spoke. "I've never brought two of you here before. There was no reason before for such communication. Is that better?"

Anton bowed his head. He managed to make it look classy and courtly even while treading water. "Much. Thank you."

Matt gazed from the Goddess to Anton. His arms were beginning to ache and he was growing tired. "My Lady," he said, mimicking Anton's formal address. "I'd really like to get out of the water."

Her laughter sent shivers along his spine. "Of course. I forget. . . ." She sighed. "The water is life and it has been so long . . . I am sorry. I haven't run with wolves in . . ." Her words drifted away on a lonely note as Matt dragged himself out of the pool and sprawled bonelessly on the shore.

Anton and the Goddess followed. Anton took the lady's hand and led her from the pool. Soft air currents flowed over Matt's wet skin, cool but not cold. A shaft of light warmed him, though when he looked up, there was no sign of the sun. Just perfectly clear, perfectly blue sky.

"Where are we?" He glanced at the Goddess as she lowered herself to the soft grass. "How did we get here?"

She dipped her head, acknowledging his questions. "I brought you here. This is my home." She swept a hand to encompass the forest in all directions. "My own when, my own where. It is everything I want it to be—the where I want, the when I want." She tilted her head and sent a smoldering glance at Anton. Then she focused her energy entirely on Matt. "The ones I want."

He felt a shock of energy, a visceral burst of heat that charged from his head to his balls down the length of his cock. Stunned by the power of a single glance, Matt shifted his eyes to gaze at Anton and realized he was every bit as aroused, his erection just as high and hard as Matt's.

Matt jerked his head around and caught the Goddess smiling at him. Her gamine expression disguised the power that was as much a part of her as breathing, but instead of fearing her, Matt's arousal expanded. His heart pounded and he rose to his knees. Reached for her without waiting for permission, without checking first with Anton as his pack's alpha.

"You are beautiful beyond . . . beyond anything," he said. He stumbled over the stupid words. What did a guy like him say to a goddess? Somehow, though, he knew she didn't seem to mind that he wasn't smooth or practiced. Feeling a little more confident, Matt ran his fingers through the impossibly long strands of blond hair that flowed over her shoulders and pooled on the grass beside and behind her. Stunned, feeling insignificant and inadequate, he whispered, "Beautiful and sensual. Finally, the voice in my head makes perfect sense. You make sense."

"I chose well," she said. She smiled, nodded her head. Then she leaned forward and kissed him.

Her lips were soft, her breath sweet. The seductive scent of her body wrapped him in a cloud of need. Groaning, Matt reached for her, cupped her shoulders in his palms, and moved his lips over hers. Her mouth parted on a sigh and she kissed him back. Slowly, Matt traced the damp curve of her lower lip with his tongue, tangled his tongue with hers, sucked hers into his mouth.

Her fingers scampered over his ribs, touching him lightly, inflaming him further. Matt sensed Anton, knew he lay on the grass beside them, watching, but it was all about the Goddess. All about the vibrant woman whose fingers shimmered over his heated flesh, who filled his mind with images of the two of them touching, kissing, loving.

Emboldened by her touch, Matt tangled his fingers in the thick strands of her hair and pulled her close. Kissing her, nibbling at her lips, at the long, pale column of her throat, he tugged on her hair, pulled her head back, bared her throat to his lips and tongue and teeth.

Their bodies had come together now as they knelt knee to knee, thighs pressing against thighs. The taut nipples crowning her full breasts brushed across his chest, and her hands were around his waist, her fingernails scoring deep crescents in his back.

Matt thought of Millie, of all she'd taught him about pleasing a woman. Thought of Daci with all her fire and youthful innocence. With Millie's sweet smile in mind, with Daci's sense of wonder, he slowed his frantic kisses along the Goddess's throat, fought the rush of desire begging him to throw her to the ground and take her here in the woods, without thought or care.

Swallowing back a groan, he leaned his forehead against hers. "With your permission, My Lady. I want to make love to you. I want to please you."

She pulled away just far enough for him to focus on her beaming smile. "You do please me. Just as Anton pleased me before." She cast a sly smile in Anton's direction. "As I would like both of you to please me now."

She swept her hand to one side and a soft blanket covered the grass. Before she could pull another bit of magic out of the air, Matt lifted her in his arms and held her close to his chest, held her there for a long moment. Felt her heart beating, sensed the rush of blood in her veins—the life in her that was so familiar, so utterly feminine.

She was a woman, like any other woman. Soft where she should be, round in the right places, with a woman's needs, a woman's desires. He glanced at Anton and caught the wizard's gentle smile and the memories that filled his mind. Memories long forgotten of the nights and days he'd spent making love to the Goddess.

Memories buried so deeply that even Keisha hadn't discovered them. He was wondering if they would be buried once again, if he'd be able to show his mate where he'd been, who he'd been with, knowing that it would matter more to him than to the woman he loved. Wanting to share this moment with her, the magic of the impossible, the joy of finding answers to so many questions filling his mind.

Matt almost laughed. Here they were in some kind of paradise with the world's most gorgeous woman, and Anton was wondering what questions he could ask her! Deacon and Daci had described him perfectly.

Thoughts of Anton fled as Matt laid the Goddess in the middle of the blanket. She stretched out and arched her back like a cat in heat. He sat beside her, admiring her perfect form, running his fingers over her silken skin. Anton moved to her other side. He caught Matt's eye and shared his visual of all of them together.

Touching, tasting, sucking, licking . . .

For the pleasure of the Goddess.

Matt nodded. He leaned over and suckled one perfect nipple between his lips, knowing Anton did the same. Together they sucked and nibbled, licked and teased as her arousal built. Matt skimmed his fingers along her ribs, found the slight indentation of her navel, slipped lower to slide his fingertips through the silky curls between her legs.

His fingers tangled with Anton's and he smiled around the nipple trapped between his tongue and the roof of his mouth. Together he and Anton slowly separated the soft petals of her sex. Together they stroked the damp folds, slipped over the taut bud of nerves, dove inside the tight channel.

Her body arched and she cried out. Her fingers tightened in the blanket beneath her. Emboldened by her response, Matt freed her breast with a final lick and moved between her legs.

Glistening with moisture, her nether lips were pink and soft, and absolutely perfect. Matt knelt between her thighs, lifted her legs, and draped them over his forearms as he raised her to his mouth. The first touch of his tongue against the tiny bud left her gasping. When he suckled it between his lips and drove his thumb deep inside her pussy, she arched her back and cried out.

Her muscles clenched and rippled around his thumb, and her sweet release flowed over Matt's tongue. Without even thinking whether it was acceptable to her or not, he lowered her legs and shifted, driving his wolven tongue deep inside in time to catch the tremors and spasms of her climax. Licking with quick strokes, he curled the tip of his long tongue against her inner walls, nibbled at her clit, and took her once more to the edge.

Anton lay beside them both. He rolled her nipples between his fingers and made love to her mouth with lips and tongue while Matt as the wolf licked greedily inside her warm pussy.

She whimpered and cried and her hips bucked against his muzzle until he pressed his forelegs over her thighs and held her down. Anton swallowed her cries with his mouth while Matt took her from one climax to another with hardly a moment's pause between.

Finally he sensed when she'd had enough, when her body quivered with sexual exhaustion and her muscles trembled. Matt shifted and sat back on his heels. The Goddess lay across the tumbled blanket with her eyes closed. A sheen of sweat covered her breasts, and the curls between her legs were damp and matted with both her release and the wolf's saliva.

The three of them rested. Neither Anton nor Matt had climaxed. Matt enjoyed the powerful buzz of arousal, the sense there was more to come. If only he knew what she wanted.

Finally, the Goddess raised herself on one elbow and waved her fingers. A tall glass filled with ice and clear liquid appeared in front of each of them. "Drink," she said.

Matt glanced at Anton. *Is it safe?* Anton merely shrugged. Matt lifted his glass and sipped. "It's water!" Laughing at himself, he drank until only ice remained.

The Goddess frowned. "What did you expect? Aren't you thirsty? Do you have so little trust?"

He dipped his chin and felt heat rising across his face. She'd made him blush, and knowing he was blushing made it worse. "I'm sorry. The magic . . . I don't know what to expect, but I was. Thirsty, that is. Thank you."

Matt focused on the glass in his hand and decided he'd better just shut up. It was full again. Once more he quenched his thirst. As aroused as he was, he realized his body was surprisingly relaxed. He'd brought a goddess to climax, and he'd done it more than once. He hoped she was pleased. He glanced her way and realized he wanted to do it again.

Anton lounged beside them on the grass. His cock was as erect as Matt's, but he appeared to ignore it. Instead, he studied the Goddess. "I have so many questions," he said. "Why Florida? Why are so many of our pack from the same area? What is it about this place that seems to draw Chanku? Where are we from? Did you create us? Were we brought to this world from another? And why are Matt and I here? What is it you need from us? So many things I have to know. You have the answers, My Lady. Will you share them with us?"

She laughed and reached for his hand. "Ah, Anton. You had even more questions before, even though you had no idea what to ask! Then, you knew nothing of your birthright. I imagine your mind is bursting right now. The more knowledge you have, the stronger your need to know. You will never be satisfied, not as long as there are questions deserving answers."

She leaned close and brushed her hand across Anton's forehead, sweeping away a thick lock of dark hair that had fallen over his eyes. "If I answered all your questions, dear Anton, you would have no purpose. Your life's goal is to find answers. I can't take that away from you. Not when you mean so much to me."

"Not any of them? You're not going to answer . . ." He frowned, reached up, and grasped her wrist. There was no anger in him, but he wasn't smiling, either. Matt glanced at the Goddess. She merely raised an eyebrow and stared at Anton. After a long moment, he released his grip on her wrist and lowered his eyes. "I am so sorry, My Lady. Please accept my apology."

She dipped her head in acknowledgment. "I know answers

are important to you, so I will give you this: You are what you seek, Anton Cheval. When you understand that, you will have at least some of your answers." She arched one imperious eyebrow. "When you find your answers, you shall have your young man back, and not before."

The water glass fell from Matt's grasp. He jerked his head to the right and stared at Anton. Anton lunged for Matt's hand and held on tight just as the Goddess waved hers.

Light flashed and the brilliance pulsed around them. A change in pressure made Matt's ears pop, as if he'd taken off in a plane. He blinked and the light faded. When he raised his head, the Goddess looked at him and smiled, but it was a sad sort of smile. Then she did something he didn't understand. She shrugged. The simple act reminded him of Anton.

Matt glanced down at his empty, outstretched hand.

Anton Cheval had disappeared.

Anton grabbed the marble counter to keep from falling. He shook his head, vaguely aware he'd been doing something with someone, somewhere. There was a loud buzzing in his head, a sense of unexplainable disorientation.

Then slowly, as if fog faded from a mirror, he remembered. He raised his head. Called out. "Matt? Matt, are you here?"

Anton stepped out of the bathroom, vaguely aware he was naked. Naked and aroused . . . and alone. He distinctly remembered his dark slacks and a fresh white shirt. Remembered the passionate embrace the two of them had shared. The out-of-body sensation, a burst of power and light. Now Matt's backpack lay on the bed where the kid had tossed it, but Anton knew, even without looking, that Matt was gone. He checked the clock by the bed. Only a few minutes had passed since . . .

He turned and stared at the bathroom. Walked back in and looked around, carefully, this time. At the wet towel on the counter, Matt's rumpled jeans on the floor, his T-shirt dumped on the seat of the commode. Anton's fresh pair of dark slacks and his white shirt piled together next to Matt's jeans.

As he stared, the memories slowly returned. The forest and the beautiful blonde. Trees so tall they couldn't see the tops, and the silver wolf who was the woman—the woman who cried out in ecstasy when she climaxed.

And then, with the speed of an oncoming freight, it all came back. Anton slumped against the marble counter, gripping the edge so hard his knuckles turned white.

He saw Matt's eyes, the fear on his face, felt the tight clasp of the young man's hand in his. He heard the voice of the Goddess as her words replayed in his mind.

You are what you seek, Anton Cheval. When you understand that, you will have at least some of your answers. When you find your answers, you shall have your young man back, and not before.

He'd lost Matt. Not here. Not in this world he understood. No, Matt was in her *when*. Her *where*. And all Anton had was a fucking riddle and absolutely no idea where to begin looking.

4

"Daciana, I am so sorry. I don't know where he is, even what time he's in. It's hard to explain, but she controls all of that. I'm sure he's okay. I have to believe that. We all do. I know he's with the Goddess, but it's not . . ." Anton sighed and held the phone to his ear. "I don't think it's anywhere that any of us can go to find him. I will do my best. I want you to keep your hearts and minds open. He may be able to reach your thoughts in some way. I just don't know."

He ended the call and set the phone back in the cradle. *I don't know.* Always when he'd said those three words, he'd felt the challenge, the need to find out. Now, though, the words of the Goddess rested heavy in his thoughts.

You are what you seek. What did he seek? Anton sat on the edge of the bed and rubbed his temples. *Questions. Always questions, but what answers? What, specifically?* He was in Florida to find out why so many of them came from this particular state, specifically the Tampa Bay area. Baylor, Tala and Lisa Quinn, Eve Reynolds, Mei Chen. He'd lived here. He'd met

Oliver here, though the circus had overwintered closer to Winter Haven than Tampa.

Okay, so he was Chanku and they were Chanku, but why did that make him the one that he searched for? What the hell did she mean?

The tones of his cell phone pulled him out of the spinning thoughts that seemed to go nowhere.

He stared at the phone through the third clip of Beethoven's "Ode to Joy" before he picked it up. He hated questions when he had no answers. Hated disappointing the ones he loved. Then his mate's voice brought him up short. "Keisha? Are you okay? Is Lily . . . ?"

Everyone was fine. Stefan was on his way—he'd gotten out of his meetings a day early. Unwilling to sever the link with his mate, Anton slowly ended the call. He breathed a sigh of relief.

Stefan. With Stefan on the way, maybe things weren't as hopeless after all. Now, if he could only figure out what the fuck the Goddess meant. He had to get Matt back and he had to do it now. Somehow, he needed to set him free.

Well, this sure sucks. It was one thing to be in this place with Anton beside him, quite another to be here—wherever here was—on his own. *With a Goddess.* Matt's heart thundered in his chest. He took a deep breath, forced himself to calm down, to find his center and relax. He was here because she'd called him, and he had answered—hopefully, of his own free will, though he wasn't quite certain of that. It looked like he was stuck here for a while, which should probably scare the shit out of him.

Except he was just too fascinated to panic . . . so far.

Fascinated and totally pissed. Getting yanked out of his life in the middle of living it to serve as her private stud was more than a little degrading. Not knowing how long she intended to keep him had his nerves a bit on edge.

Right. Okay, a little more than a bit.

She'd given Anton some kind of riddle he had to solve before Matt could go back to Deacon and Daci. He could handle that, knowing Anton would get on it immediately. Having faith that if anyone could solve it, the wizard could.

Anton had said time was different here, that he'd spent weeks with the Goddess, but it had been barely more than an hour in real time. If she'd given Anton a riddle, it would take longer than an hour in their time. It made his head spin, trying to figure it out. He hoped he wouldn't be gone too long or Daci and Deacon would totally freak.

What had Anton done when the Goddess called him? All he'd said to Matt was that he'd loved her. Given her whatever pleasure he could, and that was before he even knew he was Chanku. Before he'd had a clue who or what their Goddess was, before his superpowered Chanku libido had actually kicked in.

Matt knew he had that in spades. No problem there. Giving a beautiful woman pleasure? Beat the hell out of a lot of other options, but following in Anton's footsteps could be a challenge. Before he'd ever met the man, Matt had heard stories about his sexual prowess. His was definitely a standard to live up to. Matt bit back a stupid grin.

He loved a good challenge.

His cock pulsed in response. His balls tightened between his legs. He didn't fight it. Why should he? That was the only reason he was here. To pleasure a goddess, for whatever reason. If he was going to do it, he'd damned well better do it right, even though it still pissed him off when he thought about it. He wasn't sure he liked being nothing more than a convenient stud.

So, fix it. Change the dynamics.

He raised his head and studied her. Each beautiful curve and hollow, the way the shadows defined her breasts and hips. It was an easy chore—to study perfection—no matter the reason.

Hours? Minutes? Time had a strange way of passing in this

where and *when*. Matt stared into the Goddess's ever changing eyes. Green, gray, amber . . . the color shifted with the light, the tilt of her head, her moods.

He'd known her for such a short time. It seemed weird now, when he thought about it, the fact he knew what her intimate flavors were like but not if she had a name. He could recall the shape and taste of her nipples, the scent on her silken skin, but he had no idea who or what she really was. His body remained aroused even as he wondered exactly what she planned for him, why she'd kept him, what she wanted.

He knew what he wanted, and it wasn't merely sex with a beautiful woman. There was something distasteful about fucking someone so perfect without any kind of relationship, without a connection. He'd had more than enough of that kind of sex when he'd worked the streets. He'd sworn when he left it, never again.

Like Anton, Matt wanted answers. Why him? What for, and for how long? And the Goddess—he wanted to know more about her. He was absolutely positive there was a woman behind the beautiful façade. Before he touched her again, he needed to know who that woman was. He wanted her to know him. Without that connection, it was repugnant . . . sex with a woman who saw him only as an object for her own pleasure.

She stretched out beside him on the blanket, propped on one elbow with her chin resting in her palm. Beautiful. Desirable.

"You look at me as if your mind is bursting. Your body is aroused, yet you've not approached me again. Why?"

She flirted as if he mattered. Matt knew better.

"Do you have a name?" Matt didn't disguise the impatience or the belligerence in his tone. He hadn't intended to sound so angry, but damn it all, he felt disgusted. He spun around and sat up with his legs crossed and his elbows resting on his knees. "I can't keep calling you Goddess if we're gonna fuck."

Her eyes went wide with his crude language. Good. He'd gotten her attention.

"You ask me, a goddess, for my given name?" Slowly she turned her lithe body and sat exactly as Matt did. With her knees akimbo and ankles crossed, she bared herself entirely. It might have been sexy, except for the frown wrinkling her forehead, the defensive anger in her stance.

It appeared he'd pissed off a goddess.

Probably not his smartest move, but then, when had he acted particularly smart?

The night you declared your love for Daci and Deacon?

What a story he was going to have for those two! Matt bit back a smile. Now was not the time to think of other lovers. For one thing, he had no idea if the Goddess read his every thought. For all he knew, she was just playing with him.

He took a deep breath and reached once again for a sense of calm. It had to be hiding, somewhere behind the resentment coursing through him. Didn't she care what happened to his life? How could she hold him here, a prisoner?

He tamped his anger down and nodded in response to her question. "Yes, My Lady. I am asking, politely, I might add." He smiled to take the resentful edge off the question. "Have you always been a goddess? Weren't you ever a young girl with dreams? With a name given to you by a loving parent? Have you had any life but this one—all powerful, filled with magic?"

She tilted her head. Her lips pursed and she appeared bemused by his question. "In all the eons, the many centuries when I've called men to me, you are the first to ask."

Matt felt the aggression flow out of him. She actually sounded sad. Lonely and sad. Who was she, this woman who held the power of life and death in her hands? Maybe there really was a woman behind the Goddess. He glanced at her silky smooth body, at the tuft of blond curls between her legs. He imagined he saw those soft, feminine lips flutter, as if inviting him. His cock ached. His balls were so tightly drawn against his body that they felt like twin stones.

Still, he needed more from her. Millie had taught him that. Sex was nothing more than a physical act, like walking or breathing or sleeping. Making love required a connection. A depth of knowledge he didn't yet have.

He could fuck the Goddess or he could make love to the woman. Seeing the look of longing in her eyes, he realized fucking was out of the question.

"Will you answer me?" He touched her knee and lightly ran his fingers up her leg, along the crease between thigh and groin, across her pubic mound. There they rested, trapped in her silky curls.

She shivered in reaction. "Liana. I was called Liana in another time, another place."

Her eyes sparkled. Tears?

When she brushed her hand across her face he knew. And somehow that soft, almost breathless whisper, the sign of her vulnerability—her humanity—went straight to his heart.

Matt rolled forward to his knees and lightly kissed the end of her nose. "I bet you were a cute little thing, Liana. I see you with pigtails and scrapes on your knees and laughter on your lips. You have such perfect lips."

He gathered her up in his arms and sat back on his heels with Liana close to his chest and her warm bottom resting atop his thighs. She wrapped her legs around his waist, sighed, and buried her face against his heart.

"I'd forgotten that little girl. She was always in trouble, teasing her brothers, getting underfoot." She sighed. "Another life. Another woman." She looked up at him. Her eyes were darkest amber now. "I was offered my role and I chose this path freely, with full knowledge of the future it meant. 'Tis a lonely one. I knew that, though I will admit I did not fully comprehend how lonely forever could be. Still, I came to it with a full heart and my mind wide open."

"Is it worth it?" He nuzzled the silky fall of her hair and drew in a deep breath. *Vanilla.* Like Millie. She reminded him of vanilla cookies and cream.

She nodded. "Even on my loneliest days, it's worth it. To have the power I have, the joy I feel in protecting my people, in watching over all of you. You pray to me, you curse me, you call out to me when you need my help. For so long, I feared your kind would not survive, but now I have hope for your future. For my future, as well."

She raised her head and gazed directly into his eyes. "Now I ask a boon of you. Make love to me, Matt. Your energy will give me the strength I need. Your kindness is an added gift. Give me something of yourself to carry me through when you're no longer here."

He went to lay her down on the thick blanket, but suddenly the light shifted, the ground swayed, and he was kneeling in the middle of a huge four-poster bed in the midst of a massive room made of stone.

He exhaled a nervous breath of air. "Warn me when you do that, okay?" He gazed around him, at dozens and dozens of colorful tapestries lining the walls, at the high, narrow windows at least twenty feet overhead. Thick wooden beams crossed the upper reaches, and torches burned steadily in dark iron sconces along the walls. "Where are we?"

She laughed and the sound was free and clear, like the laughter of a young girl. Then she stretched out on the thick coverlet with her long hair flowing around her. "Another of my *wheres,*" she said. "This is my castle, the home I've kept now for almost a thousand of your years."

"Did you bring Anton here?" It was easy picturing Anton in a setting like this. Almost funny thinking of himself here, but Anton Cheval would fit perfectly. *To the manor born . . .*

"No. We stayed in a small cabin in the woods. He was a wonderful lover. The energy was . . . exquisite." She turned and stared at a beautiful tapestry on the wall beside the bed.

Matt glanced at it. Then looked again. The scene was stitched in silken thread—a dark forest of tall trees, a perfect little log cabin nestled half-hidden between the thick trunks. It reminded him of Anton's cabin in the redwoods, the one Tala and her guys had taken Matt and his friends to, where they'd made their first shift and run as wolves for the very first time. In the tapestry, a silver wolf prowled in front. A tall, slim, dark-haired man stood beside the door. Anton?

The other tapestries showed similar scenes. Cabins, stone buildings, what appeared to be a monastery. The silver wolf appeared in each one. A different man, with clothing styles reflecting the ages, though Anton's was the only one that appeared remotely modern. "Were all of them your lovers?" Matt turned just in time to catch Liana's wistful expression.

She nodded slowly. "Yes. Some good. Some not so good." Laughing she rolled to her side and propped herself on one elbow. "Some, like Anton Cheval, exquisite. I shouldn't have brought him back when I called you, but he was there and the two of you were so beautiful together. I watched you, a voyeur to your arousal, your desire for each other."

She looked away for a moment, and her eyes were shadowed when she turned to Matt again. "I stole the energy, you know. Your sexual energy. I needed it to bring you here. That's why I couldn't let you climax."

Sexual energy? She'd mentioned that before. Was that the reason she needed them? Did her power come from . . . She ran a finger along Matt's shoulder, raising shivers in her wake. He put the question aside, for now.

"You and Anton have much in common."

Matt snorted a laugh. "Me? And the wizard? How can you say that? He's brilliant, powerful."

"You're both good, kind men. Powerful men. Strong without any need to act the braggart. You love with all your heart. Your love for the two you left behind is real, as is theirs for you. You are loyal. Even when you're with me, you think of them. If I were a woman searching for a man, I would choose such as you."

"Isn't that what you are, though?" Matt caught her fingers in his hand and brought them to his lips. "A woman, searching for a man? Tell me, Liana. Why am I here? Why do you steal men away? Why do you bring men here to your own *where* and *when*? You're a goddess. I would imagine you could create your own man if you wanted."

She dipped her chin and wouldn't meet his eyes. "If only it were so simple." She sighed, and then she looked at him. "I am not your creator, I am your guardian. I exist because of you, not the other way around. Without your worship, your life force, *your sexual energy*, I would disappear as a mist on the wind."

"Like the sex magic I've heard Anton does?"

She nodded. "Very much like that. I take my strength from you, and give it back in my guardianship. It's all give-and-take. I cannot give unless I take."

This didn't sound at all the way he thought things worked. "Then who did create us? Where did the Chanku originate? Anton said the scrolls . . ."

Shaking her head, Liana pursed her lips. "The scrolls were the only way I could save what history I knew of the Chanku. The only way to pass on what little there was when Anton went looking for answers. He still doesn't realize that the one he'd made love with is the same one who sent him on his quest. It wasn't easy." She laughed. "The poor man didn't even know the questions. He only knew he had to search until whatever he was looking for was found. He did an admirable job."

"So, you really can't give Anton the answers he seeks? What about the riddle? You said I can't go home until he solves it."

"Have no fear, Matthew Rodgers. Anton won't forsake you. There are answers to some of his questions. I have no doubt he'll discover them, but as far as your beginnings . . ." She reached out and stroked her fingers along his jaw. "So beautiful," she whispered. "All of you, so very beautiful. The most perfect of all creations. Your kind existed long before I did. Sadly, your origins are lost in time. You as a people were almost lost as well."

"I don't understand." Matt caught her hand in his, wrapped his long fingers around hers.

"The story isn't so unusual. There is a greater spirit that rules us all. The Great Mother is a silent, yet powerful force of energy. The sentient life of all worlds depends on her existence, but she is not one to explain how any of us came to be. We are. We exist, therefore we must do everything in our power to survive."

Matt focused on one point. "But what do you mean, we as a people were almost lost? Do you mean the Chanku?"

Liana slowly nodded. "It was long ago. I was still young and newly turned to my immortal self when your kind left the place of your birth, the mountains you call the Himalayas, and left behind the nutrients you needed to shapeshift. Only a few of your ancestors survived the ages with their genetic heritage intact. When I realized you were gone, I couldn't find you."

Matt snorted. "You lost the people you were supposed to be guarding?"

She frowned at him. "It's not like I sit and look over you like a shepherd with his flock. One day you were there in your caves and stone houses, then poof! You were gone. But I searched until I found Anton."

"Anton? You mean you lost track of your Chanku for thousands of years?"

She waved her hand, dismissing him. "Time is different for a goddess. Since finding Anton, I was able to backtrack. I've learned what happened to the earliest of you. Some interbred with the people of West Africa and came to this country as slaves carrying the Chanku birthright. Some went to Romania. The Rom didn't have the grasses, but they found other ways to access their shapeshifting abilities. Other Chanku made the long trek to the New World across the Bering Strait, where they shared their genetic heritage with native Americans and became spirit guides. I found only one family that managed to continue on as Chanku by nurturing the special grasses through many generations—the end of that line was Anton's mate, Keisha—a line that continues now with their daughter, Lily. So few of your kind exist, but enough that you will continue."

Matt listened, barely able to comprehend what he was hearing. "We're talking thousands of years, here," he said. "Where were you when all this was going on?" Her fingers tensed within his grasp. "What kind of guardian would let her people scatter and die?"

"I did not let anyone die." Liana pulled her hand free of his. "Enough talk." She glared at him with icy disdain. Then she rolled her hips against his. In spite of himself, Matt's arousal spiked. His cock swelled against her belly.

This wasn't the way he'd wanted to take her. Not like a stud at service. Obviously he'd asked questions Liana preferred not to answer. He looked at his erection in disgust—it appeared the Goddess would have her way. He searched again for the little girl, the vulnerable young woman with too much responsibility, but she was lost.

Lost in the steely gaze of a woman filled with her own power. A woman who didn't want or need his love.

She wanted only what his body could do to strengthen hers.

"You are what you seek?" Stefan stared at the doodles he'd made all over his notebook and shook his head. "Haven't got a clue."

Anton stood with his back to the large picture window, watching his closest friend and lover. Then he turned away and stared at the darkness on the other side of the glass. "Me either," he said. "You are what you seek . . . I am what I seek. But what the fuck do I seek? It doesn't make sense."

"Well, why are you here?"

As if he hadn't already asked himself Stefan's question a million times? Anton sighed. "I'm here because of the dreams. I dreamed of Matt and he dreamed of Florida. I wanted to check on the hotel, so it seemed like the perfect time to make the trip."

"Not true."

Anton turned as Stefan shoved his chair back and walked across the room to join him at the window. Their images reflected back at them in the glare of light against glass backed by the nighttime sky—two tall, lean men with amber eyes. "What do you mean, not true? Of course it's . . ."

Stefan grabbed Anton's shoulder and squeezed. "You're here to find out why so many of our Chanku came from this area. Remember? What is it about Florida that drew them here in the first place. What drew you here?"

Anton shrugged. "I came with the circus. We spent the winters near Tampa."

"Why? Why not Arizona or maybe New Mexico? There are other places where winters are warm."

Something flittered through Anton's thoughts. "But not where the water is life."

"What's that mean?"

He shook his head and tried to remember where he'd heard the phrase. "I'm not sure. It's something the Goddess said when we cooled off in a pool of water after we ran, but I just realized I've heard it before."

"You're not thinking of the religious reference, are you? The fountain of life, the baptismal waters that . . ."

"No." Anton spun around and clasped Stefan's wrist. "Not the fountain of life . . . the fountain of *youth*. Some legends place it in Florida. The owner of the circus I worked for came here because he dreamed of finding the fountain of youth." He shook his head. "But to tie that to . . ."

"What do we know of the others?" Stefan counted off on his fingers. "The Quinn family, for instance. Mei and Eve's mothers. When did they come? Why were they here? What drew Oliver to this place?"

Anton stopped him. "That I can answer. He started out as a stowaway on a cruise ship. Got a job in the kitchen and worked his way from Barbados to Miami."

"Miami's a long way from Tampa. How'd he get to your winter headquarters? What drew him?"

Anton turned and stared at Stefan. "The circus. Oliver figured it would be a good place to work. They didn't look too closely at his lack of proper documents, so . . ."

"Not so. It was more than that." Stefan cocked his head and stared at Anton. "I know it was more because I asked Oliver before I left this morning. What specifically drew him to this part of Florida, to that particular circus. He told me he had heard of a magician and the guy's name was stuck in his head. He found out that same man was overwintering with a circus not all that far from Miami—a magician named Anton Cheval."

"Me? He joined that circus because of me?" Anton shook his head. "He's never said anything. I wonder why?"

Stefan laughed. "Probably didn't want to feed your insufferable ego."

Anton glared at him. "Funny, Stef. Real funny. That doesn't explain the others."

"You're right. So we look from another angle. Before I left, I called Luc and Tinker and asked them to do their magic on the computers. They're going to call if they find any connections. In the meantime, I think we need to run."

"Run? We don't have time to run."

Stefan began unbuttoning his shirt. "We don't have time not to run. We need to clear our heads, get to the heart of the problem. What better way than to shed the human side that wants to convince us we'll never find Matt? I don't know about you, but my feral side usually makes better sense. It ignores the rules. Run, fuck, hunt. Eat and fuck again. Works for me."

Anton stared at him for a long moment. Then he flipped off the interior lights, throwing the room into darkness before he began unbuttoning his shirt. "Sometimes, Stef, your convoluted logic scares the crap out of me."

Stefan laughed. Then the only sound was the slight rustling of fabric as both men undressed, and the soft slide of the glass door as Anton opened it to the outside.

He'd picked this cottage because of the proximity to the swamp with its thick tangle of trees and vines and the privacy afforded by its distance from the main part of the luxury resort he'd bought so many years ago. Now he wondered exactly why he'd felt compelled to buy this particular property, this piece of Florida swamp.

Could it have been that unusual effervescent pool?

He'd never run this way before. Never explored the swamp beyond the manicured lawns, the golf course, the paved walkways. The night was dark and the wild path into the murky swamp was unfamiliar. The smells were all wrong and the sounds made no sense. What rustled and slithered in a Florida swamp was nothing at all like the life surrounding a nighttime run through pristine Montana wilderness. Well aware there were things here that could bite and stab and sting, Anton led with care along the narrow trail following a sluggish river.

They splashed through a stagnant patch of shallow water, senses alert to the sounds of the night. A low growl reverberating on the still night brought both wolves to a stop.

What the hell was that? Stefan's ears pricked forward.

The growl sounded again, an eerie boom so low it was almost out of range of their sharp hearing.

Alligator, Anton said. *Watch your step.*

Stefan's unfiltered thoughts drifted toward Anton. *Watch your step, he says. Shit. What the fuck are we doing in a swamp full of alligators after dark?*

It was your idea, big guy. Run as a wolf, he said. Get close to your feral nature. Let the beast rule your thoughts.

Shit. Stefan grumbled as he trotted after Anton. *I didn't think the fuckin' beast wanted to eat me.*

For the first time since losing Matt to the Goddess, Anton actually felt like laughing. Leave it to Stefan! He took off at a slow trot, scanning the path with all his senses. Stefan followed close behind.

Stefan's disgruntled voice echoed in Anton's head. *You never mentioned alligators.*

I didn't mention coral snakes or cottonmouths, either. Stop!

Stefan skidded to a halt. *What the . . . ?*

Cottonmouth. Left side of the trail. The dark snake in the thick brush alongside the trail had coiled into a tight ring. Only the white of its mouth was truly visible.

Anton growled. The snake silently uncoiled and disappeared into the brush. Without another word, Anton headed along the trail. Stefan stayed right on his tail. He'd stopped grumbling.

They didn't run so much as meander, trotting along narrow, tree-covered trails, cutting across shallow creeks and marshy grasslands, wending their way deeper into the swamp, farther from the hotel and any sense of civilization.

Anton heard more than one alligator. The deep growls in a frequency so low they barely registered made his hackles rise. Every once in a while he heard a hiss, followed by a splash and the sound of a heavy body moving through the water.

Stefan was right. He hadn't thought about Matt or the Goddess for the past couple hours. No, he'd been more concerned with not getting eaten.

He wasn't sure where they were. The trees and vines grew thick here, the fetid stench of rotting vegetation and stagnant water lay heavy on the humid air. There was no moon tonight, but the ambient glow of a million stars gave them enough light to see the trail.

Anton felt a subtle tug, as if a barely perceptible force pulled him along the trail. He sped up, drawn to something, somewhere. He ran faster, until his paws were fairly flying over the ground.

Without warning, he felt drawn in a new direction and turned to his right with Stefan on his heels. They burst through a wall of tangled vines and tumbled out into a small meadow.

A familiar meadow, with a shimmering pool in the middle. A pool of water churning and bubbling in the moonlight, glowing silver with a natural effervescence.

Moonlight? Anton stopped so fast Stefan ran into him.

What the . . . ?

I was here. This pool . . . Anton shifted and walked toward the water. The thick grass beneath his bare feet felt freshly mowed. Cool air wafted across his shoulders. Anton raised his head and sniffed. Clean, fresh air with none of the foul miasma of the swamp. Ahead of him, the water boiled and bubbled. Moonlight glistened off the surface.

He walked out into the water. It fizzed and bubbled around his ankles, his knees, his thighs.

Still in wolf form, Stefan waited on the shore. Anton turned around with the water lapping at his chest, and grinned at him. "C'mon. No alligators here. Just cool, clear water. It's wonderful." He took another step, into water over his head.

Stefan shifted. "Said the spider to the fly." Grumbling, he waded into the pond and followed Anton to the center. He dove forward and came up, shaking his head and flinging water in all directions. "It's a spring of some kind. Look at the bubbles."

"Or a fountain." Anton waved his arms in a lazy fashion, treading water near the center of the pool. "The water is life. Could this be the infamous fountain of youth?"

Stefan laughed. "You still look like the same old fart to me."

Anton dipped his head and said dryly, "Thank you for that. You're so good for my self-esteem."

"I try." Stefan dove under water. It was at least a full minute before he popped to the surface again. "Can't find the bottom, but I can feel the water shooting out of more than one spot. Sort of like jets in a hot tub but without the heat."

"This is really strange." Anton began swimming back to the shore. "When I was with Matt and the Goddess, we ran through miles of forest without ever seeing any swamp, yet we ended up here. Tonight we ran though stinking, alligator-infested swamp and came to the same place."

"And your point is?" Stefan rose to his feet in the shallow water at the pool's edge.

"My point is, Toto, I don't think we're in Kansas anymore."

Stefan frowned and shook his head. "I don't get it."

Anton raised one eyebrow. "Neither do I, but I have a strong suspicion we're no longer in a swamp in Florida. Somehow, I believe we've entered our Goddess's *when* and *where*."

5

Matt tugged at the silken bonds holding him to the four posts of the huge bed and cut loose with a round of wasted curses. She'd restrained him with an angry flick of her fingers, leaving him stretched out so tightly he couldn't move beyond a frustrated twist and roll of his hips.

At least she hadn't gagged him—yet.

Liana knelt over him, just high enough that his erect cock brushed the damp lips of her sex. He was so damned horny he felt like his balls were ready to burst. He glared at her perfect body, so totally pissed all he could do was pull ineffectually at his restraints and cuss.

Not so much at the Goddess—she was merely obeying her own nature—but damn it all, he was pissed off at himself. How the hell could he be so turned on, so ready to make it with her when she had the nerve to treat him like this?

Trussed up like a damned offering with a boner like he'd never had in his life, and if he didn't get tab A shoved into slot B real soon, he was going to lose it. Was she making him this hot on purpose? Was this almost-unendurable arousal an accumulation of the events of the past . . . had it been hours? Days? He had no idea. Time just wasn't normal with her. Nor was the fact he'd been hard since the moment he and Anton had been swept into this strange experience.

They'd both brought her to climax. Then Anton had literally disappeared before either of them had achieved their own orgasm. Matt couldn't remember ever staying hard for this long. His cock ached, his balls ached worse, and with his hands restrained, he couldn't even beat off to get any relief.

And still the Goddess—Liana, damn it—hovered just out of reach, teasing him with her beauty, infuriating him with that damned attitude, with her perfect body and bitchy disposition.

"If you're trying to make a point, Goddess, I'm missing it."

She blinked and then smiled sweetly. "No point, Matt. None at all." She ran her fingers along her sides and cupped her breasts. Lowered herself just enough that the broad tip of his penis brushed her damp folds, though try as hard as he might, Matt couldn't lift high enough to slip inside her warm, wet sheath.

"Then why?" His voice sounded strangled. He wanted to strangle her, damn it. "Why are you doing this?"

She backed down his legs and knelt between his knees. Leaned over and ran her tongue over the weeping slit in his cock. "It's easier this way." She wrapped her lips around his glans, swirled her tongue over the slick, sensitive surface, and then backed away.

He almost howled. "Easier for you, maybe. Certainly not for me, Goddess." He put enough emphasis on her title so that even an idiot would know it was a perfect euphemism for *bitch*.

"Take it as you wish. I was growing weak. I need energy. You wanted to bring up topics I do not wish to discuss. It's more effective this way."

She ran her fingers over his balls. The light touch almost sent him over the edge. *More, damn it!* He needed more. "I've always thought of you with love," he said, practically snarling the words. "Now I'm learning your true nature. It's not as pleasant as the Goddess I imagined."

She stared at him for a long, long time. He had no idea what she was thinking, what she intended. He should have been afraid. Instead, his anger seemed to fill him until all he could see was himself taking her, rolling her slim body beneath his large one, and filling her, thrusting hard and deep until she begged for mercy.

He would not beg. Ever. But she would. She'd beg him for more, beg for him to take her again and again. His chest heaved with each angry breath, and he jerked at the restraints.

And suddenly he was free. Growling, Matt rolled forward and tackled her, spinning her slight frame beneath his and straddling her thighs. He clasped her wrists over her head with both hands, leaned forward, and, almost nose to nose, snarled, "Okay, sweetheart. Is this what you want?"

Logically, he knew she had to have freed him. Knew she wanted this, wanted him angry and hard and in charge. When she nodded her head, the movement was barely perceptible, but there was no doubt in his mind.

And none in hers. Still holding her wrists over her head with one hand, he nudged her thighs apart with his knee and slipped his broad palm beneath her firm buttocks. He lifted her hips until his erect cock rested in the slick moisture between her swollen lips.

He glared at her, angry with her, with himself that the love-making he'd wanted had come to this. Sex, pure and simple. Hard, angry sex.

With one powerful thrust of his hips, Matt filled her tight sheath. She cried out, arched her back, and raised her hips to meet him. Her inner muscles clenched his shaft, rippling along his length as he drove deep. He hit the mouth of her womb and slipped into the space beyond, bottoming out against the far reaches of her vaginal passage.

She wrapped her legs around his waist and he lifted her. Sitting back on his heels, Matt set up a pounding rhythm that forced his thick cock deep inside. Over and over again, faster, harder until she was whimpering with every forceful penetration. Her arms clasped his shoulders and the long curtain of her hair tangled around and over both of them.

She climaxed hard and fast, and still he took her. Anger and need and pure carnal lust held him in thrall—he was a slave to her baser needs, to his own impossible desire. He'd tried, damn it. He'd tried to know her, to love her, to give her the attention a woman deserved. The same love and attention he'd given Millie, the same worship he gave to Daci.

She'd thrown it back at him. He'd wanted to know the woman behind the Goddess, yet after a simple glimpse into the one she once was, she'd shut him out.

"This is what you want, right?" He clamped his teeth on the soft skin between her neck and shoulder and bit down hard. She convulsed beneath him, climaxing again. His cock was still hard, his anger harder still, yet she held him tight. He knew she loved this side of him, knew she wanted even more.

Matt lifted her away from him. She whimpered and reached out, but she was small enough and light enough that he merely tossed her to the bed. She sprawled on her belly across the multi-hued coverlet with her legs hanging over the edge. Matt spun off the bed and stood between her legs, knotted her long hair in one fist, lifted her hips with his free hand, and drove into her from behind. Harder this way, forcing her submission with each powerful thrust.

She shoved her hips against him, taking him deeper, telling him with her body that she wanted his power, the intensity of sex without boundaries. She needed his passion, the unbridled lust of a man pushed to the edge.

Telling him with each twist and jerk of her body that she was a woman willing to do anything, wanting it all.

She climaxed again, her body writhing and twisting beneath his. Matt's muscles trembled, but he hadn't come yet. His cock filled her. He let go of her hair, wrapped his fingers tightly around her flanks, and held her tightly against him as her muscles rippled and pulsed around his erection.

His chest heaved with each breath. So did hers, but she turned and stared at him out of wild eyes. "More," she gasped. "I need more."

He slipped his cock free of her pussy. Her muscles tightened around his length, holding on to him even as he pulled out. She was wet with her arousal, her lips swollen and pink, her inner thighs slick with her fluids.

Her upper body sprawled across the coverlet, her legs hung almost to the floor and her perfect ass filled his vision. Matt swept his fingers between her legs, up the crease separating her buttocks. He found her tight anal ring and pressed none too gently. She pushed back against him, harder, and his fingers slipped through the taut muscle. In and out, thrusting deeper until the muscle relaxed.

He pressed his cock at her back entrance, looked up and caught her watching him over her shoulder. Could he do this? Take a goddess this way?

"More," she growled. "Now."

Demanding, ordering him. *Meat. I'm no more than a fucking piece of meat.* Anger, such deep, overwhelming anger, drove him forward, blurred his vision, made him bigger, harder than he'd ever been. He wrapped his big hands around her flanks and with one powerful thrust of his hips breached her anus and pushed deep inside. She screamed as she shoved back against him, forcing him deeper. Her muscles pulsed and rippled around him, and her sphincter clasped the base of his cock so tightly he couldn't have come if he'd wanted to.

He didn't want to. He wasn't done with her. Not yet. She buried her face in the coverlet and he drove deep, withdrew, then deep again. She was hot and slick, her channel so tightly fitted around his cock he felt as if she sheathed him in molten bands of liquid steel.

His fingers tightened around her flanks and he pulled her close as he thrust forward. He was a machine. A fucking, tearing, rending machine, and she was his to do with as he pleased.

Even as he pleased her.

Then her mind opened to his. A joining unlike anything he'd ever experienced, a link to a mind so alien, so unlike his own, that it took him a moment to realize it was indeed the Goddess whose thoughts he heard.

There was no love in her. Only a powerful drive to take, to feed her hunger for the energy that kept her alive. To feed from him, to take from him. That little girl may have existed once in eons past, but she was gone now. Replaced by a creature of power, a guardian who took as much from her people as they ever received from her.

She was keening now, a long, high-pitched cry of dark and utterly sensual delight. Her mental images were bereft of light, lush and carnal, a visual, visceral replay of every move they made, every sensation rippling through her body and her mind.

He knew she'd never felt so full, never had so many climaxes with one man at one time. Raw and brutal, tender and sweet— over the past hours he'd shown her every side of these most intimate of acts. She wanted him. Needed him. Never, not in all her uncounted years as a goddess, had she ever wished to name one man her consort.

She wanted this man. Matthew Rodgers. Forever.

The word slammed into Matt's head. *Forever.*

"No!" He plowed into her, growled against her ear. "Love is forever. Love is me with Daciana and Deacon, two people who care about me. About what I want. Two lovers who want what's best for me, just as I want what's best for them. This isn't love. It's nothing but sex. You're getting fucked, Goddess.

That's all you want from me, so that's what we're doing. Fucking."

She screamed. Shoved her hips back in time with his powerful thrust and climaxed. He shoved her forward and crawled up on the bed behind her, his cock still trapped within her anus. Hot muscles rippled and clenched around his cock. Matt's entire body jerked with the force of his orgasm. Ramming deep and hard, he wrapped his hands around her belly and dragged her up against his, reared up on his knees and lifted her, still plunging deep and hard, still filling her with his seed.

It would never end, this climax inside the Goddess. His semen spilled out and ran down his thighs, and still his cock jerked and spasmed. Her body trembled with his, her head lolled back against his collarbone, and her eyelids fluttered.

She was boneless in his grasp. Boneless and barely conscious. Slowly he lowered himself, still kneeling, to sit back on his heels. Liana melted into his grasp. One of his hands covered her lower belly. His fingers brushed her damp curls and the curve of her pubic mound. His middle finger rested on her swollen clit, and he felt it throb in time with her racing pulse. His other arm pressed beneath her breasts where his fingers pressed into skin like silk. Her chest heaved in and out with each deep breath she took.

Matt leaned forward and rested his chin on her shoulder. His cheek pressed against hers. His cock was still buried in her backside while her body continued its rhythmic clench and release.

Her thoughts were blocked. She'd gotten what she'd wanted, and then she'd shut him out. Matt tilted his head and kissed the line of her jaw. Gently. Dispassionately.

He took a deep, calming breath and waited until his heart rate finally settled down before he finally whispered in her ear. "You should want more, My Lady. You should want what we all want. Even a goddess needs love."

He heard her sigh. "What of you, Matthew Rodgers? Do you need love?"

He nodded slowly against her cheek. "I do, My Lady. More than you, even with all your powers, with all your knowledge of our kind, will ever know. But I'm the lucky one here, because I know I need love and I've found it."

"Not with me." It was a statement, not a question.

"No, My Lady. Not with you."

This time Anton followed Stefan's lead, but Stef seemed to have a better feel for the trail. Exhaustion had left Anton's thoughts sluggish, and the events of the past twenty-four hours weighed heavily on his mind. Their pace back toward the resort was slow, but at least they'd found the trail.

He'd wondered if the Goddess had somehow taken them into her world—her *when* and her *where*—but they'd crawled out through the thick tangle of vines and stumbled into the stinking swamp with all its nasty critters, right where they'd left it.

He wanted to go back again when his mind was clear and his body not so tired and see if the pool was still there. He still wasn't certain it even existed in this time and place, but he'd felt confused and disoriented ever since the Goddess had sent him away.

Confused, disoriented, and aroused. As exhausted as he felt, he was still so damned horny he'd actually thought of trying to talk Stef into a quickie back there by the pool. He'd felt aroused ever since he and Matt had been together. Thinking about the young man's body so close to his, the way Matt's hands and mouth had felt on him, made him hard again. Picturing Stefan's long, lean body diving into the depths of the shimmering pool made the situation even worse.

Was it really the infamous fountain of youth? He chuckled silently. As horny as he was right now, it might have been, if only he wasn't aching in every joint and muscle. If it were the infamous fountain, he should feel a hell of a lot younger than he did right now. Damn . . . his mind seemed to be working in aimless circles. He needed to figure out that stupid riddle and get Matt away from the Goddess.

Daci and Deacon would never forgive him.

He'd never forgive himself. He'd forced Matt to heed the call of the Goddess. If not for Anton, he'd still be back there in Colorado, perfectly safe and happy with people who loved him.

Not true.

Ah, Stef . . . eavesdropping?

I had to. I figured by now you'd be beating yourself up over Matt. I was right.

Anton snorted. *Well, don't get cocky about it.*

Stefan's silent laughter raced through his mind as they reached the edge of the swamp and crossed the short stretch of manicured lawn to the cottage. Anton glanced at the sky. There was no moon overhead, and stars blanketed the heavens.

There'd been moonlight shining on the fountain.

Another question without an answer, one that would have to wait. The back deck was shrouded in dark shadows, and they'd not left any lights burning inside the cottage. Stefan leapt over the high railing and hid in the darkness until Anton joined him. Anton shifted, quietly slid the door open, and stepped inside. The wolf followed close behind, but it was Stefan who walked across the room and flipped on the light.

Anton leaned against the closed door and laughed at the couple startled awake on the big bed. "I had a feeling you two would show up."

Deacon pulled the blanket up over his head. Daci rubbed her eyes and rolled to a sitting position. Her lovely breasts glistened in the soft light of the bedside lamp. "Where's Matt?"

Anton grabbed the pair of sweatpants Stefan tossed to him,

slipped them on, and sat on the edge of the bed. "He's with the Goddess, though that could mean a lot of things. As she explains it, her *when* and her *where* are hers to choose."

"Is he okay?" Blinking owlishly, Deacon popped out from under the covers and scooted up against the headboard. "Will she hurt him?"

"No." Anton shook his head emphatically. "She needs him for the sexual energy he can provide. She took me for the same reason many years ago. Then she wiped my memories clean." He glanced at Stefan and struggled with the anger blossoming in his gut. "You have no idea how much that infuriates me. It's bad enough to take a man for sex, but to wipe away the memory . . . it disgusts me."

"That could destroy Matt." Daci looked horrified. "I've been worried about this ever since you told me she'd kept Matt. It's awful." She glared at Anton. "And selfish of her. Goddess or not, she's a bitch."

"Daci's right." Deacon glanced at the beautiful young woman beside him. "Matt loves with all his heart—Daci and me as his future mates, Millie and Ulrich, Beth and Nick . . . There's no halfway with Matt. It's all or nothing, and if he's forced to go against his nature . . . "

Anton crossed his arms over his bare chest. "It can't be that serious. . . ."

Daci interrupted. "You don't know him like we do. Matt loves. Sex for him is all about love, about connecting. If the Goddess wants his body, she's going to get his heart, whether that's in the deal or not."

Anton was reminded of the time, not so long ago, when Daci had been his prisoner, the daughter of their oldest enemy, raised to hate everything about Chanku. So much had changed since then. She'd taught him so much. He covered her hand with his. "But he loves you and Deacon. I don't understand how . . . "

Her fingers clenched into a tight fist. "Did you love her when you were with her?"

He felt as if she'd pinned him in place with the intensity of her gaze. "No," he said. "I was young and there were always women—or men—available. I had no idea she was a goddess. She was just a woman who loved sex, and when it was over, I had no memory. I wouldn't even know this much if the memories hadn't resurfaced when she took Matt and me."

"If Matt has sex with her, he'll want to love her. He'll try and forge a connection, make her feel something for him." She turned and stared into Deacon's dark eyes. "If he succeeds, I'm afraid she's not going to let him go. And if he fails and she still wants sex, it's going to tear him apart."

Matt stared blankly at the wall across from the bed. He'd lost track of the days, the weeks. He ate, he slept, he awoke, and he fucked. There was no lovemaking. Not anymore. She'd stripped him of his dignity. Turned his Chanku libido, his very nature, against him, and used him. There was no more talk of her past, no attempt on his part to connect. She'd made it plain what his purpose was.

He was here for one thing only—to replenish her stores of energy that she might continue in her role as guardian. "Every thirty of your years or so," she'd said. Anton had been her last. Now it was Matt's turn.

He wondered if he'd remember when this was over. Wondered if it ever would be over. She loved the fact he fought her, that he fought his own nature. He'd tried acceding to her wishes, screwing her however she liked, but she merely degraded him further until his anger won out and he fought her again.

She'd finally admitted the truth. There was more energy when he was angry. He was the first in her long line of lovers to struggle against her desires. She'd never realized before how powerful anger could be. How much it made her want him—want what he was unwilling to give her of his own free will.

He could hardly recall when he'd not been her prisoner. He'd tried shifting, but his restraints shifted with him. As a man his arms and legs were shackled. As a wolf he wore a collar chained to the bed. He'd chosen his wolf form this morning with the vague thought of biting her, but he knew it wasn't in him to ever actually hurt her. It didn't matter how angry he got.

That wasn't his nature.

Any more than it was his nature to fuck someone he didn't love, to not keep trying to connect, to understand. Exhausted, frustrated, and terribly sad, he rested his chin on his crossed paws and sighed.

There was a slight rustle of fabric and a change in the air pressure. He didn't have to raise his head to know the Goddess had entered the room.

Liana. He had to remember her name. Liana, at least, had remembered her humanity. The Goddess had long forgotten.

The bed dipped slightly when she sat on the edge. He opened his eyes. Her back was to him. She wore a white robe, and her blond hair fell in a long, silken curtain across her shoulders and swept along one hip.

He grew hard in spite of himself, and growled, a low, menacing rumble that started deep in his chest. She laughed. Music . . . her laughter reminded him of music, and the sound was much too pretty for her, now that he knew what her true nature really was.

How could a goddess, a guardian of a people as honorable as the Chanku, be so heartless? So unwilling to love? How could she hold him prisoner, keep him from returning to the ones who loved him, and force his compliance in an act that should be freely given, never taken? He lifted his head and glared at her, but she'd locked him out and his thoughts remained his own.

"I have decided you will stay." She turned and faced him. "You will remain as my consort. We will mate as wolves, and when we bond, my powers will be shared with you. My knowledge will become yours. I will remain the Goddess, the guardian of the Chanku. You will be at my side."

He remained a wolf and didn't reply. Instead he thought of Daci and Deacon. He wondered how close Anton had come to solving the riddle, if time had passed in the real world the way it seemed to pass here. He didn't look any older, but he felt older. Damn, he felt absolutely ancient. What chance did he have against the power of a goddess?

She shifted. The world shifted with her and they were back in the meadow by the shimmering pool. The collar was off his neck and the beautiful silver wolf stood in front of him. Her tail was in the air, her coat glistened like molten silver, and her heat was upon her.

The rich scent of her musk drew a low growl out of him. He felt his cock swell and knew the moment it slipped beyond his sheath. His humanity struggled for control. He thought of Daci and wondered if she missed him. If she worried. And what of Deacon? He missed Deacon's strong arms and gentle nature, his peaceful, loving soul. Matt's ardor for the Goddess cooled as the images of his beloved packmates filled his heart.

Then the silver wolf turned and snarled at him. Nipped his shoulder and spun once again, presenting herself for mating. Her scent teased his sensitive nostrils. He fought it, fought against the call of the receptive female, but his feral nature ruled. Inflamed, both body and mind aroused by her scent, he stalked her on trembling limbs.

He didn't want this. Did not want to bond with her in a mating that would seal his fate for all time. He wanted love, not subjugation. Liana might be more beautiful than any woman, might have more power than any human alive, but she wasn't Daci. She wasn't Deacon.

She wasn't love.

Mate with me. Now. Your Goddess commands you obey.

Her powerful mental voice after silence for so long brought him up short. *You say such sweet things, Goddess. Makes me go all twittery inside.*

She spun around and snarled at him. *You mock me?*

I do.

You prefer death? Death to mating with me?

He thought of Daci and Deacon again. Of Millie and Ric and all the ones he'd known and grown to love. He hated the thought of never seeing them again, of never holding Daci in his arms, of not laughing and loving with Deacon, but there was no hesitation when he answered the Goddess.

I do.

No!

She stared at him, nose to nose. He felt her power in his mind, flowing through his body. He fought the involuntary bunch and flow of his own muscles. The Goddess couldn't command his thoughts, but she had taken complete control of his body. Fighting every step, he walked stiff-legged around behind her, brushed her shoulder with his paw.

Mounted her.

His cock was hard and his hips thrust forward against his will. Her thoughts were in his head, and he knew she searched out the mental synapses that must connect for them to link. She had the power to force the mating bond upon him, and he was powerless to fight her.

His cock slipped between her silken lips, and with one powerful thrust of his hips he penetrated her tight channel. Anger welled up in him, anger that she could force this most sacred act upon him when he fought her with everything he was. Anger when he'd promised this bond to the ones he loved, with Daci and Deacon.

He'd promised! He'd never broken a promise, had never

had sex in his wolf form before. That was reserved for mating with his true mates, but he recognized the thick swelling at the base of his cock and knew the Goddess had won, knew that any chance for following his own course in life was ending.

Her thoughts were in his head, crawling deeper into his memories, into parts of his mind that had always been his and his alone. The intrusion disgusted him. She was powerful, she was the Goddess who watched over his kind, but she was raping his mind along with his body.

He held his own thoughts back as best he could, but she drew him into her head even as she held him with her body. He felt the first harsh jerks as he climaxed deep inside her tight sheath. Felt the weakening of the barriers inside his head—and did the only thing he could think of to stop her.

He shifted.

She'd not expected it. That was more than obvious when she turned on him, jaws wide and ears flat to her skull. As a wolf, the two of them had been intimately tied. As a human, his cock slipped from her passage when she turned and attacked. She lunged for his throat. Without thinking, he reached out to protect himself and grabbed her around the neck.

Empowered by rage, by the pent-up anger and self-disgust that had consumed him as her prisoner, he locked his hands around her throat and held her at arm's length. Her snarls turned to panic-stricken yips as her feet scrabbled vainly for purchase in the thick grass, but he held her too high. He tightened his hands on her throat and shook the wolf. She twisted in his powerful grasp, struggled to break free, struggled to breathe.

Her wolven body fell limp in his hands. The dark rage cleared from Matt's mind. He turned her loose and the wolf crumpled to the ground. He fell to his knees beside her.

"Oh, shit! Shit, shit, shit . . . I'm sorry, I . . ." He brushed his hand over her broad forehead and then pressed his palm against her chest. He moved his hand and pressed again, and again, but there was no steady beat, no sound of life. Could a goddess die? He leaned over her, held her jaws closed, and blew air into her nostrils. Slammed his open hand against her rib cage and breathed for her.

After a moment she began to stir and breathe on her own. Matt sat back on his heels and watched as she shifted. The wolf disappeared and the Goddess sprawled on the grass. Her long hair was tangled about her naked body. Dark bruises disfigured her slim throat.

Matt bowed his head. He'd never consciously hurt a woman, not once in his life. He looked at his hands and wanted to cry. He wasn't a killer. He couldn't fight her. She was a goddess, and her power over him was absolute.

There was no fight left in him.

He thought of his packmates and felt the hot tears coursing over his cheeks. His chest ached with what could only be a broken heart, but he had no other course left to him.

He took a deep breath and thought of all the things he wished. Then he said the only thing he could.

"I'm sorry, Liana. I never meant to hurt you. That was never my intention." He raised his head and gazed into her ever-changing eyes. It was almost impossible to speak over the huge lump in his throat. "Whatever you wish, Goddess." He bowed his head. "I will obey."

6

Anton figured Stefan would be asleep when he finished his shower, but Stef was sitting up in the big bed with all the pillows behind his back, looking over an auto club map of the surrounding area.

"There's no sign of your pond anywhere." He jabbed his finger in the middle of the page, glanced up at Anton, and then back at the map.

Anton paused in the doorway and rubbed his wet hair with a dry towel. "I know. Doesn't show on Google Earth, either. I checked the computer while you were showering. It's not there, but you saw it and so did I." He yawned and tossed the towel back into the bathroom. "I'm too tired to try and figure it out tonight. I just hope I can sleep. . . . I'm really buzzing."

Stefan pulled a couple of the pillows from behind his head and tossed them at Anton. "I slept on the plane, but it wasn't enough. I'm not worried a bit about sleeping tonight."

"How'd the meetings go?" Anton crawled in beside Stefan. His body still thrummed with arousal, but he was too damned tired to care. He turned off the lamp beside the bed and stretched out under a light blanket. Then he lay there and stared into the dark.

Maybe if he counted sheep . . .

After a moment, Stefan answered him. "Everything went really well, but I missed you." He sounded sort of wistful. Then he chuckled. "It's never as much fun to handle a crisis without you." There was another short pause—the only sound the two of them breathing softly. Then Stefan leaned over and tugged the blanket down to Anton's knees. "Let me help you get to sleep."

Anton's partially erect cock surged into full tumescence. "That certainly isn't helping." He rolled his head to one side and smiled in Stef's direction. It was too dark to see him.

"Just give me a minute." Stefan's soft lips closed over the plump crown of Anton's cock, and a line of pure fire raced along his spine. Sensation increased exponentially when Stef cupped his full sack in one hand and wrapped his fingers tightly around his engorged cock with the other.

It had been so long since Stefan had taken the lead like this. Too long. Anton lay back and lost himself in pure carnal bliss, in the soft, wet suction as Stefan took him deep, the cool brush of air across the damp surface of his shaft when Stefan dragged his lips back to the very tip. His tongue dipped in the tiny slit at the end, his long fingers kneaded his sensitive balls within his sac. Stef dragged one finger over his perineum and teased the tight pucker of his ass.

Press and release . . . press and release . . .

Anton had nothing to do but lie still and enjoy every sensation, every flick of Stefan's tongue, every scrape of his teeth. The pleasure seemed to go on forever, yet it was over in a heartbeat. Anton turned himself free to selfishly enjoy Stefan's talented mouth and fingers. After just a couple of minutes of pure heaven, he slipped almost gently into orgasm.

Groaning softly, Anton came in a simple rush of pleasure, an arch of his hips, a tensing of muscles, the rhythmic pulsing of his cock as he spilled his seed between Stefan's lips. Stef sucked him dry, licked the last drop from the tip, and then gently drew the light blanket up to cover his body.

He leaned over and kissed Anton good night. Then he curled up beside him, close enough that their bodies connected from shoulder to thigh. Close enough that they sighed as one, breathed as one. Anton drifted off to sleep with Stef's damp lips against his biceps and his warm fingers curled against his belly.

Something awakened him out of a sound sleep. The room was dark and Stefan slept soundly beside him. Anton lay back, alert to the silence.

A cry! He crawled out of bed, careful not to awaken Stefan, slipped into his sweatpants, and padded silently into the main room of the cottage. Soft whispers came from Deacon and Daci's room. Whispers and the sound of weeping. He tapped lightly on their door, but he entered without waiting for permission.

A pale shaft of light from the parking area spilled across the room, casting the two occupants in a soft glow. Deacon sat in the middle of the big bed with Daci in his arms. Her face was pressed against his shoulder and her body trembled as she cried.

"What's wrong?" Anton sat beside them on the edge of the mattress.

"She had a nightmare." Deacon nuzzled Daci's tangled curls. "It's okay, sweetie. You're awake now. It was just a dream."

She shook her head. "No. It was Matt. Something horrible is going to happen if we don't . . ."

"It's okay," Deacon soothed.

"Don't what?" Anton ran his palm over her hair.

Daci shook her head. "I don't know. I can't remember, but I know he was trying to tell me something important."

"Deacon, can you read her dreams? Maybe . . ."

Deacon shrugged. "I tried, as soon as I realized what had happened, but I couldn't see anything."

"What's going on?" Stefan wandered into the room. He'd slipped on a pair of sweats, but, like Anton, his chest was bare.

Anton reached out and squeezed his hand. "Daci dreamed of Matt. I'm wondering if he was trying to reach her. Their connection is much closer, more powerful than his to me. Daci, are you willing to let me try?"

"Anything." She took the tissue Deacon handed her and wiped her eyes.

"Come sit in my lap. Lay your head on my chest. Sometimes contact . . ."

Before he could finish, Daci had scrambled across the bed and crawled into his lap. Anton wrapped his arms around her slim, naked body and held her close. Her heart pounded and her scent, all warm woman, filled his nostrils. He rested his forehead against hers and let his thoughts wander deep inside Daci's mind.

He'd been here before and her brain was familiar territory to him. Her thoughts opened immediately to his. She was nervous, so close to him, remembering the trouble she felt she'd caused when Anton and Stefan had first caught her spying on the pack in Montana. Stronger than that, though, she missed Matt terribly and worried about him.

And she had complete faith that Anton could make everything right. Such total trust weighed heavily on him. This was all his fault. He'd been the one who lost Matt to the Goddess. What if he couldn't bring him back?

Delving into Daci's most recent memories, Anton sifted through her worries until he touched on the thread of her dream. He'd been right—it was more than a dream. Matt had reached through to Daci, and Anton heard his voice, faint and far away, yet very clear.

What he heard almost made him laugh out loud.

The answer to the riddle.

He stayed long enough to hear everything. Then Anton straightened up and hugged Daci. "Thank you. You're right. Matt was trying to reach you, but I think he's given me the answers we need to save him. *I am the one I seek.* Matt showed me the right question." He glanced at Stefan. "You were right, too. It's not why were so many Chanku drawn to the Tampa area . . . it's what happened when I was here so long ago."

Stefan folded his arms over his chest. "Okay? So what happened?"

"Matt's discovered that I was our Goddess's first Chanku lover. Until thirty years ago, she'd only been with human men. She had no idea how much power came from sex with one of us. She's not our creator. She was our guardian, newly assigned to watch over the Chanku about the time our ancestors started to disperse, but she absorbed energy whenever Chanku mated with one another. Matt said she was so busy enjoying her new powers and taking human lovers that she wasn't paying attention when we all sort of slipped away and spread out around the globe.

"Time passed, and without the nutrients Chanku began growing old and dying off without knowing who they were, without mating their own kind. Without that sexual energy to feed her, the Goddess's powers began to fade. That's when she realized she'd fucked up."

"Subtle way of putting it," Stefan said. He parked himself in a chair. "How'd she end up in Florida?"

Anton cocked his head to one side and grinned at Stef. "Would you believe she was drawn here by a spring-fed pool that somehow revitalized her? She stayed, found human lovers for what little sexual energy she could take from them, and slowly regained her strength. Her presence is what drew other Chanku to this area. Nothing conscious, but somehow they must have sensed their guardian was nearby. It wasn't until she

CHANKU SPIRIT / 95

took me as a lover—purely an accidental choice—that she realized something was different. I was Chanku, though not yet
awakened—her very first Chanku lover, the first to give her the
sexual energy she needed. That's when she realized what she
was missing. Knowing she'd failed her people, she saw me as
the answer to her problems."

He stared down at his hands for a moment, frustrated to
have forgotten so much. She might be a goddess, but she'd been
dead wrong in taking away his choice, not only in remembering
but in what became a life-altering journey to Tibet. "She's the
one who sent me on my quest, the one who made sure I found
the scrolls. I am the one I seek." He shook his head, amazed by
the simplicity of it all. "Once she found me, I found others of
our kind, and her power began to return."

He reached for Daci's hand and squeezed her fingers. "Now,
though, we need to hurry if we're going to save Matt."

Deacon hugged Daci close. "What's going on?"

"The Goddess intends to make Matt her consort against his
will. He loves you and Daci, but he sees no way out. He said
the mating is supposed to take place at dawn."

Stefan nodded slowly. "Her when, her where. Will it be our
dawn, or hers?"

"I don't know." Anton glanced at the bedside clock. "It's almost four. We need to get moving, and hope like hell she's in
the same time zone we are."

Anton hid a bag of clothing at the edge of the swamp, just
out of sight of the resort, in case they returned in daylight. Four
wolves slipped into the heavy undergrowth. Anton took the
lead while the others followed closely behind. He should have
been exhausted after only a couple of hours of sleep. He wasn't.
He was much too excited, too aware of the moment, the risks.

So many questions answered, yet for the biggest question of

all, he had absolutely no idea what to do. How were they going to save Matt if the Goddess wanted him? How were they going to find him if she wanted to keep him to herself?

He led them down the familiar trail, through swamp and bog, across shallow creeks and stagnant pools. They heard the bellow of alligators nearby, and barely missed an angry cottonmouth along the way.

Stefan was the one who spotted the tuft of wolf fur caught in a tangle of vines leading away from the main trail.

Here. This is the way to the pond.

I missed that. Anton sniffed at the fur. *It's yours.*

The four of them burst through the thicket and tumbled out into a small meadow. There was no sign of the shimmering pool. The grass was short and ragged, but not neatly manicured as it had been the day before. The meadow stood silent and empty in the gray light of predawn.

The four of them shifted. Daci turned to Anton. "Where's Matt? Are you sure this is the right place? Where's the pond you were talking about?"

Anton glanced around the meadow and recognized various trees. "I wish I knew. Another astral plane, perhaps? Stef? What do you think?"

"Do any of you sense Matt? Or even the Goddess?" After a moment, Stefan glanced at Anton. "She works on sexual energy. Can we call her with that?"

Anton shrugged. "I imagine that's our best..." The air shimmered and the ground bucked beneath his feet. Daci let out a tiny shriek. Deacon grabbed her arm to steady her.

The pond appeared, shimmering and bubbling in the center of the meadow. The Goddess stood at the water's edge, gowned in a long, silvery robe. She held a leash attached to a huge, golden wolf. Matt was so thin and haggard, Anton barely recognized him. His thick fur was dull, the expression in his amber eyes one of despair and sadness.

Daci shoved her knuckles against her mouth. "Matt?" She glared at the Goddess and demanded, "What have you done to him? Why is he wearing a collar?"

With imperious arrogance, the Goddess raised her head. "I am your Goddess. Speak to me with respect."

"No!" Daci lunged toward her. Anton and Deacon grabbed her arms. She jerked and struggled in their grasp. Anton tightened his grip so she couldn't break free.

Daci's frustration spilled out as she cursed and then cried. She raised her head and screamed at the Goddess. "You don't deserve my respect. Not if you treat someone who's always honored you like he's a dumb animal. How could you? Matt? Are you okay?"

The wolf lowered his head and looked away. Daci turned to Anton and stared at him with tear-filled eyes. Anton shook his head in disgust. He glared at the Goddess. "She's right, My Lady. How can you expect us to honor you when you treat your subjects with so little respect?"

She frowned, as if she were perplexed by his question. "He will be my consort. As you loved him when he was among you, you will love him as my mate, and me as his."

Matt's voice slipped into Anton's mind, so hopeless and filled with despair it was physically painful listening to his soft words.

Daci, Deac . . . I'm sorry. I don't know how to get away. I tried, but . . .

Before Anton realized what she intended, Daci shifted. Snarling, she broke free of his and Deacon's grasp and lunged at the Goddess's throat. The Goddess met her, all silvery fur and gnashing teeth. The two came together in a tangle of teeth and claws and vicious snarls.

Stefan and Deacon backed out of the way. Anton rushed to Matt's side and removed the collar, but when he turned to help Daci, Matt shifted and caught his arm.

"No! Look. Daci's got her down!"

The dark wolf had her jaws locked around the silver wolf's throat. Daci held her in a choke hold, but she delayed the killing strike.

The silver wolf went limp. Daci let go of her throat and backed away. Her ears were flat to her skull and her lips pulled back in a frustrated snarl, but she didn't attack. Instead, she paced back and forth in front of the fallen wolf.

After a moment, the wolf shifted and the Goddess rose from the ground. Silently she turned and grabbed her gown up in her fists. With her back to the five of them, she stared down at the twisted fabric in her hands for a long, silent moment before slipping it over her head. The shimmering folds draped around her ankles, and she carefully lifted her long blond hair free of the gown and arranged it over her back.

When she finally raised her head and looked at Matt, there were tears in her eyes. She bit her lip and stared at him, as if she struggled to understand what had just happened.

She glanced at Daci, and then she gazed at Matt as if he were the only one in the meadow. She nibbled at her lip and took a deep breath. Again, the Goddess nodded toward Daci. Finally, when she spoke, her soft voice cracked on the words.

"She is not yet your bonded mate, yet she was willing to die for you. I could have ended her life with a single word, and she knew that, but it didn't stop her."

The Goddess shook her head again, as if unable to comprehend what had occurred. Tears ran freely down her cheeks. She tried blinking them back and then grabbed the full sleeve of her robe and wiped at her streaming eyes. "You mattered more to her than life. Just as you were willing to die rather than break your spoken bond to her and the other. Not a mating bond. A spoken bond." The Goddess shook her head in silent denial.

"A promise, My Lady. Not to be taken lightly." Matt touched her shoulder.

She raised her head and stared at him a moment. "I understand, now. I am so sorry. I did not understand before."

Tears ran freely down her face. She looked at all of them, but her gaze settled on Anton. He fought a powerful urge to go down on his knees. He had revered her for so long. To find she was less than perfect, that his beloved Goddess had feet of clay, was unsettling and almost impossible to accept.

Almost.

She smiled at him, and he knew she'd been inside his head, reading his thoughts. "Is it so difficult, my dear Anton? As hard to accept imperfection in your Goddess as in yourself? I find I truly have much to learn." She shook her head. "And much for which I need to apologize."

She turned to Matt and Daci and took their hands in hers. Included Deacon and Anton in her tremulous smile. "Forgive me, please. I have wronged you. All of you, beginning with you, Anton Cheval. I used you, and for that I must apologize." She shrugged and smiled at him. "Though I can't be too sorry, as I got the results I prayed for."

It startled him to hear the same words he'd spoken to Keisha. The same excuse he'd used more than once when he'd made decisions affecting someone else's future. Wrong. He'd been just as wrong as the Goddess.

Anton's mind was still spinning with questions when the Goddess focused on Matt. "Matt, your love has reminded me what I gave up when I accepted this role. I thought to take it from you. I understand now that love must be freely given. I promise to remember the lesson you've taught me."

She dropped their hands and stepped aside. Instead of appearing diminished by her admission of fault, she somehow glowed brighter, looked more beautiful in the early morning light that now spread slowly across the meadow. "I have been strengthened by my time with you, Matt. I hope I have also learned what I should have known so many eons before."

Anton stepped forward. "My Lady? What of you? Will you still watch over us? Will our requests for your help, for your guidance, be answered?"

She dipped her head in a slight bow to him. "You are what you seek, Anton Cheval. So many of your questions have answers you will find only within yourself, but know that I will always be here for all of you, for all my people. The Chanku will survive because of you . . . because of what you have done, not because of me." She shook her head and sighed. Then she turned to Matt.

"I didn't understand. Truly, I know nothing of love, but I am learning." She touched the side of his face with her fingertips. "Because of you, Matthew Rodgers, I am learning."

Then she slowly and silently faded away.

Light shifted, and the ground seemed to quiver beneath their feet. Blinking, Anton gazed about and realized the pool was gone, the manicured lawn no longer in evidence. High in the brilliant blue sky, the sun shone down on the ragged meadow in the midst of the Florida swamp.

Anton locked gazes with the others and then, as one, they shifted and headed back to the cottage.

Within a couple of hours they were in a small chartered jet and headed west. It seemed almost surreal to Matt, surrounded now by people who loved him, who had risked their own safety to bring him home—people who thought he'd been missing only for a couple of days.

He knew he'd been held captive by the Goddess for months. His hair had grown more than an inch, though for some reason he'd not had to shave. He'd lost weight, and his ribs felt like a washboard beneath his fingers, but Daci sat next to him and Deacon was across the aisle, and the voice of the Goddess was no longer in his head.

It was no longer her *when*, her *where*. He was going home.

Home to Millie and Ric. Home with Daci and Deacon and the mating bond he'd dreamed of for so long. There was nothing now to stand in their way. Not his own fears, not the Goddess.

Nothing.

Daci squeezed his fingers, and he turned to her. She reached up and brushed tears off his cheeks.

"It's okay, Matt. I love you. We're going home and everything will be fine."

Deacon got out of his seat and squatted down next to Matt. "She's right, you know. It'll all be fine." He leaned over and kissed Matt. "Damn, I was so worried about you. Don't ever do that to us again."

Matt's laugh sounded shaky even to him. "Got it," he said. "No more kidnappings by goddesses. I'll make a note."

Anton walked back a few minutes later. "We'll be landing shortly. You gonna be okay?"

Matt gazed up at him with his mind wide open. "What do you think?"

Anton nodded. "I think you're pretty amazing, if you want the truth. She told you her name?"

Matt nodded. "Liana. Her name's Liana. There was a time when she was a little girl who had parents who loved her and brothers who teased her." He dipped his head. "I made her remember. Maybe that was a mistake."

"Never. Even a goddess needs to remember her own humanity, if there's any to recall. I'm glad we got you back, Matt. I was worried." He grinned at Matt. "The worst thing about this whole episode for me is that I learned an important lesson, one my mate's been trying, unsuccessfully, I might add, to teach me as long as I've known her."

Matt realized they had Daci and Deacon—and even Stefan's—undivided attention.

"I learned what it means to have your ability to choose your own course taken away from you." He shook his head and then he grinned at Daci. "The Goddess took me as a lover, sent me on a life-changing journey without giving me a choice. Not that I would have chosen differently, but the decision that altered my life was not made of my own free will. She stole that from me."

He rested his fingers on Daci's shoulder. "Once again, Ms. Lupei, I owe you an apology for taking away your free choice in the matter of your Chanku birthright."

Daci grinned and shook her head. "Anton, you don't have to apologize. Knowing what I know now, I wouldn't want it any other way."

"Oh, but I do." He laughed and then sighed dramatically. "You're my dress rehearsal, Daci, for the apology I'm going to have to make to Keisha. I'm never going to live this one down."

Laughter followed Anton back to his seat. Matt leaned his head back and closed his eyes. He knew all about having choices taken away.

He knew even more of the joy of having them returned.

"You're sure you're not too tired?"

Daci paused in the doorway as Matt popped the top buttons open on his shirt. It was barely dark in Colorado, but he was still on Florida time. He shook his head. "No, and I won't sleep until we do this. I've thought about it for so long. I know for you it's only been a couple of days, but . . ."

"I'm ready, too, Matt." Deacon already had his shirt off and bent to untie his boots. "Daci, quit messin' around and get your clothes off."

"Yes, sir!" She giggled and stripped out of her jeans and sweatshirt before the guys were completely undressed. Then she was out the door and running on all four paws across the stretch of open ground between the cabin and the forest before Deacon cleared the deck railing.

Matt was right behind them. Damn, how he'd missed the fresh, clean smell of the Montana woods, the crunchy sound of pine needles beneath his paws, the ripe female scent of Daci and the familiar male musk he recognized as Deacon's unique scent.

He didn't have as much energy as he'd had before this all began, but they seemed to know he couldn't run as far as they normally would have. When Daci paused in a small meadow bathed in starlight, when she presented, it was Matt who pawed her shoulder and mounted her.

She flattened her ears to her skull as he filled her with his sharp wolven cock. It was all new, a totally unique experience to mate as wolves. It was just as new and surprisingly sensual when Deacon mounted Matt and took him from behind, when the three of them somehow found the proper rhythm to ease three separate bodies into a single bond, to open three disparate minds for a mating link that left no secrets among them.

Not even the long nights and days of Matt's captivity. Not the sexual demands the Goddess had made on him, not the anger and violence those same demands had forced out of one who was by nature gentle and loving.

The good and the bad, the memories long hidden, the mistakes once made, all of it part of the bond. All of it melding among three minds, three people who loved without barriers, who opened themselves without fear of pain or mistrust.

Orgasm swept over them. Not a burst of stars and the shock of lightning, but instead a gentle climax to so much they had come through to reach this point. As Daci gave up the last of her guilt over her father's persecution of the Chanku and his horrible treatment of Millie's daughter, as Deacon came to terms with the life he'd led for so many years on the streets, so did Matt give up the pain he'd felt over the sexual bondage the Goddess had forced on him, the confused tangle of love and hate he'd felt for her.

They lay in the thick grass with the sound of crickets chirping and the distant hoot of an owl. Panting, bodies still tied in a tangle of limbs and paws, muzzles and tails, they quietly absorbed all the new memories, the shared knowledge that connected them even more powerfully than their linked bodies.

Matt rested his head on Daci's shoulder. Deacon's chin was on her flank. The sounds of the night and the cool mountain breeze laden with the fresh smell of pine washed away the last sense of the Florida swamp. Cleansed the long days and nights of Matt's captivity.

Still, he thought of the Goddess now, as his thickened penis still pulsed deep inside Daci's hot vaginal sheath, as Deacon's swollen cock stretched his ass to the point of pain.

But not beyond. He hadn't really thought through the logistics of tonight's three-way bond, but damn it felt good. Sex with love. Making love.

He wondered if the Goddess would ever understand. He realized he thought of her now through three points of view—his own, Daci's, and Deacon's. Thought of her with love in spite of what she'd put him through.

But then, he realized he'd always think of her as Liana. As that little girl who still remembered love. Maybe she'd find it again, someday.

Matt slipped free of Daci's sheath as Deacon pulled carefully out of him. He stood up and shook himself, feeling a little dazed by the images still sorting themselves out in his brain. He touched noses with Daci, with Deacon.

And then, as one, they shifted, and the three of them stood together, wrapped in one another's arms, in the dark forest.

"I'm in your head." Daci touched his temple with her fingertip. There was a look of pure amazement on her beautiful face. She turned and stroked Deacon's jaw with her other hand. "And yours. I'm in both of you, but it's like my own because you have my thoughts, my memories. I love you both so much."

She stretched up on her toes and kissed Deacon. Then she

turned and did the same with Matt. He felt the smooth slide of her breasts over his chest, the warm softness of her lips on his.

A soft glow filled the meadow. Matt raised his head and wrapped his arm tightly, protectively, around Daci. Deacon stood at his side. United, the three of them faced the Goddess.

"Don't fear me, please." She nodded to them but came no closer. "I come only to give my blessing on your mating. And to thank you once again. All of you, for reminding me of my own humanity, my own worth as Chanku. For showing me the power of love. Real love, given freely. You have honored me with your honesty, and the purity of your emotions." She held her hands out before her, bowed her head a moment as if in prayer. Then, just as she'd left them in Florida, the Goddess slowly faded away.

Matt felt her presence even after she'd gone, a faint impression of her power. Power he'd helped her regain.

He shook his head and laughed out loud, breaking her spell. Then, as one, the three of them shifted and raced down the narrow trail to their home.

Running Wild

Kathleen Dante

Prologue

Fear had her heart pounding, a dire sense of being hunted. Something bad was going to happen, she just knew.

A squeal, a long screech, another metal shriek, then silence. For a long moment, the world stood still.

Then the bottom dropped—

Arms flailing, Deanna jerked awake, a scream frozen in her throat, her side aching with ghostly pain.

Plain cream walls met her eyes, not crazed glass, broken trees, and scarred mountain. She lay in a bed—Graeme's bed— not her car. A blanket twisted around her waist, not the seat belt. Afternoon sun warmed her clammy skin.

She exhaled loudly, forcing out the air trapped inside.

A metallic smell clung to her, acrid and harsh to the nose— fear, she realized to her disgust. She pulled the other pillow over, buried her face in its softness, filled her lungs with Graeme's wild, dark scent. His strength and his steadiness. His unyielding courage. He had come for her.

It was over. She was safe.

Her heart slowed as the nightmare eased its grip.

1

_____

Some days it didn't pay to get out of bed. Graeme certainly wished he hadn't left his. Of course, he had an excellent reason for feeling that way, one any red-blooded male would agree with. At least his shift was over for the night. *Serve and protect* would take on a more personal meaning for the next several hours.

A dark-colored Miata was tucked beside the house when Graeme got home in the early hours of Monday, occupying his usual spot and leaving him to park his Jeep by the road. The rental company had made good on their promise, then. The sight filled him with mixed emotions, compounding the distasteful but not unexpected news that he'd received at the start of his shift.

News he didn't know how to break to Deanna.

The light shining through the kitchen windows welcomed him home. For the first time in the six years he'd lived here, that was precisely what it felt like—home. No longer just a place where he sacked out, but one he shared with his mate. And just like that, the day's frustrations were forgotten.

Like a bird dog, his cock went on point with the alacrity he'd come to expect. Thinking of Deanna was a sure recipe for a hard-on. It didn't help that her scent lingered in his Jeep, keeping him in a constant state of semi-arousal.

He was still taken aback by how quickly she'd gotten to him. Sure, she was single, pretty, brave, steady in a crisis, sexy as all get-out, heterosexual—and smelled like his most carnal dreams come to life. That didn't explain his bone-deep certainty that she was the one for him.

Graeme had moved away from the clan to improve his chances of finding a mate. Woodrose had the advantages of a forest to run wild in, good people worthy of protection who believed wolves in the mountains are so last century, a steady stream of hikers and other tourists—plus lack of competition. He was the only male werewolf in miles. But he hadn't expected to meet a potential mate while halfway down a cliff.

He'd invited Deanna to stay with him after the cabin she'd been renting was torched by a bunch of drunk idiots trying to scare her away. She'd accepted, with reservations, but that was still a step forward.

The knowledge that her stay was temporary hovered in the back of his mind, a thundercloud ready to rain on his picnic. Many of her experiences in Woodrose hadn't been pleasant, starting with Henckel ramming her car. The presence of the Miata only drove that point home. She could leave now, anytime she wanted. It was up to him to convince her to stay a little longer. He got out of his Jeep, a spring to his step, the front porch rumbling under his eager feet.

The mouthwatering aroma of freshly baked cinnamon rolls greeted him at the door. Delicious, but no comparison to Deanna's scent.

Graeme was all set to join her, but a better look at the entry stopped him in his tracks. The brown leaves of the plants by the door had been trimmed. The glass in the picture frames over the fireplace gleamed in the half-light from the kitchen. There probably wasn't a square inch of dust left in the place. The hall closet was ruthlessly arranged: coats and jackets by season, umbrellas to one side, vacuum tucked in the corner. His running shoes were parked on the rack beside his steel-toed boots, waders, dress shoes, moccasins, and flip-flops. He wasn't a slob, but he wasn't anal about lining them up, either. From where he stood, he could see his books squared on the shelves, the cushions plumped up on the couch and off the floor, and a bunch of mail in a neat stack.

It all added up to a raging case of stir-crazy to him.

Someone wasn't used to sitting still, even when she was supposed to be on vacation. It probably hadn't helped that what passed for downtown in Woodrose was a twisty drive away. When he'd gone looking at houses, he'd been more concerned about privacy than convenience. A county road in the middle of nowhere, with God's own forest for his backyard, fit his requirements to a T.

Shaking his head in amusement, he toed off his shoes and hung his hat, his service weapon an accustomed weight on his hip. Out of respect for the tension that the cleanliness about him implied, he set the shoes in the empty spot on the rack.

The smell of sugary goodness, melted butter, and cinnamon tickled his nostrils, stronger than gun oil and pine cleaner. He followed their trail, rounding the hall closet to the brightly lit galley kitchen where sharp smacks announced Deanna's industry.

She stood with her profile to him, her shoulder-length brown hair pulled back into a pert ponytail, looking cool and together in her tank top and shorts as she pummeled dough on the counter.

Male that he was, the jouncing of her generous breasts snagged his attention. He'd always been a breast man and hers were fantastic—a nice handful, high, firm, and round with just the slightest hint of sag, a damned fine pair of knockers. He'd seen them up close and in less, but no matter how many times he'd fondled and kissed them, the sight still managed to reduce his wolf brain to raging hunger.

Deanna looked so good in his kitchen, so right—like she belonged there. God forgive him, but he suddenly understood the hankering for barefoot and pregnant.

She glanced up from her kneading, a bright smile blooming on her face when she saw him. "Hi!"

Going by instinct, Graeme walked up behind her to wrap his arms around her waist. "Hi, yourself." She squirmed in his arms, giggling as he nuzzled her neck in greeting. He couldn't help an appreciative growl at the perfume that enveloped him. Female ambrosia and oh so good that he got hard just from one sniff. He couldn't help it—her scent short-circuited his control. He ached to bury himself inside her, to have her hot, wet pussy tight around him, to hear her gasping for pleasure.

Damn, he sounded like a horndog—even to himself. It was almost like an addiction!

He sighed, his weariness and frustration melting away on a surge of desire. "You can't imagine how much I needed that."

Her smile softened to one of commiseration as she leaned into him. "Long day?"

Graeme eyed the flattened dough under her hands, wondering whether to tell her. He hated being the bearer of bad news, but he found he particularly disliked bringing Deanna bad news. It didn't help that he had mixed emotions about the matter.

"What is it?"

He filched a cinnamon roll cooling on a tray and bit into it to give himself time to think, and was momentarily distracted by the explosion of sweetness. Pure heaven. The other deputies would turn pea green if they tasted this. He licked warm syrup off his lips as he gathered his thoughts.

Bite the bullet, Luger. Better that she hear it from him than from someone else. "Henckel made bail."

Fred Henckel was Woodrose's golden boy, the star quarterback who'd led the local high school football team to state championship last year. He and his team also had a history of underage drinking and DUI plus various misdemeanors, one the sheriff and most of the townsfolk willfully turned a blind eye to, excusing it as *boys will be boys*. The latest incident had Henckel crashing his truck into Deanna's car, nearly killing Deanna—but it was also what had brought her into Graeme's life. If it weren't for that, she might have driven right through Woodrose without him ever meeting her.

Her hands stilled on the dough, her mood visibly darkening. "That's insane."

Graeme shook his head in weary disgust. "Son of upstanding members of the community, strong local ties, not a flight risk, a promising young man." He made a face at the last. "No one was killed, so the sheriff's soft-soaping it as *an unfortunate incident*. Judge bought it." No one wanted to tarnish the golden boy and risk him losing his football scholarship.

It was little consolation that the rest of Henckel's band of idiots remained behind bars and no one was giving their babble about wolves any credence. The arson charges seemed to have put the fear of God in them—or at least the fear of being tarred and feathered. The property damage was stirring some outrage in the community, so it was unlikely the judge would be inclined toward leniency. But it galled him that as a deputy sheriff he couldn't do more.

She shook her head, the tail of light brown hair bouncing about her shoulders, as she plunked the dough into a bowl. "That's totally bogus."

"No argument there." He couldn't think of anything else to say that might make her feel better. He'd never been much for small talk, but suspected now wouldn't be a good time to haul her to bed. "How about a run?"

A run sounded like just the thing to blow out the cobwebs from her nightmare that her cleaning binge hadn't succeeded in eliminating. Deanna followed Graeme into the trees behind his house, her eyes adjusting easily to the night. The bright light cast by the gibbous moon brought out the liberal dusting of white in his short-cropped black hair, giving him something of a halo. She hadn't been looking for a lover when she left Boston. She'd been hoping for peace, an end to the strange restlessness that had afflicted her for the past year. Perhaps even family. An orphan, she'd yearned for roots and something of a heritage.

She'd gotten more than she'd bargained for with Graeme. First, there was the instantaneous animal attraction of their first meeting. Her lover stirred something untamed inside her, something she hadn't known before him. Her inner wolf, as he called it. Her shock at his explanation that his family name, Luger, was a corruption of *loup-garou* was still fresh.

Without any ceremony, Graeme stripped off his shorts and T-shirt, leaving them folded on top of his flip-flops. He stood with moonlight gilding his body, totally unconcerned about his nudity.

Once again she was struck by how big he was—all over. He was built like a tank with hard, rippling muscles and legs like tree trunks. Her mouth went dry. Seeing him like this against a backdrop of trees and dark sky, like a primeval god incarnate, brought to mind other things they could be doing besides a run through the forest.

Before she met him, she hadn't been this ravenous. The restlessness that had plagued her in Boston had made her picky and kept her celibate. Now, whenever she was around him, she felt like a sex maniac.

It didn't help that his cock hardened under her eyes, thick with promise. A promise she knew he was more than capable of fulfilling. Just as she knew he'd be hard and hot and smooth to the touch, velvet and peach fuzz to her itching fingers.

He gave her a self-deprecating smile and a shrug, the gesture excusing his response as only natural.

Deanna hesitated, fiddling with the button at the waist of her shorts as she wrestled with melting arousal. "You're sure no one will see us?"

Graeme's pale eyes twinkled like crystal, obviously amused. "My nearest neighbor is more than a mile away on the other side of the ridge. But if it will make you feel better, I'll go first and make sure no one's around."

An enormous gray wolf settled on all fours in his place, his Change so quick she might have mistaken it for heat lightning. Even in his other form, Graeme was a sight to behold. He was bigger than normal wolves, his head coming up to her chest. Thick fur, big paws but perfectly proportioned to the rest of him, and the same arctic blue eyes made more striking by the dark fur around them. A magnificent animal.

He turned his head, sniffing ostentatiously, then wagged his tail in encouragement—which meant the coast was clear. Like ordinary wolves, his sense of smell in this form was sharper than a human's, able to pick up scents a mile away.

She pulled her shirt off hesitantly. They'd been lovers for only days. She wasn't accustomed to undressing before him while not caught up in the throes of passion, much less doing so in the woods.

Graeme pressed his damp nose to her belly, a soft rumble rising from his deep chest. The spot of coolness made her jump. He gave her a wolfish grin, his tongue lolling out one side, then rubbed his narrow muzzle against her bra.

The brush of thick fur along her side sent a shiver of pleasure rushing through her. Her pussy clenched, suddenly wet.

"Alright already. Hold your horses." Whether she spoke to him or herself, she didn't know. She wasn't into bestiality, but that one time when Graeme had gone down on her in wolf form was an experience she'd never forget. It had come as a shock since she hadn't known he was a werewolf at the time, but she couldn't deny he'd driven her wild.

Just the reminder made her nipples tingle and tighten, another shiver sweeping through her. Thinking of it was enough to get her hot and very bothered. Her heart gave a distinct thump as her arms prickled.

Deanna released the front clasp of her bra, freeing her breasts to a growl of distinct approval from Graeme and a sigh as he rubbed his muzzle against her. His fur felt so soft against her she was tempted to forget about the run. "Keep that up and we'll be here all night."

To her disappointment, he backed off, leaving her to finish undressing.

Leaves crunched underfoot while the warm night air embraced her naked body. Heat swept her cheeks as she stood there, still somewhat scandalized by her behavior. But she'd turned her back on her normal world when she'd chosen to pursue a relationship with Graeme—and to delve into her heritage. This was no time for second thoughts.

Imagining a wolf, Deanna Changed. Heat flooded her, rising from her toes to the ends of her hair in a wave of tingling sensation. The next thing she knew, she was fanged and furry. She shook herself, the wolf form feeling like second skin. Though she'd undergone her first Change only yesterday, it felt like she'd been a wolf forever.

She flexed her claws, watching them dig into the soil. The Change continued to astound her—that she, ordinary Deanna Lycan, was a werewolf. The stuff of legend. When she'd imagined discovering some mysterious heritage, her fantastic pipe dreams hadn't included werewolves.

Graeme rubbed against her, ending with a nibble behind her ear that made her shiver. He stepped away, tail wagging, then tipped his head to the trees, apparently suggesting she follow him. That was one disadvantage of the wolf form: communication depended on body language. Telepathy would have been so convenient.

Her muscles flexed, her gait smooth, as she trailed after Graeme. Unlike her, he knew the forest.

In no time at all, she was running through the trees, the wind ruffling her fur with gentle fingers and desire a quiet bubbling in her veins. Running with Graeme beside her, a large, protective presence. Running until her breath came in gulps. Exulting in the power of her wolf form.

Until the last lingering shadows from the afternoon's nightmare disappeared and the restlessness lost its hold on her.

Freedom.

He'd been right to suggest a run. She felt so much calmer now, the frustration from his news and the tensions of the day flushed out by exuberance. Except for sex, this was more fun than she'd had in months. The freedom was seductive.

Graeme seemed to sense the change in her mood. From hanging back, he now sprinted ahead, the grin he threw over his shoulder challenging her to a race.

Deanna overtook him, her slimmer form easing her passage between the bushes. They were headed back now. She recognized the stump they'd passed earlier on the way out.

She glanced back at him, laughing, and saw the look in his eyes turn urgent. Feral.

In the space of a heartbeat, the race became an erotic game: a chase. From protector, Graeme became hunter and she his rightful prey. Desire and excitement bubbled up at his game and she ran, her heart pounding, knowing what would happen when he caught her.

She Changed as she reached the trees where they'd left their clothes. She regained her human form, scrambling on all fours, her heart thundering against her ribs.

Graeme closed the gap, pouncing before she could grab her shirt. She landed on her back on the grass, naked as the day she was born. He grinned down at her in playful triumph, his fangs a formidable sight.

Deanna froze instinctively. She should have been afraid; instead carnal awareness streaked through her in a chill wave that left her nipples tingling and her pussy wet. It didn't seem to matter what shape he took, she craved his touch anyway.

A happy growl above her said Graeme hadn't missed her reaction. He settled on top of her, his fur tickling in a full-body caress. He licked the sweat on her breasts, his rough tongue doing that flick-flick-flicking that sent shivers down her arms.

"God!" She sank her fingers in his thick fur, still incredulous at the turn of events, hoping he wouldn't get so carried away that he'd take her in his wolf form. Foreplay was one thing, but she wasn't sure she was ready for penetration. That other time had been different. She'd been caught up in the moment: her first Change. Mixing it up struck her as a bit too kinky, unless she was also a wolf. But if he tried . . . she wasn't sure she would stop him. Her heart tap-danced against her ribs, trepidation and arousal wrestling for the upper hand. Wondering if this time, *she* would forget herself.

He crawled up her body, the rasp of his agile tongue fanning the flames of desire—both hers and his. The heat of his turgid cock was distinct against her thigh.

"Condom?" Deanna reminded him breathlessly, poised on the edge of suspense. Would he take her right then? Would she let him? She rather suspected she wouldn't protest.

For several heartbeats, it seemed he hadn't heard her, too intent on licking her to madness. Then he rose off her, Changed, and grabbed a foil pack from his shorts, tearing it open and sheathing himself in one smooth motion. He was so thick and large, the sight made her core spasm with sudden, urgent hunger.

Too impatient for finesse, she hooked her legs over his hips and urged him into her. She'd thought about this all day; cleaning and baking hadn't distracted her for long. She'd been on pins and needles waiting for his return, lust and longing simmering into heady anticipation.

Graeme worked his way into her with short, hard thrusts that only fanned her hunger. So careful with his strength. As if she'd break!

"Faster," she urged, hungry for that breathtaking release. Slow and steady could wait; she couldn't.

"If you're sure." He drove into her, pounding her with a tender ferocity that sent brutal pleasure crashing through her.

All her anticipation boiled over in a violent eruption of molten rapture, rolling thunder shattering her senses. Deanna screamed, helpless before so much sensation. "Oh, yes!" This was what she'd been craving. This was what she'd needed.

Another burst of ecstasy flung her to the heavens. Higher and faster. Until she could touch the stars. Until she floated free, lighter than air. Free as the wind.

He continued to pump his hips, stretching it out. Pleasure washed through her in wave after wave of delight, gentler each time. Easing her descent, then taking his release.

Wonderful.

After a short rest, they stumbled back to the house and the bedroom, not bothering with dressing first. Deanna's knees felt curiously weak with a surprising tendency to fold at the oddest times on the walk back. She wanted to blame it on the run, but that was wishful thinking. Graeme just had that effect on her.

Giggling at her foolishness, she stretched out on the bed, her body still humming. The past hour certainly put the day's frustrations into perspective. Life was for living. So she'd nearly died. All the more reason to celebrate. To reach out and take what she wanted.

He grinned down at her, a thin wolfish smile that said he had plans. "That's gotten the edge off. Ready for more?"

The urge to laugh faded when he mounted her again, slipping deep inside as if he'd been made for her.

"Oh, yes." She couldn't imagine ever tiring of the sweet ache of his possession. The slick friction of his cock stretching the delicate muscles of her pussy only fanned the fire in her belly. She locked her legs around his hips, drawing him deeper until he was nestled against her core. She was definitely ready for more.

Graeme rocked his hips in a slow, steady rhythm that promised a long ride this time.

Deanna rocked along with him, content for now. The coarser friction of his crisp chest hair against her breasts sent pleasure tripping over her nerves, reigniting the embers of her earlier hunger. She twined her arms around his neck, pulling him down to add kisses to the sweet mix of sensation.

The lazy give-and-take kindled a crazy warmth in her chest. Her lover. The thought made her heart skip on a surge of possessiveness.

She could hardly believe they'd known each other less than a week. He seemed to know her body better than she did, homing in on her pleasure points and taking such exquisite care to ensure her orgasm.

But for now they took their time, in no rush to attain the heights of rapture and end the discovery of sweet delights. Lovemaking could be play. And despite his job, it seemed Graeme wasn't always serious. Certainly his playful nibbles on her lips and along her throat were proof otherwise.

"You taste so good, I could eat you up." His stubbled cheeks rasped on her skin as he worked his way across her shoulder. His motions ground his pelvis on her mound, setting off fireworks all along her nerves.

Deanna gasped, the memory his words evoked making her shiver, and not from fear. She arched involuntarily, rubbing herself against him, her breasts tingling and throbbing. Her sheath spasmed in reaction, emphasizing his girth. "You already have, remember?"

He laughed, a low chuckle that reverberated through her. "Yeah, I have, haven't I? No reason why I can't do it again. Something that great deserves repeating."

"Promises." She had to force the word out, her chest tight.

Hunger bared its fangs and bit deep and suddenly their leisurely pace wasn't fast enough. She arched up again, deliberately this time, tempting him to do his worst.

Or best.

In Graeme's case, they were one and the same.

A groan met her efforts. "You're really asking for it this time." He started to move, a slow, thorough stroking, rubbing her with his cock and his chest as he pulled out and out . . . and out. Then just before he slipped free, he returned, pressing in and in. And in . . . until he was tucked against her womb.

So very deep inside he felt like a part of her.

Then he reversed his motion, repeating the exquisitely slow, delightful friction. His shoulders bunched above her, so broad they blocked out all else but him. He dominated her senses— his heat, his heft, his hardness.

Digging her heels into the bed, Deanna met his thrusts, writhing against him, adding her own twist to the intimate dance. Pleasure zinged straight to her core, little bites of sharp delight, like a string of firecrackers whirling inside her. Gasoline to the fire blazing in her veins.

Even more thrilling was Graeme's reaction.

His grunts and growls were undeniably complimentary,

even if technically some were swear words. Obviously she hadn't been alone in her craving.

Laughing at her success, she nibbled on the slab of muscle flexing above her.

That incredible control of his snapped in a breathtaking surge of speed and raw sensation. Anchoring her with his hands on her shoulders, he switched to a vigorous beat. His pounding thrusts drove the air from her in startled cries of pleasure. He stared down at her as he moved, his irises a thin ring of electric blue around black. "I can't get enough of you."

A sudden yearning pierced the storm of pleasure buffeting her senses: the hope that would never change.

Graeme was relentless, riding her to breathless release over and over without pause, not satisfied until she was hoarse from screaming her pleasure. Only then did he give in to his own orgasm with a howl of triumph. Was that stamina of his innate to werewolves or was it just him? She'd never had a lover quite like him.

Of course, she'd never been so insatiable herself.

Deanna floated on a wave of euphoria, wrung out from so much pleasure. Even her toes tingled from clenching.

They'd wreaked havoc on his bed. The sheets were well on their way free, clawed off the mattress. A pillow slumped on top of the drawers, half out of its case. The other was nowhere to be seen in the dim shadows. She would have been tempted to laugh if she didn't feel so blissful.

Prang!

The sound of breaking glass shattered the soaring sense of well-being from her orgasms. She froze. "What's that?"

Graeme rolled to his feet, a gun in his hand, naked yet bristling with aggression.

2

Deanna grabbed the lamp on the nightstand, tugged the cord free of the socket, and followed Graeme out the bedroom. Though she'd have felt better dressed, she knew he wouldn't wait. She wasn't about to leave him to face danger by himself.

He flashed her makeshift weapon a startled glance but refrained from ordering her to stay behind. He knew better and proved it. "I go first."

She nodded, not about to argue. She might pride herself in her self-sufficiency, but he was the cop and she recognized that. Besides, unless she Changed, he was the one properly armed. Her heart raced, trying to leap out of her throat. There'd been too many emergencies lately—the crash, getting trapped in her car, the fire—and her nerves insisted this was another one.

Holding his gun pointed to the ceiling, Graeme eased through the door, slow and cautious. Completely naked. Quite unlike the cop shows on TV. He stopped there, blocking her from leaving the room, his head turning as he scanned the shadows.

Deanna rose on tiptoes to peek over his shoulder. The exterior security lights threw long shadows across the furniture. At first glance, the dark living room looked undisturbed.

Deanna waited for Graeme to be satisfied that no one lurked in the darkness. He was the professional, after all.

He cleared the doorway, stepping around furniture and making straight for the front door.

She followed at his heels and finally saw what he must have seen. One of the living-room windows was broken. Anger out of proportion to the damage flooded her. After all the effort Graeme put into helping people, he didn't deserve this.

His back to the wall, Graeme peeked outside, then swore under his breath. She caught a flash of red taillights vanishing around the curve—probably the vandals making good their getaway. Pretty insolent of them, hitting the home of a deputy sheriff.

After a moment, he lowered his gun. "It's not usually this exciting around here. Really."

"You mean it's only since I arrived?" About to join him, Deanna stubbed her toes against something rough and heavy. "Ow!" She staggered, pain shooting up her leg. Hanging on to the lamp in her hands made her lose her balance and tumble into Graeme.

He caught her easily, his arm steady around her waist. "Hey, are you okay?"

"Just—" She was about to say *clumsy*, except she hadn't walked into any of the furniture. She looked around for the culprit, then pointed to a rectangle of darkness on the floor. "What's that?"

Graeme switched on the entry light, revealing a black brick like the ones edging the flowerbeds in the front yard; clumps of soil lay scattered around it on the hardwood floor she'd mopped just that afternoon. But the vandals hadn't been satisfied with just a brick. This one had a sheet of paper crumpled around it and held in place by a rubber band.

He muttered something under his breath, then got a pair of gloves and a pen from the hall closet, using the pen to remove the rubber band and peel the paper off. The other side of the sheet had large, block letters printed in a wavering hand: THAT BITCH ISNT WELCOME HERE. THIS IS ALL HER FAULT.

Dismay pricked Deanna at the hateful message. She hadn't done anything to merit such venom. She was the one whose car was bumped, whose worldly possessions lay at the bottom of the gorge, who'd been burned out of her cabin! She hadn't asked for any of that. "Why are they doing this?"

"Damned if I know. Maybe they're just idiots. This is plain stupid." Graeme's nostrils flared. He brought the paper up to his face and drew a deeper sniff.

Rising on tiptoes, Deanna leaned closer and copied his sniff. Acrid sweat, stale cigarette smoke, and fresh beer on one corner. She flinched from the miasma; ever since her first Change her sense of smell had sharpened, a development that wasn't necessarily for the better. "Can you tell who threw it?"

He made a face. "Maybe, but just because I can doesn't make it admissible as evidence."

She couldn't interpret the glance he gave her, but the second look—the one that flashed downward with sudden awareness—reminded her of her nudity. She'd been so focused on the brick, she'd forgotten neither of them had a stitch on!

Shifting her grip on the lamp, Deanna shuffled her feet, suddenly acting uncertain and uncomfortable. With a muttered excuse, she retreated to the bedroom.

Graeme took the opportunity to bag the brick and the note, sweep up the broken glass, and call in the incident. He'd have to file a report when he went in, but that was for later.

When Deanna came back minus the lamp, she was wearing one of his T-shirts. Since she was obviously no longer in the mood for lovemaking, he pulled on a pair of shorts, then suggested a late meal. The cold fried chicken he took out of the refrigerator wasn't his usual bachelor's fare, but he didn't mind. Deanna so obviously enjoyed cooking, he hadn't objected when she took over his kitchen and didn't regret it. She was a great cook.

He dug into his meal with relish. This was nice, sitting across from her at the kitchen table, eating a meal together, almost as if they were an old mated pair. He looked forward to making it reality.

Despite their run and the energetic sex that followed, she picked at her food, eating just enough to be polite. After the brick, her reaction was only to be expected.

Graeme cursed the vandals in silence, the sneaking, idiot cowards. He didn't really mind the broken glass—the damage was minor—but this incident made convincing Deanna to give their relationship a chance more difficult.

"I've been thinking, since Lycan is a werewolf name, would you happen to know my father's family?"

The question shouldn't have taken him by surprise. Deanna had told him she'd grown up a ward of the state, therefore had no relatives who'd been willing to take her in. But he'd expected her to ask about the brick thrower.

"'Fraid not." Running a hand through his wiry crew cut, he grimaced in apology.

"But you recognized it as a werewolf name," she protested, setting down her fork to stare at him.

"It's not that simple. Werewolf packs make for uneasy neighbors. Packs don't share territory well. Back then"—his gesture encompassed the centuries as he cudgeled his memory for old history lessons—"there were as many as four packs in what's now West Virginia. But with the wolf hunts, then the Civil War, we lost track of the other packs."

She blinked at him, her mouth moving silently. *Civil War?*

Graeme nodded, grinning at her expression. "In 1728 or

thereabouts, werewolves of German and French descent settled here and eventually formed packs. Luger, Verrue, Dewulf, Lycan—those are the major ones that I remember."

"So there's only your . . . pack?" Deanna propped her elbows on the table and rested her chin on the cup of her hands, her eyes wide with fascination. "How did they manage to survive?"

He toyed with a drumstick, uncomfortable with the track the conversation was taking but soldiered on as best as he could. "Werewolves can interbreed with ordinary humans. That's why only one of your parents has to be a werewolf. Many of my aunts were in your situation, no idea of their heritage before they"—*mated*—"married into the clan."

"There's nothing you can tell me?"

"I can check the histories, but I think the last time a Lycan was mentioned in them was the Battle of Charleston. None of my aunts is a Lycan."

"Battle of Charleston, that's 18—what?—62?"

"Sounds about right." History hadn't been his favorite subject.

Deanna straightened, her enthusiasm fading. "You're right. That won't help me find my father's family." She stood up and gathered her dishes, her hands slow, hesitant. "You know, I'm not doing anything here. I have a car. Might as well go on to Hillsboro and research my folks."

Selfishly, Graeme wanted to disagree. He wanted her by his side where he could protect her, his inner wolf raising territorial hackles. But he'd promised her that distance was no problem. Insisting she stay in Woodrose when he had work and couldn't stay with her was a surefire way to send her running.

Before accepting his invitation, she'd warned him she still intended to continue on once her belongings had been recovered. He wasn't adverse to driving down to visit her, but he'd hoped her stay with him would be longer.

"No problem." He pasted a smile on his face. He could only hope that giving her room would reassure her she could trust his word.

It would also give him time to find out how serious this threat to Deanna was. He thought he knew the brick thrower. Beneath the sourness of anxious excitement and the odors he associated with the Hogg Wylde, a local bar that Henckel's team used as a hangout, was a vaguely familiar scent. Male. Possibly one of the idiot's teammates itching to join the rest behind bars. But he doubted the lab would get anything off the note— and if the techs did manage that much, he suspected the sheriff would dismiss it as a prank.

3

Deanna stared glumly at the glowing screen of the library's aging microfilm reader. The article from the local paper didn't mention anything she didn't already know about her parents' deaths.

> . . . *Officials say white-out conditions caused the pileup along Route 219. Up to 12 vehicles were involved in the crash.*
>
> *Police reported two fatalities. Peter and Marissa Lycan of Hillsboro were killed when a semitrailer crashed into their car, pinning them against the pile.*

Another dead end. Her inquiries had been equally fruitless. No one at the Marlinton office of Monongahela National Forest had been working there at the same time as her parents. The people who owned the house they'd rented didn't remember anything besides the accident. Her parents had been the nice, quiet couple who kept to themselves, giving no one any cause for alarm. They'd had no close friends, no one who knew them from before their work with the Forest Service.

In this day and age of the Internet and genealogy buffs, she couldn't find a single reference to her parents' previous employment or schooling or even birth records. It was as if Peter and Marissa Lycan had deliberately pulled up stakes and moved to a town where they would be anonymous.

For a crazy second, Deanna wondered if they'd been in the witness protection program, then dismissed the thought. What would have been the point when they used a werewolf name? The fact that she could Change was proof of that heritage. She also doubted the powers that be would have allowed them to choose their name.

She rubbed her temples in frustration, trying to head off the ache from the glare of the microfilm reader's light. It didn't help that she hadn't been sleeping well the past couple of days, responsibility for which she laid entirely at Graeme's feet and not because he kept the nightmare away. The man was too potent for her peace of mind.

Switching off the reader, Deanna finally faced her problem—she'd gotten used to his heat, the dip in the bed his big body made. This morning she'd woken up to find she'd tried to mash the pillows into a harder shape she could snuggle against. She who prided herself in her independence, who'd always lived alone, who'd been surprised by the amount of mattress Graeme took up, missed his presence at her side.

At least she wouldn't have to worry about that for the next two nights. Today was the first of his days off and Graeme would be driving down to spend them with her. The reminder put a bounce in her step as she returned the microfilm to the librarian on duty.

For the first time in months, she had a love life and she intended to enjoy herself. She allowed herself a shimmy of delight. Sometimes it felt as if she hadn't really lived until she met Graeme, as if she'd just been marking time in Boston.

Out of the corner of her eye, Deanna saw a familiar figure pass the open door. Her heart leaped in recognition. Graeme! There was no mistaking that walk and those broad shoulders.

She rushed out, then stared in consternation at his uniformed back as he bought a drink from the vending machine. It was supposed to be his day off. Had something come up and he couldn't stay?

No matter. At least he was here now. She ran to him, anticipating one of his aggressive kisses that made her weak in the knees.

He straightened and turned to her with that sure-footed fluidity that was so incongruous in such a large man. "Can I help you?"

The question took Deanna aback, stopping her headlong flight toward her lover. She stared into cat-green eyes, that shade of hazel caught between gold and green, then checked the name pinned on his chest to confirm her mistake: A. Luger. "You're not Graeme."

Her cheeks heated at her mistake. She'd nearly thrown her arms around a stranger!

"Unfortunately not. Should I apologize?" He arched a brow in good-natured inquiry that sharpened to interest as he got a better look at her. His shoulders straightened, pushing his chest forward. He took a deep breath, the light in his eyes suddenly blazing with awareness. "His loss, my gain."

"Not quite. Hello, cuz."

She couldn't suppress a start of surprise at her lover's voice behind her. The man before her had so dominated her attention she hadn't noticed Graeme's approach.

"Deanna, meet my cousin, Ashley." Dressed in a yellow polo shirt and khaki pants, her lover smiled down at her and hooked a hand on her waist, blatantly possessive.

"Heh, so formal," Graeme's look-alike chided him, a glint in his eyes. He extended a large hand to her with a bladelike smile so similar to Graeme's. "Ash Luger."

In a daze of wonder, she took the hand—only for him to press his free hand on top of hers in a gentle squeeze instead of a businesslike shake. The heat encompassing her hand gave the friendly greeting an intimate flavor she felt all the way to her toes. "Pleased to meet you."

"Believe me, the pleasure's mine," he growled in a deep bass that rang her chimes.

Good heavens! If she hadn't had the benefit of experiencing Graeme's voice, she would have melted into a puddle at his cousin's feet—even then, she was halfway to melting already. None of the men back in Boston had radiated quite so much raw virility as these two Luger males.

She looked from one to the other. Face, hair, height, physique, the way they held themselves—the semblance was uncanny. They could have been twins. Even their voices were similarly deep. Aside from their clothes, only their eyes were different, Ashley's a greenish yellow to Graeme's icy blue.

Twice the eye candy.

"This is uncanny."

"The bane of our boyhood," Graeme commented with a wry twist to his lips contrary to the tension of his fingers at her side. "Got us into all sorts of trouble."

His cousin nodded easily, as if he hadn't noticed Graeme's less-than-welcoming manner. "Do you live around here?"

"I used to. I'm moving back."

"That's great. We can have dinner together sometime."

Deanna blinked, nonplussed by his blatant interest. Couldn't he tell she was with Graeme? That the two of them were more than just casual friends? She looked at Graeme, wondering how he was taking his cousin's invitation.

Graeme tugged her hand out of his cousin's hot clasp. "You

can find us in Woodrose. Deanna's staying with me for the time being."

Ashley looked at her, arching a bushy eyebrow.

She nodded confirmation, if that's what he sought. "I'm staying with Graeme in Woodrose at the moment. We're . . . together." She blushed at making such a blatant statement, but she couldn't let him think she was free.

"Convenient." Graeme's cousin glanced around them. No one was within earshot.

"But—"

"You're not mated yet. It's still anyone's game." The smile Ashley shot at Graeme was a challenge, nearly a snarl, confidence and aggression in every line of his body.

Mated? To Graeme? Did she even want to be mated?

She turned to her lover. "What does that mean?"

Graeme stiffened, a muscle twitching at the corner of his jaw. "A woman's scent changes if she has frequent sex with one male, caused by constant exposure to his pheromones. It usually takes at least a month to happen—what we call a honeymoon. When that happens, she smells like kin to other males of his clan, therefore off-limits."

"But you're not."

Ashley's intent look sent a frisson of feminine awareness zinging through Deanna, her core pulsing in response.

The arm around her waist tightened, drawing her against Graeme's side, the move unmistakably possessive. She stiffened, sensing undercurrents between the two men, the testosterone so thick and heavy there should have been fog.

Entertaining though the posturing was and flattering to the ego, she whistled, shrill but soft, adding a hand on her lover's wrist. "Cool it. I'm not a bone to be fought over."

Ducking his head, Graeme cracked a smile, suddenly bashful and boyish as he gave her an affectionate squeeze. "You're nothing so skinny as that."

"Never meant to imply you were, ma'am." Ashley rubbed the back of his head. "Just wanted to make sure you know you have other options." The look he shot her made his meaning clear—he was sincerely interested in her, not just trying to get a rise out of Graeme.

Deanna couldn't suppress a shiver, her nipples tingling. For a wild moment, she wondered what it would be like to be between them, to have these two men making love to her.

What was she thinking?! She blushed so furiously her cheeks felt scorched. Where did that thought come from? She'd never been the type for a ménage! Still, it floated in the back of her mind, like a guilty pleasure, taunting her with possibilities.

Graeme trailed the purple Miata to the outskirts of Hillsboro and the cottage Deanna rented. He paid little heed to the cottage, except to note the distance to her neighbors. Far enough for some privacy, but not that much. Most of the terrain had been tamed within an inch of its life with trees farther apart than the wolf in him liked. A run here was out of the question.

Not an issue.

Unlike the two nights without Deanna. Those had stretched like weeks. A lifetime. He hadn't been able to sleep in their bed for missing her. But he couldn't bring himself to change the sheets or clean the interior of his Jeep to remove Deanna's scent. He wanted her beside him. It didn't help that he hadn't discovered much about the threat to Deanna. There'd been no follow-up to the thrown brick. It was starting to look like his caution was unwarranted—two nights he'd been deprived of her company.

His thoughts churned, thrown into turmoil by his cousin's unexpected appearance.

Talk about a stroke of bad luck, running into Ash that way.

Now that his cousin knew about Deanna, he was bound to join the chase. The two of them had so much in common that there was little to choose from between them . . . or so it had seemed when they were younger. They'd even gone into the same line of work and attended the state police academy together. Ash had always been competition.

Even worse, there was no denying Deanna reciprocated Ash's attraction. The day was warm; it wasn't cold that had her nipples poking at her thin T-shirt.

The wolf in him wanted to tear Ash apart. That only made him feel worse. While he'd bloodied his cousin's nose on countless occasions when they were younger and had his bloodied in turn, he'd never felt this clawing, gut-churning need to do violence, to eliminate his rival.

But if he couldn't get at Ash, maybe he could do something about strengthening his claim on Deanna.

Deanna could practically feel Graeme's intensity warming her back. He was at her heels almost as soon as she'd climbed out of the Miata. The short walk to the porch brought to mind their first time together, all straightforward sex and lots of it. She'd known her mind, known she'd wanted him in her bed and between her thighs. No complications, none of this second-guessing herself. The possibility of a repeat had pure lust tightening her throat and her skin prickling with awareness.

Graeme shut the front door behind her and rested his forearms on it, forming a cage around her. There was no mistaking his intent as he caught her eyes.

Her heart thrilled to his aggression, her knees feeling weak. She slumped against the door, suddenly needing its support. "Something on your mind?" She sure hoped it was the same as what was on hers.

"Ash turned you on." He leaned forward, pressing into her,

his large body hot and unyielding, carnal hunger stark on his face. His cock was a hard ridge against her belly, thick with promise.

Heat flooded her cheeks as Deanna remembered her unbidden response to his cousin. The memory of the two men side by side, both wanting her! Her pussy clenched, musk filling the air.

His nostrils flared, no doubt picking up her body's inadvertent betrayal.

Deanna pressed her thighs together, squirming in embarrassment. It only made the ache worse. "Of course I was attracted. I couldn't help it. He looks just like you!"

Graeme's eyes darkened, the sharpness turning intent. Hot. Intimate. "You mean that?"

"That's what I said." She wanted to believe it, too. But she couldn't help but wonder if it was a result of pheromones. If a female werewolf's first Change was triggered by prolonged, intimate exposure to a male werewolf's pheromones, could her response to Ashley be due to chemistry? And if she followed that line of thinking to its logical conclusion, was the basis of her attraction to Graeme as cut-and-dried? That nonsense pop psychologists babble about, survival of the species? Was it just biology? Let's hop into bed and make little werewolf cubs?

Was one Luger just as good as another?

Was she as fickle as all that?

She'd thought—hoped—that it was more than physical. She had nothing against sex, but the knowledge that she'd jumped into bed with Graeme less than twenty-four hours after they first met, after only a couple of hours or so of acquaintance, still made her squirm. Sure, he'd saved her life in the meantime, but such behavior was completely unlike her. The one lunch they'd shared barely counted as a date.

Graeme's kiss—hot, deep, and possessive—swept away her questions. He claimed her mouth with hungry strokes of his tongue, his carnal intentions clear. He lifted her off her feet without any obvious effort, as though she were some willowy size zero. That casual display of strength was arousing beyond belief. He got her wet without trying.

He was fierce, even rough, but the lapse in his control only served to excite her more. There was no way he would hurt her. She was sure of that.

Supremely conscious of the strength of his big body, Deanna clung to his shoulders, returning kiss for desperate kiss, wanting to fill the emptiness inside her, needing to sate the hunger from their time apart. She locked her legs around his hips, grinding her aching mound against him.

"Oh, yeah." Graeme walked them to the couch, his strides rubbing the ridge of his erection against her throbbing flesh. Bowing his head, he nipped her shoulder, right at the bend where it met her neck, sending a bolt of sensation through her body. Her nipples tingled, need blooming in the sensitive tips.

She groaned. "Hurry."

Sitting her on top of the back of the couch, he pushed her shirt up, then used his teeth to drag her bra down and free her breasts. He plumped her breasts together and buried his face in her cleavage with a groan. "God, I missed this."

Pressing her cheek against his short-cropped hair, she inhaled, smelling sun and sweat and that wild, dark scent that was uniquely Graeme. Two days away from him and she'd already learned to miss it. She wanted to rub his scent all over herself so she wouldn't ever be without him.

Rub his scent all over herself?!

Shock at the thought rendered her immobile. The desire seemed so natural—yet it wasn't exactly the sort of thing a normal person considered. Nothing could have driven home the truth of her werewolf heritage so completely. But to want Graeme's scent on her?

"A woman's scent changes if she has frequent sex with one male . . . she smells like kin . . . therefore off-limits."

Graeme was a fantastic lover, but she'd known him for less

than a week. Surely that was too soon to be thinking about anything permanent, especially if it was just physical attraction talking? An affair was one thing, a commitment—*mating!*—was something else entirely.

The hot clasp of his mouth on her nipple broke her train of thought. The suction sent her lust spiraling higher, shoving her doubts to the back of her mind. Her hormones broke out in a wild dance, cheering him on.

Deanna locked her arms around his head, holding him tight as pure lightning crackled inside her. *Oh, God!* She didn't think she could ever tire of his lovemaking. He had an instinct for knowing precisely what would drive her crazy.

Working her breasts like a master, he drew on her, his lips insistent. Licking. Nibbling. Sucking. Igniting a furious wildfire in her body. His approving growls said he was enjoying himself almost as much as she was.

It was too much.

Incandescent rapture exploded in her core, an eruption of raw sensation that took her by surprise. She cried out in disbelief as another toe-curling orgasm followed the first.

Just from his attentions to her breasts!

He gave a knowing laugh, low and intimate. Joyous. The laugh of a man who knew he'd pleasured his woman. "There's more where that came from." He turned her around, bending her over the back of the couch as he dragged her shorts and panties down her legs. His hands on her thighs raised her off her feet, leaving her teetering on the couch.

"Graeme!" She clutched at the cushions below to anchor herself and not a moment too soon. He'd freed himself and took her from behind with a single hard thrust that forced the air from her lungs. He felt so huge! His thick cock stretched her to overflowing, the angle letting him grind down on her G-spot with single-minded purpose. The sudden penetration sent another orgasm streaking up her spine.

"That's right. Say my name."

Deanna gasped, stunned by his aggressiveness. Obviously, his cousin's appearance brought out the wolf in her lover.

"Say it."

A thrill swept her, tingling excitement curling her bare toes. Her body rocked to his pounding, seesawing with each brutal stroke. She chanted his name over and over, as he took her with relentless intent. Flooding her senses with pleasure.

Even her heart picked up the beat: *Graeme, Graeme, Graeme.*

He gathered speed, his grip on her hips like steel. He raised her hips higher, the change letting him drive deeper, magnifying the effect of his possession. Raw sensation swirled inside, lightning striking her core.

Balanced on the back of the couch, she could only hang there, taking him, glorying in the storming of her senses. Wave after wave of molten rapture battered her, his hammering forcing cries of pleasure from her throat.

Ecstasy knew no bounds. It overwhelmed her, flinging her through the sky on winds of sensation, faster and higher. She screamed his name as she soared free of all cares.

A triumphant roar rose above her, all territorial male, as Graeme took his release. Loud and low and unmistakably carnal, announcing to all the world his conquest. She didn't mind. She couldn't. He was well within his rights: he'd rung all her chimes, up, down and sideways.

And she'd enjoyed every second of it.

Panting, Deanna hung on the couch, boneless from that last endless orgasm and too spent to move. When Graeme pulled her shirt the rest of the way off and removed her bra, she couldn't muster the energy to open her eyes.

He picked her up, cradling her in his arms, his shirt a gentle roughness against her back. He walked a short distance, then laid her on what felt like a bed. After some rustling of cloth, he lay down beside her, naked, his weight making the mattress dip.

"Did I hurt you? Was I too rough?" His hand patted her side as if checking for fresh injury.

Deanna laughed at the questions, savoring the ache between her thighs. The horizontal tango had never been this much fun before. "You won't get any complaints from me." Especially when he went to such lengths to ensure her orgasm.

His arm around her waist tightened, drawing her into his heat. His hard body made a surprisingly comfortable blanket.

They lay spooned together, saying nothing for several minutes. She'd missed this. Funny how quickly she'd gotten used to it when she'd never lived with a man before.

"How'd it go? Find out anything about your parents?"

She grimaced at the reminder of that spectacular failure, then rolled over to face him. "No, nothing at all. It's so frustrating."

The news article of their deaths flashed before her mind's eye, giving her the willies. Was that why she'd been dreaming of the accident? Déjà vu? Her parents had died in a car crash, then she nearly did, too.

Graeme brushed her hair out of her face, his touch strangely soothing. His smile was rueful, his eyes a warmer blue than usual. "If it were so easy, we'd have found the other packs by now. We're still looking, but it's like when they scattered after the war, they lost the pack structure."

Quite possibly she'd been building castles in the air, thinking she'd find family—just like that. Like snapping her fingers. If that were the case, she wouldn't have grown up in an orphanage, longing for roots, dreaming of what she didn't have.

But right at that moment, she didn't mind it quite so much. Graeme's presence seemed to have quieted the restlessness. Apparently, he satisfied her hankering for wildness. She shifted to a more comfortable position, hooking her leg over his thigh and resting her head on his shoulder. "I'm not giving up."

4

Graeme breathed in Deanna's scent, the vanilla and lavender fragrance of her shampoo, the faint sweat and musk from lovemaking, and felt something inside him relax enough that his conscience could make itself heard. What it was saying wasn't exactly happy making.

What the hell had he been thinking, demanding she say his name, acting like a caveman? What if he'd come on too strong and scared her off with Ash panting in the sidelines? Obviously he hadn't been thinking.

"You're lucky to have family, to know where you came from." Deanna's voice was wistful, holding none of the outrage Graeme deserved for his manhandling.

He'd taken her so forcefully, pounding into her like that. If she'd been an ordinary woman, he might have hurt her. He'd never lost control that way before, not even their first time together. Thankfully, she really didn't seem to mind.

"I suppose." He grimaced at the thought of being *lucky* that Ash could drop in on them in Woodrose. "They can be a pain at times."

"You're thinking of Ashley."

Graeme blinked at the accuracy of her guess. "You a mind reader now?"

Deanna snorted softly. "The progression was logical." She snuggled against him, tucking her head against his shoulder. "What was it like, growing up with family—a werewolf family?"

Her contentment was infectious; it made him want to wrap himself around her and settle in until spring. This was nice. Actually, it was more than nice. It was the next thing to perfect—the two of them in bed. It wasn't just sex he'd missed in the past days. He'd needed the quiet time, too.

Lying here with her beside him was restful.

He stroked her side, pleased to see that the massive bruise from the accident last week was gone. Quick healing was one of the benefits of their werewolf heritage.

"We lived something of a distance from town, far enough to be safe from curious eyes. Our nearest neighbors were all family. You could say we lived in each other's pockets."

"But what did you mean about family being a pain?"

"My brothers and cousins were hellions."

Deanna giggled as her fingers played with his chest hair, a happy, carefree sound that had a smile tugging at his mouth. "Just your brothers and cousins? Really?"

"I'll have you know I was well-behaved," Graeme protested mildly. "At least compared to them."

"And?"

"We got worse after puberty." Male werewolves underwent their first Change upon sexual maturity. Their quick healing only encouraged their roughhousing to get rougher. But it was a good life—for both boys and wolves. They'd tested themselves against each other and against nature and learned their limits.

She stared up at him, her expression expectant. Obviously one sentence didn't satisfy her curiosity.

He dug deeper, unaccustomed to talking about himself. Secrecy was a habit, ingrained after a lifetime of knowing—all the way to the bone—that werewolves were different. Discovery would mean persecution; the wolf hunts before the Civil War had a prominent place in the clan's history lessons. Now, she wanted him to talk. Talk about do-it-yourself dentistry.

"With the Monongahela as our backyard, we ran wild. Of course, there were lots of adults to come down on us—not that we didn't deserve it. Now and then." They hadn't gotten into anything like the trouble Henckel and his teammates got into, but they hadn't been angels. "I remember thinking it wasn't fair, since they had more experience hunting and running as wolves. There was no hiding from them."

"But you know they're there for you. If something bad happened."

Like being orphaned?

Deanna's longing for family was clear in her voice. She ducked her head, hiding her face from his gaze—as if she'd confessed to something embarrassing, instead of a very natural yearning.

Her reaction touched him, the wolf in him needing to fulfill her unspoken desire. She was his mate; he had to help her. Presented with a problem, everything male in him ached to solve it for her.

"Yeah, there's that." If his parents had been killed when he was younger, someone would have taken him and his brothers in. No way would they have ended up wards of the state.

Should he ever need help, Graeme knew he could depend on clan—not just his parents and brothers but also aunts, uncles, and cousins. No question about it.

His brothers and cousins were competitive as all get out and had the scars from bloody fights to show for it, but they were quick to close ranks against outsiders who thought to try the same. Family came first.

Deanna didn't have that. Moreover, she'd pulled up stakes, turned her back on the familiar sights of Boston to move to Hillsboro. She hadn't mentioned any friends, either. Small wonder she was searching for her roots.

Graeme wanted to offer to share his family, but he knew Ash's reaction was just the tip of the iceberg. There were several more males in the pack who were unmated. He could just imagine the riot that would break out if he were to introduce her to the clan. Fights would be inevitable—and that was the last thing he wanted Deanna to associate with Lugers.

At least he could be sure Ash wouldn't tell the others. He could think of a few cousins who would spread the news simply for the added challenge. At a loss on how to deal with introducing her to his family, he decided to leave it for later.

"Why'd you move away? Why to Woodrose?" She tilted her head back to look up at him, the expression on her face saying she couldn't imagine anyone wanting to leave family.

He shrugged. "Sometimes you need a bit of distance to keep the peace. We're all strong personalities. Woodrose is close enough for visits but far enough not to trip over each other."

Time to lighten the mood. And he knew just how to do that.

"Speaking of Woodrose, I have a piece of good news." He smiled at her, drawing out the suspense, anticipating her excitement. This was something he could give her.

Deanna peered at him from under her lashes. Her fingers toyed with his chest hair, her short nails scraping random patterns around his nipple. "Well, aren't you going to tell me this good news?"

"If you ask nicely."

She wound her arms around his neck, incidentally pressing

her fabulous breasts against him. "How nicely?" The corners of her mouth curved up as her tongue darted out to lick her lips suggestively. She rocked her hips against his stirring cock, a teasing bump and grind that did unbelievable things to his self-control.

Graeme sucked in air. "That would work." Her effect on him was extraordinary. Like a shot of bourbon, she went straight to his head.

Deanna nibbled on his jaw, her gurgling laughter making it clear she knew the effect she had on him. She took his lobe between her teeth and licked it like candy as she undulated over him in a full-body caress. Definitely in a mood to play. She really didn't mind his earlier loss of control.

Another polishing pass of her smooth belly and his cock was once more quivering on point, and he'd forgotten what they were talking about. Who cared? Talk was overrated anyway.

He grabbed another condom, giving silent thanks for the foresight that made him bring a box along. If this kept up, he'd need every packet.

Her tongue explored the curve of his ear, her breath adding a cool contrast.

Pleasure streaked through him, headed straight for his balls. Bull's eye. Suddenly he couldn't think of anything but getting deep inside Deanna. He grabbed her hips, her musky perfume filling his head with memories of ecstasy. His hands shook as he fought for control.

"You're insatiable." Despite the teasing complaint, she reached between her thighs, guided his cock to her slit, pressed down. And took him into her tight heat. Took him so deep his lungs seized.

His eyes nearly rolled back in his head at the sensation. Sweet fire licked his cock, running up the length of him. Shivers tripped up his spine, threatening to spill his load before he was ready.

Deanna arched her back, the slopes of her breasts flushed a beautiful pink, her nipples stiff peaks aimed straight at him. Her inner muscles clamped around him, squeezing him. Every pulsing, quivering inch. She added a little bump and grind, milking him for everything he had while she laughed that delighted, carefree laugh of hers. Unbelievably, his cock swelled even harder.

Damn, but he could never tire of making love with Deanna. He wanted this.

Forever.

With her.

No one else.

He couldn't imagine sharing this with another woman. Didn't want it with another woman. And he couldn't bear to think of Deanna doing it with another man.

She was his. Every independent inch of her.

Catching her hips, Graeme joined her in her game, trying to keep it light as their bodies strove together. Sex before had usually been a race for sensation: the fastest with the mostest. He'd rarely been tempted to take the time to play, to linger, to stretch out the time together.

Until Deanna.

With her, he wanted to savor the journey as well as the end. Seeing her pleasure, the changes in her expression, the surprise and delight added as much to his enjoyment as the tight grip of her pussy.

He answered her little dance with short thrusts of his own, breathless laughter rewarding his efforts. The game fanned the flames of their desire all over again, rebuilding their carnal hunger as they scaled the heights. Together.

This time there was no mad rush for completion, no driving

need for fulfillment. The journey was the goal. The flush of growing arousal across Deanna's cheeks and the slopes of her breasts. The shivers of delight that swept her body. The startled squeals when he got a particularly good stroke across her G-spot.

But his control only went so far. Eventually distracting himself from the fire blazing in his balls didn't work anymore—he needed release like he needed his next breath, but not alone. Reaching down, he found her clit for that extra push.

With a wordless cry, Deanna convulsed above him, her face going blank in a look of glorious transport. She squeezed down on him, urging him on.

More than willing to obey, Graeme dropped all restraint and let go, coming in a storm of rapture, the fire in his balls blowing through him in an endless orgasm. He gave himself up to the moment, thunder filling his ears and his chest.

Peace settled over him as his mate relaxed into a boneless armful of female approval. Quiet contentment. He lay there, confident in his perfection of manhood: the sure satisfaction of his woman. Life didn't get better than this.

Deanna stirred on top of him, her magnificent breasts rising and falling in distracting friction, her cheeks flushed from her last orgasm. "So what's this good news of yours?"

What? Graeme racked his brain for the answer—all that mind-blowing sex had reduced it to Jell-O. How she could remember what they'd been talking about was a marvel, especially when her pussy was still pulsing around him, milking him of the last of his strength. Thinking took a monumental effort. "Oh, right. Your car's been recovered. You can claim your things whenever you're ready."

A bright smile rewarded his mental feat. "I thought you said Friday was the earliest it would be recovered. Something about paperwork and needing to borrow equipment?"

"The sheriff gave it a push." An attempt to sweep the incident under the rug, he suspected. The sheriff—and many of the townsfolk in Woodrose—treated Henckel as if he were God's gift to football. "It doesn't look good, but at least you'll have your things."

"We can do it tomorrow."

5

Deanna's first sight of her car in the impound lot was a shock, despite Graeme's warnings. She gripped his arm to steady herself. She hadn't imagined anything quite this awful. There was no way her sporty CR-V would run again. It was a wreck, and the recent rains and a week at the bottom of the gorge hadn't helped. The collision and subsequent ride down the mountainside had reduced it to junk on wheels.

All that remained of the windshield was a border of fractured glass, like frost on a windowpane. The crumpled front, the stove-in door where the truck had rammed her, and the mud clinging to it made her poor car look like a giant pug having a hell of an ugly day. The sides and rear were almost as badly battered, their glass wide swathes of crazing. Even the insurance adjuster would have to agree it was a total write-off.

But what caught her eye were the dents on the warped frame of the window of the driver-side door—where Graeme had set his hands, straining to widen the opening to get to her. She couldn't forget that if not for his rescue, she'd have been a crash-test dummy along for the ride. The seat belt that had saved her life in the collision had jammed, trapping her in the car as it tilted on the ridge.

The sight of those dents brought it all back in squealing, shrieking color. The starburst of pain. The bottom of the world dropping. The tree's groans. The car shuddering around her.

Her face went cold, blood draining at the memory.

Graeme had risked his life to free her while the tree supporting her CR-V slowly lost its battle against gravity. A second later and he would have been dragged along when the car continued its descent.

There but for the grace of God.

"You okay?" He laid his hand on top of hers, his touch gentle, though hotter than usual. Her fingertips ached. Her nails dug into Graeme's arm, but he didn't complain, his concern all for her.

She leaned into him, absorbing his warmth and using it to drive away the flash of fear. "Thanks to you."

A wash of pink touched his cheeks with endearing color. "Just doing my job."

The technician had to force open the hatch door, releasing a dribble of muddy water, metal squealing in protest. The shrill sound made the hairs on her arms stand on end.

Deanna didn't bother cataloging the condition of her belongings until after they'd loaded them into Graeme's Jeep and arrived at his place. She didn't have the heart to look, not wanting to expose her distress to the uncaring eyes of the technician.

She carried out the most important first. The handmade wood box wasn't much, the carving fairly crude, but she'd bought it with her first paycheck, to contain her childhood treasures—a dried flower to remember a school trip to a nursery, a ribbon for a school project, a hand-drawn card. Little things made more precious because she didn't have anything of her parents. The box came apart as she set it on the kitchen table, falling in damp pieces.

Revealing its ruined contents, black with mold.

Surprise forced a sob from her, tears filling her eyes. She bit her lip, fighting for control. She'd put the box on the floor of the passenger compartment, where she thought it'd be safe. She'd taken such care. . . .

The tears sent panic whirling through Graeme. At the impound lot, it had bothered him to see Deanna grow dispirited and not be able to do anything about it. This wasn't at all what he'd expected when he broke the news of the salvage to her. He'd hoped she would be happy to get her things back. Instead, it had blown up in his face.

He hated feeling so helpless. Pounding on Henckel might relieve his anger, but it would do little to cheer her up. Sex would distract her, but he didn't want Deanna to think he was a horndog—though his cock sure gave a good impression of one.

But tears—

Graeme stood behind her, not knowing what to do with himself. Knowing how independent she was, he doubted she'd welcome his sympathy. Sure as sin, his sisters wouldn't have. But he couldn't just stand there.

Feeling awkward as a newborn cub and completely out of his depth, he put his arms around her. "I'm sorry."

She stiffened, as he'd expected, but didn't pull away when he drew her against him. "Not your fault." Her voice was muffled against his shirt as she struggled for composure.

Thud, thud, thud.

Deanna jumped away from him as if she'd been caught shoplifting. Despite Graeme's pique at her reaction, the knock came as a relief. At least Deanna didn't look like she was going to cry anymore.

She gestured at him to answer it, then ducked into the bathroom where the sounds of running water and splashing suggested she was erasing any evidence of tears.

The knock repeated, steady and patient.

His nose identified their visitor before he opened the door. Irritation pricked him at being taken unawares. He should have known he'd show up at the earliest opportunity.

For a split second, Graeme considered not answering the knock, but the weight of Deanna's expectations constrained him to politeness.

A man stood on the porch, practically a doppelganger down to the faded academy T-shirt, cargo shorts, and hiking boots he wore. It was like looking at a mirror.

"Ash." The knob creaked under his hand. A visceral anger woke at the threat his cousin represented to his claim on Deanna, hot emotion he'd never felt for one of his clan. It mingled with frustration at his helplessness. Shutting Ash out wasn't an option. Still, Graeme was woefully tempted to slam the door on his cousin's face.

Determination hardened features so similar to his own. He'd known Ash all their lives; they'd grown up in each other's pockets. It'd take a bomb to shift his cousin once he'd decided on a course of action. "Afraid she'll prefer me, cuz?"

Graeme felt his nostrils flare at the challenge.

"Who is it?" Deanna came up behind him, her scent raising his territorial hackles.

Ash's eyes paled to gold as he waited for Graeme's answer. His back straightened, his shoulders squared, bracing himself for a fight.

It was tempting to give him one, since he expected it. But a fight would make Deanna uncomfortable.

"Extra hands," Graeme replied, grinning at the suspicious look his cousin gave him. Ash's casual attire implied that Graeme wouldn't get rid of him anytime soon. He might as well put his cousin to work, since Ash insisted on forcing his presence on them. Though, on second thought, it was good to have another man around in case Deanna got weepy again. Moral support and all. He'd like to see him face her tears.

Graeme opened the door wider, watching as Deanna greeted Ash. He couldn't force her to become his mate. She had to make her choice freely . . . and if she preferred Ashley, he'd have to accept her decision.

The wolf inside him bared fangs in protest. Deanna was *his* mate. His to protect. His to cherish. His to love. Ash knew nothing about her, save what his snout told him.

Graeme forced his inner wolf back. Laying down the law was a surefire way to send her running. They'd been through a lot together. He had to trust that the bond between him and Deanna was stronger than just physical attraction.

"What's this about extra hands?" His cousin shot a cautious look at him, clearly aware of Graeme's internal struggle.

"You can help us unload." He jerked his head toward his Jeep where the rest of Deanna's belongings waited.

They trooped outside.

"What the hell?" Ash made a face of consternation as he lifted a soggy box, his fingers digging holes into the brown carton.

Graeme waited for Deanna to carry her laptop inside before he explained the situation in a low voice. She could probably hear him if she tried, but why remind her of the accident if he could avoid it?

Just relating it roused his anger all over again. He'd underestimated his reaction to seeing what remained of Deanna's car. The sight of the CR-V tumbling down the mountain flashed before his eyes. It had turned over several times. He'd seen too many wrecks to harbor any illusions about her chances, had she been inside. Werewolf heritage or not, her injuries would have been fatal.

Ash's expression darkened. "And this bastard's still alive?" he asked half-seriously.

"Don't tempt me."

* * *

Deanna bit her lip as another grating sound came from inside her laptop bag. That didn't bode well for its condition.

She looked over her shoulder to check on the Luger men. Graeme and Ashley were still by the Jeep, apparently engaged in some male bonding ritual judging from the pugnacious expressions on their faces.

At least she wouldn't have to guard her reaction. She smiled, remembering Graeme's heroic attempt to comfort her earlier despite his discomfort. He'd been so sweet. The memory gave her the courage to unzip the bag.

Glass shards showered out. She raised the lid of her laptop to survey the damage. The screen was broken. Though she half expected it, the reality came as a blow. Fixing that would probably cost as much as replacing the whole thing. With a heavy heart, she started gathering the glass. It wouldn't do to leave it lying around where someone might step on it.

Graeme and Ashley walked in, each carrying a box, as she picked up the bigger shards.

Her lover took it in with a single glance and went to the kitchen without a word. He returned with a box cutter, a small dustpan, and a brush. "*Hsst*, leave that to me. See to the rest."

Deanna sighed. "I seem to have a theme going." Glass from the windshield, the broken window, and now her laptop screen.

"Not your fault." Graeme handed her the cutter, sweeping up the shards without waiting for thanks.

She watched him for a moment. It was probably chauvinistic of her, but there was something sexy about seeing him clean. His questioning glance got her moving, though; she didn't fancy trying to explain why she was staring, not in front of Ashley.

The carton boxes she'd used for her clothes were somewhat waterlogged, with holes gouged through the sides. Her nose picked up a faint whiff of mildew even before she slit the tapes. The clothes inside were wet and dirty, hopefully nothing a spin through the washer wouldn't fix. No big loss if she had to re-place a few. It was mostly casual wear. One of the advantages of working for herself as a Web designer was no dress code.

"Damn, I have lousy timing, don't I?" Ashley murmured, a wry twist to his mouth. He crouched by the other box, using a fingernail to slit the tapes. The stance made his thigh muscles bulge attractively, something she tried not to notice—without much success.

Box after box yielded more of the same. Deanna sorted her clothes automatically, but the sheer amount of drudgery they represented was daunting.

Ashley made a strange sound, like a strangled groan or a choked breath. He clutched one of her balconet bras, its cham-pagne lace marred with mud, his face brick red.

Her cheeks blazed hot when she realized which box he was going through. If she remembered correctly, she'd packed all her underwear in it.

Graeme's hand connected with the back of his cousin's head. "Get your mind out of the gutter." Her lover took it all in stride, transferring one pile to a laundry crate. "Let's get that started. Leave the smalls to me if you can't control yourself," he added in a growl at the other man.

His straightforward manner was soothing in its normalcy. At least he didn't make a big deal about it. Hot in the sack and handy with chores. She smiled reluctantly. What a man!

Ashley aimed a scowl at Graeme. "I was surprised, okay?"

"I'll do that," Deanna insisted, dragging the box with its sensitive contents away from Ashley.

"Sorry about that. No offense meant." He handed her the bra, the speculative glint in his eyes spreading the heat in her cheeks down her body. Now that he'd recovered his balance, he didn't look like he minded the surprise.

"None taken." And that was only the truth. She forced her-self not to squirm. What was it about these Luger men and her underwear? She could imagine the thoughts going through Ashley's head, but instead of wanting to slap him she felt complimented.

His obvious interest didn't help, either.

The beeping of the washer as Graeme programmed it seemed to chide her for her response to Ashley's overture. Graeme was the one who'd risked his life for her—more than once. He was the one she'd taken to her bed.

God, from a dormant libido and a dismal love life to two hunks—prime racks of beefcake—vying for her attention! She was tempted to laugh. Despite her losses, she couldn't quite resent the unexpected turn her life had taken.

Deanna made short shrift of her underwear. Too much attention would have invited Ashley's scrutiny, and she didn't want to think about replacing the ruined ones when the memory of shopping with Graeme for lingerie—and what followed shortly after—was still fresh enough to singe.

She kept her hands busy while she fought the inconvenient awareness threatening to overwhelm her better judgment. Graeme and her and Ashley? She shook her head impatiently. It was as if her first Change had let loose all sorts of crazy thoughts.

Graeme had made it clear he wasn't inclined to share her with Ashley—and *how!*—so she could toss that outrageous notion right out the window. She didn't know why she'd entertained it even fleetingly. She'd never been interested in taking on more than one man. Graeme alone was more than enough for her—adding Ashley fell under the category of Too Much of a Good Thing.

Never mind that.

Her spices were a lost cause. She'd squeezed the spice rack between bigger stuff when loading her CR-V, and it had gotten loose. Days in the stream and the recent rains hadn't helped. They'd have to be replaced. Luckily, her baking stuff—pans, measuring cups, bowls, and her precious mixer—had survived intact if somewhat dinged.

The rest of the work went without a hitch. Graeme had handled the laundry quietly while Ashley had disposed of the cartons and everything else beyond mending—including her box of childhood treasures. The reminder of her loss sent another pang through her. At least she hadn't had to face their disposal herself.

The afternoon had passed in an uneasy calm, Graeme and his cousin conscious of Deanna's distress. Ash had responded by toning down his overtures, but that didn't stop Graeme from anticipating his cousin's departure.

He wanted Deanna to himself for some cuddling to, he hoped, ease her pain. Or at least distract her, even if just for a little while. Though she didn't say much, he suspected her losses hit deep. She wasn't the type of woman to cry over the little things.

So when Ash checked his watch after demolishing his share of pizza, Graeme just about cheered. "Time to head back? It is getting late." He managed to inject a note of disinterest in his voice, but that didn't fool his cousin.

"I thought I'd hang around another day. Camp out tonight. You've work tomorrow. I really ought to hang around, in case there are troublemakers." Ash finished off his can of Dr Pepper in a similar show of casualness.

Graeme narrowed his eyes at Ash. He couldn't say there was no need, just because nothing had happened since the brick throwing. And he had to admit his cousin could protect Deanna as well as he. But the thought of leaving her alone with another male didn't sit well with his inner wolf—especially one who had openly declared his interest.

Ash gave him a thin smile. "Don't worry, I'll take good care of her."

"Then we'll see you tomorrow." Graeme shut the door on his cousin's smug face, the knowledge that Deanna was sharing his bed doing little to soothe his hackles.

He hadn't said, "Touch her and I'll gut you." But he'd thought about it. A lot.

6

A sudden chill started the dream rolling. Deanna was asleep and she knew it. She dreamed and she knew that, too. But fear mingled with memory, and the result felt so real.

Smoke filled her head—more smoke than there had been, but that detail didn't change her fear. Trapped. They were trapped, and the fire would get them.

A hole appeared, and she lunged toward it. Cool air met her muzzle, bringing with it the smell of rain and forest. Fear clinging to her fur, she scrambled forward, her claws clicking on wood, then dropped down.

Alone.

Graeme didn't follow her out.

Deanna spun around and found him stuck in the hole. He bared his fangs, growling as he fought to get through.

She caught a furry foreleg between her jaws and pulled. Nothing happened. No matter what she tried, nothing she did helped. She couldn't get him out.

The acrid smell of smoke strengthened, making her dizzy.

He was going to burn.

She blinked, and Graeme was gone. Fire filled the hole, its heat making her flinch, driving her back. *Graeme!*

Deanna jerked awake—into hard arms.

Graeme's arms.

Sitting beside her, he rocked her gently, a blanket of heat and male. "Hey, it's okay. You were dreaming."

Morning light peeked between the blinds, casting stripes on the walls and across the bed and Graeme. She clutched at him. "You were gone."

He stilled. "I just went to take a leak."

"You were gone," she repeated, her heart in her throat, choking thick. Her fingers tangled with his chest hair as she held on to reality. "You were trapped in the fire." Her breath shuddered between her lips as she fought back tears.

"Ah, damn." Graeme pulled her onto his lap, his hand cupping her nape as he planted kisses on her hair and temple. "Shh, shh. I'm fine. We got out. It's over."

Deanna pressed her cheek against him, soaking in his heat, immersing herself in his wild, dark scent. "It felt so real."

He tipped her chin up. "That was a dream. This is real." He took her mouth in a searching kiss, firm and insistent—all reassuring male strength. Allowing nothing to intrude. Demanding a response she was only too willing to give.

Surrounded as she was by hard male, the fear lost its grip on her, drowned by rising desire. She welcomed her hunger, embraced the electrifying sensations of life. This was real.

The kiss changed, gentled. Graeme nibbled on her lips, teasing, flirting. Playful licks invited her to relax and forget her cares, a side of him she rarely saw. Usually making love with him was intense, a storm of sensation and fury, passion and desperation. Not fun and games.

While she enjoyed his intensity, she found she liked his

coaxing as well. Last time, she was the one who'd initiated the game. This time, it was all Graeme.

Ashley showed up bright and early, just as Graeme was coaxing another climax from Deanna. His knocks were steady, insistent—and completely lacking in urgency.

Graeme ignored the sound and its subsequent repetitions, more interested in the woman in his bed and the music they made together—the slapping of wet flesh, her gasps and sighs, the thundering of their hearts. He had her hips propped up on pillows and had mounted her from behind, and she seemed to like that position a lot.

Just because Deanna had gone through her first Change didn't mean she didn't deserve just as good. This was no time for complacency. She might put up a strong front, but clearly recent events haunted her. The nightmare about the fire and her tears were proof she needed reassurance.

What better way to do so than sex?

Besides, he wasn't about to give up the hot, sweet grip of her pussy, not unless there was blood, flood, or fire. A man had to have his priorities right. The scent of her arousal, of her pleasure, went straight to his head—both of them.

The knocking repeated, slightly louder this time.

"What's—" Deanna broke off on a gasp. "Oh, yes! Right there. Yes!" He loved hearing that hitch in her voice. It made him feel strong.

"Just Ash. He can wait. I can't." Graeme had to admit there was something particularly satisfying in knowing his rival might be hearing Deanna's breathless moans of ecstasy.

After that last shout, the noise stopped, allowing Graeme to concentrate on pleasuring Deanna. Just the way it should be.

Maybe his cousin would learn a thing or two about patience.

She pushed back against him, her round ass brushing his

belly, welcoming his thrusts, her enthusiasm unabated by the interruption. The tight ripples along his cock electrified him, sending tongues of delight flicking over his balls and reducing his irritation at Ash's presence to a distant memory.

None of his previous lovers got to him the way Deanna did. From his first sight of her, fighting her way out of her car, something inside him had responded to her—and that was before he'd gotten wind of her scent. Her effect on him couldn't be simply biological; pheromones only went so far. She felt right, the other half of him, and he intended to do everything in his power to make sure she became his—in every way.

His mate.

She swayed before him, sweat beading down her back, the strong line of her spine so graceful and feminine as she writhed with pleasure. Man, he really had it bad if he was admiring that. Breasts, legs, face, ass, hell, yeah! But her spine?

Surrendering to the inevitable, he pressed a kiss on the base of her nape, resting his weight on one hand and cupping her breast with his free hand. There was no denying it, even her back looked perfect—not *perfect* perfect, but just right for her.

"Oh, oh, oh! Oh, yeah! Just like that." Deanna's soft whimpers of approval spurred him on. The little mewls and gurgles of relish said he was on the right track. He pushed harder, clinging to the shreds of his control as he thrust slowly back into her. The firm grip around his cock ratcheted up the pressure in his balls.

Just a little more.

He got her to that last peak, driving home his message: she was his, he was fine, and everything was okay. Right and tight. Safe and sound.

A shudder ran through Deanna, her tight pussy convulsing around him yet again. The wordless gasp of delight that escaped her was the last straw.

Graeme couldn't hold back any longer, his heart a pounding,

thundering drumbeat in his ears. The firestorm raging in his balls blew through his cock, ecstasy exploding up his spine in a blast of pure sensation.

His trembling arms gave way. He slumped on top of Deanna, his heart going forty-five over the speed limit. And still his limp cock gave a twitch when he slid out.

Before Graeme got his breath back, Ash started his patient knocking again, that steady triple thud that said he would keep knocking until someone answered the door.

Deanna broke out in giggles, muffling her laughter against his chest. "Oh, God. He's been outside all this time?" She gulped air as she regained her composure. Her cheeks were rosy from all their exertions, he noted, well pleased with the results of the morning's labor.

"I guess we can't stay in bed all day." She sighed, then pushed herself off him.

So much for a postcoital snuggle.

"Bastard's putting a crimp in our love life."

She smothered another burst of giggles against her fist. "That's so inhospitable."

"He invited himself."

His body still humming with the mind-blowing explosion of his last orgasm, Graeme debated answering the door fragrant with the evidence of their lovemaking. Tempting, but he suspected it would put Deanna on the spot—like mounting a loudspeaker on his Jeep and driving through town announcing she'd lost count of how many orgasms she'd had that morning—embarrassing as hell and not the sort of thing she'd appreciate. He managed to talk her into sharing a shower, pointing out that dried sweat was pretty uncomfortable. She agreed readily, sparing him the admission that he didn't want her bathing when she was alone with Ash.

Despite the friction and temptation from close quarters, he didn't prolong their shower. That would have been on the edge of rudeness, especially since his cousin was—technically—doing him a favor by staying with Deanna while he worked his shift. Someone had thrown a brick through his window.

"I'll get the door." Pulling on a pair of shorts for the sake of decency, Graeme waved Deanna to the kitchen and prowled over to the front door. The clock over the fireplace pointed to a little past noon.

A blast of summer accompanied Ash's scowl.

"Oh, it's you," Graeme said mildly, still feeling too good to inject genuine heat into his greeting. He lounged against the door, a sappy grin probably stretching his face. He didn't care. All was right with the world.

His cousin shot him a narrow-eyed look of disgruntlement. "I've been waiting for hours." The knuckles of his upraised fist were red from knocking.

"Yeah? Imagine that."

"You're an ass."

Graeme raised a brow at his cousin. "You didn't have to be this early. My shift starts at five—as you well know."

"And deprive myself of Deanna's company? C'mon, Gray. You know me better than that." His cousin rolled his eyes in mock disgust as he walked past, making a beeline for the kitchen, where Deanna was heating cinnamon buns for a late breakfast.

Resigned to his cousin's presence, Graeme followed Ash. He'd have suspected something was up if Ash hadn't come early.

The slight breeze of Ash's passage brought Graeme a whiff of ferns and moss mixed with his cousin's scent. He must have spent the night in wolf form in the forest outside.

Graeme couldn't help but smile. His cousin might have gotten more than he'd bargained for by staying so close.

Breakfast was a casual affair, everyone pitching in and getting in each other's way until Deanna shooed them to the breakfast nook. She looked happy, claiming his kitchen as her domain. She was already putting her stamp on it. Her mixer was stashed in that little rollup cabinet he'd never known what to do with. Her pans were snuggled beside his plates on the drain board. And flowers brightened a corner of the kitchen, tucked into a vase—hers, since he didn't own one.

The sight of their belongings mingled together gave Graeme a warm feeling that the intent looks Ash gave Deanna couldn't dispel, not even when he finally had to leave for work.

"All alone. Finally, just the two of us." Ashley flashed her a thin grin as he closed the door behind Graeme. "Whatever are we going to do with ourselves?"

God, how to answer that? She'd never had two men vying for her attention quite the way these Luger men were. Ashley's blatant interest had her on pins and needles, uncertain how to handle it. That was one difference between him and Graeme: her lover had never been so aggressive; instead he went out of his way to put her at ease.

Deanna muffled a nervous giggle behind her fingers. "Tell me I didn't hear you say that."

"What? I've been trying to get rid of the guy all afternoon," he protested jokingly. He'd moved closer without her realizing, so close she couldn't help but notice the damp spots where the thin cotton of his T-shirt clung to the ridges of his abs and pecs. So close his body heat made her flush with heat of her own. Her core pulsed, her clit swelling in readiness.

His hair was still damp and spiky from his shower—Graeme had said something about getting the forest off him, so now he smelled of Graeme's soap. Distractingly so. His nose flared; he could probably smell the musk of her arousal.

This was so awkward.

She found herself in the kitchen, eyeing the contents of Graeme's pantry. "You really don't need to stay to protect me, you know. That other time . . . those guys were drunk, and anyway, they're in jail."

"Gray doesn't think so. And I'm on my own time, so why not hang around? It'll ease his mind." The flicker of a wink he added said easing Graeme's mind wasn't his goal. The gesture felt strangely intimate, something between friends or lovers, not acquaintances who'd met only twice before—and under fairly ordinary circumstances. His cavalier behavior didn't sit well with her.

"You're yanking his tail." Hearing her words, Deanna laughed in surprise. They'd just slipped out without thinking. She'd said *tail* as though she'd known about werewolves all her life. The reminder that he was no ordinary man—and neither was she—wiped the smile from her face. The strength of her carnal response to him wasn't ordinary, either.

Her heart skipped a few beats. It seriously freaked her to be so aware of Ash.

Flour, butter, brown sugar, apples, and other pie fixings appeared on the counter, gathered while she'd tried not to babble like an idiot. Baking helped her relax—she wouldn't have to think about what to do with her hands. And she needed desperately to relax before she made a fool of herself.

Ashley wasn't going to jump her, for heaven's sake!

But try telling that to her nerves. They weren't listening.

"After making me wait this morning, he deserves it."

Remembering what she and Graeme were doing while his cousin waited, Deanna blushed, her cheeks burning. Not that she would have wished away that morning's lovemaking. Graeme had been so different, playful and gentle, though just as thorough in seeing to her pleasure as before. And he'd done it to drive away that nightmare. Sure, it hadn't been a sacrifice on his part, but the caring behind his lovemaking was unmistakable.

A sudden groan broke her train of thought. Ashley was staring at the ingredients on the counter like a man who'd just been offered a blow job. Lust and greed shone in his cat-green eyes, giving them a distinctly golden hue. "Are you making what I think you're making? Apple pie?"

The seam of his mouth rippled as if he'd surreptitiously licked his lips. It seemed Graeme's cousin had a weak spot.

Now that she thought about it, Graeme enjoyed her baking, too. Maybe something about the werewolf metabolism burning lots of energy gave them a sweet tooth.

Deanna bit her lip, fighting a smile, as she added her battered pie pan to the collection. "Only if you drop all the innuendos." It wasn't that she was choosing Graeme over him—she was no more ready to settle down than she was a week ago—it just felt tacky, as if they were going behind his back.

Ashley eyed her dubiously.

"The cinnamon rolls this morning were homemade, baked from scratch." She pulled out her measuring cups and spoons, then paused in her preparations to give him a meaningful look. "I also make a mean pie."

His throat worked. "That's dirty pool."

"No more innuendos?" That much was nonnegotiable. She didn't think she could handle hours of tap-dancing around the subject. Yes, there was an attraction between them, but she wasn't sure she wanted to explore it. His semblance to Graeme wasn't reason enough.

A loud sigh signaled his surrender. "No innuendos."

She set Ashley to work preparing apples and sought safer conversational waters. "Graeme said the similarities in your appearances got you two into trouble. So you grew up together?"

"That's right," he replied absently, his attention on not breaking the peel as he worked a paring knife around a Granny Smith, his hands moving steadily.

Deanna had to shake her head at his game. How like a man to make a challenge out of something so minor. "What sort of trouble?"

"Skipping class to go fishing, baiting skunk traps, filching pie, that sort of thing. When they couldn't figure out which one of us was responsible, we were both held responsible. Gave me a better appreciation for a frame." The peel fell free, completely intact. He popped it into his mouth, crunching down with relish as he moved on to the next apple.

"*Graeme* framed you?" She paused in her measuring of ingredients as she tried to imagine a Graeme who would deliberately set up his cousin to take the blame for a prank. It wouldn't jell.

Ashley snorted, not looking up as the apple twirled beneath his knife. "I suspect he got the short end of the stick, there." The corner of his mouth quirked. "It did teach us to be more . . . inconspicuous, you might say."

That explanation sounded more like her lover. "What was it like, growing up with him?"

"It was an ordinary childhood, for the most part, up until our first Change. Nothing interesting. Why don't we talk about you?" He slid her a sidelong glance, another intent look full of unspoken flattery. There was no need to guess at his thoughts; the tenting of his cargo shorts made them more than obvious.

"In that case, I'm even less interesting," she protested, wrenching her eyes away from temptation. She tried not to notice the breadth of his shoulders or the way sunlight glinted on the silver in his hair or the confident motions of his hands or how they made his arms flex. "I grew up thinking I'm plain vanilla. What's to talk about?"

"That isn't exactly a local accent you have there." He pointed out, gesturing with the paring knife. "You're in the process of moving, so how'd you meet Gray?"

Talking with Ashley might have been a mistake. He was a

nice guy, easy to talk to, when he wasn't giving her intent looks, though he did refrain from innuendos. She'd thought it would make the time pass more easily. And she was right. It did—too easily. When she didn't see his eyes, she could almost forget he wasn't Graeme.

If she hadn't met Graeme first, she might have taken Ashley up on the invitation he was so obviously extending, jumped into bed with him without a qualm. Maybe. She liked to think the life-or-death circumstances of her and Graeme's first meeting had forged a bond between them.

However, if she'd met Ashley first, would she have been more attracted to him? His rugged good looks were just as easy on the eyes. Were her feelings for Graeme simply serendipity? Was their relationship an accident of timing? Would she have fallen into bed with the first werewolf she encountered—no matter who he was? Doubts cropped up, one after another.

The overwhelming awareness she'd felt with Graeme on their first day together was like a dream now. That humming anticipation. That exquisite hunger. The breathless uncertainty. Her nerves singing with tension. She'd known he wanted her and she'd wanted him just as desperately—the only question was if they would act on their desire. It didn't seem possible she could have wanted someone so much. Yet she had. And they'd come together like gasoline and fire. She squirmed, the memory washing her body with heat. If not for that, would she have been more welcoming of Ashley's advances?

Deanna sighed as she kneaded the dough for the pie crust. Maybe she was overthinking the whole situation.

7

Graeme forced himself to drive away, to act normal when every instinct demanded he return to Deanna's side. He was a man, despite the existence of his other self. He had a job to do, people depending on him. He was no cub to consign all that to the wind and do what he wanted.

He could only trust that the bond between him and his mate was stronger than werewolf pheromones. That might be jumping the gun, but Deanna hadn't pulled away when Ash mentioned mating and the honeymoon. That had to mean something.

He prayed it meant something.

The knowledge that his cousin was with Deanna was like a thorn in his paw, one he couldn't pull out. All the way to the station, his thoughts kept wandering back to Deanna and Ash.

It didn't help that his fellow deputies knew Graeme was spending time with Deanna.

Mitchell hailed him as he headed for his patrol car. "How's that pretty lady?" The older man had been the first deputy on the scene when Henckel rammed Deanna's car and had seen how close she'd come to dying.

"Better than last week."

The other deputy snorted, a wry smile twisting his genial features. "That's good. Word is, Old Man Henckel's going to pony up for damages, sweep this all under the rug for his little boy."

"When'd you hear that?"

His smile widening into a grin, Mitchell smoothed his uniform shirt over his potbelly. "Yesterday, while you were off. After everything that's happened, that lady's due for some good news, eh?"

Graeme nodded. The sheriff might try to whitewash Fred Henckel's record, but there was no denying the idiot's culpability in the destruction of Deanna's car. She deserved compensation.

He drove out on patrol with one less worry to occupy his thoughts. Leaving them to circle back to Deanna and Ash. Lucky—or perhaps not so lucky—for him, the night was undisturbed.

With most of the high school football team still cooling their heels in jail, the Hogg Wylde was quiet. Nothing about the low building squatting in the early evening sun belied that impression. The patrons lounging at the picnic tables clustered near the bar were mostly locals: a bunch of coal miners celebrating the end of another work week, some oldsters blowing their Social Security checks on beer regular as clockwork, a few others.

Not a teenager in sight—so far. Henckel's team had been a fixture at the bar the past months, exploiting their popularity as state champions to buy beer and get falling-down drunk. Until recently, until the arson, nothing was too good for Woodrose's golden boys—people let them get away with stupid shit. Even the sheriff had given explicit orders to ignore the blatant flouting of state law. That was politics for you.

As Graeme drove by on patrol, a group of bikers rode into the graveled clearing that served as a parking lot for the bar. He made a mental note to check back later, but that was routine; nothing about their demeanor suggested trouble.

Even the chatter on the radio was routine.

Too bad. He would have welcomed something to break the monotony. Nothing major, just a small ruckus would do. As it was, the end of his shift couldn't come soon enough. The hours stretched endlessly with nothing else to think about but Deanna and Ash. Alone in the house. Together.

And the worst of it was, he'd left them on their own. Knowingly.

His inner wolf continued to bristle at him for leaving the field clear, giving another male a chance to claim his mate. But he'd had to. He couldn't exactly take a leave of absence until Deanna agreed to be his. Duty could be a pisser at times.

He didn't think Deanna would jump into Ash's arms, but for sure Ash would do his damnedest to get her there. Not with force, that he was certain would never happen. But Ash had had a fair amount of success with the opposite sex—and Deanna wasn't blind to his attractions.

The sweet musk of her arousal taunted Graeme, the memory making his cock twitch and stretch to the point that he had to adjust his pants. That first day together he'd spent hours immersing himself in her glorious scent, slowly going insane with desire as he struggled to act normal, without any idea if he'd get lucky.

Ash had turned her on, too. How far would his cousin push his suit?

The end of his shift couldn't come soon enough.

On his next pass by the Hogg Wylde hours later, he spotted Henckel entering the bar. Someone must have dropped him off, since his truck was still in impound.

At least the idiot seemed to be sober. Graeme didn't trust that to last, though. Give him a few hours and all bets were off. Then there'd be trouble. Someone who hung around the Hogg

Wylde had thrown that brick—not Henckel himself, but someone who hung out with him. Probably one of his teammates.

Once he'd completed his reports, Graeme didn't linger at the station. Tension gripped him as he drove home, the narrow county lane stretching empty before him. The half moon rising through the trees lent a serene beauty to the shadowed mountains. Normally he enjoyed the early morning stillness, the stars in the dark sky, the night air smelling of forest and freedom, the peaceful solitude, just him and the road—but he was in no mood to appreciate any of it tonight.

Now one thought dominated his mind: Deanna had been alone with his cousin for hours.

Ash's pickup gleamed in the moonlight, parked behind Deanna's Miata rental in the exact same position as when he left that afternoon. They hadn't gone out, at least not driving. He drove past them and pulled into his usual spot beside the house.

The light shining through the kitchen windows wasn't as welcoming as before, not when he knew Deanna wasn't alone. His feet slowed as he neared the porch. He sniffed the air for a clue on what to expect. Exhaust fumes from the Jeep, bruised grass, and the aroma of freshly baked pie teased his nostrils.

The door opened before he reached it, spilling light across the front porch. Then Deanna was there, Ash right behind her, the light throwing her face into shadow.

"Hey." She walked up to him and hugged him tentatively, not quite the enthusiastic greeting he'd hoped for, but that could be because of their audience. The scent of her; of cinnamon, butter, and tart apples; of pine cleaner and lemon liquid soap; and beneath it all a faint hint of him—and none of Ash—rose to his nose in a blanket of gentle welcome. Whatever she and his cousin had done to occupy themselves while he was gone, it hadn't involved much physical contact.

Graeme returned her hug, the wolf in him relaxing slightly,

appeased by the evidence. "Hey." He buried his face in her hair, filled himself with the scent that was uniquely Deanna and the vanilla and lavender of her shampoo.

With a sigh, she snuggled against him, her lush body a welcoming softness from his chest to his groin and thighs. With her pressed to him that close, there was no hiding how happy he was to have her in his arms—just like there was no missing the heady musk of her arousal as she melted into his embrace.

Ash tossed his head in greeting, then stepped back inside, clearing the doorway. Nothing about his cousin's expression gave any clue how their time together had gone. He just stood there expectantly, a silent demand for him to release Deanna.

She stepped away with a laugh, the light showing flags of color on her cheeks. "You must be hungry. I'll pull something together. We left some apple pie for you."

"Quiet night?" Graeme asked his cousin as Deanna headed for the kitchen. He made for the hall closet, trying to act normal while he manfully ignored his hard-on.

"Quiet enough." Ash closed the door and leaned on it. Out of the shadows, his cousin had an air of . . . discontent about him, a humming tension or restlessness that put Graeme on alert. What had brought on this reaction? Deanna didn't act as if anything untoward had happened.

"You spent the whole time here?"

"Yeah, we talked." Ash gave him a sardonic look, a smudge of what looked like pie in the corner of his mouth.

"Should I be worried?" Graeme hung his hat, then toed off his shoes and put them in the shoe rack.

His cousin's wry smile only deepened. His scent strengthened slightly, bringing with it an edge of irritation along with a tang of apples . . . and pine cleaner.

Graeme felt his eyes widen as the evidence added up. "Don't tell me she put you to work, too."

"She found dust bunnies." Ash crossed his arms, his jaw so

tense Graeme's molars ached in sympathy. "I couldn't leave her to do it all by herself."

"Dust bunnies?" After her cleaning spree at the start of the week, that must have taken some doing. As much as Graeme might empathize, a shout of laughter fought to escape. He pressed his lips together, but choking it down made his belly quiver and his shoulders shake despite himself. "You mean she's skittish around you."

His cousin narrowed his eyes at him. "She's attracted. You can't deny it. The smell of her musk was incredible."

I couldn't help it. He looks just like you! Deanna's voice rang in Graeme's head, that memory helping him maintain his calm against the territorial urges of his inner wolf.

Ashley hadn't so much as laid a hand on Deanna. Graeme had the proof of his own nose for that. His cousin hadn't gotten far, hadn't stolen his mate away.

"That's just pheromones." Not wanting to continue that train of conversation, he went to the bedroom to change out of his uniform.

When he stepped out, feeling much cooler in shorts and a tank top, Ash was waiting for him, perched on the low back of one of the armchairs, bouncing his leg impatiently. "How about a run after you've eaten?"

"You didn't go earlier?" Graeme eyed his cousin's stance. This sort of tension was unlike his cousin. He couldn't see any reason for it. Just because they hadn't driven anywhere didn't mean they'd stayed indoors the whole time.

"Said so, didn't I? She was afraid we'd be seen."

More likely she hadn't wanted to get naked with only Ash in the house. His cousin could bluster all he wanted, but Graeme knew better—Deanna was fighting the attraction. He didn't rub Ash's nose in his error, though. Some of their cousins wouldn't have behaved as well as Ash; Graeme owed him some respect for that.

Deanna's smile when Graeme put the question to her was all the answer he needed. She wanted to run; they would run.

Graeme made short work of the snack, his inner wolf straining his control at the prospect of letting loose, his mate at his side, running as a pack. Not that they were really a pack, but he wasn't a lone wolf at heart. If living near clan didn't reduce his chances of finding a mate, he wouldn't have moved away.

"You done?" Ash scooped up the dirty dishes and dumped them in the sink almost before Graeme took his last bite. "Let's go."

"Okay, okay, hold your horses." Laughing at his cousin's impatience, Graeme turned to Deanna. "You might want to Change here."

"Good idea." She gave him a smile and retreated to their bedroom, her step quickening as Ash pulled his shirt off.

"Showoff." Graeme shook his head at his cousin in mock disapproval, but Deanna's modesty—additional proof of her skittishness—heartened his inner wolf.

Ash shrugged, then continued stripping down to bare skin. "Can you blame me? Better she see what she'd be missing before she chooses a mate."

Competitive as hell. As always. Some things never changed. But in light of Deanna's comments about family, Graeme found it hard to resent him. He was only behaving as any other unmated, red-blooded male would.

But Graeme's instincts, too, were riding close to the surface. Until he and Deanna were mated, he couldn't view the presence of another male with any equanimity. Right then, his cousin stood squarely in the category of competition.

Ash Changed in a quick glimmer of light into a muscular wolf with gray-speckled black fur very similar to Graeme's. He shook his big body once, settling his fur, then stretched, working through the tingling afterglow that always accompanied the Change.

Graeme waited. Someone had to stay human to handle the door. Unfortunately for him, he couldn't put in a pet door—much less one that would accommodate his wolf form—without questions from visitors. It wouldn't matter if they were family, but the townsfolk would wonder . . . and talk.

Moments later, Deanna emerged, a graceful wolf, all amber-ale fur with a cream-tipped tail. She paused, ears pricking as she eyed Ash. His cousin faced her fully, head high, tail up, ears forward—the stance of a dominant male.

Though tempted to whack his cousin on the snout for that bit of vanity, Graeme stood back, wondering what she would do. It went against every instinct, but he stayed where he was. Force wasn't the answer, not in mating. Not with Deanna.

When Ash approached to sniff her muzzle, she sidled away, keeping her distance. Her hackles stayed flat. Hesitation, not rejection. She didn't display any aggression; on the contrary, she continued to eye his cousin, her tail slowly swaying from side to side.

There was definitely some attraction there.

Graeme let them out and locked the kitchen door behind him, leaving the house dark. The summer night embraced him in warmth and the dissonant, directionless chorus of cicadas. This deep in the forest, there were no streetlights to challenge the early morning darkness. He breathed deep, taking it all in. It was a good night for a run. The waning moon still cast enough light that they could keep a good pace. He could already feel his muscles stretching, his heart picking up its pace.

He followed Deanna into the trees, her wagging tail brushing his thigh with every other step. He had to move sharply to keep up with her. Obviously he wasn't the only one looking forward to a run.

Remembering his first primal response to Deanna's scent, Graeme kept an eye on his cousin. Ash seemed to have his wolf self under control, but who knew when instinct would raise its head? Just the memory of that time he'd run down a scent in the forest only to discover Deanna was enough to tingle his balls.

Ash stuck close by Deanna's side—too close for Graeme's tastes. He matched her pace, his fur in definite contact with hers, the body contact communicating his sexual interest.

She sidled away, her ears flicking with—he hoped—irritation. Graeme couldn't be sure, though. Before Deanna, he'd never been in the presence of an unmated female werewolf who wasn't kin. That ear flick could have been a come-hither for all he knew.

He swore silently. Now wasn't the time for doubts. Deanna already risked her life and fought by his side. She was his mate. He had to believe that.

Graeme hooked his fingers on the bottom of his tank top and pulled it up. And froze at the touch of something cool and damp on his belly. With the shirt around his head, he couldn't see what it was.

A delicate woof came from the same direction.

He jerked the tank top all the way off to find Deanna sniffing his crotch while Ash glared from the side. She'd never done that before; of course, he'd usually Changed first.

She rubbed her muzzle across his thighs, the contact unexpectedly ticklish—and arousing as hell. It sent a flash of sensation zinging straight to his cock. She gave what sounded like a happy grumble, then did it again, rubbing him with the tip of her nose to her cheek—where wolves have a scent gland. Like she was scent-marking him.

Claiming him as hers.

Graeme froze, shock and hope drowning out arousal. Did she know what she was doing? Did she understand what it meant?

Probably not. Maybe it was just instinct. She liked his scent and acted on that liking. Just as she could walk and run smoothly immediately after her first Change, chances were this, too, was automatic.

Ash thrust his head between them, then his body, trying to shoulder Deanna away. She bared her fangs in response, her hackles rising. His cousin snarled back.

Graeme snapped his tank top at Ash, catching him on the snout, instinctively jumping back after the shirt connected. No red-blooded male wanted any of that near his dangly bits.

"None of that," he warned, holding the cotton taut in front of him, at the ready. "You want a fight, you fight me." The shirt would be of little protection against fangs, but it would buy him time to Change if it came to that.

His cousin stared at him, testing his nerve, looking for weaknesses. A silent contest of wills. Then he flicked his ears and looked away, conceding the argument. For now.

This was precisely the sort of behavior they could expect if he introduced Deanna to the rest of his family now. Worse: the unmated males wouldn't be satisfied until it got physical. What kind of impression would that give Deanna? She held such high hopes for family that he hated to disappoint her.

Deanna swirled her tail between his thighs, the contact catching him off guard. As if Ash hadn't interrupted, she gave him a wolfish grin, her tongue lolling on one side mischievously. Was she flirting with him?

He tried to scratch the fur behind her ears, but she backed away with a glance at Ash. Skittish even with him. That surprised him since she hadn't displayed any reservations before. Maybe she felt more comfortable when there were no witnesses.

Ah, well. It was early days yet.

She nudged him, then took a few steps away.

Right, the run.

Time enough later for speculation. Tonight, they had the moon and the forest. The future could fend for itself.

Reaching for his other self, Graeme Changed, welcoming the tingling heat flooding his body in waves of power. His already sharp senses sharpened. The wind brought him the smell of a squirrel in one of the trees around them, some field mice in the dry grass, and the fainter whiffs of apple pie and far-off traffic. His ears picked up the rapid squeals of flying bats amid the rustling leaves and the scurrying mice.

The night felt richer, the moon brighter. They called to him to stretch his legs and run!

Then another scent demanded his attention: Deanna's. In his wolf form, he could smell her so much better. And she smelled damned receptive—fabulous, in fact. That blood-hailing perfume that short-circuited good judgment. He could feel it working its magic on him. No wonder Ash was so edgy.

Before instinct could get the upper hand, Deanna headed out, leaving him and Ash to follow. Clearly the other night's run had given her confidence in the forest.

Deanna ran, wishing she could outrun the demons of temptation. The urge to let Ashley sniff her had been bad enough. It had taken some grit to keep her distance and not give in to the urge to reciprocate with a few sniffs of her own.

But worse, she'd given in to the urge with Graeme. She'd found herself rubbing against him before she could stop herself. And it had felt right.

It still felt right.

Her lover's wild, dark scent lingered in her memory, all musk and light sweat and that earthiness that she associated with him, taunting her with her delight in his virility. She'd never done anything like that before. In this other form, she was like a writhing mass of instinct, her sense of caution lost in the Change. She wanted to do it again. Graeme's and Ashley's scents were so tantalizing, they woke a carnal response deep inside her.

If she wasn't careful, she just might give in to the urge—and do more. Sex as wolves. Just the thought sent heat flooding her veins.

So she ran.

She ran from her feral instincts, from her stirring emotions, from the extraordinary man she'd welcomed into her bed, from the strange twist her life had taken.

How ironic that that very twist was what let her forget her confusion in the primal simplicity of the run. To challenge her body. To stretch her muscles without thought of destination. To forget her human cares.

Before, she'd run to escape the restlessness plaguing her in Boston. She'd thought finding family was the answer—and perhaps it had been, in a roundabout way—but it had taken Graeme and the discovery of her werewolf heritage to soothe her.

Now, it was the reality of her werewolf side and the instincts that went with it that gnawed at her—the same instincts that drew her to Graeme and Ashley. She'd thought she'd chosen Graeme on her own accord. Was it a false freedom, then? Was it all chemistry and genetics? It galled her to think she could be so mindless, a slave to her hormones.

But she couldn't outrun Graeme and Ashley. They remained at her side, darting in playfully, teasing, racing, never letting her forget their presence. She couldn't resist their game.

Graeme bodychecked Ash and scrambled to catch up with Deanna, his heart flying at the laughter in her eyes. This was the life: sharing the night with his mate and his pack. It brought to mind his younger days before he'd moved away from his clan. He'd envied his mated uncles their happiness, that settled contentment they'd found with his aunts. That was what he hoped to have with Deanna.

His cousin cut in, initiating a mock fight. But that didn't last long since something caught Deanna's attention and she made to investigate. They broke off at once to accompany her.

Despite the close attendance Ash gave Deanna, she looked like she enjoyed the run. Not just the exercise, but the interplay. The sight sent a pang through Graeme. She'd love running with the pack, but that was something he couldn't offer her— not yet. He couldn't take the risk.

Just then Ash growled, a low rumble of warning. His cousin had come to a halt behind them, in the middle of the clearing, and stood looking over his shoulder, his ears pricked and swiveling. Obviously he'd sensed something, but only the cicadas rattling in the trees could be heard, nothing else.

Graeme raised his nose to test the wind. At first he smelled nothing unusual, then fresh exhaust fumes and a sour sweat stench flowed up the mountainside, so strong their sources had to be nearby. He trotted back, joining his cousin to stare downslope.

The road lay that way.

Ordinarily, he would have dismissed it as random traffic. But the sweat stench wouldn't be this strong if its source were a passing vehicle.

Deanna stepped into him, pressing against him in a nudge for attention. When he turned to her, she stared at him in question, a furrow between her brows. Probably wondering why he and Ash stopped.

He sniffed audibly, exaggerating the motion, in answer. That sweat stench was still in the air, still strong. She copied him, then sneezed, shaking her head as if trying to throw off the unpleasant odor.

Graeme sympathized with her difficulty. The sour scent remained constant, not fading despite the wind. Which definitely meant its source was relatively stationary.

They'd come nearly a full circle, back to the ridge above his home. This close to his house, it could be someone looking for him, except he wasn't expecting anyone. This early in the morning, that couldn't be good.

His first thought was an emergency. But Dispatch would use the phone to contact him, not send someone to knock on his door.

Graeme looked at Ash, who twitched his ears in agreement. They had to investigate. They headed downslope with Deanna trailing behind and found the source of the exhaust fumes readily enough.

Someone had driven a pickup off the road, into the bushes, and left it there. Recently. Graeme could still smell the heat of the engine as it cooled. Rather than walk along the road, the driver and passenger had blazed a trail through the brush, marked by broken branches, sweat, beer, and piss.

From the scent trail, two people were sneaking around in the trees. Since Deanna was with him, sneaking around automatically meant *up to no good*. A threat to his mate.

8

Graeme dressed quickly, not waiting for the tingling afterglow of his Change to fade. This close to his place, he couldn't risk someone seeing him in wolf form. The local belief that no wolves roamed the surrounding mountains was one of the reasons his pack had managed to escape discovery all this time. They couldn't afford inconvenient questions.

"Stay here. I'll handle it."

Ash simply flicked his ears to indicate he'd heard Graeme. His cousin kept watch at the edge of the trees, making sure no one approached while Graeme Changed.

Deanna, on the other hand, gave him a thoughtful look that said she intended to guard his back—whether he liked it or not. He shouldn't have expected otherwise, not from a woman who took things into her own hands instead of waiting for rescue.

He grinned. "Fair enough."

It wasn't difficult to find the intruders once the three of them got closer to the road. Whoever it was might be keeping to the shadows, but their scent trail through the bushes was as obvious as a marching band. It led toward his house but veered to the road before they reached his security lights.

Disgust curled his lip at the reek that assaulted his nose. They were stinking drunk, literally. Must have been drunk already when they arrived for him to smell them with his less sensitive human nose. He had a feeling he knew his intruders.

Two figures crouched in the trees a short distance from Deanna's and Ash's vehicles, egging each other on in low tones. In the early morning quiet, their voices carried.

"You sure about this?"

"It's all her fault I've got no wheels."

Graeme swore silently, recognizing the voices. Fred Henckel and one of his teammates, the big Assenmacher boy. What was his name? Emmitt, that was it.

A guard on the offensive line, Emmitt Assenmacher was one of the few on the football team who hadn't been scooped up in the arson case. Graeme had hoped Assenmacher would steer clear of trouble, but obviously he hadn't; his scent matched the one Graeme picked up on the brick.

Worse, they hadn't left the beer behind at the Hogg Wylde. Henckel sucked down on a longneck bottle like a thirsty man.

"Yeah, but . . ."

It sounded like Assenmacher wasn't quite sold on whatever idiocy Henckel planned. Maybe there was hope for him.

Henckel rolled right over his teammate's objection. "Ma's a mess. Pa's talking about me taking some stupid student loan to pay him back."

"You're fucking kidding me. No way." The larger figure turned slightly, presenting a gaping profile silhouetted against the moonlit road.

"No kidding." The idiot took another swig and belched. "If she won't go away, we make her go away. We gotta do this."

Graeme circled around toward the break in the trees lining

the road, conscious of Deanna by his side, her fur brushing his leg.

Hissing leaked through the quiet, too loud if they were letting air out of the tires. Then a whiff of acrid fumes violated the early morning air: spray paint. They were engaging in a spot of graffiti. And chances were, they weren't painting the trees.

"Hey!" Graeme barged through the brush.

The two geniuses froze, hands outstretched, in the midst of defacing Deanna's rental and Ash's pickup. Paint streaked the windows and bodies of the vehicles with rather creative spelling on the indecencies. The moonlight was bright enough for reading. Talk about digging a deeper hole for themselves.

"Fuck, it's Luger." The can dropped from Assenmacher's hand, landing with a resonant *thunk* as the beefy drunk retreated a step.

"You guys just bought yourselves a heap of trouble."

Henckel glared at Graeme, spray paint can raised defiantly. "He's alone, Em. We can take him."

"Ah, c'mon, Fred."

"He shouldn't have brought her back."

Perhaps they could take him. Assenmacher was almost as big as Graeme, and Henckel didn't lack muscle. Two against one. Add to that the shoes they wore versus his moccasins and the scales were probably tipped against him.

None of that mattered in his calculations.

Driving drunk, Henckel had rammed Deanna's car, nearly causing her death. His teammates had burned her cabin while she was inside. Assenmacher had thrown that brick.

And now this.

It was too much.

They weren't kids anymore.

The knowledge that the sheriff would turn a blind eye to *boyish shenanigans* curdled his stomach. Not this time, not if Graeme had anything to say about it.

"That's enough. If you come quietly, I'll go easy on you."
Graeme purposely shifted his gaze to Assenmacher. Him, he
was willing to excuse. The big guy had managed to avoid most
of the trouble Henckel and his teammates had gotten into.

"Easy?" Henckel scoffed, obviously used to speaking for his
teammates. "Easy like shelling out hush money?"

Hush money? He thought restitution for destroying Deanna's
car and nearly killing her was *hush money?* The idiot wasn't
just drunk and irresponsible, he was a spoiled brat.

Graeme smiled—though the tightness of his face felt too
fierce for a simple smile. He'd been wanting to get his hands on
Henckel since the accident. It looked like he was going to get
his chance. "You're lucky you didn't kill Deanna."

The idiot scowled, the beer fumes rolling off him threatening to turn Graeme's stomach. He faced Graeme, planting his
feet and hunching forward aggressively. "Not my fault. The
bitch got in the way. Like you're in the way."

Adrenaline flooded Graeme, his heart picking up speed,
moonlight etching the night with knife-sharp clarity. "I'm in
the way? Man up and take responsibility for your mistakes."

"You—" Flinging the spray paint can at Graeme, Henckel
lunged forward, leading with his fist.

Deanna planted her paws, resisting Ashley's efforts to herd her
away. The memory of the fire was still fresh. Graeme had been
trapped and might have died if she'd left as he'd ordered her to
do. She couldn't leave him to face these hooligans alone.

Her heart skipped a beat as the can went tumbling through
the air. Graeme dodged the missile, then blocked a punch at his
face.

Why wasn't Ashley helping him?

She snarled at the other wolf, furious at his intervention. He
was preventing her from helping—

Her mate.

The realization was like a bolt out of the blue: *Graeme* was her mate. Her place was by his side.

Talking would do no good. This idiot needed some sense beaten into him.

Sidestepping another wild swing, Graeme planted a fist in Henckel's cheek, ignoring the jolt of pain when his knuckles split. He landed another blow, the nose this time.

Blood spurted as his enemy staggered away with a yelp. "Em!"

The young drunk had it coming. Since the sheriff refused to throw the book at him, Graeme intended to inflict some punishment of his own. He threw a flurry of punches at Henckel's face, drawing more blood as he broke the idiot's nose.

Assenmacher waded in, his blows slow. Reluctant. Fighting stupid. His heart wasn't in it.

Not Graeme's problem. The wolf wanted to tear their throats open, Henckel's in particular for what he'd done to Deanna and the nightmares she struggled with as a result. No one threatened Deanna and got away with it.

Frustration powered Graeme's blows. The stupidity of it all. The idiot's sense of entitlement. The sheriff's willing enablement. With his blood up, it was a relief to let loose.

This time Deanna snapped at the wolf beside her, who wasn't Graeme for all the similarities in their appearances—and dared to stop her from going to her mate. He stood his ground, but recoiled when her fangs caught fur.

Now was her chance!

Too late. Beer spilled as the bloodier of the thugs smashed a bottle against the Miata, leaving a big dent and gouged paint. What the hell was it with them and broken bottles?

Even as she lunged forward, he raised his weapon, his gaze

fixed on Graeme's back, and she couldn't do anything about it. She was too far to stop him.

Her scream of warning emerged as a high yelp.

A sharp yip from the trees warned of more trouble. Knocking Assenmacher a step back, Graeme stole a glance over his shoulder, found Deanna bounding forward with Ash behind her—

And light glinting off broken glass, lending it a deadly beauty. The wicked points came at him. A wordless shout—

Time spun out on a rush of adrenaline, stretching like cotton candy. The fight flowed on in slow motion. His heart took forever between beats.

Dodging with dreamlike leisure, Graeme deflected the strike and punched Henckel in the arm. If he'd been an ordinary human, he might have risked it, let himself be cut and charged them with aggravated assault. But as a werewolf, he healed too quickly. Exposure affected more people than him—his family was a matter of public record.

Tawny fur flashed past, followed by gray and the loud, hollow *thunk* of skull on solid wood.

Henckel released the bottle with a grunt of pain, his motions sluggish. A kick to the belly folded him in half, but Graeme's moccasin lacked the stopping power of steel-toed boots. He wasn't down, not yet. But his jaw met Graeme's rising fist—with all of Graeme's weight behind it.

Henckel dropped to the ground, as limp as a poleaxed steer. He wouldn't be going anywhere for a while. Neither would Assenmacher, who'd apparently brained himself on a tree, courtesy of Deanna.

Exhaling sharply, Graeme stepped back, and time resumed its normal pace.

Deanna planted her paws on Henckel's back, a steady growl

coming from deep in her chest. There was no danger there; the idiot was out cold.

"Easy, he's done for."

She didn't let up, her ears back and flat against her head, her snarl low and steady. Ash pranced on his forelegs, nose wrinkled as he glared at Graeme.

Holding back laughter at his cousin's frustration, Graeme threw an arm over Deanna's shoulders and kissed her muzzle. "Thank you. Now, don't let them see you." She eyed him so dubiously he had to grin. "There's just the two of them. I'll be fine."

Her ferocious growl stopped.

His cousin simply tossed his head, then went ahead.

"Go on. You'll want to Change, and I have to secure these guys."

As she left, casting doubting looks over her shoulder the whole time, Ash stalked up in his shorts, his hand held out. "Here, you'll need these."

Two sets of cuffs and a cell phone. His cousin had anticipated him. "Thanks."

Ash jerked his chin at the bloodied mess that was Henckel. "That who I think it is?"

"Yeah, the golden boy of Woodrose." It gave Graeme a lot of satisfaction to put the cuffs on the idiot.

"Make sure he does time for this." Ash's face darkened as he inspected the damage to his pickup and Deanna's rental. Probably tallying the cost of repairs.

"I intend to."

As soon as Graeme walked through the door, Deanna threw herself into his arms, wrapping hers around his neck with gratifying intensity, her breasts plumped against him. She must have dressed in a hurry. Though she wore a pair of shorts and a T-shirt, she hadn't managed a bra—the hard nipples poking him stood testament to its absence. "You idiot, what was that about?"

He shared a grin with Ash at her ferocious greeting. "Henckel threatened you. I just exacted some punishment."

"Caveman." She thumped his shoulder, then dragged his head down for a deep, thorough kiss full of tongue and teeth and heat. As fierce as her snarls earlier. Possessive.

Graeme's heart and cock sprang to attention. Did that mean what he thought it meant?

"Oh, yeah. Sorry about that." Ash swiped a hand across his crew cut, a sheepish look on his face. "She wouldn't leave."

"Of course I wouldn't!" She directed a scathing glare full of righteous outrage at his cousin. "And you were no help."

"Big oaf didn't need it."

"I'm surprised she didn't bite you." He'd meant it as a joke, but the two exchanged startled looks before Deanna shifted her eyes away guiltily.

"You did?" Laughing, Graeme hugged her. He'd bet she'd be just as fierce protecting their children. "What a wild woman!"

"Are you sure you're not hurt?" Deanna pushed him away, then ran her hands over his chest and down his arms, her eyes widening with alarm when she got to his torn knuckles.

"That's nothing." He didn't regret the fight . . . and it sure felt good to lay into that idiot.

"Won't you get into trouble?"

"They can try. Two against one. Near my home. With the brick throwing on record. We have the spray paint cans with their fingerprints and the bottle. Henckel will get his bail revoked and more charges pressed against him. Anyway, I called it in. They'll be picked up."

Even if the sheriff got pissy about it, Graeme intended to bring the full force of the law down on Henckel, no matter how unpopular it might make him in Woodrose. Henckel might be responsible for bringing Deanna into his life, but Graeme refused to turn a blind eye to threats against her.

Red and blue lights flashed through the trees, announcing the approach of a patrol car. Must be a slow night. He hadn't expected a response this quick.

Deanna twitched the curtain aside to watch Graeme meet the patroller responding. The deputy was a lean, older man with a hipshot stance that gave him a cynical air. His acknowledgment of Graeme seemed congenial enough, but she couldn't help but worry. "Will he really be okay?"

Joining her by the window, Ash laid his hand on her shoulder, the contact a jolt of heat. "He heard them sneaking around and went to investigate. The commotion woke us. When we got there, he'd already subdued them. Simple enough."

To her surprise, she felt a tingle of awareness but nothing more—nothing like that melting arousal that rattled her composure. What had changed?

Not the run. It couldn't have been. That was her fleeing her demons, clinging to her past, afraid of abandonment.

Was it the fight?

Now that fear for Graeme no longer fogged her mind, she could consider her actions rationally. She'd thought her attraction to the Luger men based merely on chemistry—biology at work. But the need to stand beside Graeme wasn't chemistry. If there was no difference between Graeme and his cousin, why had she fought Ashley? Why had she struggled to stand by Graeme's side? Clearly at some subconscious level, she didn't think they were identical.

Deanna glanced at the man beside her, seeing his semblance to Graeme. "Is that our story?"

"It's the truth, or as much of it as possible. Don't worry. Just leave it to us. We'll handle it."

His light words made her mouth twitch with irritation.

When push came to shove, fighting brought out a man's true nature. Ash tried to protect her, but his protection came with the expectation that she would stand aside and leave him to handle the problem, let him play he-man to her helpless female. Graeme did nothing of the sort. He respected her independence and her need to take an active part in solving her problems.

That was the difference between the two men.

And sometime when she wasn't looking, her heart had gone and made her choice. Sure, Ash's presence still gave her a thrill, but it was Graeme she wanted beside her.

She'd been using their semblance as a shield to keep Graeme at a distance, blaming their attraction on chemistry. Because she was afraid she would lose him the way she'd lost her parents? The answer came to her in a wave of certainty. She'd focused on finding out more about her heritage, so she wouldn't have to risk going forward with Graeme.

But avoiding loss meant keeping people at a distance. No wonder she preferred to work for herself and to work from home. No wonder she'd been able to pull up stakes in Boston so easily—she hadn't set down roots to begin with.

Not anymore.

At peace with her decision, Deanna stepped out from under Ash's hand and went to the kitchen.

"What're you doing?"

She smiled. "If you guys are going to stay up, we might as well have coffee."

A sense of relief left Graeme's shoulders lighter as he watched the taillights of Elsworth's patrol car disappear down the road. He was just glad the other deputy had agreed to file a complete report. Elsworth initially warned him about the repercussions of pursuing a complaint against Henckel, but ultimately supported his decision. Probably hard to do otherwise with Ash standing a few paces away, scowling at the graffiti on his pickup.

Deanna's offer of coffee and pie had been the perfect touch, winning Elsworth over. He'd taken their statements, documented the scene, and gathered evidence with his usual thoroughness. Then they'd bundled the two idiots, still unconscious, into the backseat of his patrol car.

"I'm glad that's over." Deanna put her arm around Graeme's waist, holding him tight to her side, her breast a yielding softness as she smiled up at him, her face luminous in the moonlight. Or perhaps it wasn't just the moonlight. The gesture looked like an overt display of preference, and her eyes held a warmth that made his heart skip a beat.

Apparently Ash read it the same way. The resigned twist to his cousin's mouth conveyed understanding better than words. At least it looked like he wasn't going to force the issue.

Deanna's smile widened when Graeme reciprocated with an arm across her back. The quiet intimacy of the open embrace felt complete, like uniting two halves to form a whole. "You'll have to excuse us. I think the next discussion should be private."

"I have to head back anyway. I'm running late." Ash shrugged, then suddenly grinned, a wicked gleam brightening his eyes. "You'll have to introduce her to the clan, you know."

Graeme aimed a frown at him. "Yeah, well . . ." He'd face that when he had to. But when he did, he'd be secure in the knowledge Deanna had chosen him. Probably. "Maybe in a few weeks. A month might be better."

A snort of laughter escaped Ash.

"Don't forget the paperwork on your complaint." The more pressure on the sheriff, the better. This time Henckel wasn't going to get off scot-free. Since Ash babied that old pickup of his, there was little chance he'd just let the graffiti slide.

The reminder wiped the amusement from his cousin's face. "Ah, man. Now I'm really going to be late. Those shitheads." Scowling, he stalked to his pickup.

Graeme urged Deanna into the house and closed the door, shutting out the rest of the world. A motor started, then faded into the distance, and they were finally, truly alone.

Leaning against the door, he studied her smile. He could almost touch the contentment she radiated. "I got the impression you were undecided earlier. Not to look a gift horse in the mouth, but . . . what happened?"

Deanna traced his lips with a light finger, the contact making them tingle. "I realized something when you were pounding on those idiots."

He had to swallow twice to get his voice to work. "What's that?"

"Just because I haven't learned much about my parents doesn't mean I have to be stuck in the past." She gave him a shy smile. "I want what we have together. And I want it with you."

Graeme reined back a yell of triumph, stealing a kiss instead, with the promise of more to follow. "No problem. If you haven't figured it out, I'm yours."

Heart of the Wildcat

Devyn Quinn

1
_____

Kathryn Dayton didn't like the looks of the men walking into her camp. Sometimes you could tell with a glance that certain people in this world were bad news. She had no doubts about these two.

They definitely weren't up to any good.

Gaze steady and unflinching, Kathryn stayed down in a crouch, leaning in closer to her campfire, establishing her territory. She neither said a word nor made a reach toward the hunting knife strapped at her hip. She just watched as the men casually ambled into the perimeter she'd staked out as a place to roost after sundown. Other than members of her own crew, she hadn't expected company this far into the back country.

One of the men stepped boldly up to the fire. "Howdy." The second man lingered a few steps behind, as if watching his partner's back, one hand wrapped tightly around the strap of the rifle slung over his back.

Kathryn's gaze narrowed. "Howdy." Both wore backpacks and bedrolls and walked with the gait of men who spent a lot of time on foot in treacherous terrain. Hard-core mountain men,

202 / Devyn Quinn

right down to their ruddy skin, shaggy beards, faded jeans, flannel shirts, jackets, and heavy hiking boots.

But that wasn't what disturbed her.

The guns did.

Both carried hunting rifles. Both had dangerous-looking knives strapped on for ease of access. More horribly, each man carried a set of claw-tooth traps commonly used for large game such as bear. *Illegal* traps.

A chill scurried down her spine. *Shit.* She was all too familiar with those vicious creations. Once an animal got a limb in, it didn't get loose. Men carrying weapons and traps meant only one thing.

Poachers.

They were fairly safe from prosecution because of the remote location. No towns existed in the immediate region, and it had taken a helicopter to get her and four crewmates into the remote area. An isolated remnant branching off the Appalachians and carved out of the Blue Ridge by erosion, much of the South Mountains of North Carolina were almost as pure as the day God created them. Even the rush of gold fever in the eighteenth century hadn't inflicted much of an impact on the old growth forests.

Still, snakes lingered in paradise.

Kathryn ran a quick mental check of her own supplies. Aside from basic food and water, she carried a few hunting knives, a walkie-talkie, a small tent, and a sleeping bag. She'd deliberately turned her radio off, detouring away from the rest of the crew to spend the night alone. She'd needed some time to herself. The recent news her team had received hadn't been encouraging.

Her mouth quirked down. *So much for time alone.* The knot of automatic distrust settled deep in her guts.

Kathryn had no respect for men who committed brutal crimes against nature. There were plenty of other places to hunt throughout the state. Legal places. Not that she condoned killing wildlife for pleasure. She found nothing sporting in shooting down beautiful animals through the sights of a high-powered scope.

The stranger held out his hands, palms down, soaking in the welcome heat. A cheery glow radiated from the flames consuming the wood. High summer in the mountains didn't necessarily mean the nights were warm or dry.

"Got cold," he said by the way of starting conversation. The wind kicked up, tugging at the wide brim of his hat. "Feels like a front's about to come through." His words were laced with the slow, down-home cornpone accent so familiar in the South.

Gaze lifting to the brewing sky, Kathryn felt as if the coming storm warned her something wicked had arrived. Lightning scratched the sky's leaden underbelly the way a predator would rip open prey. Thunder crashed through the night's uneasy silence. "Yep. Sure is." Another ten or twenty minutes and they'd all be driven out of the clearing by the rain.

The stranger eyed the blackened tin pot she'd positioned at the edge of the fire. "You mind if we sit a spell and drink a cup?" He inhaled, drawing in the smell. The enticing scent of pure dark Columbian coffee mingled with the pungent smoke. The chilly night air was doubly fragrant with the aroma.

Since she couldn't very well tell these two big boys to fuck off and find their own place to sit a spell, Kathryn shrugged. "Take a load off."

The stranger grinned. "Much obliged, ma'am." He slid the heavy backpack off his shoulders and set it down. His hunting rifle followed, barrel propped an angle pointing away from the camp. His silent companion followed suit, nodding in agreement before stepping up and relieving himself of his own load.

The first man reached over, offering a brief handshake. The odor of stale tobacco, whiskey, and sour male sweat assailed her nostrils. "My name's Willie. Willie Barnett."

Kathryn warily accepted his offer. Her hand practically disappeared in the maw of his calloused grip. She gave as good as she got. "Kathryn." She didn't offer a last name.

The slight wasn't noticed.

Withdrawing his hand, Willie's elbow jerked toward his companion. "This here's my little brother, Skeeter."

"Howdy, ma'am." Scrawnier and scruffier than his brother, Skeeter also offered his hand. His fingernails were caked with what must have been a lifetime of grime. He looked like he was many years shy of a good hot shower and hard scrub. No telling what kind of vermin might be living inside his less-than-clean clothes.

After a week of hard hiking and camping, Kathryn didn't exactly smell like a daisy herself.

She shook his hand, keeping her lips in that rictal smile of friendly acceptance she'd perfected through the lifetime trial of being a congresswoman's daughter. "Skeeter's an, uh, interesting name."

Skeeter grinned, more snaggles than actual teeth. "That ain't my real name," he confessed. "It's, uh, Waylon."

Kathryn resisted rolling her eyes. Oh, God. Willie and Waylon. The parents of these two were probably first cousins, and country music fans to boot.

Broad face breaking into a grin, Willie explained. "We call him 'Skeeter' 'cause when he was born, he weren't no bigger than a skeeter bug."

Skeeter cackled as though hearing the story for the first time. "But I sure growed up big," he filled in, hammering in the impression that he wasn't the brightest of the two. He smiled at Kathryn again. "You sure are purdy."

Kathryn refused to be baited. "Thanks."

Willie gave her a head-to-toe eye-fuck. "Don't see many women up here."

She gritted her teeth and glowered back. Terrific. Just what she needed. Two horny mountain men. "Wasn't like I expected to see any men, either."

Willie shrugged and smiled. "I know what ya mean. Been months since we laid eyes on 'nother human face." His attention moved back to what had lured them to her camp. "I sure could use a cup of that coffee, ma'am."

Kathryn forced herself to relax. At least they were polite. Not that she was accustomed to hearing that word applied to her. She was only thirty-three, many years away from that moniker best suited to half-deaf old ladies with walkers.

She nodded amicably. "Sure." Maybe if she gave them each a cup, they'd drink it and move on.

The small old-fashioned percolator wasn't exactly the newest or most modern piece of camping equipment, but it made a drinkable cup of coffee. Dinged and more than a little battered, it had traveled the world with her. That it had been a gift from her late father made it that much more valuable. Unlike her career-oriented mother, he hadn't been too damn tied up with work to spend some time with his kid. He'd patiently fostered her love of wide open spaces and the freedom of the wild, untamed lands.

The two men dug cups out of their packs.

Kathryn filled, careful not to spill one drop of the precious black gold. After walking for hours without a break, she'd been looking forward to a good hot cup of the mud-thick brew to restore her flagging energy.

Her supplies were limited to what she could comfortably carry in her own backpack. Before leaving base camp, she'd pared down to the bare essentials in preparation for the rigorous hike. Survival in hostile and remote regions was a part of her profession as an ecologist and wildlife conservationist.

Willie lifted the cup to his nose, inhaling deeply. "Christ, that smells better than anything Skeeter ever made. His fuckin' coffee's like drinkin' pure horse piss, and just as unhealthy." He gulped, smacking his lips after the drought was swallowed. A moment later every last drop was drunk.

Kathryn sipped her coffee, relishing the soothing warmth settling into her bones. Hot and strong, but hardly the way she liked drinking it. She'd already decided to keep the sugar and few precious cans of condensed milk out of sight.

Skeeter wasn't as quick to drink. He apparently had his own stash of luxury items. He fumbled inside his coat, fishing out a small bottle of Wild Turkey. "Coffee'd taste better if you'd add to it." He poured a liberal dose into his cup, then tipped the bottle toward Willie's cup.

Willie held his not-so-empty cup out. "I'd be much obliged if you'd fill'er up again, ma'am."

Resigned, Kathryn refilled. "Glad you're enjoying it." *Yeah, just what these two need to mix,* she thought acidly. *Guns and alcohol.*

Skeeter offered her a tip from his bottle. "Have a bit," he offered with all the amicability of a true southern gentleman. "It does keep the chills away."

The icy wind whipping up the fire hastened her acceptance. "Thanks."

"Welcome, ma'am."

Kathryn sipped again, tasting the strong Kentucky bourbon mixing with the tar-black brew. It went down smoothly, leaving a comforting glow in its wake. The temperature was definitely dropping, and would go lower before the night ended.

For a few minutes everyone concentrated on their drinks. The coffee went fast, leaving the two men sharing the bottle between them. The lower the whiskey went, the more they grinned like fools.

Willie scooted closer to Kathryn. By the fire's glow she saw his thick brown hair and bushy beard were heavily tinged with gray. "So what's a nice lady doin' out here all alone?" A big hand settled on her knee. "You lost?"

Kathryn caught a whiff. God! He smelled worse than a pig living in shit. No telling when soap and water had last touched his skin.

Brushing off his hand, she quickly resettled herself a few inches away. "I don't like things easy. Parking an RV, that's not real camping." Probably better not to reveal that she worked for the Wildlife Resources Commission. They were natural enemies.

Skeeter snorted his agreement. "I hear you there."

Kathryn eyed the traps on their packs. "You catch anything with those?"

Willie scooted in and patted her leg again. "Not a goddamned thang," he said. "Haven't been able to bring one of those fuckin' cats down for weeks."

Nervous about the way he kept invading her personal space, Kathryn scooted over again. "Cats?" The region was home to most common wildlife. Bobcats were plentiful, and not endangered.

A smile played around one corner of his tobacco-stained mouth. "The *anitsasgili wesa,*" he breathed.

"The what?"

"What the Cherokees call the ghost cat. Cougars."

Kathryn didn't believe him. "Impossible." The eastern cougar was extinct. "There are no cougars here."

Taking a shot straight from the bottle, Willie solemnly disagreed. "You're dead wrong, little girl." As if expecting to see one that minute, he cast a quick glance over one shoulder. "There's cougar in these mountains, as sure as we're sittin' here now."

Swallowing more whiskey, Skeeter backed him up. "There's good money in 'em. Asians want 'em, from the pelt to the teeth. Hell, even the goddamn paws and claws." He carelessly tossed the empty bottle. "Catchin' the damn thangs is the hard part."

Eager to tell more tales, Willie cut back in. "Those cats . . ."

He visibly shivered. "They're smart, like men. They're mean as Satan, too."

Kathryn doubted she'd be very nice if these assholes were hunting her. "I can imagine."

Leaning closer, Willie pushed up the heavy sleeve covering his right arm. The firelight easily revealed the long scars marring his entire forearm and part of his hand. "See that?"

She momentarily held her breath. "Yes."

Willie pulled his sleeve back into place over his mutilated arm. "There's the proof. Fuckin' cat nearly took my arm off once." His heavy gaze bore into hers. "I'm gonna get that bastard someday, too. I ain't the only one that took some scarrin'. I got him a few times with my knife. Ol' Scar 'n me, we're gonna tangle up ag'in. When we do, I swear I'll have that cat's balls." Exacerbated by the alcohol he'd consumed, his words were almost unintelligible.

The thunder boomed at that exact moment, hammering in his vow of vengeance.

Heart racing, Kathryn's mind worked furiously. Could it really be true the *Puma concolor couguar* had somehow returned to the area? Herds of white-tailed deer, a primary food source for the cougar, had recently increased in number. Given the almost pristine preservation of the old growth forest, it was also possible that a few hardy cougar holdouts had survived undetected—perhaps breeding themselves back into significant numbers. If that were true, efforts to conserve the region would be more vital than ever.

Then Skeeter belched and farted. " 'Scuse me," he mumbled.

Kathryn reconsidered her sources, both rude and socially unacceptable. The cougar tales might be Wild Turkey coupled with a couple of good ol' boys telling some tall tales to impress her. She regarded her now-drunken companions and sighed. *Until an actual cougar sighting is confirmed, hearsay is all I have.*

The storm kicked up again. More fat drops fell, sizzling

when the water contacted the crackling flames. Seconds later the rain pelted a little harder.

Tugging the wide brim of her hat lower to shield her face, Kathryn reached for her coffeepot, removing its lid and dumping the grounds into the fire.

"Well, fellas, it's been nice visiting," she said, tucking her cup and coffeepot into her backpack. "But I really want to get out of the storm." Earlier, she'd made plans to head for a nearby ravine. The low cliffside would provide a good windbreak and place to spend the night. Come morning she'd head back to base.

Warmed by the whiskey in his gut, Willie's big hand closed around her wrist. "Hang on there," he slurred. "Where ya goin' all the sudden, sweet thang?"

Jerked out of private concerns, Kathryn shot him a glare. She tugged but couldn't break his iron grip. An unbidden surge of anger obliterated sense. "Let go of me."

Grinning like a monkey eating shit, Willie held tight. "Just enjoyin' the pleasure of your company," he said softly, ominously.

Kathryn planted her weight and yanked harder. "I'm not enjoying the pleasure of yours!" Heart thumping hard in her chest, panic clawed her throat. "Let me go, asshole!"

Willie grinned. "Yes, ma'am." He let her go.

Driven by her own velocity, Kathryn stumbled backward. Tripping over an unseen stone protruding from the ground, she landed on her back. Head striking the ground, a smattering of white stars sped in front of her rapidly blurring vision. A mass of thick hair tumbled out from under her cap. Arms and legs akimbo, she lay stunned.

Both brothers got to their feet, casually inspecting the damage.

Pulse pounding in her ears, Kathryn made a quick grab for the knife sheathed on her hip.

Willie guffawed and expertly knocked it out of her grip.

Skeeter stepped between her open legs, settling a heavy boot at each of her ankles, effectively pinning her legs in place. Swaying, his gaze never strayed from her crotch. "We could have a l'il fun here now."

Willie knelt beside her. He reached out, fingers skimming the inch-wide expanse of bare skin between her jeans and coat. "Been a long time since we had a taste of pussy fine as this," he leered.

Head pounding, their words reverberated through Kathryn's mind. Suddenly her body quaked, their intent setting off a chain reaction deep inside her. If they raped her, they would probably kill her. Concealing a body in these dense woods would be a piece of cake. Every second she squandered put her that much closer to dead.

Fighting to clear the haze in her mind, she swallowed hard and struggled to sit up, move away from the range of danger. Unable to find her footing, she scrabbled backward like a hermit crab. She got a foot, maybe two, away.

A grin hitched up one corner of Willie's mouth. "You ain't goin' nowhere, honey."

Hands like manacles captured and pinned her wrists to the ground above her head. Dazed and confused, she hadn't even been aware of Skeeter coming around to cut off her retreat. He'd moved a hell of a lot faster than she had.

Grinning and straddling her body, Willie's big hands worked the zipper of her coat. He fumbled her shirt, ripping it open when he couldn't undo the buttons fast enough. Pushing up her sports bra, his big calloused palms settled on her breasts. "Nice tits." He squeezed. "Bet it makes you wet when they're sucked."

Fear jetted through her veins. She kicked, scratched, but nothing would break the men's dominance. "Get off me, you big apes!"

Skeeter snarled, twisting her arms. "Be still. We're just gonna have a little fun."

Kathryn spat toward the ugly face looming over her. "Fun, my ass!"

"Fun with your ass," Willie cheerfully unbuttoned and un-zipped her jeans.

Kathryn moaned but didn't stop fighting. "Don't, please."

Her plea went unheard.

Fingers hooking in the waistband, Willie slid her Levis down her thighs. Her panties went down, too, leaving her to-tally exposed. "Nothin' I like better than stickin' my dick up a nice, tight asshole."

Kathryn clenched her eyes against the chill rush of fear spi-raling through her. She considered her options and realized there were none. Zero. No way she'd get out of this one. Maybe if she just gave in and gave them what they obviously intended to take she'd have a better chance of getting out alive. Damn. She should have trusted her gut, not let her guard down.

I don't have to remember this . . .

Hard to forget as thick fingers probed between her naked thighs. "An' this sweet piece o' poontang. . . . Hot damn, it's nice an' slick."

The stroke of his fingers against her clit sent tiny little tremors of disgust through her. "No—ah . . . hell . . ." The abil-ity to speak all of a sudden eluded her.

Goose bumps tripping over her exposed skin, Kathryn gasped. Her stomach clenched into tight knots and a wave of mortified disgust washed over her. She felt absolutely para-lyzed. Nothing in a woman's life could adequately prepare her for such a brutal assault. She swallowed hard, fighting to keep her wits about her and stay calm. Staying alive meant getting a grip on her emotions. Lose control and she would most likely lose her life.

Willie stroked deeper. A smile curved the corner of his

mouth. "Goddamn, my cock's rock hard jes' feelin' her cunt." He grinned up at his brother and winked. "Hold this li'l wild-cat still."

Skeeter's grip tightened on her wrists, his steely fingers digging in painfully. "Don't use it all up," he chuckled.

"Plenty here," Willie breathed. "Enough for both o' us."

She started to pray. *Please, God, this isn't happening. . . .*

But it wasn't stopping. Not until the men were done with her.

Lungs burning with the need to drag in air, Kathryn opened her mouth. A horrifying wail ensued, turning the blood in her veins to icy water. Yet the oh-so-terrible terrible scream tearing against her ears hadn't come from her throat.

Something else screeched a high wild howl of vengeance.

Some*thing* fierce and terrible.

Both men immediately let her go. "Shit! Cougar!" they bellowed simultaneously. "Get the guns."

Eyes immediately snapping open, Kathryn lifted her body off the ground, pawing stupidly at the remnants of her clothing. Between flashes of lightning and fire, she saw at least half a dozen big cats circling around them with dizzying speed.

Taken aback by the sight, air filtered out of her lungs. "My God." To her utter shock she felt strangely calmed by their unexpected arrival. Even the drenching rain couldn't stay the thrill of sexual awareness, sending a hot tremor all the way to the tips of her toes. "They're beautiful."

The cougars were magnificent, sheer poetry in motion. In addition, they were huge; at least three times the size of the average animal, all fur, sinew, and muscle. Cold brutality simmered in glowing amber eyes.

With a subtle display of intelligence, the big felines were canny enough to cut the men off from the campfire, and their guns. If they wanted to fight, it'd be claw to hard steel, and no guarantee the humans would win.

Knives drawn, both men watched the cougars weaving around them, stalking closer to their prey.

Willie swiped his blade at the closest animal. "Ya ain't gettin' a taste o' me!" he bellowed.

Wrong.

Sharp claws tore across his hand.

Willie screeched in pain. "Oweee!" Blood dripped from the gaping wound.

Drawn by the scent, the big cats turned loose and waged an all out attack.

Kathryn jumped, violently startled by the detonation of motion surrounding her. Right in front of her eyes, she saw one of the big cats leap on Willie, bellowing in displeasure as the frantic slash of a knife penetrated vulnerable fur. Shocked by the violence of the attack, her mind vaguely processed two more of the cougars pouncing on Skeeter. He screamed and ran, unwilling to try and fight.

But there were more cats, and not all were occupied with the hunters.

Kathryn vaguely registered one of the cougars breaking off from the fight. Its unblinking gaze settled on her. A wild cougar stared her in the eyes with the intent to kill. The hair on the back of its trunk-thick neck rippled.

She started to pray. "Oh, Lordamightygetmeoutofthisnow . . ."

Bounding into motion, the cougar sped at her with lethal precision. It leapt into the air, all four paws sailing off the ground in defiance of gravity.

Scrambling madly to her feet, Kathryn looked around frantically for a way to escape. All she could do was run.

She wasn't fast enough and couldn't get far enough. In that instant everything around her took on a surreal quality, as if she now viewed events in slow motion through a distant lens.

Two huge paws made contact with her shoulders, the mass of its weight forcing her back to the ground.

Hardly able to think through the thudding echo of her heart, Kathryn automatically rolled over onto her back to find herself pinned under the gargantuan beast. Shards of pain radiated through her head and neck. The cougar's huge head simultaneously came down over her face. Hot, moist breath misted her face.

Her mind struggled to compute the fact the cougar was about to eat her for dinner. Tears of pure shock stung her eyes. *I'm toast.*

The cougar's head dipped lower. Broad pink nostrils flared, drawing in her human scent. Fangs bared, an intense hiss rippled over the cougar's tongue. Ears pinning down, perilously sharp fangs were bared.

That was all it took for her to lose control.

Kathryn frantically beat at the big cat, twisting and struggling to free herself from its domination.

Her struggle failed.

The beast would not be deterred from claiming its prize.

Stray bolts of lightning struck the ground nearby, instantly electrifying the atmosphere around them, creating a corona of crackling, spluttering sparks all around them. Shimmering distortions of crimson and orange glimmered, dizzying and swift, wrapping like grasping fingers around their downed bodies. Thunder snapped the air asunder in a tremendous bashing, and the ground beneath them quaked.

Disoriented by the blistering power the lightning had unleashed, Kathryn vaguely heard the creature bellow, felt the weight of its big furry body envelope hers. Terror consumed her as her body unwillingly arched into the muscular feline frame, joining and merging. For a moment the impression that she was becoming a being of sinew and fur bewildered her. In the same instant the cougar's face blurred, momentarily appearing to metamorphose into distinct and recognizable human features. Behind the mask of the cougar, a sentient soul lived and breathed.

The strange effect lasted only seconds, no more than the time it took her heart to beat a single time.

Moaning in delirious agony, Kathryn felt herself slipping into the grasp of unconsciousness, tumbling downward as if the earth beneath her had mysteriously crumbled. Her mind short-circuiting from too many impressions force-fed into her brain at quantum speed, she willingly sacrificed herself to the over-whelming grip of absolute shock and terror.

Time and space ceased to exist, and her world went entirely black.

2

Kathryn swam painfully out of the abyss swathing her senses like thick cotton bandages. Cracking open crusty lids, she was assailed by a series of unfamiliar sights. A veritable ocean of stone crowded in, and a rough rock ceiling loomed overhead.

She turned her head a little. She was in some sort of a cavern. A frown turned her mouth down. *Where am I?* More important, how long had she been unconscious? A twinge here and there warned her she'd been through a rough time, but the pain wasn't enough to be unbearable. In fact her body was swaddled in comforting softness.

Awareness slowly seeped back into her fuzzed brain. Her strange world wasn't all darkness. Vision adjusting, she saw a fire burning nearby. Contained in a hollow dugout of the ground and ringed with stones, dancing flames cast mysterious shadows in a play only they understood. The pungent scent of burning wood mingled with the smell of crisp, damp air winnowing in.

She looked for the source of the air. The cavern's entrance was clearly visible from her safe cubby. An unrelenting rain pattered outside, punctuated by flashes of lightning and rumbles of thunder. Worse than ever, the storm raged.

Kathryn yawned and rubbed her eyes, grateful she wasn't exposed to the elements. *I'm safe.*

Disjointed fragments of recent memory returned, but she could make very little sense of the events. Her clearest memories centered on the two scraggly mountain men, their vicious traps, their obscene attack. She remembered how they'd handled her, tearing at her clothes, dirty hands touching her skin in the most indecent way. They'd caught her as flat-footed as a greenhorn, and when they'd attacked there hadn't been a damned thing she could have done but hope the assault wouldn't end with her throat cut.

Kathryn shut her eyes against the ugly images. *Oh, my God. They tried to rape me.*

Frantically she sorted through the blurry images, seeking more answers. Finding them in the jumbled attic of her skull, she relaxed.

Pulling in a calming breath, she relaxed. The men hadn't succeeded in taking her.

Strangely, how she'd gotten away from them was hazier, not as clear in her mind. She thought it had something to do with cougars—abnormally huge cats that had somehow turned into men.

Rationality scoffed. Her brow wrinkled. No, no. Wasn't possible. Cougars didn't shift into human beings. Cougars were extinct.

Someone else had come to her rescue.

Kathryn struggled to remember more. Digging deeper, she insisted on sorting through the shards and flashes of random images. For her own peace of mind she needed to put the facts together in a way that would make complete and perfect sense. She'd probably only imagined cougars had rescued her because that's what the poachers said they hunted and killed.

She dug some more, stopping to turn over and examine every bit of memory she found. More disembodied images seeped back into her fuzzy brain. At the forefront loomed a stunning man with amber eyes, lean torso, and legs a mile long.

Ah, there he was.

How could she have forgotten him?

Kathryn clearly recalled the stranger bending over her, gathering her up in his arms. As though looking right at him, she almost believed she could reach out and touch the long black hair streaming wildly around his broad shoulders. She remembered aching to kiss his stunningly sensual lips, yet being unable to move in his powerful grip, as though some strange force had welded her limbs in place. . . .

A sudden burst of pain rattled her skull. Everything slipped through her fingers like tiny granules, her memories once more sinking back into the quicksand inside her skull.

Kathryn paused for a moment to blink away the brief surge of dizziness. She took a deep breath to steady herself, and then sat up. She winced, feeling every scrape and bruise mottling her skin. After taking a hard fall, she'd been manhandled to the max and then some. The aftereffects of the violence apparently still lingered.

Kathryn scrubbed both hands over her face, grimacing a little when she felt a twinge of pain under her fingertips. One of her cheeks was a little swollen, tight. "Wow," she mumbled softly. "I've been through some hairy shit."

She was pleasantly surprised to learn that she hadn't been sleeping on a hard stone surface. A blanket of soft fur had been spread out over a thick bed of wild grass clippings. An acre of luxurious fur covered her body.

Her naked body.

Every stitch of her clothing had been removed.

Her clothing—what remained of it—lay neatly folded nearby.

Her hiking boots, topped with a misshapen ball that she recognized to be her socks. Great care had been given to their treatment and placement, easy to locate should she want to get dressed. Whoever had come to her aid had taken a lot of trouble to make sure she was secure and comfortable. The setup was wholly primitive, but it did the trick.

A mental picture of her mystery man wavered back into sharper focus. It was easy to imagine him carrying her to his hideout, laying her on the soft furs before undressing her. His fingers would have skimmed her skin, touched every inch.

Kathryn groaned under her breath. Her nipples automatically tightened into tight little peaks. A thrill of anticipation sped through her. The possibilities of what he could have done to her spun through her mind. The fantasy of being taken by a strong male she desired was one she often wove. The sensual images of their bodies locked together on top of the soft fur blankets aroused some primal urge inside her. . . .

God! She'd just been nearly raped, and instead of being grateful she wasn't, she was fantasizing about having sex with the man who'd gotten her out of harm's way! Aside from work, sex was constantly on her mind. She thought about it twenty-four hours a day, seven days a week. When she wasn't having sex, she was daydreaming about having sex.

I'm a psycho, she thought. *Abnormal.*

Despite herself, she could feel the pull of untrammeled desire. She shivered. Something stirred beside her.

Startled, Kathryn immediately yanked back the fur blanket. A weak sigh of relief broke from her throat. For some reason she'd halfway expected to see a cougar.

She stared in spellbound fascination. No cougar here.

Stretched out full length, the man beside her was all muscle and sinew. The soft glow of the nearby fire caressed his exposed flesh, hinting of the unleashed power and invisible hungers stirring inside his soul. With one look, without even a single touch, she felt instantly connected to him. A feeling she couldn't conquer, deny, or even begin to explain.

Heart as trippy as her respiration, Kathryn threw her hand over her mouth before her gasps disturbed his slumber. She visually searched his face. His severely chiseled features bespoke of his strong Native American heritage. Lusciously naked, he stirred beside her, one strong hand loosely cradling his very obvious erection. Tribal symbols etched into his skin in black ink ringed both sinewy biceps. Three words were inked in the center of the design. *Death Before Dishonor.*

Sexy. Definitely a turn on.

He snored softly, his chest rising and falling steadily. He clearly wasn't feigning sleep.

Strangely, his presence calmed her. Even though naked and vulnerable in this strange place, she felt no fear of him. It almost felt as if she knew him, that they shared a connection so deep it went past the conscious and into the psychic.

Recognition seeped in. This was the man who'd appeared out of nowhere to help her. Seeing him in living, breathing flesh reassured her that she hadn't imagined him. She'd have fainted dead away if she'd found herself beside one of her attackers.

Fighting to breathe past the lump in her throat, she just had to check out every inch of him.

Kathryn visually traced the lines of his broad chest, stopping for a moment at his dusky flat nipples before moving over the ridges of his cobbled abdomen.

Such a specimen of arresting male beauty nearly robbed her breath. Oh, he was gorgeous, in a way that almost hurt her to look, a fairy-tale hero straight from the great wilds of the forest that had birthed him. The sight of his stunning body kickstarted that particular liquid ache between her legs all over again. Her clit pulsed softly, begging for the touch of a hand, the wet pressure of a tongue.

Her visual sweep continued toward his narrow hips. She wasn't disappointed. A smile tweaked up one corner of her mouth at the sight of his penis. Her tongue strayed out, tracing her lips.

Awesome.

In sleep her rescuer had a damned impressive hard-on, something she hadn't seen in a long time. A beautifully erect cock; a good eight inches and thickly veined. With equipment like that he had to be an excellent lay. Its length and weight begged her to stroke it even as the wide, flared crown demanded she taste and tease it with her mouth. Talk about an eyeful of flesh impact. This hunk was definitely hot enough to incinerate a woman on sight.

The ache between her legs increased to an almost painful degree.

Drawing in a shallow breath, Kathryn clenched her teeth. She'd always been hypersexual, needing sex the way some people needed regular meals.

However, needing lots of sex didn't always mean there was a suitable partner.

Kathryn was careful with her choices—maybe too selective. The last year had been a total drought in the lovemaking department. Her reliance on masturbation and sex toys to get her through had begun to border on the ridiculous. But the truth was, she hadn't ever found a man whose physical needs rivaled her own. Sex, when she did have it, was usually unsatisfying.

Her gaze drifted back to the magnificent beast sleeping so peacefully beside her. His sheer presence, however innocent, threatened to overwhelm her. Just looking at him made her feel like a wanton bitch in heat.

Wake him up and fuck his brains out.

The thought sent embarrassed heat to her cheeks. Her eyes firmly fixed on his lovely cock, voyeuristic discomfort blossomed inside her. Invading his body while he slept wouldn't be right, however much he might welcome the gesture.

Still, he had to wake up soon.

Meanwhile, Kathryn had to do something about the throb between her legs. At the moment she'd have to handle the problem herself.

Easing back slowly, she stretched out on the fur-luxurious blanket. The strong odor of an animal-scented musk tickled her nostrils, not unpleasant at all. The smell ushered in images of wild carnivores hunting down and overpowering the weaker prey.

Breathing deeply to steady her pulse, Kathryn closed her eyes, imagining what it would be like to make love to the stud sleeping beside her.

"Like this," she murmured softly.

Using just the tips of her fingers, she touched herself softly, tracing her lips, chin, neck, and then the soft hollow between her breasts. Sexual heat simmered as she circled soft erect peaks, gently tugging the tender nubs. A thrill swept through her, increasing her neglected clit's need for proper attention.

Gasping under her breath, she tugged her nipples a little harder. She pressed her thighs together, applying just the right pressure to her clit. She wanted to enjoy the sensations without climaxing too fast. That would ruin everything.

Right then her companion shifted, turning his body to one side and lifting his weight onto his elbow. An audible gasp escaped him. "Oh, wow!" he murmured in a voice still thick with sleep.

Oh, hell! She'd just been caught masturbating in a strange man's bed.

Kathryn cracked one eye open. Sure enough, her unnamed companion was now wide awake. Looking right at her. And grinning like a very happy man. His smile softened well-etched, masculine features.

Hands falling away from her breasts, she opened both eyes all the way. She blushed hot. "Sorry," she breathed, her voice husky with the strain of her craving.

Darkly tanned skin intensified the white flash of his teeth. "Don't be," he drawled in perfect English. "This is the best entertainment I've had in a long time." His voice was lush, like crushed velvet over smooth, cool gravel.

Kathryn's heart pounded so hard that she felt her throat quiver. "I was just, uh . . ." Shit. She sounded like a teenager busted for having a boy in her room.

His gaze skimmed her naked body, and his brows rose suggestively. "Waking up?" he suggested politely.

Thank God. A true gentleman.

Brushing her long hair away from her face, Kathryn nodded. "Yeah."

Her rescuer glanced toward his pelvis. His cock still very much had a mind of its own. A little hiss escaped. "I have to admit it's nice to wake up with a lovely naked woman in my bed."

She nervously cleared her throat. "It's nice I'm getting to wake up at all." She swallowed hard, and finished, "Considering what I got myself into."

Sensual speculation vanished from his face. "That was too close," he said tightly. "I'm just glad we got you away from those assholes who tried to rape you."

Frustration and confusion poured into her. Rescue was still so vague in her mind. "I—I don't remember much of what happened after you came," she admitted softly. "I guess I passed out."

He reached out, catching a lock of her long hair between thumb and forefinger. "It's no wonder. Things were pretty tough on you." He used the tip to trace a bruised patch on her left cheek. "You're safe now, I promise. Those men don't come here."

His intimate gesture slammed into Kathryn's gut like a ram-rod. Body trembling, she felt a thrill of sexual awareness race down her spine. "Do you know them?"

He brushed her chin with the thick strand. "I know them the way they know me—like mortal enemies," he answered gravely. By the look on his face, the idea of the poachers disturbed him deeply. "We got you away from them as fast as we could."

His words triggered more memories. Images of more cougars turning to men unspooled on the screen of her mind's eye. She shivered violently, as nothing about the disjointed vision made sense.

But cougars didn't turn into humans. The idea was absurd.

Kathryn frowned as seeds of doubt about her sanity took root. "I thought I saw others, but I can't get a clear picture in my mind."

Leaning closer, he stroked her face softly as if willing her to forget. His gaze visually swept hers. "I had some friends with me. . . ." he explained. "But I don't expect you to remember. You took quite a bump on the head. How do you feel?"

Looking into his eyes, Kathryn gasped and her heart fluttered. *Oh, his eyes.* His eyes were the windows to a savage's soul. The dark brown irises were smattered with shining amber flecks. Just looking into his eyes mesmerized her, communicating a silent message that she belonged to him, and him alone. If she didn't have him she'd be doomed to remain forever unfulfilled, her search for her mate unending.

The desire to make love with him shimmered through her. The muscles in her abdomen rippled as sensual anticipation bubbled up inside all over again.

Suppressing her shudder, Kathryn drew a breath. The air felt deep and heavy inside her lungs. She forced her frozen mouth to move. "I know it's strange," she started to say, "but I'm horny as hell." Her hands ached to stroke the marble-hard planes of his body. She didn't believe in love at first sight.

Lust, yes.

Yet what she felt right now went deeper than simple carnal hunger. Hers was a desire she couldn't explain in words. Mere words wouldn't make sense. It didn't even make sense when she tried to rationalize the thought in her mind.

Kathryn just knew this man was the right man for her.

Period.

No point in denying that he was attracted to her, either. That was obvious.

His chuckle floated back with tender reassurance. "Must be some kind of delayed stress syndrome."

Kathryn drew in a shuddering breath to steady the need jolting through her. She didn't know what it was, or care. She just wanted to feel him . . . take what he so clearly had to offer. "Does it sound crazy that I want to have sex with you right now?" Her voice was taut, as ragged as her respiration.

Her rescuer couldn't control the quiver that ran through his body. He searched her eyes for an intense moment. "Are you sure?" he asked softly. "I won't take advantage." He visibly swallowed. His words were husky with the strain of holding himself back. "If you want me to sleep somewhere else, I will."

Definitely the last thing she wanted.

Kathryn felt heat rising up from her core, scorching her from the inside. Biting her lower lip, she shook her head. He was the sweetest of taboos, the forbidden too enticing to deny. "I want you to stay," she said softly. "Make love to me."

He reached out, tracing the curve of her lips with a single finger. "I can honestly say I've never met a girl like you before." The simple caress was soft and sexy as hell.

Kathryn groaned with that first skin-to-skin touch. Aching, aroused, she turned her naked body toward his, closing the already narrow distance between them and offering all. "You mean *easy?*" She trembled with anticipation, hoping—no, praying—that he wouldn't turn her down.

He shook his head and smiled. "I mean like me." Weight supported on one elbow, he leaned close to her ear. "I know why you're here," he whispered presciently. "What you need . . . what you've always craved deep inside."

Kathryn waited breathless, hungry for his caress. She couldn't think of any reply. Silence fell. They simply looked at each other. The impact of his gaze sent liquid tremors through her veins.

What she saw in the depth of his eyes mirrored what he saw in hers: the need to satisfy the lusty beasts lurking in both their souls.

3

Turbulent thoughts swirled through Kathryn's mind. She knew what would happen between them, what *must* happen between them. They couldn't stop it any more than they could stop breathing. The energy both their mutual desires generated was enough to power an entire city.

Her rescuer's head dipped lower. His mouth settled on hers, his need a hungry, devouring thing. His tongue easily slipped through the seam of her lips, sweeping in with an erotic intent to overwhelm every inch of her mouth.

Kathryn responded, melting against him. He couldn't seem to get enough of her, each break for air only ending in another deep kiss. Amazed and disoriented, she willingly let him take control.

One thigh moving possessively over hers, he broke their kiss to concentrate on other parts of her hungry skin. His mouth traced the curve of her chin, her neck, down to the soft hollow of her throat, tracing the path her own fingers had forged. Her senses purred with immediate response. "I can't believe this is happening. It's too damned incredible to be true," he murmured. "I don't even know your name."

She blinked at the statement. Normally she'd be the one asking that question. She hadn't even bothered. It already felt like she'd been connected to him through an entire lifetime. "Do you need to?"

Lifting perfect brows, he smiled reluctantly. "Believe it or not, I don't often drag naked women to my cave to make love to them." Gaze filled with unflinching honesty, his words were tinged with the simplicity of truth.

Hand on his chest, she felt the heightened beat of his heart. There was a hint of apprehension under his sure demeanor. "Kathryn," she murmured. "Kathryn Dayton."

A short silence, as if he weighed revealing his own identity. Then his heart took on a faster beat as more flares of the forbidden came alive inside him. "Joe. Joseph Clawfoot."

Kathryn rubbed her body sinuously against his, her senses soaking up and basking in every sensation. Her nipples jutted, hard and rosy nubs. "I like your name. Very native."

His dark eyes sparked with primal power. She gasped lightly when his hand cupped one of her breasts. His cock pressed against her bare thigh. "That's because I am *very* native."

"How native are you?"

Rumbling a greedy sound, he pounced. "As in a wild, savage Indian who is about to ravish a naked white woman." His head dipped, and his mouth descended over one quivering peak. He sucked softly, then harder. Suddenly taut muscles tightened in her abdomen as he suckled the sensitive tip.

She moaned, the low supple sound of pure appreciation slipping through parted lips. "Oh, damn . . . ravish away!"

His head lifted a fraction of an inch. "Enjoying?" he asked, tongue flicking over her tender nubbin.

Lust flooding her with a rush of fluid desire, she laughed with delight. "Oh, you don't know how much."

He moved to her other breast, beginning the sensual tease all over again. His tongue briefly painted her pink areola. "I'm only just getting started." He clearly intended to sample every inch of her with his mouth.

Kathryn threaded her fingers through his luxuriously thick hair, marveling at the fine bluish-black sheen. In the nearby firelight it was like a thing alive, spreading across his shoulders and down his back like a cloak. "And doing an excellent job, too."

Joseph flicked her nipple again, his sultry breath heating the tender bud. "Oh, you have no idea what I've got in mind."

A thrill surged through her. "Then show me," she answered, all innocence.

He did just that.

One hand slid down the flat plane of her abdomen, stopping just before making contact with the rise of her Venus mound. The heat from his palm seemed to burn into her skin, as though he were somehow marking her, branding her with his touch. She gasped at the sensation, enjoying the ripples of pleasure emanating from her core.

His hand went into motion again, caressing her bare mons. "Oh, I like this."

Kathryn shivered under his touch. "Thanks." She had so much hair down there that it often felt like a Brillo pad in her panties. A Brazilian bikini wax made wearing tight jeans uncomfortable.

Joseph slid an experimental finger through the narrow crease. "Mmm, nice . . . and wet." At the same time his mouth resettled on a supple nipple. He suckled and caressed, giving clit and nipple simultaneously slow strokes.

Her body responding with a powerful surge of white-hot lust, Kathryn's hips automatically arched upward, a silent encouragement for his finger to penetrate deeper. "And ready," she hinted, voice a little on edge. She parted her legs a little more, giving him better access.

The suckling and stroking didn't stop for a second. "Don't rush. Just let it come," he breathed against her breast before claiming the sensitive peak again. He skimmed a finger across her clit, lightly at first, then with harder pressure until she moaned and writhed with pleasure.

Fingers clenching the soft fur beneath her back, Kathryn's entire body undulated with pleasure. The blood pounding in her temples felt like molten silver, flowing and beating a tom-tom rhythm that echoed against the walls of her skull. She gasped in delight when he skimmed his fingers through her creamy labia. Control was beginning to slip out of her grasp as her orgasm set to simmering inside her. The blood rushed from her head, spilling into her loins. Dizziness enveloped her senses as he simultaneously flicked and teased both her nipples.

Just when Kathryn thought she couldn't take another second of caressing, her lover penetrated the folds of her velvety sex. The narrow channel of her vagina closed around his thick finger, inner muscles undulating to pull him deeper. "Oh, please . . ." Twisting and shivering, she heard her words morph into a primitive cry even her own ears didn't understand.

Without saying a word, Joseph added another finger. Using his digits like a cock, he stroked her damp sex with steady thrusts. Her strong muscles clenched and tried to hold him.

"Go deeper. As deep as you can."

Joseph wouldn't be commanded. He was the one in control and intended to keep it. Leaving her breasts, he suddenly slid lower, positioning himself between her open thighs. Nothing was concealed from his hungry gaze. She was fully exposed, spread open like a freshly bloomed rose. The raw power of what he was about to do encased her.

Kathryn bit her lower lip as his hands slid under her ass, lifting her, positioning her. *Oh, yes . . . Oh, God, yes . . .* She could not breathe. She could not think. So few men did oral well.

He inhaled, breathing in her scent, an intensely erotic and personal act. "Nice." Head dipping, his lips circled her clit with a ravenous intensity. Teeth scraped the sensitive nub, tearing a sultry cry from deep inside her gut. She pressed into him, fingers twisting through his thick hair, pulling him closer as her hips danced to the rhythm of his tongue and suckling lips.

At some point Joseph slipped his fingers back inside her. His tongue flicked and stabbed her clit even as his fingers sawed in and out of her drenched sex.

A guttural cry of sheer animal release tore out of Kathryn's throat as all the sensations he gifted her with detonated, sending her into a world far beyond planet earth. A dazzling display of multicolored rockets went off behind her eyes, filling her mind with sounds, colors, and sensations she'd never dreamed possible.

She floated back to earth as though borne on the wings of the angels. Every muscle throbbed with pure satisfaction.

Joseph gave her no time to process what had just happened.

Rising to his knees, he captured her hips in both hands. Corded biceps bulged as he angled her body to his. Impatient with need, he penetrated her with a single hard thrust. He'd satisfied his female. Now he would claim and take what he needed to sate himself.

Cock sheathed in her sex, he leaned forward, supporting his weight on outstretched arms. Face to face, she could see the sexual haze glazing his eyes.

This was exactly what she needed, what she'd craved.

Total domination over her pleasure.

Nerve endings sizzling, her body was alive for the first time in her life, her spirit finally embracing the lust driving her to search for that elusive something she couldn't quite identify.

Without a word, she circled her arms around his narrow waist, palms splaying possessively over the taut cheeks of his ass. She squirmed with pleasure, firmly pinned down by his colossal weight. His pelvis ground against hers in such a way that made her clit sing with joy.

Their gazes locked. Something mysterious and erotic passed between them, an unspoken understanding of what each wanted and expected from the other.

His head dipped, and his lips brushed her, giving her a hint of what her own female spices tasted like. "You're so damn tight," he murmured against her parted lips. "It's like having a virgin."

Her tongue snaked out, tracing his mouth. Tasting. Enjoying. "You're so damn big," she countered. "It's like being a virgin."

He pulled out, then slowly slid back inside, making sure she felt the sensual glide. "Is it?"

Gritting her teeth, Kathryn dug her fingers into his ass. She was sure she felt him all the way up to the back of her throat. "Yes."

He rumbled, a low, impatient growl. "Want more?" he challenged, as if she had a choice.

The fierce look of arousal fed her desire all over again. "Yes." The single word transformed to a gasp when he withdrew, then slammed in again.

Suddenly there was no more time for words.

Hips rolling into motion, his cock went deeper with every thrust. His weight pounded against hers with a speed bordering on excruciating fury. He drove into her again and again.

Caught in the dark, powerful surge of his lust, Kathryn held on tightly, meeting the hard pummeling with an intensity that matched his. He used his cock like a weapon, making sure she felt every damn inch invading her sex. The sizzling heat of flesh on flesh numbed her wits to every sensation but the climax he drove her toward with the unerring determination of a speeding bullet. He intended to take her to the edge and toss her over.

She held on tighter, determined not to be left behind.

Without warning, Joseph wrapped one fist into Kathryn's long hair and pulled her lips to his, tongue stabbing the depth of her mouth at the same time his cock pounded her sex, straining for release. Control deserting him, he shafted her repeatedly with long, driving strokes. His plundering mouth ravaged hers, a hunger bordering on desperation. He was lost, beyond the grip of anything but physical gratification.

His frenzied need to devour her—claim her completely—hadn't just materialized because a willing female had made herself available. His insatiable eagerness, his intense lust, all was for her.

Only her.

Breath sucked away by the sheer frenzy of an all-consuming pleasure, Kathryn dug her nails deeply into his taut flesh and held on as carnal sensuality laid siege against her senses. Her skin burned as if set afire, her breathing ragged, her swollen breasts flattened against the hard slab of his chest. The animalistic scent of two people in mad sexual heat singed her nostrils.

Joseph slammed his hips hard into hers. "Do you feel me?" he growled against the depths of her mouth.

Pulsing with a pleasure that bordered on pain, Kathryn's rising hips met his, thrust for brutal thrust. "Yes," she gasped back against his lips. Her core was a steaming pool of pure, molten lust. "Hurt me more, dammit. . . . Make me come . . . as hard as you can." If he had wanted to eat her alive, she couldn't have sacrificed herself fast enough. Deep inside she knew this kind of raw, savage sex only came once in a lifetime. She was determined to enjoy it as long as she could.

Joseph redoubled his efforts, every muscle in his shoulders, back, and thighs straining, his hips striking like a jackhammer crushing concrete. Giving her no mercy, the ram of each long stroke threatened to trigger the climax wrapping around her tender clit. Breath-snatching pleasure dangled on the edge of her reach.

Kathryn closed her eyes tight and grabbed for heaven. *Pound me harder, harder . . . One more, baby. Just one more. . . .*

Her thought had barely formed when crackling sparks of lightning flared outside the mouth of the cavern; thunder splintered the air into fragments with a tremendous rolling boom. A vibrant force swept through their coupled bodies, an invisible pulse of energy drawn from the essence of creation.

Quivering under the siege of intense carnal gratification, Kathryn heard a savage wail—ragged and raw—barely recognizing the guttural, throat-scraping howl as a sound made by human vocal cords.

Senses exploding in fire, orgasm shimmered through her with the power and majesty of a star gone nova. Glittering sensations as sharp as shards of glass poured through her veins, scraping every last nerve ending. The merciless sensations bombarded her from a thousand directions. Like a surfer riding storm-tossed waves, the crest of orgasm was barely savored before another climax roared in to claim her all over again. . . .

It wasn't over yet.

Last barrier shattering, a terrible cry tore from her lover's throat as though climax would obliterate some piece of his soul. Agonized delight scorched his vocal cords, twisted his face with brutal precision.

Delivering a final thrust, Joseph's body abruptly stiffened. Every inch of his magnificent body shuddered as his cock throbbed and released its burden, delivering a jet of hot semen. Flushed, beaded in sweat, and trembling head to foot, he collapsed on top of her in the most beautiful surrender she'd ever witnessed. He groaned against her mouth, unable to say a single coherent word. His cock pulsed inside her, milked of every last drop by her voracious core. His semen filled her to overflowing, the peak physical and spiritual perfection.

Silence followed, broken only by the sound of their breathing and the sounds of the storm outside. They lay spent in the aftermath, enjoying the fading sensation of shared orgasm.

Limp and worn in the aftermath, it was the sweetest and most complete release Kathryn had ever known. Pinned beneath his weight, she'd been not only claimed, but conquered. No gentle seduction this, but he'd touched her in places no other man had ever come close to. He'd taken her with an intensity she'd never experienced in another man's arms.

A little smile crept to her lips. *Works for me,* she mused. And judging by the feel of the collapsed man on top of her, it'd definitely worked for him.

An eternity seemed to pass before Joseph rolled onto his side, bringing her with him so that the connection between their bodies remained unbroken.

Joseph slid a hand under her thigh, lifting her leg onto his hip so that he could burrow deeper. "That was amazing." His heated gaze burned hot and strong, a warning that he was nowhere near finished with her. Not by a long shot.

Trembling inside as they lay face to face, Kathryn automatically adjusted her hips to meet the new rhythm he created. Pebble-hard nipples brushed his damp chest, igniting all sorts of liquid vibrations in her belly. His semihard erection pulsed and lengthened. Deep inner muscles automatically clenched in response, holding him.

He wants me again.

The thought thrummed through her mind like an invading virus. *He really wants me.* What a bloody miracle, a man whose heat, fire, and passion matched her own. He'd taken her like a starving man at a banquet, filling himself to the brim with erotic delights—and still wanted more. His seething gaze and burgeoning erection told her that he was ready—no, burning— to make love again.

Kathryn dragged in a quick breath. Not even a cold shower

could douse the heat blazing through her now. "Mmm . . . yes. The best." It was true. She'd never known a desire so intense, or felt the urgency to have a man so fiercely. Giving herself to this man was the most natural thing she'd ever done. And it was the first orgasm she'd ever had that wasn't self-induced.

Pretty damn amazing. This Indian definitely had all the right moves.

Hungry for more, Joseph cupped her rear, leaning forward to reclaim her lips. "I'm sorry I got a little rough," he whispered, sampling the moist heat of her mouth. "I wanted you so much I couldn't help myself."

Kathryn nibbled back. "Good," she whispered, flexing her stomach muscles so that deep inner muscles would also tighten.

Feeling her tighten and undulate, Joseph's cock grew even harder. One big, warm palm cupped her breast, tugging pleasurably at the erect tip. "I can feel you around me."

She laughed low in the back of her throat. "I meant for you to."

Joseph gave a low, sexy chuckle "You're all piranha, honey. Teeth. Devouring me." He plucked her erect nipple harder. "I've spent most of my life fantasizing about a woman like you."

His proof was nice and hard. And getting harder. "And now that you've got me here," she asked, "what are you going to do?"

For an answer, Joseph rolled onto his back, keeping her firmly seated as he lifted her into a sitting position. Straddling his hips, she was suddenly the one in the position to give or deny pleasure. A sense of power flooded her. She felt like a witch, a sorceress of sexual charms who could bring this man to his knees simply by granting him her favors. Deny him and he'd be bereft.

A smoldering look filled his face as he slid his hands over the soft flare of her hips. "Fuck you again, as often as you'll let me." His voice came out strangled with longing.

Control slipped through her fingers. Kathryn wanted him so much she shook with anticipation. She could hardly believe that this big male animal had ever suffered a single day of anguished, unsated arousal.

Unbidden tears stung her lids. She quickly blinked them away. "I'll let you fuck me, all you want," she promised softly. And meant every word.

"I've waited for you, Kathryn. I waited because I knew you'd come someday. . . ." His hands slid around to caress her spine, fingers tracing the soft curve of her spine even as he guided her body forward so that a nipple hovered over his mouth like a tempting morsel. He tongued the tip, drawing circle after delicious circle.

Hungry for more, Kathryn found her hips automatically followed the slow dance he was leading her into. Every pulse of his hard shaft inside her tore through her senses even as he suckled at her breasts. "You're not waiting anymore."

Wide palms settled around her ass cheeks. He lifted her up until the tip of his penis almost slid out, then lowered her again until it was again consumed by her insatiable core. "I want to feel you climax around my cock again." This time he was taking things slowly, making sure she experienced every sensation in rapturous detail.

Hands clenching his thick hair, Kathryn groaned when he eased her up, then slid her back down. Her clit twitched when making contact with the base of his erection, and all sorts of delicious melting sensations poured through her veins.

"Trust me," she moaned in guttural submission. "I will. . . ."

4

Hours later, Kathryn opened her eyes on a most incredible sight. Joseph Clawfoot, totally nude, tending the fire. A thrill of pure appreciation swept through her. That sight alone was enough to bring a girl back to consciousness as soon as possible.

She stretched and propped herself up. It would be a pleasure just to stay in bed and watch him all day. Clear, radiant sunshine shone outside the mouth of the cave. Last night's thunderstorm had dissipated just as quickly as it had raged across the land. The day promised to be warm and bright, and absolutely perfect.

Noticing her stirring, Joseph glanced up from his preparations. He was in the process of roasting some fowl he'd cleaned and prepared. Rigged on a splint fashioned out of green wood, the bird sizzled. Fat and other juices dripped into the fire, creating the most incredibly delicious aroma. "Good morning. I hope you're hungry."

Kathryn inhaled deeply. The smell of real food set her ap-

petite to the edge of hysterical. "God, yes. I'm starving." Her
stomach growled, seconding her words.

Joseph nodded and turned the roasting bird. "It's almost
ready, I think."

Kathryn crawled out of the soft fur nest and reached for her
clothing. Every muscle in her body ached, but it was a good
ache. A well-earned ache. A smile tugged at her lips as a small
shudder rippled through her. Her inner thighs felt as if she'd
been riding a galloping stallion for weeks. "Good. I think I
might pass out if I have to wait much longer."

Concern creased his face. "Are you feeling okay?"

Anxious to reassure him, Kathryn nodded. "I'm good. A little thirsty."

He reached for the canteen near the fire. "Ah, I think I can
take care of that. Rescue is on the way."

Rising out of his crouch, he bridged the distance separating
the sleeping area from the cooking area. Magnificently nude,
even his most casual gestures were filled with uncanny grace.
"Here you go. I'm sorry it's only water and not wine."

Kathryn accepted the canteen. The closer he was to her, the
more she felt the raw energy that simply radiated from the man.
He was all sparks and nerve.

And certainly a very creative lover. Intense, focused. Not to
mention relentless. Joseph had given her more orgasms last
night than she could possibly count. Every time he'd touched
her, she'd popped like a balloon. His stamina was equally endless. That cock of his had a will of iron.

Remembering what he'd done to her last night was enough
to make her blush hot—and want to do it all over again.

Kathryn forced her numb fingers to twist the cap off the
canteen. Cool liquid splashed into the lid doubling as a cup.
Thirstier than ever, she drank it down in one big gulp. She refilled and drank again.

Joseph smiled. "Better?"

Lowering the cup, she nodded. "I'm good now. Thank you." She recapped the canteen and set it aside. She also deliberately cleared her brain of thoughts related to his incredible sexual abilities and refocused her full attention on him. She wanted to know everything about him, who he was and what he was doing in the South Mountains. He'd mentioned he had friends. Where were they? She hoped she would get to meet them later, thank them for helping her.

Back at the fire, Joseph turned his attention to the cooking, taking care to keep twirling the bird so it wouldn't burn. "I think another ten minutes and this beauty will be done. Wouldn't want it raw at the bone."

Kathryn shook her head. "Definitely not." As good as the cooking bird smelled, she wasn't interested in courting a nasty case of salmonella.

A feeling of fullness in her bladder warned her of nature's call. It was never a comfortable thing for her to get up and parade around naked in front of a lover. She'd always been the kind of woman to get up and go after the sex. Waking up in a man's bed was an entirely new experience in her world. She usually had sex for the physical gratification, not to satisfy any emotional connection.

Joseph appeared comfortable enough running around bare-assed in front of her. And he'd seen—and explored—every inch of her. No reason to turn into a prude now, she decided.

Still, there were some things in this world that shouldn't be shared.

Kathryn scooped up her clothes and nodded toward the rear of the cave. "Um, I need to use, ah, the facilities, if you don't mind."

He grinned. "Sure. Help yourself."

Clothing pressed against her breasts, Kathryn forced herself to go past him without scurrying or trying to hide her rear. No droop there yet, thank God. A lifetime of hiking and climbing in strenuous conditions had kept her leg muscles toned and firm.

Far from being damp and cramped, the cave was wide, spacious, and airy. A short tunnel near the rear branched off into a separate antechamber that functioned as a bathroom of sorts. A crevasse in the high rock ceiling allowed water from outside to trickle down into a sinklike basin hollowed out of the stone halfway down one wall. Fresh, cool water from the recent rains filled it to the brim. A pile of rags and cake of rough soap had been piled nearby for easy reach. The loo was a smaller hole a few feet away, seemingly bottomless.

She grinned. A roll of toilet paper was perched on a rock nearby, giving the uninitiated a prompt as to its use. During a trip last night she'd been happy to have it. It added a nice touch to the primitive conditions. A kerosene lantern chased the darkness back into shadowy corners.

Taking care of her libations, Kathryn dipped a cloth into the water and wrung it out to wash a few vital private parts. The urge to wash her matted hair had her wishing for a hot, steamy shower. Not possible, so she did a quick braid of her tresses, then knotted it into a bun. No hair ties at hand, so she improvised and used a stray strand of hair to make the band, tucking it under so it would stay tight. A few curling wisps hung around her face and neck. She hoped it looked sexy and not stringy.

Attention turned to her clothes. Slipping on her bra and panties, she hiked her ass into her jeans, a little dirtier for the wear. Her heavy flannel shirt had suffered under Willie's rough hands. Most of the buttons had been ripped off. She compromised by tying the ends together, making a halter out of it, then slipping into her jacket. By the time she'd put on her socks and boots, she felt almost whole.

Washed and dressed, Kathryn made her way back into the

main part of the cave. Her host was still occupied with the food. "I like the homey touches you've added to the place."

"Thanks."

She walked around. Little cubbyholes and shelves were carved into the stone. Odds and ends of camping gear useful for surviving in the wilderness were stored for easy access. "You stay here often."

He glanced up from his cooking. "More often than not."

Biting her lower lip, Kathryn stared at him. Crouched by the snapping fire, Joseph's coppery flesh glowed. Memory of the musky scent of hot male skin swirled through her skull with aphrodisiac intensity. Violent desire shimmied down her spine. Her palms ached to stroke the marble slabs of his chest, his abdomen, and his back. Remembering what he could do with that cock of his tied her insides into knots all over again.

Knees threatening to buckle under her weight, Kathryn pulled in a quick breath. "If you feed me first, I won't mind at all." She smiled and rubbed the bare swatch of skin between her jeans and shirt. "I'm past starving. If I don't have food, I'll faint."

He made a sympathetic face. "Can't have you go unconscious on me again." A folded blanket in front of the fire offered a soft place to settle. It hadn't been there when she'd gone to dress. "Have a seat."

Kathryn gratefully settled down in front of the fire. Despite the surge of desire, the fatigue of her short night's sleep hung on, making her wish for a strong cup of coffee liberally laced with lashings of condensed milk and lots of sugar. Right now she'd kill for a shot of caffeine. She didn't see her backpack, but maybe there was a slim possibility he'd managed to salvage it. "I hate to be a pain, but I don't suppose you managed to get my pack."

Maneuvering the roasted bird off the splints and onto a tin platter, Joseph shook his head. "Sorry. Didn't get it. We just wanted to get out before anyone got hurt."

Kathryn shrugged. "No problem. Couldn't expect you to under those circumstances, I guess." The flash of a cougar taking a blade to the shoulder seeped into her brain space.

Not cougars, she reminded herself, trying to shake the images of the big cats she'd swear had come to her rescue. She couldn't. The cougars insisted on roaring through her skull. *My sanity is clearly slipping.*

The question nagged, but there was no time for answers. She needed food in her belly. The sooner, the better. Joseph had a delicious roasted fowl that she intended to tear into like the hungry carnivore she was.

"We can go back to your camp," he said, using a stick to roll something out of the embers, a darkened mass that looked like leaves.

She nodded. "That would be great. Thanks. They probably took everything I had. I had a walkie-talkie with me, too. If it's still there, I need to let my team know I'm still among the living."

"If your radio isn't there, I'll get you back to your people." Unrolling the mass produced a selection of freshly baked vegetables—small brown potatoes, wild carrots, and onions. He piled these beside the roasted bird.

The smell of hot food twisted her stomach into knots. "Thanks."

Joseph presented the food. "Dig in."

Kathryn took the loaded platter. "Thanks. Wow, this is more than I expected. I've been eating nothing but MREs for an entire week now." The food smelled delicious, prepared with nothing except fire and the natural juices heat engendered. "I don't know how you did it, but it looks great."

He grinned. "It should taste pretty good, too. Definitely better than precooked, dehydrated stuff."

She grimaced. "It's easy to carry and doesn't spoil in the field. We weren't going to be here long. Just a few weeks to do our survey and turn in the report." She gestured at the bounty. "You don't want any?"

Joseph shook his head and grinned. "I ate before you woke up. I felt half starved and just couldn't wait. I hope you don't mind."

Kathryn pulled a drumstick off the bird. "I can understand. My stomach has been rumbling since I woke up." She took a bite of the meat. The skin was crisp, the meat moist and tender. It tasted vaguely of onions and smoke.

He watched her eat. "Edible, I hope."

She swallowed her bite. "Perfect." She picked the leg clean, then went for another. "In fact I've never had better," she said between swallows. "What kind of bird is this?"

"Grouse. They're plentiful around here."

"Never thought to eat one." She picked up a carrot and bit into it, enjoying the taste of the roasted vegetable. "You're pretty good at surviving off the land."

He laughed. "I've been in these mountains quite a few years, Kathryn. If I don't know my way around by now, I'd have a problem."

She selected a potato and bit into it. "Really? As in living here?" She'd had the feeling that he spent a lot of time alone but couldn't put her finger on the exact reason why she felt that way. "Most of this land is privately held."

He nodded. "As in living here, you might say. But don't worry. I'm no squatter like those two good old boys you met last night. Eighty-five hundred acres of these mountains belong to the *Tlvdatsi* clan, a tribe of the Cherokee Nation."

Kathryn swallowed the last few bites of her potato. She didn't recognize a couple of the words he'd spoken, obviously part of his native language. "I didn't know. So that's what you meant when you said those men don't come here."

He answered quietly, "Yeah. We guard our perimeters pretty fiercely. No outsiders are allowed here."

She chewed thoughtfully, then swallowed. "Guess I was about to stumble in on you."

He nodded. "I have to admit we've been watching your people pretty closely."

A smile tugged at one corner of her mouth. "Wanted to know what we were up to, eh?"

Joseph spread his hands palm up. "Actually, yes."

Kathryn poured a splash of water into the cup and drank. "I'm with the Wildlife Resources Commission. I'm a wildlife ecologist."

Relief instantly colored his features. He reached up and pushed a stray lock of hair away from her face. "Care to tell me what your people are doing here or is it top secret?"

His gesture of understanding settled the brief awkwardness between them. Kathryn's pulse set to racing all over again. Each time he touched her it got harder and harder to fight off the urge to make love to him all over again.

She took a breath and her heart eased its thudding. "No secret at all. As you probably already know, your tract of land closely borders that of the South Mountains State Park."

He nodded. "That's a given. Go on."

"Much of the parkland is undeveloped. And many of the private owners whose land abuts the park are also interested in preserving the land for future generations. I would imagine your tribe is also interested in preserving its holdings."

"We are," he interjected, his voice tight with suspicion. He still didn't completely trust her presence. "Go on."

She did. "However, one significant tract of land has come up on the market recently—and it's caught the interest of a developer who's eyeing the possibility of building a vacation resort. The Wildlife Resources Commission is moving to block purchase of the land."

Clearly disturbed by her words, Joseph ran his fingers

246 / Devyn Quinn

through his hair, exhaling a long stream of air. "Damn. That's just what we don't need or want."

Kathryn cleared her throat, forcing herself to spit out the rest. "I know, but the news isn't getting better. We're losing a significant amount of our grant money due to budgetary cuts in federal programs. We'd hoped to have the money to partner with a private buyer, but it doesn't look like we'll get it."

Her words put Joseph Clawfoot on edge. Clearly not liking the idea of civilization moving closer to land that had already been yanked away from under the feet of his people once, he visibly struggled for calm. "Not a prayer, huh?"

Kathryn licked her lips, suddenly dry from the tension building inside her. "There's one chance to block it, and it's already hanging on a wing and a prayer. About six weeks ago, word filtered out that a cougar had been shot and wounded outside Connelly Springs. They're saying it was someone's pet, turned out to the wild or escaped."

His jaw tightened. "I heard."

"That's why we're here. If we can prove wild cougars have returned to this area, we can block the sale of the land for commercial development, have it declared a federal preserve for the animal." Her life's work was devoted to maintaining the ecosystem that would allow nature to thrive unimpeded by man's invasion. Too many species had already been irrevocably destroyed by the heavy tread of civilization.

Joseph Clawfoot looked thoughtful for a moment. By the expression on his face, a lot of things were going through his mind at once. None of it looked good or encouraging.

Finally, he drew a breath and spoke. "I think I can help you prove the cougar has returned to these mountains," he said slowly, as if carefully weighing every word. "It's something my, uh, people, are intimately connected with."

The eye-to-eye impact of his gaze sent a hot tremor through her. "Can you?"

He nodded and leaned closer. "It's something we show very few outsiders, Kathryn, but one I feel is vital you know about. Once you see for yourself, you'll know why this land and its resources are sacred to my people."

Excited by his confession, Kathryn felt her breath rattle tremulously. "Are you telling me there are wild cougars here?"

Joseph Clawfoot unspooled a slow, intimate grin that slammed into her gut like a fist. His bandit's smile and incredible good looks rolled all over her female senses, drenching her in nervous perspiration.

Standing up, he stretched like a lazy feline. "I'm not only telling you, Kathryn. I can show you where they are." He glanced down at his naked body. "That is, as soon as I get dressed. Sometimes I forget I'm just dressed in plain old skin."

Any physical lag she'd felt earlier instantly vanished. The sheer grandeur of his masculine presence threatened to overwhelm her. Her hands started to tremble. She clenched them together in her lap. Like a caveman who'd conked her over the head and dragged her to his cave, he'd somehow grabbed on to her most primal instinct to be conquered and possessed. If he wanted to walk around buck-naked all day, that would be fine with her. For now she was learning something new: it was possible to go drenching wet just watching a man get dressed.

Walking to a far corner of the cave, he retrieved a leather knapsack. Traipsing through the mountains, however, required something a little tougher than a bare ass and unshod feet. He pulled out a pair of well-worn blue jeans, stepping into and pulling them up to cover his well-muscled thighs. A dark gray T-shirt with the sleeves cut out followed. After pulling it over his head, he tucked it neatly into his jeans.

The T-shirt's logo belonged to some Goth band she'd never heard of.

Kathryn's brows rose. "Now there's an oxymoron. An Indian in a heavy metal T-shirt."

Joseph grinned and put on a folded red and black bandana that doubled as a headband. Between the fall of shiny black hair brushing his shoulders and the tribal tattoos inked into his skin, he looked every bit the hard-core rebel outlaw. Taking names and kicking ass definitely wouldn't be a problem for this man.

"I never said I was a fucking savage, Kathryn. I may be reservation born, but I've got the white man's education."

She cast her eyes down, clearing her throat. "Sorry. That came out totally wrong."

Joseph sat down to put on his shoes, a pair of black leather steel-toed cowboy boots. "I get what you're saying. I learned a long time ago the only way for an Indian to get around in this world is to know how it works." He shrugged. "Not knocking it. That's just the way things operate, you know. The inability to adapt means extinction. It's been that way since the beginning of time."

Scowling at the picture he presented, Kathryn climbed to her feet. "Guess the world will keep right on fucking us all over until the day we die."

Joseph's intimate gaze raked her right back, his eyes glinting with all-male glee. What he was thinking about was sexual, pure and simple. Dark eyes narrowed with amusement. "Guess we'll have to keep on fucking right back and breed ourselves back into the majority."

His hint kick-started Kathryn's heart all over again. Desire bubbled low in her belly, wet warmth trickling between her thighs. It was easy to remember the way their bodies had twined together, the pressing heat of his cock filling every inch of her. If they'd had more time, she might have considered picking up the sexually charged gauntlet and showing him a thing or two about nature.

She pulled a deep breath to clear her head. *Not now.*

That was very hard to do. She couldn't decide what she wanted more. To rip off Joseph's clothes and have sex with him right there, or see actual proof of the cougars that he'd promised to show her.

Disposing of the leftover food, Joseph poured a bucket filled with sand over the fire to safely extinguish the flames. "That will take care of that. No telling when we'll get back this way."

Kathryn tucked her fantasies away for later replay. *Live replay*, she hoped. "Then you're not living here?"

He shook his head. "This is just a hidey-hole I use when I get caught too far from home." He jerked a thumb toward the mouth of the cave. "The tribe has a settlement about eight miles away. It's a little bit more hospitable. Just couldn't make it there last night because of the weather. Now that it's clear, we'll be there in no time."

Kathryn hesitated. "I really should make contact with the team to let them know the change in destination. They think I'm headed back to camp. And I know they'll want to be in on this."

He considered her words. "How is it you ended up separated from them to begin with?"

She laughed and shook her head. "It's stupid, really. My team partner, Gerald, and I decided to widen the search perimeters by splitting up. The plan was to meet in a couple of hours and get back before sunset."

"I take it that plan didn't work out?"

Here was the part where she decided to lie. "The plan would have worked out fine . . . if not for the three bears. They sent me scurrying off trail and I got lost. I wasn't very worried, though, since I had the walkie and a compass. Walking north will get me back to base. I would have made it if the storm hadn't blown in."

"Most likely."

Her mind set to ticking. "If we head out now, we can reach base by late afternoon. How far away did you say your tribe's settlement was?"

Frowning, Joseph shook his head. "I'm not offering to take

everyone, Kathryn. I'll take you—alone. No one else. That's the condition. If you want to see cougar, you'll come with me now. If not, I can take you back to your people and then go back to mine."

She stared at him, mind momentarily blanking. "What?"

"You heard me," he said, then repeated. "I'll take you. Just you."

Hearing his ultimatum, Kathryn's heart rate bumped up ten notches. His conditions put her between a rock and a hard place. If she didn't make contact with her team soon, they'd send out a search party. But if she did make contact, she might lose the chance to make the discovery that would take her career to a whole new level.

She exhaled in frustration. "You're putting me in a really difficult position," she said quietly. "I can't run off chasing shadows."

Joseph's gaze narrowed, giving his dark eyes a distinctly feline cast. "I understand you have people to answer to, Kathryn. I do, too. You have to understand that the cougar is a sacred animal to my people. On our land we guard it fiercely. We will sacrifice our lives to keep its secrets."

Throwing her hands up in the air, Kathryn tried a different tack. "You say there are cougars here, and I'm willing to believe you. But believing isn't documentation—and with no documentation, there's no reason for development not to go forward."

A few steps bridged the distance separating them.

Standing like a tower, he stared down at her defiantly. "Just you, Kathryn." His hands reached out and wrapped around her upper arms and pulled her closer. His head dipped, brushing her ear. "I'm willing to take you—an outsider—into our world because I believe you can help us."

The space between the rock and the hard place narrowed,

blocking her in from all sides. Tension rolled between them in thick waves. "I guess I haven't got a choice."

He relaxed his grip, then let her go and stepped back. "I know this is hard, but I have to ask that you trust me."

Walking to the rear of the cave, Joseph strapped a bowie knife on his hip and picked up the hunting rifle, propped unseen in one shadowy corner. He hitched his knapsack over his back.

Rifle in hand, he winked. "Are you ready for the adventure of a lifetime?"

5

The hike through eight miles of trees and undergrowth so thick it could barely be penetrated on foot had taken every bit of stamina Kathryn possessed. She'd been on some hairy explorations in her time, but she'd never gone this far inside the old growth forests. Her shoulders, back, and legs ached. Muscles she didn't know she had screamed with tension and fatigue.

Hours passed with little conversation exchanged between them. Joseph Clawfoot clearly wasn't a talker. During their trek, he'd kept his attention on barely discernable trails, ones he obviously knew like the back of his hand. Using no compass, no map, and only landmarks he knew, he'd navigated the dense woods the way other people would city streets.

Just as Kathryn had convinced herself Joseph was yanking her leg and then some, they finally broke free of the grip of trees that had surrounded them through mile after mile.

Her eyes widened as a gasp broke from her lips. The Garden of Eden unexpectedly burst to brilliant life right before her eyes, a little slice of heaven on earth. Water gushed over the edge of the mountain, millions of gallons pounding the jagged rocks below. Cutting through a gorge that had taken centuries to carve, a veil of liquid silver caressed the sides of steep boulders.

Captivating the senses with the fluid beauty of its power, the waterfall thrilled even as it snatched the breath away. A variety of wildflowers were in full bloom, including jack-in-the-pulpit, lady slipper, and delicate yellow sunflowers.

Kathryn could only gape. The waterfall was magnificent, at least a hundred feet high. Maybe more. She propped her fallen jaw back into place. "My God, it's gorgeous." All her earlier misgivings evaporated.

Sliding a hand across her back, Joseph grinned down at her. "I know you had your doubts, but this is it."

Kathryn welcomed his touch, the first intimate gesture between them since departing the cave. She grinned, tilting back her head to look up at him. "Wow. I knew there was a lot of undiscovered beauty in these mountains, but this is the most wonderful place I've seen."

"You like it?"

"Yes." She laughed and wiped her sweaty brow, thankful the trek had come to its end. Her legs felt like stumps. Her feet seemed to have fallen off ages ago. "It was definitely worth the trouble to get here. Does it have a name?"

He led her closer to the waterfall. Droplets from the powerful stream of icy water misted the air. "We call it *invigati ama,* the tall water."

"Tall water," she repeated. "Makes sense."

Joseph laughed. "Pretty much says what it is, I guess." He pointed away from the falls. "And there's home. I think you'll find it a little more comfortable than a hole in the side of a mountain."

Kathryn squinted into the sun. It took a moment to find the settlement nestled at the base of the mountain, constructed in such a way as to seem a part of the foundation of the rock wall instead of an invasive blight. The sturdy cabins and adjoining corrals looked as if they had stood since the days of the pioneers.

"Very nice," she murmured.

"This is part of our main site. The rest of our settlement is on the other side of the gorge. All in all, we have about seventy members."

"Ah, impressive. And you're really the chief?" Tumbling around with the head honcho didn't hurt any girl's feelings.

He nodded. "Yes. The clan always votes, but I make the final call."

"So bringing me here was your decision?"

Joseph's intelligent gaze took on a thoughtful cast. She almost heard his mind working, carefully putting every word in place. His people were naturally cautious of outsiders. Trust wasn't easily given. It had to be earned. "We've been watching your group since it arrived in the area."

"You told me."

"And it wasn't exactly an accident that we happened to be nearby when the Barnett brothers attacked you."

Kathryn's brow crinkled. "Your men were following me?" Her quiet question brooked no denial.

Joseph's mouth twitched up into a rueful grin. He had no option but to continue his confession. "Just you." His eyes were filled with unflinching honesty. "We'd already decided you were the one we needed to, ah, make contact with."

"So you specifically picked me out of the group?"

"Yes."

She considered a minute, then shrugged. "I don't know whether to feel creeped out about the stalking or honored I made the cut with a tribe of wild Indians."

Joseph released a rich chuckle that sent a whisper of desire across the back of her neck and tied her insides into knots. "It's not that you made the cut with the clan, Kathryn. We're not exactly a democracy."

She gave a wry smile. "Oh? Then how does voting work around here?"

Grinning wide, he reached out and pulled her close against him, so close that she could feel the erection beginning to rise against the front of his jeans. "You made the cut with me. As chief, I have the final decision who we invite into our world. Not just any outsider is allowed to see inside our society. You're not like the rest of your group. You belong here, and they don't."

Caught in his hold, Kathryn stared up at him. Deep inside she knew this kind of—was it love? lust?—came to a person once in a lifetime. She'd barely known him a single day, yet being in his arms felt so right, so absolutely perfect. How many people actually found a companion they could hold onto and love forever?

She flushed hot. Recent events were still a crazy whirl in her mind. Everything was so jumbled that she could barely tell up from down. Just a day ago she'd been worried how some stupid budget cuts might affect her job. Life really had a way of changing on a dime. "Wow. You really know how to make a girl feel wanted."

Joseph's hips nudged hers. "Let me get you into that cabin and I'll be glad to show you how much you are wanted, Kathryn." As if to add an extra enticement, he added, "There's running water, if you don't mind an old-fashioned pump, and a wood-burning stove to heat it. It's also got a bed, one with a nice, soft feather mattress."

"I've never slept on a feather bed." Memories of their earlier lovemaking flooded her mind. Visions of his strong, muscular body pressed against hers sending a thrill down her spine all over again.

He grinned wider. "Then you're in for a treat." His hands settled on her waist and slid around to her back. His chest was a wall of cobbled muscles. "I've been dying to hold you since we left the cave."

"Have you?"

An insistent bulge nudged through his jeans. "I think my body speaks for itself."

Kathryn laughed and playfully broke out of his hold. "And I think my body stinks for itself. Before you lay another hand on me, I need a good wash. I've smelled myself for hours."

His nostrils flared suggestively. "Nothing more enticing than the smell of a female in heat."

She cocked her head. "Is that how I smell to you?"

"You do." His gaze, fixed on her body, glittered like chips of smoky obsidian under the unrelenting sun.

"You're just going to have to give a lady a minute to freshen up." Hating the feel of sweat-beaded skin, Kathryn slid out of her jacket, much too heavy now that they'd left the cool overgrowth of the forest. Letting it drop to the ground, she walked to the edge of the pool and knelt. The water was so clear she could see its rocky depth. Tiny minnows and other small fish darted back and forth.

She dipped a hand into the water, soaking in the feel of its icy temperature. It felt wonderful against her hot, sweaty skin. "God, I'm filthy."

She untied the knot around her waist and slipped off her torn shirt. Her sport bra provided a decent amount of coverage.

Cupping her hands together, she bent over and splashed water onto her face. It felt like every insect in the forest had taken a bite out of her skin. She'd scratched herself red and raw from all the itchy attacks she'd taken from gnats and mosquitoes.

"Feel better?"

Kathryn eyed the waterfall. "I will, as soon as I get a bath."

She plopped down on her butt and plucked the laces of her heavy hiking books. Her swollen feet felt heavy as lead weights. "God, it feels good to get them off." She plucked off her socks and wiggled her toes. "Ah, freedom." She quickly shimmied out of her jeans. Showing some remnant of modesty, she kept her white cotton panties on. The ensemble was no more offensive than an actual swimsuit.

Kathryn stepped forward, easing experimentally into the water until it reached her knees. It was brisk, icy. To lessen the shock, she dunked herself quickly under the water. She came up spluttering, wiping dripping water out of her eyes. "God, that's cold, but feels so good."

She went in deeper until the water reached her waist. The pebbles under her feet were round and smooth, a little slippery. Noticing that he still stood on the edge of the bank, she made a "come here" gesture. "Join me?"

Joseph readjusted the knapsack and rifle riding high on his shoulders. "That water's too damn cold for this Indian," he said. "I think I'll head to the cabin and put away my gear. I'll be back in a few."

She waved him off. "Okay."

Left alone, Kathryn swam over to the waterfall. The pounding water had flattened and smoothed the rocks at its base, forming a perfect shelf under the spray. Hefting herself onto the wide ledge, she stood under it. Icy cold water pummeled her from head to toe. She rubbed her arms, shoulders, abdomen, and legs briskly, scrubbing away the heavy film of sweat and trail dust mucking her skin and underclothing.

Teeth chattering, but squeaky clean, Kathryn dove off the ledge. She knifed through the water, making clean, strong strokes toward shore.

Joseph waited for her at the edge of the water. Grinning, he held a blue mass in one hand.

Clearing the water out of her eyes, Kathryn smiled. "Just

what I needed." She scrambled up out of the water to claim her well-earned prize.

Handing over the towel without a word, Joseph stared at her, clearly mesmerized by the sight. "A minute ago I was hoping you'd take those things off." He swallowed thickly. "Now I'm glad you left them on." His gaze was hot enough to set fire to the countryside.

She glanced down. "Oh, my." The tips of her nipples poked through her wet bra, hard and ripe as little buds.

By the look in his eyes, bath time was definitely over. Joseph surveyed her body, snugly embraced but barely hidden by her nearly transparent undergarments.

Without giving her a chance to say another word, he picked her up. "The sight of you is enough to give a man an instant hard-on."

Arms and legs automatically circling his girth, Kathryn groaned into the soft hollow between his neck and shoulders. The casual strength he displayed without a second thought amazed her.

She shivered, but not from the cold. Her soft curves molded perfectly to his hard angles. His hot skin smelled of male musk and sweat, a totally enticing aroma.

Feeling the pressure of his erection pressing against the front of his jeans, she tightened her thighs around his hips. The combination of wet panties and warm denim set her clit to demanding more creative stimulation. "Guess I'll have to handle this one."

Big hands slid down to cup her ass, heft her higher. "I'd hoped you'd say that," he murmured in her ear. "It's been too long since I last took you." His mouth brushed against hers in a slow tease. Tongue sliding past the seam of her lips, he swept in for a slow, gentle exploration.

Kathryn moaned into his mouth, parrying the thrust of his tongue with her own. A slow delicious curl of heat seeped into her core. Her body was on fire again, and all it took was a simple touch. Hormones shifting back into overdrive, she wanted nothing more than to drag him to bed and make love to him for the rest of the afternoon.

"I could take you now if you weren't so damn overdressed," he murmured against her mouth in a husky voice.

Imagine that. He considered a bra and panties overdressing!

Pulse pounding in her ears, Kathryn flexed her thighs around him. "I guess I'll have to get out of these skimpy clothes then." Her voice had a muffled sound, the tones of a woman in sexual thrall.

Joseph quickly set her feet back on the ground and stepped away. "Easier done than said." Looking her over from head to foot, his fingers flexed like a kid's over a Christmas package, eager to open it and get to the gift inside.

Gazing up at him, Kathryn silently reached for the edges of her sport bra. Her gut clenched with need. She pulled in a breath. Damn. All it took was a single look from him to turn her knees to wobbly jelly.

He caught her wrists in a light grip. "Let me," he said roughly. "I want to undress you."

She gulped. "Okay." She let her hands drop. The gleam of fire in his eyes matched the flames threatening to incinerate her inside.

Eyes dark and stormy with need, Joseph fingered the wide straps across her shoulders. "There's nothing I love more than undressing a woman," he admitted. "And I'll admit it's been a hell of a long time since I've gotten to do that."

Her brows rose. "Oh? How long has it been, if I may ask?"

A world of pain flashed briefly behind his gaze, a flicker that came and went as quickly as summer lightning.

"Let's just say it's been too long, babe." His fingers slid lower, tracing the edges sculpting her breasts into perfectly round mounds. Gaze simmering with need, his whole body quivered. "Much too damn long." His voice came out rough with inner tension.

Kathryn trembled under his electrifying touch but couldn't tear her gaze away from his. She didn't want to. Her heart flipped over with the power behind his words. Her pulse was a rebel, taking off in its own direction. Arousal blazed to life, and the first heated trickle of desire flooded the crotch of her already-damp panties. Her wet bra clung to hard, jutting nipples. Her clit ached at the memory of what his lips could do when creatively applied.

Whatever he's offering, I want it.

In her wildest dreams, Kathryn never could have hoped to meet a man like Joseph Clawfoot. His body fit so well with hers it almost felt like they'd been created for each other.

She wanted him to touch her all over, explore her most secret places with his mouth and hands before laying her down, spreading her thighs, and hammering her sex like a bed of nails.

Mouth going bone dry, need was molten lava pouring through her veins. "I guess you're doing your best to catch up. . . ."

Joseph grinned self-mockingly. "You could say that," he chuckled. "But I'd rather believe it's the absolutely stunning woman standing in front of me that's driving me wild." He dragged one strap off her shoulder, freeing her left breast. Bared to the warm sunshine her nipple peaked, a hard little berry, all ripe and tasty.

He bent, capturing the rosy tip with his mouth. He suckled with starved intensity. With thumb and forefinger, he teased her other taut peak through the material, plucking and flicking the erect nubbin.

Breathless, throbbing, a mass of hot yearning, she shivered as his warm tongue painted her nipple. Ah, it felt so good. *Heavenly, luminous delight.*

Threading her fingers through his thick hair, she felt her eyes drift shut in ecstasy. "I want you, too. . . ."

6

Fearing her knees would buckle under her, Kathryn caught hold of his broad shoulders. She tried to ignore the feel of his hard planes pressed against her or she might have climaxed right on the spot. Hard to do, but she didn't want to come early and spoil everything. She intended to enjoy his every stroke, every caress, every lick and bite.

Even as Joseph teased her nipples, he was guiding her down to the blanket he'd spread out on the soft grass. She was on her back before she quite knew how he had managed to get her there. Pressed under him, she felt every breath he took, every beat of his heart.

It couldn't have been any better if she'd concocted the fantasy herself.

Joseph lifted his head, flashing a savage's smile. He circled her areola with the tip of a finger. "Beautiful." The small tip grew harder, pinker.

Kathryn grimaced. "Small."

Joseph laughed and looked at her, all seriousness. "More than a mouthful is a waste, Kathryn. They're perfect, round like peaches." He tugged her bra up and over her head, discarding it.

Both breasts bare now, she stared at him skeptically. "I've always wanted more."

"Trust me when I say you don't need a smidge more." Catching one bud between two fingers, he softly pinched. "They turn me on, and that makes them enough."

A delicious sizzle sped up her spine. Her hands gripped his shoulders until her fingernails bit through his T-shirt and into his hard flesh. "I think you're just flattering me to fuck me."

He snorted inelegantly. "If you prefer, I can fuck you without flattery." Using just the right amount of gentle pressure, he tweaked her nipple again. "Though I thought women liked that."

Her insides kinked up ever tighter. "I don't care how you fuck me, as long as you do." She locked her arms around his neck as if daring him to get away.

He treated her to another lazy smile. The predator in him permeated her. The way he embraced her said that he'd claimed her as his woman, and would brook no argument. "I intend to have you every which way, and then some." One of his hands slipped between her thighs, rubbing against the crotch of her panties.

A whoosh of air escaped her. "Oh, goodness!" She trembled even at his simplest touch, the flares of heat inside her going off like a Fourth of July firework display.

"Ain't no goodness in it," he drawled, using the tips of his finger to draw mesmerizing circles around her clit. The pressure of his finger gliding against the material that in turn glided against her sex sent white-hot darts of fire straight to the tips of her toes.

"Oh, God. . . . This is too good." Hips bucking upward against his hand, Kathryn felt her head go all swimmy with erotic dizziness. His slow, sexy tease was putting an edge on a desire that was already threatening to flame out of control. The pressure of his fingers worked magic against her hungry clit. The idea of his cock taking the place of his fingers was enough to make her shudder. She was close to the edge of losing control.

So much for self-control, she thought wryly.

The yearning inside was beginning to build toward unbearable. Her hands roamed. The muscles of his abdomen rippled. "You'd better stop or I'm going to come," she warned raggedly.

Dark eyes probed hers. His clever fingers worked harder, circling around her clit faster. "That's what I'm aiming for, babe."

Lids shuddering, Kathryn held on to her sanity and gritted her teeth. The thrill of his touch burned its way up her spine, searing through the base of her skull, excruciating and blissful.

Submerged on the edge of a fierce climax, she wriggled to ease the pressure against her crotch. "Not yet," she gasped, barely able to string her words together coherently. "I want to come when you're inside me." She craved his thrusts, hungered to feel his hips stabbing his cock into her sex.

He let out a frustrated rush of air. "You sure?" The edge in his tone was unmistakable.

Kathryn opened her eyes and peered at his shadowed face. The way he could make her tremble with a simple look and touch defied all logic.

Gazing into his dark, cat-narrowed eyes, she felt her heart miss a beat. Lust wasn't the only thing coalescing between them. Yet she dared not to think what it might be. *Not yet,* she warned herself. *Just enjoy it for what it is.*

Joseph clearly was.

Trapped inside his tight jeans, his erection strained against her, pulsing harder and harder with each passing second. Every brush of his body against hers sent fresh shocks all the way to her toes.

She swallowed the thick lump threatening to cut off her oxygen. "Yeah," she said, then added, "But you're kind of overdressed for the occasion."

"Damn." Broad shoulders flexing, Joseph pulled away, cursing a string of unfamiliar words under his breath. "I always knew clothes were more a hindrance than help."

Catching the edges, he flicked his T-shirt over his head. His boots and jeans followed.

Drawing in a quick breath, Kathryn shivered beside him. God, the man was poetry in motion. She'd seen him naked in the cave, but never so up close, every inch of his coppery skin exposed under bright sunlight. He didn't seem to have a single flaw.

Her gaze traced every hard line, trekking lower. Anticipation built in her gut when her vision settled at his narrow waist. Harder than an iron bar, his cock was the eighth wonder of the world.

Joseph wrapped his fingers around his prize, stroking up and down its length with sensuous intent. He didn't appear one bit ashamed or inhibited about pleasuring himself.

Kathryn's jaw dropped at his erotic assault on her visual senses. Her fascinated gaze watched his hand deliver stroke after long, slow stroke. Looking at him was like looking at a piece of art. No wonder the great masters cast their most awesome nudes in stone.

A monument should be built to glorify that erection. A giddy, totally wild image flashed across her mind's screen. She knew exactly how she'd design the testimonial to his physical attribute. The round, smooth head looked as delectable as a piece of sun-ripened fruit.

Teeth nibbling the pillow of her bottom lip, she imagined

what it would feel like to slide her lips over his shaft. "That looks delicious."

Corded bicep bulging, he slid his hand up, then down. Watching him touch himself was as seductive as it was mesmerizing. Gazing down at her through heavy-lidded eyes, his lips curled into a lazy smile. "Want some?"

Driven to the brink by his erotic tease, Kathryn wasted no time rolling over onto her stomach. "Definitely."

Propping herself up on her elbows, she studied the powerful erection he presented. Surrounded by a nest of dark curls, his long, powerful erection arced up toward his cobbled abdomen. Licorice thick veins corded its length, and a single droplet of pre-cum glistened at its cherry-ripe tip.

Her hand replaced his. She stuck out her tongue, sampling the clear fluid at the top. Salty, but not unpleasant.

A choked gasp escaped him.

Kathryn swirled her tongue over the tight crown, then traced the seam between head and stalk. "Feel good?" Another bead of moisture leaked from the tip. She licked it away.

Joseph's entire body trembled. "More than good," came the husky reply. He swallowed, trying to hold on to his composure. By the look on his strained features it was a battle he was close to losing.

She smiled up at him. "A little payback." Opening her mouth, she swooped down over the blushing head of his cock like a hawk taking a rabbit.

Groaning helplessly, Joseph tangled his thick fingers into her damp curls, attempting to guide her head in a slow, steady rhythm. His abdomen brushed her forehead, his hips easing his weight forward. He was taking care not to push too hard or too deep down her throat, letting her set the pace.

Kathryn scraped his shaft gently with her teeth. He'd pleasured her in so many ways that she wanted to return the favor. Her saliva created a slippery path for her mouth and jacking palm. As she pleased him, the hot rise of arousal simultaneously swept through her own body. Her breasts ached even as her clit swelled with carnal eagerness.

Her free hand moved lower, cupping him. She palmed his balls, heavy and full with his seed. "Mmm." She squeezed lightly, fondling the sensitive sac. She wanted to take him to that razor's edge where climax threatened but remained just out of reach. The pressure in his balls surged. He was seconds away from spilling

He moaned in a tone of pleasant surprise at the same time a long shiver tore through his entire body. His cock jerked, his heart pounding heavily as more blood rushed into his loins. He thrust into her mouth a final time, then quickly pulled away. "Keep that up and I'll lose it," he warned.

Lips chafed by his sex, she smiled up at him in triumph. "Wouldn't want that to happen."

Joseph rolled her over. He quirked a threatening brow. "You're about to learn the true meaning of getting paid back, my dear." Switching their positions, he scooted lower, dropping a trail of heated kisses across her breastbone and stomach. A stab of his wet tongue penetrated her vulnerable navel. "I love the taste."

Kathryn sucked in a sharp lungful of air. "Of sweat and belly button lint?" she teased.

Joseph nipped the soft skin beneath. His darkened gaze connected with hers. "Best I've ever tasted." His fingers slid into the band of her panties. "Now let's see about getting these off you."

Settling onto his knees between her spread legs, he licked his lips like a hungry coyote. Gaze lit with delight, he slid his palms up her thighs. His hands came to rest on her hips. "I've been waiting to see these panties come down." His fingers curled into the elastic.

Kathryn raised her hips to help him when he slipped her

panties down. The elastic rolled against her hips and thighs, down past her knees, then passing her ankles. He'd barely gotten her underwear off and already her strain was growing, pulling the blood from her head and rushing it straight to her eager clit.

He flicked the flimsy garment aside like a piece of candy floss. Skimming his hands up the insides of her thighs, he caught her behind the knees and lifted her legs, spreading her wide. Studying her most private part, his gaze glittered with a feral and wanton fierceness.

Totally exposed, Kathryn felt heat creeping up toward her cheeks. Her nipples jutted, hard and pink as pencil erasers. Anticipating what he was about to do, her pulse kicked into high gear. Lust pulled at her core with silken hands. "Like what you see?"

Rumbling a hungry sound, emotion worked his throat. "Very much."

Kathryn guided her legs over his thighs, curling her feet around his perfect ass. "Then do what comes naturally."

His hands swept over her abdomen, cupping both her breasts in his hands. His fingers closed around her nipples, gently tugging them into hard little points. "You're everything I ever imagined you'd be, Kathryn."

"You talk like you knew I'd come."

Bending forward, Joseph squeezed her breasts. The pads of his thumbs brushed back and forth over her sensitized nipples. Long black hair fanned around his face like the spread of a raven's wings. His cock pulsed against the soft nest of her belly, but he made no move to enter her. His gaze searched hers. "All of us are meant to find our mates. You're mine."

Heart thudding in her chest, she looked at him, breathless. "How do you know?"

His hands slid around to the small of her back, arching her body upward. His tongue snaked out, briefly tracing one pink tip. "I know it the way I know the sun will rise tomorrow. It just is." His mouth settled around the peak, suckling deeply.

Control drizzled through her fingers.

Kathryn lifted her hips off the ground. Slipping a hand between their bodies, her fingers found and curled around his massive erection. She jacked her hand up and down the length of him, enjoying the feel of the hot, velvety flesh. She wanted him so badly that she shook.

Breath coming in short ragged bursts, Joseph moaned in the soft hollow between her breasts. "Once I get in you, I don't know how long I'll last."

Hardly able to wait another second to have him, Kathryn guided his penis toward her creaming sex. Her heels pressed against his ass, urging his hips toward hers. "I don't care, as long as you're inside me."

He surrendered without protest. The wide, smooth crown of his cock slid through her labia like a hot knife through creamy butter.

Kathryn shuddered and a moan slipped from her throat. "Oh, yess. . . ." Her words came out almost unintelligible, strangled with need.

Settling his hands on either side of her shoulders, Joseph grinned down at her. He speared his hips into hers, knifing in every inch he had. "Is this what you wanted, Kathryn?" he teased behind a pirate's smile.

Kathryn gasped and writhed against him. "Oh, hell, yes." Hands settling on his wide shoulders, she dug her fingers deeply into his skin. Aching and pulsing around him, every muscle in her body throbbed with tremors of pleasure. "It's exactly what I wanted."

Joseph retreated, pulling back briefly. "I knew you were to be mine the moment I saw you," he confessed. Gazing into her eyes, he slowly slid back in.

Biting her lower lip, she arched her back in an attempt to

take him even deeper. "I wanted you, too." Gazing up at him, her heart tightened in her chest. The look in his eyes was a mix of heated desire and haunting uncertainty, as though he wasn't quite sure that he'd finally managed to find the intangible wraith that had always eluded his grasp.

With a slow deliberation, Joseph lowered his mouth to hers. This time his kiss was slower, gentler. He took his time, using his lips and tongue to tease hers, each long, slow kiss matching the exquisite silken glide of his cock.

Time slid away, ceasing to exist. No more words were needed. Their bodies spoke for them, using a language harkening back to a more primitive, primal time. They communicated with their bodies, each perfectly understanding the other.

Mind clouded with passion, Kathryn wasn't exactly sure when control deserted them. With every gliding motion of his thighs against hers, he penetrated fuller and deeper inside her. The head of his cock was smooth, but with every plunge she felt the bulging ridges circling his erection. The driving force behind the friction was fabulously unbearable.

Suddenly Joseph wasn't so slow or gentle. He was lost, oblivious to everything but the grip of pleasure spurring him on. Face twisting with burning ecstasy, he bucked his hips against hers. His cock pummeled, driving her faster, higher, hotter, harder toward climax.

Kathryn gritted her teeth and held on. Hot muscle pulsed beneath her fingertips. Fuse lit, she was going to lose it any second now, explode like a rigged bundle of dynamite. Her grip dug into the hard slabs of his back, her nails pulling long trenches in his skin. This was what she'd always needed, craved, moments of intense release, the abandonment of inhibition to give into the lusts that had always driven her.

The delivery of pain sent him over the edge.

Bellowing like a wild animal, Joseph thrust up into her again, lifting her body off the ground before bringing her down and unleashing the very pulse of his soul inside her. His cock surged, spewing liquid fire. "Come for me, Kathryn." Raw, naked lust roughened his voice. "Let me feel that beautiful cunt drink in its pleasure."

Lost in the anguish of pure bliss, Kathryn felt every nerve in her body explode. A rising flood of tyrant sounds and sensations engulfed her, threatening to sweep her away like a hurricane making landfall.

She arched into him, her senses filled with the crescendo of sonic vibrations speeding through her head like an out-of-control freight train. Dazzling sparks crackled through her veins, the rapturous sensations heating the blood in her veins past boiling to scalding.

Satisfaction had never been so damn painful.

Or enjoyable.

A hiss, a whisper, then the flickering fire extinguished itself.

The fast and furious pace slowed, then stopped completely. As quickly as it had begun, lovemaking ended. What felt like hours had, in reality, taken only minutes.

Relieving her of his weight, Joseph rolled over onto his back. Sprawled out on the warm grass, his coppery skin glistened with sweat. He panted from his recent exertions, his breath softly whistling in and out of his lungs.

"Damn, that was freaking intense."

Inner thighs still quivering, Kathryn sat up and pushed long strands of hair out of her face. She opened her mouth to add her impressions of their recent coupling, but no words came out. A flash of color caught her attention and she froze, hardly able to believe her eyes.

As her pulse dropped from normal to deceased, her gaze settled on a tawny red-brown animal with a long, slender body; broad, round head with erect, rounded ears; and long tail. It was huge, too, at least three times the size of any animal she'd ever seen in captivity.

Cougar.

As if disbelieving what she saw, she blinked, attempting to clear her sex-hazed vision. Her eyes snapped back open. Nope. The cougar was still there. No mistaking it, either.

The big cat had them squarely in its sights. Cougars didn't chase their prey. They stalked.

Kathryn's human instinct to flee kicked in. Panic tightening her chest, adrenaline surged through her veins. Only sheer force of will kept her rooted in her spot. Any quick, sudden movement could set the animal off with a vengeance. Getting away unscathed wasn't going to be easy. Two naked, vulnerable humans wouldn't have a chance against sharp teeth and claws.

Kathryn's heart pounded so fiercely she could barely form a coherent thought. She had to stay focused. Nothing in her wildlife training covered dealing with a ferocious cougar while having sex with a hot Indian.

Gaze fixed on the animal slinking across the clearing—heading straight for them—her hand settled on her lover's chest.

"Joe—" she whispered in a strangled tone. "I think we've got a problem. . . ."

7

Sprawled out on the blanket like a sloth in half a doze, Joseph Clawfoot opened one eye and rolled his head toward the cougar stalking the perimeter of the clearing.

"It's just my brother," he said between a lazy yawn and a stretch of his long limbs. He closed his eye, obviously intending to settle down and take a nice snooze in the sun.

Seeing the two people stretched out on the blanket like picnic morsels ready to be tasted, the cougar twitched its long tail and sneaked dangerously closer.

With its amber eyes narrowing, a series of low, threatening growls rolled up from deep inside the cougar's chest. Mouth opening, pink lips curled back to reveal the perfectly white, long, sharp fangs extending down from its upper jaw. The teeth protruding up from the lower jaw didn't look any less menacing. Those strong jaws and long canine teeth made it possible for cougars to kill their victims with one bite to the neck. And a twenty-foot leap between the cougar and its quarry wasn't impossible.

In other words, there wasn't any time to run.

Kathryn swallowed hard. Another minute, maybe two, and the cougar would be close enough to take a nip out of naked human flesh.

A single thought chilled her. *We're not going to make it.*

Snatching up the damp towel, Kathryn pressed it against her bare breasts. She shook Joseph harder, an Indian apparently unconcerned about being a cougar's snack.

"Listen," she hissed. "I don't believe that bullshit about cougars being sacred spirits and all animals are really your brothers under the fur or whatever you people tell yourselves when tripping out on peyote. This sucker's coming fast and he doesn't look friendly."

This time Joseph opened both eyes. And yawned again. His calm gaze connected with hers. "I'm telling you that's my brother."

The cougar suddenly picked up speed. Bounding across the clearing at top speed, it closed the distance between predator and prey in the space of seconds. At the last possible instant powerful muscles coiled and sprung.

As though gravity didn't exist in its world, the cougar leapt into the air. Its claws and teeth bared, a loud gut-wrenching scream tore out of its mouth. It landed squarely on Joseph, pinning him down under its enormous body.

Expecting to see the tearing of flesh and the rush of blood, Kathryn covered her eyes with both hands and shrieked. "Oh, my God!" The world around her spun alarmingly. Her entire body felt paralyzed.

She expected to hear screams of terror and pain.

Nothing.

Not a sound.

Drawing a deep breath, Kathryn dared to peek between her fingers. What she saw was enough to make her believe the world had fallen off its axis.

The cougar was not only not attacking, but it was playfully

274 / Devyn Quinn

head-butting Joseph the way a house cat would a favored owner. Its purr rippled through the silence like a steam engine running on crack.

He laughed. "Get off me you big oaf." Fingers twining into the cat's tawny fur, he tried to shove its massive bulk away. "You're crushing the hell out of my balls."

Relieving Joseph of its weight, the cougar fell over on one side. It rolled in the grass like a kitten, limbs akimbo and purring up a storm.

Kathryn lowered her hands in disbelief. Catching hold of her emotions, she struggled for calm. Having had a bit of fun, the cougar didn't appear viciously inclined. "Is it tame?"

A slow smile curled the corners of Joseph's mouth. "I wouldn't call my brother the tame one," he drawled. "But if that's what you want to believe, go for it. Right now he's just showing his ass." He eyed the gamboling animal. "I hope you're happy, asshole, scaring her like that."

She scowled at both. "You act like that cat understands you." Her eyes rolled. "Your brother, the cougar. Riiiight."

Joseph didn't blink. "I'm serious. Your eyes may see a cougar, but mine see my little brother, Jesse."

Kathryn shook her head. "Ho-kay. Have your fun." She looked at the cougar. "You might have warned me you had one here."

Joseph reached for his discarded clothes. "I've got several," he countered, pulling on his pants and zipping.

Her brows rose. "You're kidding."

"Not at all."

Kathryn scrambled after her bra and panties. The sun had dried her undergarments nicely. "This I've got to see."

Joseph looked up from putting on his boots. "Oh, you will." He glanced toward the cat. "Go ahead and show her, Jesse."

The cougar got up and sat on its haunches. Shafts of sunlight danced across its reddish-brown fur, creating a scattering of gold highlights across its head and back. Amber eyes narrowed. Then it vanished.

An almost exact replica of Joseph Clawfoot sat in its place; long black hair, brown eyes, deeply tanned skin—and naked as the day his mother birthed him.

Kathryn blinked, then blinked again. Even as her mind worked furiously to process what she'd seen, the neural pathways of her brain handling reason and logic were threatening to melt down from the overload of sheer disbelief. The metamorphosis had taken place between a blink, happening too fast for the human eye to even recognize and logically compute the change.

Her senses started to wobble. The sun was too hot, the air too dry. *I've completely lost my freaking mind and no one bothered to tell me.*

The naked Indian grinned and raised a hand in welcome. "Hi. I'm Jesse Clawfoot."

Kathryn's throat began to thicken. She gulped in an attempt to keep breathing. If she lost her breath now she would pass out. "Ah, hello." Her hand scrabbled toward Joseph's. Fingers tightening around his, she leaned over. "Please tell me I've been out in the sun too long and I'm suffering heat stroke."

Joseph squeezed back. "Well, you are a little red, Kathryn, so we do need to get you out of the sun soon." He jerked a thumb toward the man he called brother. "As for Jesse, he's going to apologize for sneaking up on us like that." He shot a glare toward the naked man. "Aren't you?"

Jesse Clawfoot shrugged and grinned some more. "Yeah, yeah, I'm sorry I scared her," he said. "But you deserve to have your ass whipped, bro. Here's the first female of our kind that we've seen in a long time, and you've already staked a claim. That's so totally bogus."

His words confused. "First female of your kind? What the hell is he saying?"

Joseph Clawfoot shot his brother a *drop-dead* glare. "I haven't had a chance to tell her."

"Because you were busy getting busy?" Jesse flipped the one-finger signal that told his brother exactly what he thought. "I saw you in action, bro. That was a heap of Big Chief you pounded the poor woman with."

Realizing that Jesse had seen everything she and Joseph had done—and then some—Kathryn pressed a palm to her mouth and tried to look like an innocent virgin instead of a wanton woman.

Noticing her discomfort, Jesse laughed disarmingly. "Don't sweat it, babe. If I had found you first, I'd have done my best to get those panties off you, too."

The fiery look of desire in his eyes lit her internal fuse all over again. She squirmed with need, her clit sitting up and taking notice of this second hunk of raw beefcake.

The fresh surge of arousal confused. Physical satisfaction appeared to be her only master as the lines between sense and control slowly eroded away. Her body seemed to have no problem dismissing her personal ethics from the equation. Too many years of repressing her natural instincts had taken its toll. It was like suddenly discovering her speeding car had no brakes.

Kathryn went ten shades redder. "Um, well," she started, then trailed off into embarrassed silence. She truly hadn't been able to help herself. Her libido had taken total control. If she kept up the carnal activities at this rate, she'd soon need a trip to *Nymphos Anonymous*.

Joseph Clawfoot glowered at his younger brother. "You're overstepping boundaries, Jess," he warned with a low growl. "Apologize to her. Now."

Jesse pulled a sullen pout. "Sorry."

"It's okay." Kathryn looked from one to the other. More than a little jealously was brewing here. Over her!

She shook her head. She didn't feel drugged. And the ache

between her thighs from the recent poundings Joseph had given her didn't exactly come off as the deluded fantasy of a dreaming mind.

Time to get some answers.

She drew in a breath. "Okay, guys. Can we cut the jealousy bullshit over who got what piece of me? I think I just saw a cougar turn into a man and I can't explain it. Therefore, I must be *nuckin' futs* or this is real."

Shooting a glance filled with warning daggers at his brother, Joseph sighed. "You aren't crazy, Kathryn. Jess really did shift from a cougar into his usual ugly self. Keeping that in mind, you may guess that I can, too."

A cougar. She'd just had wild, hot sex with a man who claimed he could shift his form from human to animal. Good grief! Would that be considered bestiality?

She shook her head. "I—I'm a little confused. . . ." Check that. She was a lot confused.

Joseph sighed. "The best way to convince you is to show you." His brown gaze fixed on hers. "Just watch."

For a moment nothing happened. Then the irises in his eyes began to stretch, long and narrow. At the same time the brown tint in his eyes faded to a pale amber shade. Seconds later, he vanished.

A lean, tawny cougar sat behind her. All that was left of Joseph were his clothes, piled in a messy heap. He'd apparently shifted right out of them.

"Holy shit!" Kathryn yelped, and scooted quickly away from the big cat. The change had taken place so quickly that she hadn't time to inhale a full breath before he'd vanished.

She looked at Jesse. He, too, had shifted back into the form of a cougar. The two big cats had her pinned between them.

Still in his cougar body, Joseph nudged her arm with his nose, the familiar gesture cats made when they wanted a scratch behind the ears.

278 / Devyn Quinn

Moving more than a little tentatively, Kathryn reached up and placed her fingers behind one furry ear. She scratched, working her nails into the skin.

The big cat nudged her over and settled its weight on her chest. A darker color began to seep back into its eyes, the narrowed irises growing ever wider and rounder. Tiny gold flecks glistened in the brown.

A second later Joseph Clawfoot was smiling down at her. His bare chest flattened her breasts. "Oh, I love it when you do that."

Hand still behind his ear, Kathryn looked up at the big Indian and felt her innards begin to twist all over again. She could almost swear she caught the split second when cat turned into man.

"Unbelievable." Hand dropping, she turned her head. Jesse Clawfoot was still in his cougar form.

Joseph reluctantly relieved her of his weight. "As much as I'd love to take advantage of your position, I really don't want to do it in front of that asshole I call brother." Dragging his fingers through his long hair, he looked down at the pile of clothing sitting beside him. "Damn it, now I'll have to get dressed again." He sighed and reached for his jeans.

Kathryn laughed and sat up. "I've always wanted to try a threesome," she teased, "but he's definitely going to have to shift first." She raised a brow toward Jesse. "But I'm not into eating pussy, if you know what I mean."

Hearing her words, Jesse immediately shifted. "At your service. Ready, willing, and very able."

Joseph frowned and immediately put the kibosh on his eagerness. "Keep your pecker in your hand a minute, little brother."

"Can't help myself," Jesse said, and then grinned. "The smell of her is driving me wild."

The desire to smile abruptly deserted her. This was the second time odor had been mentioned in regards to her presence among them. Joseph had told her earlier that she smelled like a female in heat.

At the time, she'd let the remark pass. Now it boomeranged inside her skill with resounding clarity.

She looked from one man to the other. "Oh, my God. You guys aren't saying that you think I'm one of your kind?"

Jesse Clawfoot's gaze settled squarely on her. This time his eyes burned not with lust, but with anticipation of another kind. "That's exactly what we are hoping," he said softly. "Because if there's one female, there may be more."

Kathryn wasn't quite sure she understood the implications of his words. "Me?" A little giggle of disbelief slipped out. "You think I can change into a cougar?"

Both men nodded.

"Because of this, uh, *odor*, I have?" Her nose wrinkled a little in disgust.

Joseph laid a hand on her arm. "It isn't an unpleasant smell, Kathryn. Just a pheromone that helps us identify our females."

Her nose wrinkled more. "It doesn't stink, does it?"

"It's like sandalwood and musk," Jesse explained. "Very nice smell, actually. One whiff and my dick gets harder than a hundred-year-old oak."

Joseph growled a warning. "Jesse. . . . Behave." He sighed and turned to Kathryn. "Don't worry. Males who don't carry the gene to shift can't detect it."

As a scientist, Kathryn knew that meant only one thing. Logically, females who didn't carry the gene wouldn't have the odor. "How can this be?" she blurted. "I'm not Native American."

Both men laughed.

Jesse snorted and met her incredulous gaze with one reflecting his own amusement. "There's a *Tlvdatsi* Indian or two in your family's woodpile."

Kathryn raked her hair away from her face and tried to

make sense of everything. She knew for a fact that her father's people had come off the reservation in Oklahoma, but that was four generations ago. Surely the bloodlines had worn thin through the years.

But being able to shift her body into the form of a cougar. Though she'd witnessed Joseph and Jesse change, it defied reason that she could, too. Logic insisted on warring with the incredible. In their case she was willing to suspend disbelief. But for herself? Come on. That one jumped from incredible to impossible.

At that moment the sun shifted in the sky, beginning its downward arc toward the earth. Cool shadows were beginning to creep around the edge of the clearing. Beating down on her bare skin, heated rays changed from pleasant to blistering. If she kept sitting out in the bright glare, she'd go from nicely tanned to crispy critter.

After rising from the blanket, Kathryn walked over to retrieve the clothes she'd discarded at the waterfall's edge. "I'll cop to having some Cherokee blood in my veins." She picked up her jeans. "But don't you guys think I'd have noticed by now if I could sprout some whiskers and a tail and had a penchant for scratching posts?" Shoving her legs in, she tugged her jeans up to cover her ass. "I mean, hell, I don't even like the smell of catnip."

Joseph picked himself off the blanket. "It doesn't work that way, Kathryn. It's not you think you're a cougar, therefore you are."

Jesse stood up and stretched, buck naked and unblushing. It didn't go unnoticed that he was as well hung as his older brother. "It's a little more complicated than just thinking you can make the change."

Both answers exasperated and avoided.

Kathryn slipped her shirt on, knotting the shirttails around her waist. "Since you've gotten me in this far, I hope you two

intend to explain how the change happens." She finished dressing, sitting down and putting her boots back on. In her world,
well shod was well armed. She had never been one to run
around barefoot in the grass.

There was always a damn nail to step on.

A slow smile curved Chief Joseph's lips. "That's not my place,
Kathryn," he said. "That honor belongs to the *Ani-Kutani*, our
shaman. He is the one who will guide you to the inner truth of
our tribe's ancient totem."

8

Darkness had settled, and the shadows invading the forest were deep and impenetrable when the other members of the tribe crept out of the murky gloom. They came slowly, carefully, cougar after cougar daring to stalk into the open.

They were wary, suspicious, of Kathryn's presence among them. Revealing themselves to an outsider's eyes delivered fresh peril to an existence already fraught with too many dangers. Their numbers were few, too few. As members of a vanishing race they faced the extinction of their kind on both sides. Human and cougar were threatened with extinction.

Several cougars gathered around the perimeter of the clearing. It took Kathryn a moment to realize they were standing guard. If anything happened, they'd be ready to react with lightning speed.

Before the sun had disappeared over the faraway horizon, Joseph and Jesse had prepared a meeting place. They'd built and lit four fires, positioning the hearths in a square. In the center of the square they spread out a blanket.

The two men had also changed their clothing, discarding

modern styles for more traditional garb: loose-fitting shirts in a bright calico pattern tied with beaded sashes, loose-fitting trousers, and moccasins. Plain, simple, and utilitarian, their clothes were hardly the fringed buckskin costumes of many a Saturday morning B western. Hair long and straight, they each wore simple beaded headbands of an unusual design. No fancy feather headdresses or face paint either.

Kathryn had been provided with a dress of sorts, in reality one of Joseph's shirts. Tied with a beaded sash, it settled just above her knees and gave her decent cover. None of their moccasins fit her, but barefoot was fine. After combing her hair, she'd braided it. Her crown of glory, the burnished-gold shade perfectly matched her eyes. She'd always worn her hair long, resisting her mother's comments that she should cut it down to a sleek, more professional style. True, it would have been easier to keep clean when out in the field, but there was something sensual about the cascade of silky hair across her bare shoulders.

The three of them took a spot on the blanket. Kathryn found herself wedged between Joseph and Jesse. Not like they were protecting her, though. They'd clearly staked a claim.

And then the cougars arrived, silent predators haunting the land.

Kathryn shivered. *The greeting committee.*

Had she not been wide awake and aware, she wouldn't have believed such a thing could possibly happen. But she'd seen them shift with her own eyes, heard their words with her own ears. If seeing and hearing weren't believing, she didn't know what else could possibly convince.

As if acting on a prearranged signal, several men glided out of the forest. They walked in a tight group, striding with confident purpose. All were wearing the traditional clothing adopted by the clan.

Joseph Clawfoot settled a hand over hers and leaned close

enough to whisper in her ear. "Ayunkini is the oldest of all of us here. He has lived in these mountains all his life and has counseled us in the ways of rejoining with our heritage."

Jesse sat to her left, and even his flippant tongue had been stricken quiet at the approach of the men.

The old man stepped forward. His graceful moves were made slowly and with much effort. His hair was gray with age, and his face was heavily lined with the weariness of a long and difficult life. Body taut and wiry from the exertions of living off the land, his features were severe, cold, and stern, even a little bit ruthless. He might have been seventy, maybe a hundred. Hard to tell in the shadows.

Ayunkini looked to his chief. The two exchanged words in a language Kathryn couldn't understand, even though the conversation was clearly about her presence among them.

Joseph indicated the blanket in front of them. "Sit and we will talk more of her," he said, thankfully in English.

The old man took his place, sitting cross-legged. He stared at Kathryn until she began to squirm under his unrelenting gaze. "Word has reached me," he finally said, "that you are a female of our kind." He tapped the side of his nose, then pointed toward her. "This I know to be true as my nose does not deceive me."

Tense muscles unwinding, Kathryn relaxed a little. The old man seemed to be accepting her. "That's what I've been told," she said cautiously, unsure if a female was allowed to speak during such an important powwow.

Joseph moved to make a more formal introduction. "This is Kathryn Dayton. She came to the mountains as part of a group working toward the conservation of our lands. She was attacked by the *dila*, the skunks who hunt us."

Eyes narrowing, Ayunkini's forehead ridged a little. "It is good you got her away from them in time, before they discovered what she is. We cannot afford to lose any more of our clan."

Joseph nodded. "Kathryn told of a report her people had that a cougar was shot outside Connelly Springs."

Ayunkini nodded. "Dennis Wolfe took the bullet."

Kathryn's heart dropped. "Was he killed?" she asked.

A flicker of faint amusement passed over the old shaman's face. "He is alive. And he has learned where he may—and may not—show his furry face." Ayunkini shook his head. "You younger men who have lived outside these mountains still have yet to learn there are places our kind are not wanted."

Joseph nodded toward his elder. "It's why we still need those who know the old ways to guide us in this voyage of rediscovery of ourselves as members of the cougar clan."

Ayunkini's unblinking gaze settled on Kathryn. "And do you seek to rediscover your lost self or are you content to let the beast inside you sleep?"

Kathryn involuntarily shook. This was a question she hadn't been prepared for. She could never have dreamed that she'd face such a change or challenge in her life. She could deny it and walk away—or she could take a chance to take the journey that might lead her into deeper self-discovery of who she really was on planet earth. Somehow these remote mountains that modern civilization had yet to conquer with concrete and asphalt had become more than a haven. Since meeting Joseph Clawfoot, she'd actually come to think of this place as home.

Strange.

But true.

Pieces of her soul were still missing, though. It was a feeling that nagged, had always nagged her, since she'd been old enough to put cognizant thoughts together inside her own skull. Something she couldn't explain any more than she could why the sun rose in the east or why the sky was so vast. All her life she'd found her feelings a curse that set her apart from the rest of the human race. She'd never fit in, never quite belonged.

Her chin rose a notch. "I want to know the beast inside. I've always felt incomplete, alone in this world," she said simply, looking straight into the old man's eyes. "Now I know why."

Ayunkini nodded. "Brave words. But are you prepared for the changes that you will have to make?" he asked presciently in a low-pitched voice that seemed to carry to her ears alone and no further.

Kathryn heard herself say aloud, "Yes. Yes, I am."

Ayunkini drew in a deep breath. "It has been a long time since I have taken in the scent of one of our females. My own mate passed many years ago, and we had no children. You give me hope more will come, that our clan's men will have mates to carry on the *Tlvdatsi* bloodlines."

"Then the ability to shift is a genetic one directly tied to your clan?" she asked.

Joseph nodded. "Yes. As far as we know only those of direct lineage to the clan originating in these mountains carry the shifter's gene."

"So if I had children with someone outside the clan, my children would carry the shifter's gene, too?"

"Most likely, they could." Joseph shrugged. "Though we've found a few *Tlvdatsi* who can't shift. Truth be told, the people who can shift are dying off."

Kathryn shook her head. "That would be a shame, to lose such a precious gift."

Joseph's eyes crinkled around the edges. "I'm just telling you how it is, babe."

Jesse Clawfoot surreptitiously elbowed her in the side and leaned over to whisper in her ear. "Just remember, as the minority and holder of the sacred thing we all desire, you can choose your mate. Just because Chief Big-Stuff here found you first doesn't mean you're stuck with him."

Joseph leaned forward and glowered at his little brother. "I heard that."

Jesse shrugged and grinned. "Just letting her know her options are open if she decides to stay."

Joseph glowered some more. "One of these days I'll wipe that smart-ass grin off your face," he muttered under his breath.

Jesse stuck his lip out. "Try it, bro."

Ayunkini held up his hands for silence. "These things can be decided after she walks the path of revelation." The old man turned and summoned his attendants with a few words in his native language.

Taking off the knapsacks they wore, the men set to creating some kind of a ceremonial drink simmered in a clay pot passed over one of the fires until boiling. The ingredients they added were foreign to Kathryn's eyes.

After about half an hour, the brew was readied for drinking, poured in a clay bowl, and presented to the shaman who would administer it.

Ayunkini took the bowl, blessing it with words sacred to his people. He then handed it to Kathryn. "Drink so that you may begin your union with the spirit."

Kathryn took the bowl, careful not to spill a drop. She sniffed, and the smell of warm fruit assailed her nostrils, not an unpleasant aroma. "What is it?"

"We call it *Asi*," Joseph explained. "A mixture of berry wine and peyote that we use to open neural pathways in our brains blocked by disuse. Modern disbelief and logic tell us it's impossible to shift, and so we can't. The *Asi* will help you relax and focus on the metaphysical side of your nature."

Kathryn gave him a skeptical look. "In other words, I'm gonna be out of my mind?" An uncomfortable feeling knotted in the pit of her stomach. She swallowed a laugh. "I'm not sure I can do this."

Joseph nodded and laughed. "Yes, you'll trip, but in a good way." He reached out and smoothed a stray strand of hair away from her face. "We'll be here, watching. I wouldn't let anything happen to you." His touch tantalized and seduced. The heat behind his gaze seared. "I promise."

The knots inside loosened and came apart.

Something about the look in his eyes made Kathryn's heart skip a beat. A jolt of sensual awareness jerked a response deep inside her body. Her nipples rose into little points, aching for the feel of his lips and tongue. Her clit pulsed with interest, eager to get in on the sensual act. Moisture pooling between her thighs, her senses started to sway. She hadn't even taken a sip of the potent drug-laced wine and already she was on the edge. Just thinking about his cock and the pleasure it could bring made her mouth go bone dry.

Kathryn licked her dry lips. Liquid fire sizzled through her veins. Somehow she had a feeling her journey would end with more than just a metaphysical discovery.

Lifting the bowl to her mouth, she drank down a healthy gulp. The warm brew slid over her tongue and down her throat. The taste of it was sweet, almost sickeningly so, but a bitter aftertaste lingered.

Now she knew how Neo felt when he swallowed the little red pill in *The Matrix*. The choice between delightful ignorance or embracing the sometimes excruciating truth was a hard choice to make.

By imbibing the brew, Kathryn had made her choice.

I hope I don't live to regret this. . . .

Fighting the urge to gag, she swallowed down another sip.

9

Joseph Clawfoot touched her arm, sending a spray of goose-flesh over her skin. "Take it easy. That stuff's pretty powerful. You just need a little."

Kathryn took another deep drink, almost emptying the bowl. By now it didn't taste bad at all. "But I don't feel anything," she slurred.

Joseph claimed the vessel. "I think you're already feeling the effects," he warned.

Kathryn yawned and grinned. Contrary to his words, it didn't even take a full minute for the potion to set to work on her system. Her head felt light and her bones felt as if they were melting away, leaving her all loose and limp. Her skin tingled, like millions of little insects crawling over every inch.

Kathryn's world started to spin. "I need to lie down," she mumbled through gradually numbing lips. Her mouth felt as if someone had filled it with Styrofoam packing peanuts.

The two men beside her scooted over and guiding her body across the blanket so that she lay on her back, her head pillowed on Ayunkini's crossed legs.

The old man gazed down. His fingers settled on her temples, making slow circles. "Close your eyes and listen to the sounds of the fires burning around us." He massaged with gentle pressure and motion.

Kathryn closed her eyes and breathed in deeply. The old man's fingers worked against the pressure points. The gentle weight on her temples sent prickles across her scalp and down her neck and spine, setting up a sensation that felt wickedly good. The snap and crackle of the flames. The wood hissed and popped, turning to ashes.

The old man began to speak in a low, lulling tone. His fingers moved to the front of her head, lightly caressing the space between her brow and hairline. "Follow the path that will take you back to the beginning of creation," he murmured. "Then you will see how we came to be."

Kathryn kept her eyes closed. Though she lay on hard ground, the feeling beneath her body was one of lightness, as if she floated free, cushioned by nothing more than air.

Deep under the influence of the potent drink, she became dimly aware of sound and sensation slipping beyond her grasp or comprehension. Through the moment it took for her heart to beat, nothing existed. Then she sensed rather than physically felt her spirit slithering free of all earthly bonds to rise above the earth in a defiance of gravity and time.

A pinpoint of light in the far distance suddenly came rushing up to engulf her. Swallowing her in a mighty gulp, it sucked her down into a pit of ever-expanding light, dragging her beyond the constraints of the known universe and pushing her backward . . . Toward nothingness. Toward the beginning of creation itself.

With a brief tingling jolt, Kathryn found herself floating in the vastness of an all-consuming, star-splattered universe. Existing on some intangible level of reality, she hovered over a

great round rock hanging in space among a hundred other un-
formed spheres. The dim, bare globes were nothing more than
endless skies and landmasses—planets waiting to be birthed,
for life to be spawned.

And then she saw great, huge hands reaching out of the
darkness and scooping up dirt—plain dirt. Surrounded by a
nimbus of glowing power, the hands began to mold and shape
and place, giving form to the barren empty plains. More scoops
of earth, more manipulation and life began to rise, the inani-
mate became animate as little more than granules of sand became flesh and bone, and breath. . . .

Kathryn knew then that every being on earth shared the
same single tangible element of creation. The energies allowing
all living things to have form and substance could be subtly
molded, reshaped and physically manifested.

In the beginning all the tribes of mankind had been granted
these secrets, but they'd become lost, muddied through evolu-
tion's progress and civilization's march toward science to rule
out faith and belief in the spirit realm. Through the ages, those
retaining the primeval genetic coding had thinned out to the point
of extinction. Scattered to the four corners of the earth, only a
few, very few, retained the trace memories required to use the
ancient gift. . . .

Just as she was beginning to understand the beginning and
end of all things, darkness abruptly boiled up again, grabbing
and thrusting Kathryn back toward the earth.

Suddenly she was in the forest, thick with trees and shadows. Only the body she knew wasn't her own. Some unseen
force grabbed her, pummeling her into an alien shape. Submerged in a wave of bombshell shocks, she felt an agony so
swift and fierce that it snatched the breath from her lungs. Icy
pain squeezed her head, and a glare of sparks sprung up behind
her eyes. Writhing every which way, her bones twisted, muscles

and sinew stretching to fit over a new, elongated shape. Skin vanished, eaten up by a short nap of thick fur. Her jaws snapped open, sprouting teeth and fangs that could not possibly fit in a human's mouth.

Lean, new body springing into motion, Kathryn was dimly aware of huge paws slapping the ground. All her spirit wanted was to run, to be free of the constraints and restrictions of human existence. . . .

Thunder crashed, sending Kathryn slamming back into her body. She fought to regain her senses, get back to the place she belonged, yet couldn't seem to find her way. Darkness boiled in her mind like a thick cloud. Strange menacing shapes and twisted half-recognized faces floated in front of her eyes.

A sharp slap to her face brought her back to her senses.

Kathryn blinked and her blurry vision cleared. Putting names with faces, she recognized Joseph and Jesse Clawfoot and that of the shaman, Ayunkini. All three men wore expressions of deep concern.

She gasped, painfully. Her skull thudded with heaviness. A sickening up-and-down rhythm beneath her body warned that her senses hadn't entirely stabilized. "How long was I out?" she asked thickly.

"A few hours," Jesse said.

"Did I shift?" she asked through her daze. "It felt like I changed. . . ."

Joseph slowly shook his head. "You were close, but not quite." He softly traced the cheek Ayunkini had slapped. "Nobody shifts the first few times. It takes a while to retrain the mind and body. You'll learn with concentration and meditation."

Head and heart pounding, Kathryn felt her teeth chatter. My head," she mumbled. "God, my head. It feels like someone smashed my skull. So cold." She didn't yet fully comprehend the toll her near shift had taken on her nervous system.

Ayunkini pressed his fingers to her temples, rubbing in small, hard circles. "The pain will go," he promised, beginning to murmur in words Kathryn couldn't understand.

The sensations of distress gradually eased. As her heart settled into a normal rhythm, the pain began to recede, seeping away and dissipating like smoke in the night's sky. A few minutes later Kathryn felt normal again, whole. The memory of what she'd witnessed dangled in her skull, begging for further exploration and thought. Overall, the experience had been awesome.

Her mouth quirked. *Mind-bending.*

Ayunkini eased his legs out from under her head. "She will be better now." He climbed to his feet, moving a little slower, arthritically. Sitting for hours on end had clearly stove him up. He summoned his men. "The hour is late and we should go. Tomorrow, I will come back."

Kathryn sat up. "Thank you."

"Is she going to be all right?" Jesse Clawfoot asked his elder.

Ayunkini nodded. "She will be fine. Some of her senses will remain heightened, but that will soon fade." The old man turned to Joseph. "Will she stay here?"

Joseph shook his head. "We haven't gotten that far yet. She still has another life to answer to."

The shaman considered. "I think she will. . . . And others will heed the call and return to the land of their ancestors. It has only been a matter of time, and this is our sign that time has arrived for our people."

Joseph's hands settled on the old man's shoulders, and his smile was grim. "We can hope."

Ayunkini stepped outside the perimeter of the four fires. A second later he and his men had disappeared back into the forest. The cougars standing silent guard at the perimeter of the clearing also crept away.

Left alone, the three settled back on the blanket.

Kathryn dipped back her head, contemplating the clear night's sky. Millions of stars winked across the velvety darkness. "I was there," she murmured. "I swear, I saw the beginning of everything, understood how we came to be." She sighed and lay back on the blanket. "I'll never forget this night as long as I live."

Joseph Clawfoot settled beside her. Jesse flopped down on her other side, folding his hands under his head.

"It's quite a trip," Joseph agreed. He hoisted himself up on one elbow and looked down at her. "I remember my first time. It was . . ." He shook his head. "I don't think I have the words to describe what it was."

Kathryn rolled over on her side, bringing her body into alignment with his. "Awesome." She smiled. "Out of this world."

Joseph reached out, sliding his free hand around to caress the nape of her neck. He pulled her closer and his lips brushed hers. "Not half as awesome as having you here right now." His mouth settled over hers, beginning a long, slow, lingering kiss.

Suppressing her moan, Kathryn sent her tongue in to parry against his, meeting him thrust for slow, delicious, wet thrust.

Mouth still on hers, Joseph pressed Kathryn onto her back. He continued his explorations, easing a hand under her borrowed shirt to cup her waiting breast. The swelling flesh came to life under his touch, the nipple trapped beneath her sports bra rising to a hard little peak. Gut throbbing with need, Kathryn felt moisture seep between her thighs.

A disgusted voice broke into their lovemaking.

"Oh, come on, you two have been fucking like bunnies all day," Jesse snorted in disgust.

Romantic interlude shattered, Joseph and Kathryn quickly broke apart.

Kathryn wiped her mouth. "We, ah, didn't . . ." she started to explain, then stopped herself. Of course she and Joseph had intended to make love right then and there.

"Sorry," Joseph mumbled. "Couldn't help myself."

Jesse harrumphed and rolled over on his side. "Get a room, okay?" He tightened his arms around his body and rolled into a small tight ball. "You don't know how damn hard it is to watch you two make love, knowing there's nothing for me. You got to her first, and it's not fair."

Pressing a hand to her forehead, Kathryn struggled to sit up. A tremor shook her that had nothing to do with the peyote-laced wine and everything to do with the two potent males beside her. The musky scent of their skin singed her nostrils and set her senses aflame. A light sheen of sweat covered her skin, and every nerve in her body tingled with carnal desire.

Trying to ignore the pulse between her legs, she shook her head. Hard to do when every inch of her skin screamed out for kisses and caresses.

Kathryn's fragile control snapped and she made a sudden decision. She reached for Jesse, placing her hands on his shoulders. His muscles were bunched, tight with unreleased tension. "I—I think I need both of you tonight."

Jesse unknotted his body and rolled over to sit up. He looked as if she'd just gifted him with the keys to the kingdom of heaven. "Are you sure?"

She nodded.

Joseph gave a tight smile. He clearly wasn't happy. "I . . . suppose we could share you."

Nervous system buzzing from the peyote and wine, Kathryn slowly nodded. "That would make sense." Hot, feral thoughts boiled in her skull, bubbling together to form a delicious picture of three bodies locked in erotic abandon. "I can't help it." She sucked in a breath and groaned. "I can smell *both* of you and it's about to drive me wild. I don't know what was in that potion your shaman fed me, but it's like I'm in freaking heat."

"You're still in the mind of a female cougar," Joseph said

quietly. "It's normal for you to want to mate with more than one male at a time."

Climbing to her knees, Kathryn reached for the sash around her waist. "I'm more than willing." Untying it, she slowly unbuttoned Joseph's shirt and slid it off her shoulders, letting it drop to the ground. Her sports bra followed. That left her only a provocative pair of panties. She untied her braids, letting her long hair fall in loose waves around her shoulders.

She smiled, confident in the control she obviously exuded over both. "There's enough of me to go around for both of you."

Jesse Clawfoot visually drank in her nudity from head to foot. "You're so beautiful, Kathryn."

Behind her, Joseph's hands settled possessively around her hips. Trapped behind the barrier of clothing, his erection nuzzled the crevasse of her ass. "Are you sure you want to do this?"

As though she'd grabbed an electric fence, the scent of two aroused males sizzled over every nerve ending. Dewy moisture pooled between her legs, seeping into the crotch of her panties. "Please . . ." Nothing less would satisfy the ache inside.

Jesse Clawfoot rose up on his knees. His gaze skimmed the length of her slender body. "May I touch you?" he asked in a voice humbled with awe.

Kathryn smiled and cupped her breasts, offering him the succulent morsels. "Touch away."

Jesse's hands swept forward, his touch replacing hers. His thumbs brushed her sensitive nipples. He rubbed small circles around the areolas, causing the tight tips to pucker and harden even more. "You have beautiful breasts."

Kathryn's body was rigid with the sexual tension crackling in the air. "Thanks."

"I've been dying to taste them." Jesse's head dipped and his tongue flicked over one bare nipple.

Kathryn cried out. Her hands tightened into fists in his long hair, urging him to have his pleasure. In response, Jesse painted his tongue around the hard tip. Mind falling back into a pleasant haze, she clung to him.

Jesse kissed the hollow between her breasts. "Do you like that?"

"Oh, yes." She groaned and offered him the other nipple as an answer. "Every time you suck, I feel it clear to my clit."

Joseph pressed into her from behind, fingers slipping into her panties, guiding them down over the curve of her ass. "Let's find out about that."

Kathryn felt her world tip over. A low groan escaped her throat. "I can assure you that I'm very wet," she gasped, trying to catch her breath as Joseph's lips brushed the nape of her neck.

Joseph chuckled in her ear. "I'll be the judge of that."

Jesse's mouth and teeth played with her nipple, his fingers teasing the hard tip of the other breast. "You're going to need a lot of lube tonight, babe. I haven't had sex in ages."

She groaned. "Just go easy on me, guys." Jesse nipped a little nubbin, and a flash of pure liquid fire surged through her. "On second thought, don't go easy. . . ."

"We'll have you every which way and then some, Kathryn," Joseph warned. One hand catching her hip, he slipped an arm around her waist. His huge palm settled against her mound. Gliding his middle finger through the narrow channel, he stroked her dewy clit with a slow motion even as Jesse suckled her rosy nipples. "Mmm. Just like you said." He dipped an experimental finger inside her sex. "Hot, wet, and very ready."

Kathryn shuddered and lost all control. "I've got to come. . . ."

Stabbing deeper, Joseph scraped his teeth into the soft hollow between her shoulder and neck. His warm breath brushed her skin. "Let yourself go."

Voice breaking on a gasp, Kathryn exploded like a firecracker in a glass bottle, shard after shard of brutal euphoria threatening to slash her into tiny pieces. Her cries of pleasure echoed far into the night, but she didn't care what listening ears might hear her moaning like a bitch in heat. She wasn't human now at all, but all animal, driven by her inner cougar to be mated until thoroughly bred.

Gulping in breath after breath of air, she hurled back to earth. Still sandwiched between the two brothers, her night was far from over.

Pulling away from her breasts, Jesse shimmied out of his clothing. Beautifully erect, his cock arced up toward his wash-board-flat abdomen.

Joseph guided her forward, settling her onto her hands and knees. Jesse's erection loomed just inches from her mouth. "I want to watch you suck his cock."

Jesse guided his swollen penis toward her mouth.

Kathryn opened wide and took him deep. To her surprise he tasted a little different than his brother, a wilder, drier taste, but far from unpleasant.

Behind her, Joseph undressed. Free from his clothing, he positioned himself behind her, using the tip of his cock to tease her, sliding the thick head between her creamy labia.

Mouth too full to protest, Kathryn let out a whimper when Joseph pressed forward. His cock slid in with an excruciating slowness. Her sex fluttered and gripped his shaft like a silken fist. She'd already climaxed once, but it wasn't enough. Tonight it would take more, much more, to fulfill her.

Hands cupping the taut flesh of her ass, Joseph started to pump.

A thrill shimmied up Kathryn's spine. Lust coiled, coalescing in a tight, hard knot in her core.

The slide of pulsing hot flesh filling her mouth and pussy almost sent her over the edge. Sucking in a breath, she moaned. Joseph's fingers dug harder into her sides with a bruising force as he thrust up inside her, his thick cock hammering into her.

"Harder," she moaned around Jesse's cock, ramming herself back into Joseph's hips. "All the way."

Giving a cry of his own, Jesse pulled his cock away from her clenching teeth. Neck and arms thickly corded, he wrapped his hand around his shaft, quickly dragging it down to the base. Body tensing between shivers and jerks, a stream of semen erupted from the tip.

Trembling arms bracing her weight, Kathryn watched orgasm claim him.

Jesse shuddered, devoured by the intense sensations gripping and milking his body until it had wrung every last ounce of strength out of him. The beauty of such brutal euphoria inundated Kathryn.

Joseph's hips struck against hers like a jackhammer, his cock pounding deeper with each punishing blow.

Thigh muscles quivering, Kathryn ground back as he hammered her toward a second mind-twisting climax. One hand slipped around her hip, fingers ruffling the short hair of her mound in the search for the small nubbin between her thighs. Then, without warning, his index finger crooked, spearing right into the center of her clit.

Pure. Raw. Pleasure.

Throwing back her head and unleashing a cry of gratification, Kathryn arched her back as crackling jolts exploded behind her eyes like a nuke hitting ground zero.

Unable to hold back another second, Joseph moaned, impaling her a final time. His balls slapped her ass, quake-inducing jolts of power shaking both of them to the core. He moaned and held himself deep inside her. Body twitching, his seed filled her womb.

It took a few minutes for the last sweet pulses of orgasm to fade.

Panting, spent, Joseph collapsed on top of her, dragging both their bodies to the blanket. Skin beaded with sweat, his chest rose and fell. "Damn," he gritted. "I wasn't ready. That was too intense. . . ."

Kathryn had to swallow and lick dry lips before she could answer. "Somehow I have a feeling you'll make up for it later."

Jesse nuzzled her neck, stroking her breasts with a lazy hand. His erection was finding new life pressing against her thigh with unrestrained eagerness. "If he can't, I can assure you I will." He gave her an impish grin and bent to continue pleasuring her berry-shaded nipples.

Kathryn purred with silken approval and parted her thighs. "I look forward to it."

Joseph grabbed a handful of his brother's hair. Giving his head a yank, he glowered down at Jesse. "I'd said I'd share. That doesn't mean you get all access."

Jesse pulled out of the threatening grip. "I don't think that's your decision, *Kemo Sabe,*" he drawled. "Seems to me the person who holds the goods gets to decide how they're parceled out."

Lifting her weight on her elbows, Kathryn made a disapproving little rumbling sound. "Boys, play nice." Pressed between two sinewy bodies, every inch of her felt alive with new sensations—sensations she'd dreamed of but never thought possible to achieve. "If I'm going to stay around here, we're going to have to figure things out."

Joseph reared up. "What?"

Kathryn grinned. "You heard me."

Joseph leaned forward, his voice deadly serious. "Are you telling me you're planning to stay a while?"

She slowly nodded. "I have to rejoin my team tomorrow, but I'm going to come back. I can't walk away from these mountains now, not after what I've seen, experienced, with the two of you."

Light as intense as the snapping of the fires surrounding them leapt into Joseph's eyes. A slow smile crept across his lips. "Of course, I—we—want you to stay."

Jesse added just as eagerly. "Anything we can do, we will."

"We both want you," Joseph added softly. He bent close to her ear so only she heard, adding, "I want you the most."

Kathryn grinned and squirmed back down between the two men. "Good. Now that we've settled that part, I need to figure out how to handle you guys." Reaching down, she grasped both men, stroking the evidence of their arousal. "I'm thinking of alternating days, with Sundays reserved for threesomes. . . ."

10

Joseph Clawfoot pushed Kathryn back against the rough bark of a stately old oak. "Are you sure you have to go?" he rumbled. "Or could I persuade you to stay another day?"

Kathryn laughed and slid her arms around his neck. "I'm already twenty-four hours overdue. I need to radio in and let base know I'm heading back." She tightened her grip and brushed a kiss across his lips. "I promise I will be back as soon as possible."

Joseph shuddered and his hold on her tightened. "I don't want you to go, Kathryn." In a move that had rankled many, he'd ordered his braves to stay behind. Jesse threw the biggest fit to go, but in the end the Chief had overruled everyone. He'd wanted to be alone with her, make love one last time.

She nipped the pillow of his lower lip. "I still have a job and a boss to answer to." She nipped again. "But don't worry. I will be back."

Joseph drew back, sliding his fingers down to her, twining their hands together. He pulled her away from the tree. "I'm not happy about this, but I guess there's nothing I can do."

She smiled. "It's not a bad thing. I'm going to file my report and recommendation that the tract going to market be declared a cougar habitat. Once I get that in motion, I'm sure the funding can be procured for the government's purchase of the land to keep it in pristine condition." She tightened her grip on his hand. "I'm sure it will go through since we will be partnering with the *Tlvdatsi* clan to ensure the safety of the cougars."

Joseph groaned in mock horror. "So you're back to civilization for a while."

Kathryn laughed and pulled him back onto the trail leading to her camp. Barely a mile to go and they'd be there. "Yep, the modern world beckons. God, I hope the batteries on my walkie are still good. If my pack's even still there. Be my luck those assholes took everything."

Hand pulling out of her hold, Joseph hung back. "I don't like the way this feels," he commented, scanning the brush around them. He reached for the 9mm pistol holstered at his side, checked the clip, reholstered. A hunting knife was strapped to his thigh, in easy reach.

They continued the rest of the trip in silence.

Kathryn knew he was aching to shift back into cougar form but holding himself back. He wasn't comfortable being this far away from *Tlvdatsi* territories. Anyone could see him, anything could happen.

Stopping at the edge of the ridge, they peered down into the ravine where she'd built camp. Rocks still lined the hole she'd dug to contain the fire. Cold ashes filled its pit. Everything she'd carried had been dumped on the ground, scavenged. Her coffeepot had been stomped flat by an angry foot.

Anger sent a red haze in front of her eyes. "Those bastards."

Before Joseph could stop her, she shimmied down the steep ledge. He stayed put, reluctant to break cover.

"Kathryn," he hissed under his breath. "Be careful."

She ignored him.

Reaching the perimeter of her camp, Kathryn dropped to her hands and knees, frantically searching through bits and pieces of gear for her walkie-talkie. She spotted it lying along a ridge of tangled brush. It looked like it had been thrown.

She headed for the walkie. "God, please let it work." Her hand shot out to claim her treasure.

The snout of a handgun popped out of the brush. "Hang on there, honey," came the molasses-slow drawl. A man slowly rose out of the brush. "Just step back and let it go."

Hands rising to the height of her shoulders, Kathryn's heart jumped to her throat. She'd never seen this man before, a lanky redhead with pock-marked skin. "Who are you?"

He grinned. "Just someone who's got a little time on his hands." He kicked at the useless walkie. "Sorry, I broke it."

Cursing her stupidity, Kathryn schooled her features. Joseph had warned her the mountain men were crafty and she'd ignored him. Talk about a too-stupid-to-live moment. She'd walked right into the trap.

"I'm just trying to get back to my team. I'm an ecologist, with the NWC."

He nudged her with his gun, urging her back to the center of the camp, out in the open. "I'm not dumb, honey. I know where you've been. You stink like them Injuns."

She sucked in a burning breath. *Shit.* "I don't know what you're talking about." Knees trembling like jelly, she refused to let fear get the better of her. She deliberately cleared her mind and made herself stay on track. She couldn't believe she'd let her guard down over some stupid camping equipment.

This guy wasn't going to make it easy. Forcing her to her knees, he pressed the muzzle of his weapon to the back of her skull. "How many's with you?" He cocked back the hammer.

"No one. I'm alone."

He prodded. "I know you ain't alone."

Knowing the game was up, Kathryn shouted. "Don't come

after me!" Silently cursing herself for her stupidity, she hoped Joseph would heed her warning and make fast tracks back into the forest.

Something deep inside said he wouldn't.

The stranger clouted her soundly across the back of the head. The strike sent her reeling forward, face striking the ground. "Don't be stupid, bitch."

An ice-cold voice said, "I wouldn't do that if I were you."

Kathryn lifted up in time to see Joseph Clawfoot slither out of the underbrush. His weapon was locked and loaded, aimed straight for the poacher. Jaw hardening, he didn't flinch.

The man kept his weapon trained on Kathryn. "Looks like we got us a little problem, Chief." He smiled. "So who you think's gonna pull the trigger first?"

Joseph tried to evade answering. "We don't have to do this today, Rusty." He shot a quick look toward Kathryn. "She's not a part of this. Let her go, and we'll settle things between us."

Glare menacing, Rusty shook his head. "Ain't no settlin', Chief," he advised, his voice low and deadly. "You boys done laid up my cousin pretty bad. Now we're gonna take a piece outta your hide."

Joseph's finger tightened on the trigger. "I'd be willing to lay you down right beside him."

Kathryn caught a quick movement behind Joseph. "Joe," she warned. "Behind you!"

Joseph Clawfoot whirled and leveled his weapon toward the new threat.

Rifle drawn, Willie Barnett stepped out into the open. "Howdy, Chief."

All three guns were aimed and ready for firing. One false move and someone would die.

Willie Barnett spat a wad of tobacco. "Looks like we got us a l'il Mexican standoff. I got a gun, Rusty here's got a gun an'

306 / Devyn Quinn

you got one, too." He glanced toward Kathryn and chuckled. "Only one who ain't armed is this l'il miss. Now that one gun versus two, Chief. Who you think is gonna win?"

Joseph's grip tightened on his weapon. "I might be willing to take my chances just to take you out, Barnett."

Willie Barnett chuckled. "Yeh, you could get off a shot at me, Chief. But then I'm sure my cousin here would be just as glad to take a shot at the l'il gal there. Think she'd have a chance? Your boys didn't give Skeeter any chances. Tore him up bad, they did. He's barely livin'." He shrugged and clucked his tongue. "Be a shame to waste a nice piece of pussy like that."

Joseph lowered his gun. "Just don't hurt her."

Willie gestured with his rifle. "Drop the clip and lose the gun, Chief. Throw it nice and far."

Flicking the clip out of his gun, Joseph tossed the weapon.

"And the knife."

Joseph surrendered the blade. "That's all I have. I'm not armed. You can let Kathryn go now."

Rusty chuckled. "Oh, we're not lettin' her go. Once we get you taken care of, we're gonna be havin' a little fun with this 'un." He bent down and grabbed a handful of Kathryn's hair, yanking her to her knees. "My pecker's gettin' hard just thinkin' 'bout them sweet tits."

Kathryn spat at him in fury. "I'll die before you lay another hand on me."

Rusty wiped off her spittle with a hand. The next thing Kathryn knew, his open palm was speeding toward her face. He slapped her hard enough to rattle her teeth. "Do that a'gin an' I'll knock your teeth out." He grinned obscenely. "A toothless woman's easier on the pecker."

Cupping her aching cheek, Kathryn got the idea that he was dead serious about what he'd do.

Willie Barnett reached for one of the ropes he'd coiled

around his shoulder. He tossed it to his cousin. "Tie 'er up, Rusty."

Kathryn swallowed hard. Saliva slithered down her throat like lead.

Shoving his pistol in the waistband of his pants, Rusty wrenched her hands behind her back. He looped the rope around her wrists, pulling it tight enough to bite into her skin.

Kathryn hissed. "Ouch, damn it, that hurts!"

Rusty tightened the knots. He leaned close to her ear. "That oughta keep those little claws of yours from tearin' me up when I fuck you later."

Kathryn gagged. His breath was rank enough to slay. She knew better than to toss out another smart-ass remark. She'd already had a tangle with the outlaws. They'd take what they wanted and discard the carcass. The idea caused her stomach to lurch all over again. She swallowed to keep from vomiting.

A dim alarm went off in the back of her mind. *I don't think we're getting out of it this time.*

Satisfied with his work, Rusty shoved her back onto the hard ground. "Stay there an' be still."

Nodding his approval, Willie Barnett shoved Joseph down on his knees. Lifting his rifle, he clouted the Indian squarely across the temple. "A little payback from ol' Skeet."

Though the blow clearly stunned him, Joseph reeled but didn't fall.

Kathryn twisted her wrists against the ropes. The knots began to give a little. She relaxed her arms and felt the rope give. Definitely looser. "He wasn't doing anything," she protested.

Willie Barnett stared at her impassively. He snatched up a handful of Joseph's hair, wrenching his head back. "You can't trust these things, honey. They're damn sneaky, and vicious when they're riled." He tossed his rifle over to his cousin. "Don't let him blink, Rusty."

Rusty leveled the rifle. "Got my eye on 'im," he promised.

Uncoiling another piece of rope, Willie Barnett prodded Joseph with his boot. "Hands behind your back, Chief."

Stony gaze staring off into nowhere, Joseph Clawfoot put his hands behind his back.

Willie prodded again. "Lock your elbows with your hands, arm over arm."

Joseph reluctantly complied.

Willie knelt. Looping the rope around Joseph's neck, he secured his arms with several tightly wound coils and knots. "That'll hold 'im." He grunted with satisfaction. "He can't turn cougar when he's hog-tied. It'll break his limbs."

Kathryn gasped. They knew Joseph could shift!

Willie fished a few things out of one pocket, a vial and hypodermic syringe. After filling the syringe, he plunged the needle into his prisoner's arm. Joseph winced, but there was nothing he could do to avoid the shot. "This'll make double-damn sure you can't do any shiftin', Chief. Somethin' nice to relax your muscles."

Kathryn winced. The poachers weren't dumb country boys. They were a lot smarter than she'd given them credit for.

Catching the look on her face, Willie Barnett grinned. "You think we didn't know 'bout these Injuns?" He gave his prize a slap on the shoulder. "Hell, he's nothing more than an animal in human skin. These things have no souls."

Joseph's features hardened. He refused to comment.

Kathryn recognized the look on Joseph's face. *Defeat.* In his mind he was shutting down, the cougar distancing itself from the man. To the poachers he was no more than an animal, and would be sold as such on the black market. Once purchased, he'd be an oddity, a curiosity.

Someone's pet.

And it was entirely her fault he'd been captured. He'd risked his freedom trying to protect her.

As for her. . . .

Kathryn moistened dry lips and sucked in a heavy breath. Her head hurt. Her chest hurt. Her heart ached. These men would never let her walk away now. Once they'd had their fun with her body, her future most likely consisted of a cold, dark hole in the forest.

Yes, she understood the situation perfectly.

They were going to die. She knew Joseph wouldn't survive long in captivity. Somehow he'd kill himself, following the ancient code of his kind: death before dishonor. She'd wondered why he'd had those words etched into his skin.

Now she knew.

Kathryn strained harder against the ropes holding her hands. She hadn't been tied half as thoroughly as Joseph, probably because the poachers didn't know she was one of his kind.

Somewhere in the back of her mind a dim plan began to take shape. She wasn't sure what she was going to do yet. . . .

And then it hit her.

Loaded with drugs and tied in a way that would strangle a man or cougar, Joseph couldn't shift. But if she could at least work a hand free they might have a chance to escape with their lives.

Maybe, just maybe, if she concentrated hard enough, she could pull off a shift. She'd come close, damn close, last night.

If . . .

Closing her eyes, Kathryn forced herself to take a deep breath. Staying focused was absolutely essential. She ordered her body to relax, even as her fingers worked the knots around her wrists. The rope was loosening.

Baring her teeth against the burn, Kathryn yanked her left wrist free. She was careful to stay in the position of a tied person.

Barely daring to breathe, she opened her eyes.

The poachers had their attention on Joseph. Good.

"That Chinaman's been waitin' for one of these for years,"

Willie Barnett said. "He'll pay top dollar to have one alive before the shift."

Rusty nodded happily. "Never thought we'd lay our hands on one alive." He chuckled. "Sure worth a lot more than paws and claws."

Knowing she had to do something soon, Kathryn made a subtle gesture.

Interest sparked, Joseph turned his head to look at her. His face revealed nothing.

Focusing hard, she silently telegraphed her intention. *I'm going to shift,* she told him. *Help me. I don't know how. . . .*

He miraculously caught her intent. Hope flared in the depths of his eyes. "Remember," he mouthed.

Remember.

She was desperate. They were running out of time and their options were limited. She had to do this. It had to work.

Panting and damp with sweat, Kathryn closed her eyes. Seconds crawled by and nothing happened. Her body did nothing.

She refocused, willing herself back toward that single moment in her life when time had stood still . . . the great vast darkness of space, the hands that had taken and shaped all things great and small. Her nerves and muscles knew how to react if only she could summon that spark. All she had to do was . . .

Kathryn felt her body ripple. For several seconds a twitching, shuddering tremor shook all her limbs, then a series of interlocking changes began, occurring from inside out as her bones unlocked, reformed and relocked, stronger than ever. Head snapping back, sharp fangs sprouted from ever-widening jaws. Her hands shortened, fingers stubbing into implements wielding sharp claws. Wave after shimmering wave of fur coated her skin, covering her from the top of her head to the tip of her tail.

Her change hadn't gone unnoticed.

Willie Barnett had seen everything from beginning to end. "Holy shit!" he cursed. "Goddamn, she's loose!" He lunged for his rifle.

No time to waste.

Kathryn had a plan.

She hoped it would work.

But first she needed a hostage.

Setting loose a heart-stopping roar, Kathryn whipped around on big, powerful limbs. She didn't hesitate to attack, hurling her lithe feline form through the air in a single bound.

Tackling Rusty, she drove the big man to the ground. Even as he fell, Kathryn was concentrating on returning to human form, paw metamorphosing back into a hand to snag the weapon he'd shoved down the front of his jeans.

Straddled on her victim, she shoved the muzzle of his own six-shooter right between his eyes. Rusty never knew what hit him. Her shift had lasted seconds, almost too fast for the human eye to comprehend her change from human to cougar, then back to human. Somehow she'd lost her clothes in the shift, but it didn't matter. Even stark naked she felt powerful. Unstoppable.

Index finger curling around the trigger, she thumbed back the hammer. This was a weapon she knew how to handle.

Rusty's eyes widened with horror. "Shit!" he squealed. "Don't let 'er kill me, Willie!"

Kathryn dug the muzzle deeper between his eyes. "I won't hesitate to blow his fucking brains out." Her palms started to sweat, forcing her to tighten her grip on the butt of the gun.

"Don't kill 'im." Willie Barnett raised his hands, palm out. "We can work this out."

Kathryn's gaze never wavered from the poacher. "You're fucking right we can work this out," she snarled. "I'm about to

312 / Devyn Quinn

send this asshole straight to hell." She knew she had the advantage. She could put a bullet through both men and they'd never have a chance.

Her finger tightened on the trigger. All it would take is one little squeeze.

Joseph read her intent. He slowly shook his head. "Don't, Kathryn. You don't need their blood on your hands."

Apprehension burning in her gut, Kathryn hesitated. "Why not?" she demanded. "They hunt your people, Joe . . . our people."

"You're not like them, Kathryn. You're not a murderer."

Indignation seeped in. "I could be," she warned.

A grim smile hitched up one corner of his mouth. "I know. But not today. Make him a trade. We will live to fight another day."

Kathryn considered. "Cut Joseph loose, let him go," she ordered. "Do that and I'll let this piece of pigshit live."

Willie Barnett drew his knife and cut through the ropes. "I'll lay hands on you yet, Chief," he snarled under his breath.

Joseph Clawfoot climbed to his feet, rubbing his chafed wrists. The marks of the tight rope still laced his skin. "I won't be caught short again." Claiming the poacher's rifle, he swung it against a nearby tree, shattering the stock. He tossed the remnants away.

Walking over to Kathryn, Joseph slipped off his shirt. "Trade me," he said, holding out the piece of clothing. "Give me the gun."

Kathryn looked up. Emotion tightened her throat. "Okay." She reluctantly handed it over, taking the shirt he offered. Flashing him a sheepish grin, she slipped it on. "I didn't know the naked part would happen," she mumbled.

Joseph held out a hand to help her up. "You'll get used to it."

Climbing to her feet, Kathryn nearly collapsed against his

unyielding body. He was so damn calm and composed. She, on the other hand, was a nervous wreck! "Joseph," she whispered, unwelcome tears pricking behind her eyes. "I'm sorry for being so careless."

"Don't worry about it." Joseph prodded the downed poacher with one booted foot. "Move it. Now." Eyes riveted on both of them in something akin to awe, Rusty looked too petrified to move.

Joseph growled again. "Get your ass up and get gone."

Rusty scrambled toward his cousin on hands and knees.

Willie Barnett claimed his cousin. Prisoners exchanged, the standoff was over.

The older man smiled. "This ain't over, Chief." His burning gaze slid toward Kathryn. "We'll meet again, bitch."

The two men slithered into the forest like the snakes they were.

Still half-paralyzed by what had just happened, Kathryn sagged weakly against Joseph. Mouth a grim, set line, he tightened his arm around her, held her. No words were needed to discuss what had happened. They both knew too well.

The battle lines had been drawn, the war declared.

Kathryn shivered and shut her eyes, sickened. In less than two days her world had changed. Now Joseph's people were her people. His fight, now hers. She was *Tlvdatsi.* Cougar.

And could not walk away.

Turn the page for an excerpt
from the next installment
of Kate Pearce's House of Pleasure series,
SIMPLY INSATIABLE!

Coming soon from Aphrodisia!

1

London 1819

He'd made a fool of himself.

Over a man.

Lord Minshom raised the bottle at his elbow, drank deeply, then carefully set it down again. He licked the brandy from his lips and tasted his own defeat and humiliation at the hands of that upstart, Lord Anthony Sokorvsky. A man who'd had the nerve to walk away from him—from him!

All of London was whispering about how his former sex slave had forsaken him for a woman. Minshom smiled bitterly in the direction of the fire and exhaled, feeling the tug of recently healed bone. At their last meeting, Sokorvsky had punched him so hard he'd ended up unconscious at the bottom of the stairs with two cracked ribs. Luckily, Robert had been there to drag him away before Sokorvsky and his nauseating lady love had descended the stairs to gloat over him.

Minshom picked up the bottle again and drank until there was nothing left. And it wasn't as if he was "in love" with

Sokorvsky. He didn't love anyone, didn't believe he was capable of it anymore. All his sexual encounters were exercises in power, opportunities to show that he was still at his peak and able to subdue or seduce anyone he wanted.

Yet Sokorvsky had found the balls to walk away from him. And for the first time in his life, despite his threats, Minshom had given up the pursuit and allowed his former lover to follow his heart. He grimaced at his own saccharine choice of words. Was he slipping? Was he losing his touch?

"My lord?"

He turned his head toward the door of the oak-paneled study, blinked at the blurred outline of his valet and occasional secretary, Robert Brown.

"What?"

Robert came farther into the room. His dark red hair glinted in the meager candlelight, the only spot of color against his pale skin and somber black attire.

"Would you like to retire for the night, sir?"

Minshom held out the brandy bottle. "Get me another one of these."

Unlike most of his staff, Robert held his ground and didn't even duck.

"I'll get you more brandy if you take it up to bed with you, how's that?"

"Go to hell."

"I'm already there, sir; I've lived with you for far too long. You'll have to think of something else to threaten me with."

Minshom raised an eyebrow and threw the bottle toward the marble fireplace, where it shattered into a million glittering fragments and almost put the fire out. "Get me my brandy, damn you."

Robert sighed. "I'll go and get someone to clean that up, sir. I wouldn't want you cutting yourself."

"Leave it."

Robert hesitated, his brown eyes fixed on Minshom's. He was in his early thirties, had come to Minshom Abbey as a stable boy and had stayed with his master ever since.

"Sir . . ."

"Come here and kneel down." Minshom pointed to the rug in front of him.

"Are you sure you don't want to go upstairs? Anyone could come in."

"And see you sucking my cock? I'm sure they've all seen that before."

Robert looked resigned, but he did as he was told and came to kneel in front of Minshom. He eyed Minshom's groin.

"After the amount you've had to drink, I'm not sure I'll be able to get a rise out of you, sir."

"You'd better try hard then, hadn't you?"

Robert sighed again and undid the buttons of Minshom's placket, pushed aside his underclothes to reveal his half-erect cock. Minshom reached forward to slide his hand into Robert's thick pelt of auburn hair.

"Make it fast and hard; make me come."

He closed his eyes as Robert's warm mouth closed over his shaft and began to suck and pump his flesh. He hadn't been back to the pleasure house since his injury. The discovery that Sokorvsky's woman was Madame Helene's daughter hadn't helped either. Would he ever go back there? Was it time to move on?

Coward.

He could almost hear his father saying it, the way his lip would curl, the sting of the beating he would no doubt get for his impudence in begging for the punishment to end. He dug his fingers deeper into Robert's hair, heard his valet draw in a hurried breath and suck faster. Perhaps he hadn't completely lost his ability to make men sexually serve him after all. But then he and Robert had always been simpatico.

A slight commotion in the hallway below registered through his drunken arousal. He wasn't expecting guests and had told his damned butler to deny anyone who inquired. He had no desire to see the glee in his so-called friends' eyes as they recounted yet more gossip about Sokorvsky and his new love. To be fair, he'd liked Marguerite Lockwood, had felt an unexpected stir of interest in his loins despite his refusal to fuck women. She'd reminded him of someone . . .

The disturbance was getting louder, rising up the stairs, coming closer. The agitated sound of his butler's voice and the clearer high tones of a woman. What in damnation was going on? Robert stopped sucking and tried to raise his head. Minshom shoved him back down again.

"I didn't tell you to stop."

He didn't bother to turn his head as the door flew open and his butler started apologizing.

"I'm sorry, sir, she refused to leave and . . ."

And sure enough, his vision was filled with an apparition from the darkest recesses of his personal hell.

"Good evening, Robert, good evening, Minshom."

Minshom kept one restraining hand on Robert's head. He used the other to wave the butler away and waited until the door shut behind him before addressing his visitor.

"What the hell are you doing here?"

"Visiting you?"

"I didn't give you permission to do that."

She raised her eyebrows and took off her bonnet, holding it at her side by its wide blue ribbons. Her long brown hair was neatly parted in the center and drawn back into two coiled braids over her ears. At first glance, she still looked far too young to be anyone's wife, let alone his.

"I don't believe I need your permission to visit my own house."

"It's my house. Don't you remember? When you married me, everything you brought with you became mine."

"How could I forget? You've always been very good at making me feel like a possession."

He met her clear hazel eyes and smiled. "And yet, here you are. Where you are not wanted."

She sighed. "Can we stop this? I need to talk to you."

He glanced down at Robert. "I'm busy. Make an appointment with my secretary and get out of my house."

She regarded him for another long moment and then turned on her heel. "Fine, I'm going to bed. I'll see you in the morning when you are sober."

He closed his eyes as the door closed behind her, waited for the front door to slam as well and heard nothing. Dammit, where was the woman going? He sat forward and hissed as his now-flaccid cock caught on Robert's teeth.

"Sir . . ."

"What?"

He glared down at his valet who was busy wiping his hand over his mouth.

"Was that her ladyship, sir?"

"Yes."

"Did you finally send for her?"

"Of course not!"

Minshom shoved his seat back and stood up, waited for the room to readjust itself to his unbalanced drunken gaze. Where the hell had Jane gone? Surely she hadn't had the audacity to stay and bed down here for the night? He'd made it quite clear he wanted her off his property. Minshom started for the door, almost tripping over Robert in his haste.

The marble stairway was dark, and Minshom paused to listen. A door closed upstairs and he set off again, following the faint trail of lavender-scented soap Jane always left behind her.

He was aware of Robert tracking him, but at least his valet had the sense not to speak.

Minshom passed the door into his own suite and kept going down the hall. A faint light gleamed under the door of the room next to his. He entered without knocking and found his wife kneeling in front of the fireplace, encouraging a wisp of smoke to ignite the kindling.

"I told you to get out."

She rose slowly to her feet and faced him, her expression as mulish as he suspected his was.

"I am not going anywhere."

"Despite your age, you haven't put on that much weight." He allowed his lascivious gaze to flow over her, let her see it, resent it, waited for her to blush. "I wager I could still pick you up and toss you out myself."

"I'm sure you could, if you wanted to cause yet more scandal."

"You think I'm afraid of scandal?" He smiled. "My whole life is a scandal."

"I know. I might live in the countryside, but I do read the London newspapers and the gossip columns." She unbuttoned her drab pelisse and laid it over the back of a chair, meeting his gaze unflinchingly. "And I don't think you have done anything to be particularly proud of."

"And you think I care about your opinion?"

"Probably not, but there it is, all the same."

He moved toward the chair, picked up her discarded coat and held it out to her. "Put this back on. I wouldn't want you to catch a chill on your journey back to Minshom Abbey."

She ignored him and continued to unpack her small valise, taking out a long white nightgown and her hairbrush. He stared at the back of her head and realized that Robert had slipped into the room behind him. Jane was right. Did he really want more scandal? He was already out of favor with the *ton*.

Throwing his wife out into the street would certainly make matters worse.

But then, if he was already convicted, why not add to his infamy? He took a step toward Jane, then hesitated as she started to take down her long dark hair. God, he remembered watching her do this a thousand times, the anticipation building in his loins as she readied herself for bed, for him . . .

"Stop doing that."

She looked over her shoulder at him, her hands still busy in her hair.

"I can hardly sleep with all these pins sticking in me, can I?"

He throttled down his frustration and the unexpected surge of interest from his cock, knew he couldn't bear to watch her disrobe. He'd forgotten how clever she could be. Was this battle worth fighting while he was drunk and still incapacitated from his cracked ribs? In truth, he was in no state to follow through on his threats. Perhaps he should follow Wellington's example, make a strategic retreat and face her on the morrow.

"Are you sure I can't convince you to leave?"

"I'm staying." She walked toward him, and he tensed until she presented him with her back. "Can you undo my buttons and loosen my laces, please, Blaize?"

He recoiled from her as if she were a raddled old whore. When was the last time someone had called him by his given name? Dammit, he couldn't remember, never allowed anyone to get that close to him anymore, even Robert.

"I'm no serving maid. Do it yourself."

"But I can't reach."

"I don't care." He set his jaw and snapped his fingers at Robert. "Come here and help my wife, not that she deserves it."

He walked around to face her, received the benefit of the warm smile she meant for Robert, and headed for the door.

"I'll bid you good night, then."

She opened her eyes wide. "You're leaving?"

"What did you expect? Did you imagine I'd be so delighted to see you that I'd drag you straight into bed and fuck you?"

Her expression stilled. "No, hardly that. Good night, then."

He inclined his head a glacial inch and walked out, heard her start to chat with Robert and Robert's warm laughter in return. They'd always gotten along well and he'd been selfishly glad of it in the early years of his marriage. It was only a few feet back to his bedchamber, but it felt like a mile. He glanced back at Jane's door and scowled. Robert had better be quick about unlacing her, or he would feel the edge of his master's temper. How dare she turn up and act as if she had a right to be here?

He flung open his door, steadied himself against the frame and stared at his large four-poster bed. But, devil take it, she did have a right. She was, after all, his legally wedded wife.

"Are you all right, my lady?"

As her stays and gown were loosened, Jane gripped the front of her bodice to stop it from falling down and turned to Robert.

"Yes, thank you for your help."

His smile was warm, his slight Welsh accent as soft as butter. Despite her knowing he was Blaize's lover, they'd always had a good relationship.

"You're welcome." He hesitated, one eye on the door her husband had just slammed behind him. "Is there anything else I can do for you?"

"Not tonight, although I would appreciate it if you could arrange for one of the maids to help me get dressed in the morning." She brushed at her crumpled skirt. "I suppose the rest of my baggage is still in the hall, so I'll have to make do with this gown until I can unpack properly. I wouldn't want to face Lord Minshom in my nightgown."

"Neither would I." Robert bowed. "If it helps, I'm glad you

are here. The master has gotten himself into a devilishly difficult situation."

"I gathered that from your letters." She sighed. "I doubt he'll let me help him, though."

"He probably won't, my lady, but we can hope. Give me your gown and I'll have it pressed and freshened for you. I'll also arrange for a maid to attend you in the morning." He hesitated by the door. "Sleep well, and I pray I'll see you tomorrow."

"Why, are you worried I might not survive the night?"

Robert grinned. "I don't think his lordship has quite sunk to those depths, ma'am, but maybe you should lock the door into his suite, just in case."

Jane waited until he left and sank down into the nearest chair. Her knees were still shaking, her breathing as ragged as her thoughts. Blaize's study had stunk of brandy, and glass had littered the fireplace. Was that how he lived now? In a permanent drunken stupor, not caring if anyone saw him use Robert to satisfy his unnatural sexual appetite?

But perhaps having caught him at such a disadvantage had worked in her favor. He'd backed down and allowed her to stay at least for one night. When she'd first seen the cool detached rage in his pale blue eyes, she'd wanted to run away, wanted to forget her stupid notion of making peace with him.

But giving in was never the best way to deal with her husband. He pounced on any show of weakness with the speed and ferocity of a starving cat. It was her lack of fear that had first won his interest and brought about their marriage ten years previously. Jane bit her lip. Not that that had proved to be much of a success . . .

On the long journey to London from Cheshire, she'd spent many hours wondering how Blaize would look, if the depravities of his lifestyle would be reflected on his countenance. To her dismay, he was as fascinating as ever. His gaze colder, perhaps, the pure line of his jaw and high cheekbones more sharply defined, but hardly the debauched drunkard portrayed in the satirical cartoons in the newspapers.

She got up and hurried to check that the door between the two suites was indeed locked. The thought of waking up with Blaize's hands around her throat wasn't pleasant. She returned to the fire, made sure it wasn't smoking, and stepped out of her gown and stays. Her suite of rooms didn't look as neglected and unused as she'd assumed. They'd even been redecorated in soft shades of blue and lavender, her favorite colors. But then knowing Blaize's sexual appetite, they probably hadn't remained empty for long . . .

Her nightgown felt cold against her skin, and she crouched down beside the fire to warm her hands. There was no water to wash in and nothing to slake her thirst. She certainly wasn't prepared to draw attention to her presence in the house by requesting anything. She was here, and she was not going to leave until she and Blaize had explored what needed to be said.

She shivered despite the building heat. Knowing her cynical, malicious, enthralling husband, she didn't expect her task to be quick or easy at all.